Stuart James sat in the dim glow of a single desk lamp in his room at the Algonquin Hotel.

He rarely slept more than four hours a night and had been awake since three, occupying himself by surfing the Internet. Peering at the luminous screen through half glasses, he read the headline that announced the upcoming marriage of his ex-wife.

Marilee had been floating around in his mind so much for the past six months. That was why he had come back to the States.

Rubbing the stubble on his cheeks, he read the text on the computer screen and felt such emotion as made him turn away. He looked at the telephone for a long minute, before going to the closet, pulling out his bags and beginning to pack. He would not call her. He wouldn't give her an opportunity to tell him not to come. If he just showed up on her doorstep, she would see him. And he doubted she would send him, the father of her child come at last, away.

"Endearing and magical."
—Ann B. Ross, author of *Miss Julia Throws a Wedding*

"Curtiss Ann Matlock brings us characters who live long after we've closed the book."

—Lois Battle, author of
The Florabama Ladies' Auxilary and Sewing Circle

Also available from MIRA Books and
CURTISS ANN MATLOCK

COLD TEA ON A HOT DAY
DRIVING LESSONS
LOST HIGHWAYS

Curtiss Ann Matlock

AT THE CORNER
of LOVE AND
HEARTACHE

MIRA

67002923

ISBN 1-55166-917-X

AT THE CORNER OF LOVE AND HEARTACHE

Copyright © 2002 by Curtiss Ann Matlock.

Visit us at www.mirabooks.com

Printed in U.S.A.

AUTHOR'S NOTE

If you are a reader familiar with my previous books, you know what to expect. I hope you are not disappointed.

If you are a new reader picking up this book, I'm honored that you picked it up at all, considering the thousands of books out there. To be of help, let me tell you that this story is about ordinary people living lives of desperate trials and quiet triumphs. I admit to cultivating a positive outlook on life. There are enough books in the world that focus on the gutter; I like to keep my eyes outward and upward, to the beauty. This is the only view I believe worth passing on.

I sometimes think of the reader out there, picking up the book and reading the words on the page. I imagine the person smiling, or perhaps with a tear in the eye but smiling just the same, because of having read something that expressed a similar personal experience. Many readers have written to tell me this is so. Thank you all for your letters! And should you enjoy this book, please don't hesitate to write to tell me. I can be reached at www.curtissannmatlock.com.

I want to thank my family for their support all these years of writing: my husband, Jim, who knows "the look" when I come down the stairs, so keeps his silence; my son, T.J., who gives presents of my books to the many women he meets; and my mother, who rearranges copies of my books from the obscure to the prominent shelves at Wal-Mart.

And gratitude to my ancestors, too, from whom I inherited a love of books, a certain stubbornness and a deep and wide sense of humor.

My sincere gratitude to my editor, Leslie Wainger, whose calm strength and unfailing faith in me saw me through a particularly rough time during the writing of this book.

Welcome to my world—Valentine.

Curtiss Ann Matlock

"Home is the place where,
when you have to go there,
They have to take you in."
        —Robert Frost
            "The Death of the
            Hired Man"

The Valentine Voice, Wednesday, February 21

Publisher and Associate Editor to Wed
James, Holloway Announce Engagement

Tate Briggs Holloway, publisher of *The Valentine Voice*, and Marilee Roe James, associate editor, announce their engagement and plans to marry March 21, 11:00 a.m., at the First Street Methodist Church, with Pastor Stanley Smith officiating.

Ms. James is the daughter of Norma Cooper of Lawton, formerly of Valentine, and the late Frank Justus of Valentine, and the niece of Vella and Perry Blaine, of Valentine. She has served on the staff of *The Valentine Voice* for over eight years, and is the founder and director of Angel Gifts, a nonprofit organization that provides educational assistance for special-needs children to small schools.

The prospective groom is the son of Franny Holloway of Galveston, Texas, and first cousin to Muriel Porter-Abercrombie, formerly of Valentine and from whom he purchased *The Valentine Voice* last spring.

The couple will make their home in Valentine, with Ms. James's son, Willie Lee, and niece, Corrine Pendley.

New York City, 6:15 a.m.

Stuart James sat in the dim glow of a single desk lamp in his room at the Algonquin Hotel. The sounds beyond his room were becoming more frequent, footsteps in the hallway, the whoosh of the elevator, horns on the streets below, as the city awoke.

Stuart, in a navy sweatshirt, plaid flannel lounge pants and worn kid leather moccasins bought years ago while on a photo shoot on a Navaho reservation, was reared back in the chair with his feet up on the desk and a notebook computer open in his lap. He rarely slept more than four hours a night, and had been awake since three and occupying himself by surfing the Internet.

Peering at the luminous screen through half glasses, he read the headline that appeared. He became still, as if even the blood stopped in his veins.

Movement returned, first with his eyes, which ran along the lines of text that announced the upcoming marriage of his ex-wife. Then his hand came from behind his head, and his feet dropped to the floor, while he stared for long seconds at the text, his mind assimilating the news.

Then he reached for the two medication vials sitting nearby. Popping off the lids, he shook one pill from each vial, tossed both into his mouth and downed them with water from a glass that was ready and waiting.

Carefully, breathing deeply, he set the computer on the desk, his eyes drawn again to the text, which he reread.

His hand shot out and took up the receiver of the phone. But he halted the action in midair, then slowly replaced the receiver, sitting for a long minute with his hand resting there, as his mind swept back, touching on memories out of time.

In a motion more swift than he had achieved for some months, he rose and reached for his slacks thrown across a chair. Pulling his wallet from the back pocket, he opened it to the picture he had kept of her and held it into the circle cast by the lamp.

Marilee's image was there beneath the cloudy plastic. Not smiling, but fiery. He smiled softly, remembering. He had taken the picture himself, and it was the best of her possible. Marilee had never been one to take a very good picture. She posed too hard. But this one he had caught her unawares, and angry. What had it been that time? Oh, yes, it had been when he had left her a whole day, waiting at that old grocery in the Tennessee mountains.

He supposed his main mistake had been leaving her too often.

Rubbing the stubble on his cheeks, he again read the text on the computer screen and felt such emotion as made him turn away. It was just a podunk newspaper in a podunk town, he thought, and that was why the announcement appeared on the front page.

Marilee had been floating around in his mind so much for the past six months. That was why he had come back to the States, why he had found the *Voice* on the Internet and looked there every few days for the past month. He had been resisting the urge to run to her. His urge was stupid. Why couldn't he let it go?

He shook his head, and then he caught sight of himself in the mirror on the wall. Always thin, his face was bony now. In the low-lighted room, his image appeared colorless, lifeless. Fear swept down his spine and sent him turning from the sight.

He looked again at the telephone for a long minute, before going to the closet, pulling out his bags and beginning packing. He would not call her. He wouldn't give her an opportunity to tell him not to come. If he just showed up on her doorstep, she would see him then. And he doubted she would send him, the father of her child come at last, away.

One

Today—the first day of the rest of your life.
Valentine, Oklahoma, 5:30 a.m.

Streetlights twinkled through the trees, and here and there kitchen lights were popping on, as the earliest risers, or those who were just coming home, began to make morning coffee.

Up on Church Street, Winston Valentine didn't have to make coffee. His niece, Leanne, had moved in two weeks earlier and brought her fancy coffee machine with its automatic timer. She set it to come on around the time Winston awoke each morning and checked to make certain he was alive. At eighty-eight, he thought it prudent to check his vital signs each morning. He took being able to smell the aroma of the coffee as a main indication that he remained among the living.

Rising, he looked out the window, saw the frost on the porch roof and thought it a good choice that he and his neighbor, Everett Northrupt, had decided that during the winter months they would push their flag-raising time until one half hour after sunrise.

He dressed, caught up his breath and his cane, and headed downstairs, passing the closed door of the room his niece occupied and stopping to peek in the room of his elderly friend and boarder, Mildred Covington, who snored lightly with her mouth wide-open. He liked to make certain Mildred was still alive, too, since the death of his former elderly boarder, Ruthanne Bell, who, just after Christmas, had passed away sitting in a chair and they all thought she was asleep for half a day.

In the kitchen, he swallowed two aspirin, slipped into his old wool coat, poured a mugful of coffee and took it to the front porch. There he eased himself into a rocker, watched for daybreak and talked to God. He thought it best to be on speaking terms with God, since each day he came closer to kicking the bucket.

Down at the intersection of Main and Church Streets, a spotlight shone on two flags, the Oklahoma state flag and the Valentine city flag, faintly fluttering in front of City Hall. To the west, the buildings of Main Street stretched in shades of grey at this hour, the color broken on the south side by the fluorescent blue and yellow of the old Blaines' Drugstore sign.

The stray black cat that had taken up at Blaines', where Belinda Blaine fed it milk out the back door, walked across the street and disappeared beneath the only parked car on the street, a Grand Am belonging to Charlotte Nation, who was inside *The Valentine Voice* building. Light shone around the closed blinds covering the plate glass windows of the *Voice*. Charlotte, receptionist and general girl Friday, sat in front of her computer, where she had been since the early hours of the morning.

Charlotte's mother had suffered a stroke back in January, and in an effort to escape the sound of her mother's labored breathing in the other room, she often left her in the care of the night nurse and came down to her office computer, where she worked on the *Voice*'s Web site, or boosted herself with e-mail from support lists, such as ExecSecs, for executive secretaries, and MomofMom, for daughters caretaking their mothers, and RealWomen, for women with younger lovers.

A knock at the front door jarred Charlotte's attention from her computer.

"It's me, honey."

It was Sandy Conroy, layout man for the *Voice*. Charlotte threw off her glasses and raced to the door, where Sandy stood with a bag of cinnamon rolls from the IGA bakery.

"I know you're beat. I'll make us some coffee," he told her.

No one had ever considered that staunch Charlotte might need some care; it had always been Charlotte looking after everyone else. Until Sandy.

Touched to the core in that instant, Charlotte pulled him inside and into her strong embrace, kissing him ardently.

"Marry me, Charlotte," he whispered when he dragged his lips free.

Her answer was to kiss him again, so as not to have to tell him, yet once more, that no, she could not. She was almost thirty-seven, and Sandy was just barely twenty-six, and she had an invalid mother to care for. It was too much—for both of them.

Over on Porter Street, in the rear bedroom of a bungalow with a deep front porch, Marilee James came awake from a vivid dream. The dream was a repeat of one she had had earlier in the week. While not exactly the same dream, it was close enough to be a little disturbing and cause her to turn on her bedside lamp.

It was what came from listening to Julia Jenkins-Tinsley, the postmistress, who knew everyone's business and told it every chance she got. This time Julia had been telling about how Kaye Upchurch had met her husband at the door wearing nothing but a fur coat, which she flashed open to bare her altogether, as Julia put it. Julia did not know if Kaye had succeeded in heating up her husband with this stunt, but she did know that he was now receiving *Men's Health* magazine and vitamins through the mail.

Since hearing about this, Marilee had been toying with the idea of doing something similar to Tate. She thought of it now, her gaze falling to the new engagement ring sparkling on her finger. She shined it on the bedspread and admired it again.

Of course the idea was preposterous. Marilee was not the sort who did such things. She did not *want* to be that sort to do such a silly thing.

Except that Tate told her she was way too serious, and she wanted to show him that she was not. And she felt the need to stir him up, get him to take command of their intimate lives. Well, sort of.

Marilee wasn't certain exactly what need she was experiencing, except that there was a craving deep inside causing her to feel frustrated and wild.

She slipped out of bed and went to open her lingerie drawer, pulling out a long, silk, flaming red nightgown that she had, in a fit of reckless intentions, ordered from Victoria's Secret.

Two

Flying by the seat of the pants

In the front bedroom of the bungalow, Little Willie
Lee, as he was generally known by bigger kids at
school, opened his eyes and saw the fuzzy first grey
light of morning around the edges of the window
blinds. The entire room looked fuzzy. He found his
glasses on his bedside table and put them on in the
careful, almost reverent manner he always used, because his glasses enabled him to see.

There was just enough light for him to make out
his shiny red cape lying at the end of his bed. He
had loved the cape since his mother had made it for
him to be Superman on Halloween.

He looked over at his cousin, Corrine, peering hard
through the gloom. The room was yet so shadowy
that he could barely identify a lump under her covers.
Corrine, who liked a pile of blankets—Aunt Vella
said it was because she was so skinny—slept with
the covers over her head.

He held his finger to his lips at Munro, who remained with his head on his paws, although his eyes
blinked. Munro knew the plan, and to be quiet.

Slipping from the bed, Willie Lee knew how to

step so that he missed the places where the floor would creak. The wood was cool through his socks.

His shoes waited in the dark corner. He had to sit to slip them on, but he did not have to tie them, because he had learned to remove them without untying the laces. He took his coat from the hook on the door and put it on over his flannel pajamas. Concentrating as hard as he could, he got it zipped up.

Just as he was reaching for his cape, floorboards creaked. *Mama! Coming from her room.*

For an instant Willie Lee stared wide-eyed at Munro, who sat up on the bed and was also wide-eyed, and then he dived for the bed just as a slice of light came shining in from the hall. He scrambled to get himself, his cape clutched in his hands, and his bulky coat, hidden beneath the covers. Munro lay back down, up close against his legs.

There came the swish of his mother's robe and the creak of the floor as she came to the bedroom door. He saw her in his mind's eye, in her long pink robe, her hair billowy, her eyes that often searched him; he could even smell her sweet scent.

It was strange for his mother to be up this early. His mother did not like mornings. No one liked mornings the way Willie Lee did.

He heard his mother go back to her bedroom and shut the door. He peeked out from the covers and saw the empty doorway, hall light out now.

Slipping again from bed, he stood contemplating his problem. His mother might hear him go out the window. His mother seemed to have a certain knowledge about him. She might already know about him going out the window on the previous mornings.

He looked at Munro and heard clearly, *"Better not this morning."*

But Willie Lee whispered, "I have to."

He pushed his pillow and blankets until they looked like how Corrine did in her bed. He got his cape snapped around his neck and shook it out behind him so that it fell properly. Then, on his knees on his bed, with Munro twitching beside him, he raised the window blinds. He had long ago figured out how to do it with almost no noise. The window needed a tug, and then it whooshed up silently, as if with angels' help.

Fresh cold air hit his hands and face.

"Me first!" Munro jumped through the window from which Willie Lee had removed the screen a week ago. No one had noticed.

Willie Lee carefully lowered the blinds back into position, then glanced over his shoulder at Corrine. She was still beneath her covers.

There was no way to be silent in trying to get on the other side of the blinds. He did the best he could. Nothing was going to stop him now, anyway. He got his feet out the window and his rear end positioned on the windowsill, holding to the frame on either side with a hard grip. Munro was sitting on the ground, looking up expectantly. *"Come on!"*

Willie Lee braced his feet against the outside wall. Then he put his arms out in front, the way Superman did, took a breath, closed his eyes and imagined...*jump!*

For an instant he was hurting through the air, with his cape flying out behind him.

His feet hit the ground with a hard jolt, then his knees—something sharp stabbed his left knee—and he caught himself instinctively with his hands, only to lose balance and go rolling across the cold, wet ground.

He found himself staring at the brick foundation three feet from his face. Munro came over to lick his face. "I am o-kay," he told his dog.

He sat up. Everything looked funny. Oh, his glasses. He straightened them on his face. He got to his feet and rubbed his hands on his coat. He had almost flown, he felt sure. Almost. Yes, his cape was okay.

Turning, he looked up into the bare branches of the elm tree that stretched over toward the corner of the house. He looked at Munro. "May-be I need to be high-er…up in the tree."

Munro looked up at the tree and then at Willie Lee. *"I don't think so."*

Willie Lee went over to the tree and walked around on the lumps of roots spreading out at the base. He felt the rough bark. He pressed his ear against the trunk, hearing the life running through the tree the same way he could sometimes hear it in the wind or in the ground.

He looked upward again for a long minute. He raised both arms out in front and upward, hands together, closed his eyes and stood there, imagining, feeling himself begin to soar.

But when he opened his eyes, he was still on the ground.

Just then a door opened next door.

Willie Lee dropped his arms and squished himself against the tree trunk. Munro moved close.

Trash cans banged. Mr. Purvis putting out his garbage.

Next came a small meow and then Mr. Purvis saying, "Git...git outta here!"

Willie Lee risked peeking around the tree. He saw Mr. Purvis stamp one of his big boots at a small grey kitten, as if trying to smash it.

The kitten scampered under the hedges that divided Mr. Purvis's driveway from Willie Lee's front yard.

Mr. Purvis went back into his house.

Willie Lee, crouching, went along the hedge, until he saw the little kitten.

"Do you know him, Mun-ro?"

"No."

Willie Lee said, "Here, kit-ty."

The kitten, frightened of everything, scampered farther along through the branches of the hedge. Munro went ahead and tried to speak with the kitten, while Willie Lee held back and watched. But the kitten just hissed at Munro.

"Stupid cat." Munro retreated.

Then Mr. Purvis came back out to start his pickup, and at the roar of the engine—which Willie Lee's mother and just about everyone else in their neighborhood complained of—the kitten zipped through the hedge, and then it was as if it shot out and up into the air, right out into the road, unfortunately at the exact moment that a little car came speeding past.

Thud!

Willie Lee saw and heard it. It looked as if the kitten hit the car and not the other way around.

The next instant the car was gone, and the kitten lay in the road, like a dirty rag.

Munro took off like a bullet for the street, and

Willie Lee, forgetting to remain hidden, hurried as fast as he could after the dog.

He stopped at the curb. He was not allowed in the street. But the kitten was only a little way into the street. Munro was sniffing it gingerly.

Carefully Willie Lee stepped off the curb and over to the lifeless grey-striped form. Pushing his glasses up on his nose, he crouched with his hands on his knees for a closer look.

"Road-kill," Munro said.

"Well, by golly, Willie Lee, is that your kitten that got run over there?" It was Mr. Purvis, looking over from scraping frost off his windshield. Puffs of white came out of his mouth, about like the dark puffs coming out of the tailpipe of his rumbling truck.

"No, sir."

"Well, son, you had better get out of the street before a car comes and runs over you. I'm fixin' to back out."

Mr. Purvis reached for the door handle.

Willie Lee watched with alarm, and Munro pranced. *"Pick him up, quick…hold him."*

Willie Lee reached down to gather up the kitten's limp body. His knuckles scraped the pavement. He always had such a hard time moving fast. He could never move as fast as everyone wanted him to.

Then, holding the kitten close against his chest, he carried it up into his yard, stumbling on the curbing. He walked beneath the massive bare branches of the elm tree and stood there, feeling the kitten warm in his arms. He closed his eyes and imagined himself flying, and as Mr. Purvis's pickup truck roared out of the driveway, he could feel himself lifting.

* * *

Inside the house, Marilee had her face jutted toward her dresser mirror and, in the impossibly low light of the little crystal lamp, was applying lipstick, when Leon Purvis's hot-rod pickup roared in the driveway next door. She jumped and shot red toward her cheek.

Dang that man! Somebody ought to shoot him. She threw down the lipstick and headed for the bedroom door. Hearing her boot heels connect with the floor, she went up on tiptoe, lifting up the red silk nightgown as she raced across the short hallway to the children's bedroom.

She stood there, hearing her neighbor's hot-rod truck fade away down the street and holding her breath as she studied the forms in the beds.

The forms did not move. A bomb going off outside would not wake Willie Lee unless he wanted to wake, but Corrine could be awakened at times by the least thing.

It occurred to Marilee that she would feel pretty foolish should her niece wake up and find her standing there in the sexy red negligee and tall taupe cowboy boots.

She tiptoed back into her bedroom, where she stood for a moment, listening with the door cracked. Silence. No one stirred. She reassured herself that one could generally count on children sleeping more soundly on school days.

Back again in front of the mirror, she took a tissue to the smudged lipstick, then reapplied it. A last study of her image, then she dropped the lipstick and strode to the closet, where the door sat open with clothes hung all over it, got out her long trench coat and put it on. She hadn't worn it in years, usually opting for her practical and comfortable Pendleton barn coat.

Standing in front of the full-length mirror, she tied the coat around her, leaving the buttons undone. It would be much easier to whip open the coat if it were just tied.

She gave it a try, jerked the belt loose and flung open the coat and struck a provocative pose. Plunging neckline, skin shadowy beneath the filmy gown, high-heeled cowboy boots. Well. That was a picture to get attention, she would think.

Sucking in a breath, she folded the coat closed and retied the belt. Taking advantage of a sudden leap of faith, she opened the bedroom door, tiptoed again to the door of the children's room. The lumps remained still in the beds.

Turning, she tiptoed through the house and out the back door into the cold morning, and hurried across the frosty yard shadowed by the trees. She was still on tiptoe, she realized, and let her feet down.

The latch on the old back gate was frozen in place. She jiggled it, and it opened with a small squeak. She hurried through the gate and the line of cedars at the back of Tate's yard, across the expanse of lawn and up the back steps. She felt like some sort of criminal sneaking through the neighborhood.

The doorknob was cold beneath her hand. The door that had not been locked since Tate moved in opened quietly.

She stuck her head through and peered into the room. A light burned above the sink, but there was no aroma of coffee. Her nose twitched, detecting the acrid scent of old moldy wood.

Listening carefully, she thought she detected water running through pipes. Maybe so, maybe not.

She stepped into the kitchen and closed the door quietly behind her, leaned against it, catching her breath. Then she was struck with the boldness of her following through with her idea, and that the idea was actually rolling along.

Pushing from the door with a bit of eagerness now, she went to the coffeemaker, pulled it forward on the counter, then looked at the cabinets, guessing the location of the coffee and opening the door directly above.

She and Tate had been dating since last fall, and she had not spent enough time in his kitchen to know for certain the location of his coffee. This fact seemed to speak about a definite hole in their relationship. She didn't know where his coffee was kept, and she had only made love with him four times. Four rather furtive times, stolen moments that had much more to do with passionate need than commitment, which they had now made.

At the thought of her commitment, Marilee's mind did a sharp jog back to the preparation of coffee. Just to be ready in case Tate appeared, she untied the belt of her coat and did a quick practice seductive flash. Okay, that would do.

The next instant the back door swung inward.

Marilee whirled around. She had thought Tate was upstairs. What was he doing coming in the back door? *Grab the edges of her coat, pose and flash.*

She had her coat whipped open when she realized the figure stepping into the kitchen was not Tate but...a woman.

Yes, a woman coming in the door. A small

woman, in a bright pink-and-purple silk jogging suit, who gazed at Marilee with equal surprise.

Marilee wrapped her coat closed.

The woman said, "Oh, honey, I'm sorry to startle you. I guess you weren't expectin' me." She laughed. "And I wasn't you, either."

Who was this woman?

As if in answer to the unspoken question, the woman said, "I'm Tate's mother, Franny. I got in late last night." Lowering her voice, she leaned forward and held up a pack of Virginia Slims. "I took my smoke outside, before Tate got up. He will take me to task if he finds out I still smoke a cigarette on occasion. I *do* take care of myself, and one little cigarette isn't going to kill me, and I like to have it while I do my mornin' meditations. But I thought it best to go outside.... I don't want to do anything to make Tate start up again." She put a hand over her heart. "Heaven knows he had such a hard time quittin'. And I do not want to be any temptation in the wrong direction for my son."

The entire time the woman spoke, Marilee stood frozen, holding her coat around her and taking in the woman's bright green eyes, pixie-styled, carrot-red hair, dangling earrings and bangle bracelets that tingled, noticing that her features greatly resembled Tate's, although surely she was too young to be his mother, and she looked not at all like her picture on his office wall. Her accent, too, was very much like his; she said the word *direction* with a long *i,* and there was a brightness about her that was arresting, as if she glowed.

Then the woman said, "You're Marilee, aren't you? If you're not, Tate has a lot more problems than startin' up smokin' again.'' She gave a throaty chuckle.

"Oh, yes, I'm Marilee.'' Clutching her coat together with one hand, she extended the other. "Hello.''

"Hello, my dear.'' The woman took Marilee's hand, but instead of a shake, she came forward and pressed her cheek against Marilee's in a warm manner. "It is a delight to at last meet the love of my son's life.''

Then she drew back and was again assessing Marilee, who said, "I...I was just...well, I thought I'd make Tate some coffee this morning.''

"Ahh...'' The woman's gaze traveled up and down Marilee, and then she turned to reach into a cabinet for a mug, which she stuck beneath the water faucet. "I always have a cup of hot water before my coffee. I don't make very good coffee, so I'm awfully glad you can.'' Popping the cup into the microwave, she pushed buttons.

Marilee decided she had to get out of there.

"I need to be getting back home. The children are alone. I just left them for a few minutes.'' She didn't want Tate's mother to think her careless as a parent. No doubt the woman was already having plenty of skeptical thoughts about her. She moved toward the door, remembering at last to tie her belt and not keep clutching her coat together like an insane woman.

"But, honey, you haven't seen Tate.''

"I'll see him later.'' She opened the door.

"Now, I don't want to be an interruption to you and Tate and y'all's routine. I'm takin' my hot water right up to my room and leavin' you two alone to do...whatever.''

"We don't have a routine," Marilee said instantly, taking the woman's "whatever" to be something like making mad, passionate love on the floor. "I just...well, I have to get back."

At that minute Tate entered. He was pulling a T-shirt over his head. Marilee saw his bare chest, blue flannel lounge pants and bare feet. When her gaze came up from his feet, she found his head out of his shirt and his eyes staring at her in surprise.

"Marilee?"

"Good mornin', dear," his mother said as the microwave oven beeped. "I think Marilee has a surprise for you." And then, bearing her cup of hot water, the woman swept out of the room in a swish of her silk jogging suit.

Tate looked at Marilee, who said, "I just came to make your coffee. See you later."

Turning, she left him there with his confused expression, going out without so much as a kiss on the cheek, closing the door to the aroma of coffee, descending down the steps with the cold crisp air blowing up her coat and gown, a painful reminder of her foolish, audacious actions. As she hurried across the frosty grass that crunched under her feet, she listened for Tate to follow. But he did not. Bitter disappointment brought tears to her eyes.

She should have known better than to try something silly. She had never been very good at silly.

In the bathroom, Corrine heard a noise and opened the door a crack, peeking out. Light poured in the living-room windows now. She heard her aunt Marilee's steps through the house, coming from the kitchen. The question of where her aunt had been so early in the morning flitted through Corrine's mind but was pushed out by the immediacy of her situation.

Her aunt, just entering the hallway, stopped on sight of Corrine, who said, "I...I started," and thrust her panties out through the cracked door.

"What?" Aunt Marilee looked puzzled.

Corrine closed her eyes and shook the panties, which Aunt Marilee took and looked at. Corrine opened her eyes to check her aunt's response.

Aunt Marilee's bottom lip quivered, and her eyes went all soft and warm, and Corrine could breathe again.

"Oh, sugar," Aunt Marilee said, pushing open the door and pulling Corrine out. She pressed Corrine against her, saying again, "Oh, sweetheart," and Corrine had to turn her head to the side to keep from being smothered. Aunt Marilee led them into her room and sat on her big bed, all the while saying how Corrine had taken a big step into womanhood.

"Remember all I told you? All we learned?" her aunt asked.

In her dedicated effort to school Corrine and Willie Lee at home last summer, Aunt Marilee had taught Corrine all about the human body. Aunt Marilee had done such a thorough job that when her teacher this year at school had addressed a lot of the same facts, Corrine had felt she could have taught the class.

Corrine nodded that she did remember.

"Do you have any questions?" asked Aunt Marilee, who had tears flowing down her cheeks even while she smiled.

Corrine didn't think the smile reached her aunt's

eyes. She wondered what her aunt was really think-ing, but she was not about to ask.

Then Aunt Marilee was stroking Corrine's hair. "I wish sometimes that I could keep you from growin' up.... Life just gets more complicated from here," her aunt said in a sighing voice.

Corrine thought life was pretty complicated now, but she was glad to be growing up, and it couldn't happen soon enough for her. She believed that when she grew up she would know all that she needed to know, and that she would never act as stupid as all the adults she saw.

Just then Aunt Marilee got to her feet. "We need to call your mother, and you can tell her. She'll want to share this time with you. Wouldn't you like to tell her of your big day?"

Corrine read the assumption on her aunt's face and said the expected "Yes." She watched as her aunt reached for the telephone on the nightstand. Her stomach tightened, and uncertainty tumbled over her body. Apparently Aunt Marilee had forgotten that early mornings were not a good time to call her mother, who was never, even when not hung over, in a good mood first thing in the morning. When Corrine had lived at home, she had learned not to wake her mother and in the mornings to make coffee so that her mother could have a cup as soon as pos-sible upon awaking. One never spoke to Corrine's mother before she had her coffee. And one generally didn't speak of private things at all with her mother, who did not like to speak of bodily functions.

"Oh, this phone doesn't have your mother's num-ber," Aunt Marilee said, and Corrine felt an instant of relief, but then Aunt Marilee was heading for the phone on her desk in the living room.

Corrine followed, for the first time noting that her aunt had on a long coat she had not before seen, and boots. Curiosity over her aunt's dress and where her aunt had been so early in the morning flitted through her mind but was replaced by wondering if she should remind her aunt that morning was not a good time to call her mother.

She threw herself into the big chair, to hide, but then she poked up on her knees and said in a sudden, hurried whisper, "You tell her, Aunt Marilee."

Aunt Marilee cupped Corrine's chin with her hand, which was cool and smooth.

A moment later Aunt Marilee was saying into the phone, "Anita, this is Marilee. Call up here this evenin', okay? Corrine has something to tell you." She paused and added, "We love you, Anita."

Aunt Marilee put down the phone. "Your mother's probably still sleepin', but she'll call us back this evenin'."

Corrine looked into her aunt's eyes and saw the eagerness to please there. She smiled, trying to give her aunt what she wanted, while inside she felt relieved not to have to hear her mother's groggy morning voice. Guilt came with the relief.

Aunt Marilee hugged Corrine in that way she had of trying to make everything right.

Just then the front doorbell rang, causing both of them to jump, and Aunt Marilee to let out an "Oh!"

Aunt Marilee moved to answer, and Corrine hurried to stand beside her, to be ready in case. She did not know in case of what, but Corrine always felt the need to be ready for dire happenings.

It was Willie Lee and Munro standing there.

Willie Lee was in his coat and Superman cape, and holding on to a little kitten squirming in his arms.

"I have been out-side." He stated the obvious as he came forward. "And I have a new kitten."

Corrine thought of Willie Lee's bed, of the lump she had thought was him.

"Oh, Willie Lee, not another one," Aunt Marilee said.

Just then the kitten managed to spring out of Willie Lee's grasp, bolted over his shoulder and across the porch. Willie Lee turned to call to it, but it disappeared beneath the house.

Aunt Marilee tugged Willie Lee inside and told him that he could have the kitten if it showed up again. She wanted to know what he had been doing outside.

"I have been learn-ing to fly," he said.

Three

Officially engaged...

Tate came driving up in his yellow BMW just as Marilee was herding the children out to her Cherokee. Tate had been taking them to school each day since the beginning of the school year, but he was late today, and Marilee had assumed that he had decided to skip this morning because of his mother's presence. She had thought him rude for not calling to tell her so, too, and now she felt silly for jumping to conclusions.

"Sorry I'm late," he said, leaning over and opening the passenger door.

"I just figured you were spending the morning with your mother." Marilee stood looking in the door at him. She felt sharp and was annoyed with herself because of it.

"My mother generally amuses herself in the mornin'. Come on, kids." He beckoned to Willie Lee and Corrine, who were already easing past Marilee and into the back seat.

Marilee slipped into the passenger seat, keeping her eyes averted as she buckled herself in.

"Thank you for the coffee," Tate said as he

shifted into Reverse. She looked over to see his blue eyes warm upon her.

"You're welcome," she answered, thinking how nice he was being, and of how he had not followed her out the door that morning. Shifting her gaze to Willie Lee, she made certain he had fastened his seat belt.

On the short drive to the school, Tate told them that his mother had arrived in the middle of the night. He used the phrase, "She landed in about one o'clock." This caused a bit of discussion.

"Did she land on the roof?" Willie Lee wanted to know.

"Uh, no...she stopped in the driveway."

"You said she land-ed."

"I meant she arrived at one o'clock," Tate corrected. "She drove into the driveway at one o'clock...and stopped." One had to be specific with Willie Lee.

"Oh. You do not mean your mo-ther can fly?"

"I guess she could, but Valentine doesn't have an airport, Willie Lee."

"I know that. I thought may-be your mo-ther could fly by her-self." Willie Lee's voice echoed with disappointment.

Understanding dawned on Tate's face. Then he shook his head. "No, son. My mother has a number of supreme abilities, but flyin' is not one of 'em."

Marilee wondered about his mother, who did seem somewhat unique.

He went on to tell Marilee that his mother had not even telephoned him that she was coming until she was one hour outside of town, when she called for directions. When Marilee commented on her youthful appearance, he said that his mother had turned seventy years old, and that youthful appearance was a family trait.

Marilee, looking at his profile and at the way his pale hair curled slightly behind his ear, said she saw it in him.

Tate stopped the BMW at the curb in front of the school, where Marilee got out and lifted the back of the seat to let the children out. In the manner of many a single mother carrying sole responsibility and occasionally being a little manic about it, Marilee adjusted Willie Lee's backpack to the proper position and then made certain Corrine had the coins she had given her for a pay phone, in case of emergency use.

"I could always use the office phone," Corrine said, even as she showed Marilee the coins.

"I just like you to have options. You can call me anytime, and I'll come get you, if you don't feel well." She wanted Corrine to know it was okay to come home, if she wanted. She wanted things to be different for Corrine than they had been for herself. For an instant in memory, she recalled being at school and feeling the blood run out between her legs, afraid of shaming herself and not having anyone to turn to.

"I'm okay," Corrine said in a low voice, shooting a cautioning glance toward the car and Tate.

Marilee got the message to shut up. "Okay. Love you."

She kissed them both quickly and then stood there, holding the car door, resisting the urge to stuff them back inside and race home with them, to keep them there with her, safe from the hard world.

She watched them walk away up the sidewalk,

falling in beside other children, yet seeming to stand out, different, marching to a drum unheard by others. Corrine, always protective, took Willie Lee's hand. Her niece possessed a fierce heart in a thin, fragile body.

And Willie Lee...Marilee's eyes lingered on her son, on his spiky blond hair that nothing could tame, almost like Willie Lee himself, different from others and going at his own pace in a world that hated different and slow and kept pressing him to be customary and fast. But he was Willie Lee, who had been denied oxygen at birth, or some such thing she had never fully understood and felt vaguely guilty at possibly causing. His brain could not comprehend as a standard brain and would never be able to go beyond the understanding of what it was right now, a five-year-old brain in a nine-year-old body.

And what did it matter? Her son was happy, and Marilee did her best to encourage him to be exactly who he was, while at the same time trying to help him to learn to live in the world in which he had to live.

It would no doubt be easier for him in the long run. As Willie Lee's body matured, his handicaps would be more and more obvious, and the world made allowances for handicaps that could be seen.

Not so for Corrine. Her handicaps were wounded emotions, invisible and considered shameful, if considered at all. The world was frightened of wounded emotions, because everyone had a bit of their own. To admit them meant admitting to weakness, and the world had little tolerance for weakness.

Marilee slipped back into the car.

"They are fine," Tate said, and squeezed her knee.

She glanced over and saw the look of understanding on his face. She wished she could believe him. There was such a faith in life about Tate Holloway.

With this thought came a jumble of emotions, admiration, gratitude, desire, all coming in a flood so strong that she flushed warmly and put her hand atop his, entwining her fingers with his. Quite suddenly her mind filled with the image of throwing herself onto Tate and doing it right there in the school parking lot, or, conversely, jumping out of the car, which was now exiting the lot, and running far, far away.

She let go his hand and turned her head toward the window, seeing the bare-branched trees against a clear blue sky, the empty playground, and the buses pulling into the garages. To say she was in a confused emotional state probably put it mildly.

"The announcement will be in the paper today," he said, and the comment drew her head around; his expression was pleased as all get-out.

"Yes, it will," she said, putting a pleased smile on her face for him. And she *was* pleased. Of course she was pleased.

"It's already on the Web site."

There was no need to tell him that she had not looked. She felt a little guilty for possibly not paying sufficient attention to their official engagement announcement.

Tate was saying, "Charlotte must not have been able to sleep last night. She got the entire front page updated already."

"Charlotte has become something of a computer maven. She put the announcement on the front page?'' She found this vaguely disconcerting. Marilee did not like to stand out.

Tate nodded happily. ''We thought that appropriate. After all, I am the publisher. You are marryin' big-time, darlin'.'' Tate *did* like to stand out. He enjoyed attention as much as he generally liked to give it.

They had come to the corner of Main and Church Streets. *The Valentine Voice* building sat like a stanchion on the north corner.

''Take me home,'' Marilee said, giving the building a glance. ''I'll work at home today.''

He looked at her, questioning.

''I just need the quiet. I need to concentrate to finish the piece on the teachers' proposed pay raise.''

Up Church Street, a right turn onto Porter, and then they were pulling into her driveway behind her white Cherokee. Munro, waiting on the porch, got to his feet. From next to him came a flash of fur.

''Oh,'' she said. ''I think that was the kitten Willie Lee wants slipping underneath the porch. I'm so tired of all these strays. We have finally gotten down to two rabbits, the mice and the goldfish.''

''Animals are his talent.''

Marilee agreed with a sigh. ''Remember, all these animals will be living with you soon.''

''There's plenty of room over at the Big House,'' he said, using the new term he had for his house. ''And I'll build him cages in the backyard, if we have to. We could have a budding veterinarian on our hands.''

''No, we don't. We have Willie Lee.'' Sometimes Tate, who could be as imaginative as a little boy, needed reminding that this was the real world.

He said, "Yes, it is Willie Lee, but no doubt his talent with animals will be profitable in some way."

At that, Marilee had to put her hand on his cheek. "I do love you, Tate Holloway." She did not say it often. Even now, the words came as if propelled past her reasoning mind, which could hardly believe in love between a man and a woman.

Then she was looking at his lips and bending toward him, and the next instant they had melted together in a deep kiss, causing her to put her hand to the back of his neck and hold him when he would have lifted his head. She went to kissing him for all she was worth, and he responded, and soon they were slipping down in the car seat. Marilee heard the caution in the back of her brain and pushed it away. She thought of the house, now empty of children, of her bed that she had not even made that morning.

Ask him...tell him how you feel...ask him inside...no, don't you dare do that.

Then Tate was pulling away. "Well...I guess we'd better remember where we are."

Marilee was quite limp and breathless. She saw his face all hot with passion, and she let him see clearly how she felt. Or she attempted to do this, but his response was to sit up straight and say that he needed to get on over to the office.

"I'd best check and make sure everything is on its way to being ready for deadline." His sky-blue eyes flitted up to her hair, then down to her lips, and then up again to meet hers.

"Yes," she said. "I need to get to work, too."

She scooted out of the seat, taking up her purse as she moved.

"I'll call you later."

"Okay. Have a good day."

She shut the car door and gave him a wave, then headed in long strides for the porch, thinking that they were behaving as though they were very good friends, which of course they were. Marilee was always good friends with the men in her life. She knew how to be a friend. It was being a lover that she found problematic.

She turned the knob on the unlocked front door. The old wooden door stuck, and she shoved it, realizing with a suddenness how very angry she felt.

The door swung inward, all the way back to bang against the wall. Munro, coming into the house at her feet, skittered out of the way at the sound, then shot her an accusing look.

Marilee took a deep breath and carefully closed the door. She leaned against it for a moment, then pushed herself away and went to her desk, took up the phone and punched the automatic dial for her aunt Vella, tucked the receiver into her neck and picked up a fingernail file as she listened to the slow rings across the line. Just when she thought her aunt was not going to pick up, she heard a click.

"Aunt Vella? Hello?"

"Yes, I'm here, sugar." Aunt Vella's voice came with static across the line. "I'm on my cell phone...calls forwarded...I'm...way...sale...Home De..."

"Aunt Vella? You're breakin' up. I'll call you later."

Hearing her aunt's acknowledgment, Marilee hung up and sat there, thinking of her situation, which was that here she was, marrying a man to whom she could not talk about her deep need for closeness.

Who she could not manage to get alone for any length of time—in fact, with whom being alone seemed to frighten her.

Her record in previous situations of this type was not a good one. Here she was, now officially engaged to a man, the third one in her lifetime, although she and Stuart hadn't really had an engagement of any longer than it took to get a marriage license and get married, and thinking that maybe she was, yet again, making a terrible mistake.

Four

One picture is worth a thousand words....

The clock on his desk read one-fifty when Charlotte called out from her reception desk, "Paper's here."

He popped out of his swivel chair, and was out of his office in three swift strides and heading through the tall-ceilinged main room at a pace just shy of running. He jerked open the heavy steel door into what had once, during the *Voice*'s heyday, been the printing press area and was now the loading garage.

The large overhead door was up and the opening filled with the back end of the printer's delivery truck. Diesel exhaust hung like a cloud, mingling with the scents of musty wood and brick and newspaper ink, bringing to Tate's mind faint memories of his boyhood, when he delivered papers at the crack of dawn.

"Yo, Editor!" Burly Chet Harmon, their circulation manager, and two of his helpers were busy unloading the bundled newspapers, stacking them on the dock, then loading them into the *Voice* van that sat nearby. Chet pulled a rolled paper from his back pocket and tossed it to Tate. "Here ya' go, boss. One picture is worth a thousand words, so they say." He grinned widely.

Newsprint ink wafted up to Tate as he unrolled the paper and saw the announcement right there on the front page. He gazed on Marilee's face smiling out from the paper. She had agreed to marry him, Tate Holloway, who was fifty-two years old and just now getting a start on a home and family. That he was seeing his dream come to reality was almost more than he could take in.

"Congratulations, Editor," called one of the men—Durham, who did the store route.

Tate grinned broadly. "Thanks!" He shot a wave to all, then turned, slammed the door closed and strode back through the main room, waving the newspaper at their reclusive comptroller, Zona, through her opened door, "It's here!" and to Sandy at the layout counter, who grinned his young, good ol' boy grin.

When he reached Charlotte's desk, he smacked the paper over her monitor screen. "Here it is."

"I've seen it."

"Yeah, well—" he dropped the paper so she had to grab it "—look at it now. *Published.*"

Heading on to his office, he ducked behind the door and snatched his brown suede jacket from the hook, slipping it on as he returned. "You know, they say if you see it in the *Voice,* it's the truth."

"You stole that." She was on her feet and holding the paper out to him. Charlotte was tall, and today, in heels, she seemed to look down on him.

"I only *borrow* the true statements." He adjusted his shirt collar over his jacket. "It's announced now...to everyone."

"Yes, it is." She pushed her glasses up over her thick dark hair and regarded him with her dark eyes.

He finished straightening his collar and met her gaze for a moment, savoring an accomplishment.

Charlotte gave him one of her rare smiles. "Congratulations. You two are perfect for each other."

"Thank you. I think so." He couldn't seem to stop grinning. "I'm off for an hour."

"Show-off," she said with a shake of her head.

"You bet." And he was out the door into the bright winter sunlight and crisp, fresh breeze.

He slipped into his car and backed out onto the street. There was one person he had to show first. He owed it to Parker Lindsey. They had become friends, of a sort. They had shared a rivalry for Marilee—which Tate had won—and they shared the same hour in the morning for jogging, where Parker by far proved the more hearty runner. These things were ties enough. It seemed the honorable thing to do, to tell Lindsey in person, and the reason Tate hadn't told him straight away, after settling things with Marilee on Sunday, was that Lindsey had been off at a convention down in Houston and had returned only yesterday.

Guilt nagged at him that he had not gone over to speak to Lindsey last night. He didn't want the man to hear the news from someone else. But last night he'd been full of Marilee's good stew and biscuits, and crawling into bed before he thought of it. He hadn't even mentioned about Lindsey to Marilee.

Possibly Marilee had broken the news to her former fiancé that morning. But that did not take care of Tate's sense of responsibility. Okay, might as well admit that a great deal of pride was involved. Such an attitude seemed small on his part. Oh, well, such was he and such was life, he thought, grinning just a bit as he pulled into the gravel lot of the Lindsey Veterinary Clinic.

"Doc's out back, workin' on a cow," the young girl at the desk told him. She was new to him; she had dyed black hair, spiked. "You can go on back through here."

Tate, tapping the newspaper against his thigh, went through the main lab room and opened another door, stepping into the large rear room with two stalls. Parker was coming out of one.

"Hey, Editor," Parker said, peeling off a soiled glove that covered his arm to his shoulder.

"Hey, Doc." Eyeing the plastic glove, Tate said, "I admire your courage, putting your hand deep into parts unknown."

Parker grinned. "Always interesting. Found a Wal-Mart bag this time."

"Empty?" Tate asked.

"Not exactly."

Just then another figure stepped out from the stall, carefully closing the gate behind her. It was a woman. Slim, blond hair, good-looking. She had on a medical smock. Parker often had interns in training, and he seemed to manage to get the pretty females.

Parker introduced them. "Amy, this is the illustrious editor of *The Valentine Voice,* Tate Holloway. We all just call him Editor," he said to the girl. "Editor, this is Amy Lawrence, my new partner."

Partner?

Amy was a no-nonsense sort and stuck out her hand for a firm shake. "I'm Amy Lindsey now."

Tate took that with surprise, looking from the

woman to Lindsey, who blushed and rubbed his nose.

"He isn't used to it yet," the young woman said, flashing a grin. "I guess I'll have to make him practice saying it: Mrs. Amy Lindsey."

Lindsey put his now clean arm around her. "Yes, that's right. Editor, please meet my wife…Mrs. Amy Lindsey."

The two were about the same height and coloring. And they were clearly two people in love.

Tate recovered his senses. "Well, congratulations!" he said and stuck out his hand to shake Lindsey's. "This is…quite a surprise. You go away to a veterinarians' convention and return with a wife." The man had upstaged him.

"Yeah, well…" said Lindsey, whose eyes returned warmly to the woman at his side.

"It came as a surprise to us, too," she said with a laugh.

Tate said, "So, you have captured our proverbial bachelor. You must be awfully special." He looked her over. She was younger than Parker, possibly as much as fifteen years younger, he would guess. The difference was probably a good match.

And she was a talker, was Amy Lawrence Lindsey. An up-front, straight talker, who quite quickly imparted the information that she and Lindsey had met over two years ago and renewed acquaintances at the convention. "I make up my mind pretty quickly, and Parker figured he wasn't getting any younger."

She draped herself there against her husband. They were in love. It was fantastic.

Probably won't last, Tate thought, and then purposely swept that bit of uncharitable negativity out of his mind.

He was so stunned by this turn of events that he almost forgot his own news, and in fact when Lindsey asked why he had come by, he felt a little defeated. Then he held out the newspaper and showed his announcement to the man who had been Marilee's former lover and almost husband.

"Well, that's fine," Lindsey said slowly after long seconds of looking at the photograph. His eyes came up to meet Tate's. "I'm really glad for both of you, Tate. You're good for Marilee." He meant it.

"Thank you. I think I am, and I know she is good for me. And I was hopin' you would be willin' to stand up with me as my best man." He was aware asking was a tall order, but he didn't have a close friend, and he meant it as an honor to Lindsey, too.

"I'd be glad to, Tate. Thank you." The man spoke sincerely.

"You bet." Well, he'd said what he had come to say. He shook Lindsey's hand and wished the two newlyweds a good future, then walked back out into the late winter sunshine, fighting off a very foolish annoyance at Lindsey for having upstaged his news. As he got back in his car, he figured his general attitude of Parker Lindsey being a childish sort was the pot calling the kettle black.

Then his gaze fell to the newspaper lying on the seat beside him, to his and Marilee's picture. Happiness took over, for Lindsey who he no longer had to feel guilty about leaving odd man out, and for himself, because he was getting the woman of his dreams, and for the whole dang world.

He caught a glimpse of himself in the rearview

mirror and saw he was smiling broadly. He was a pretty handsome fella.

Coming back into town, stopping at the light at Main and Church Streets, he saw Mayor Upchurch, a bucket of fried chicken under his arm, crossing the street from the Quick Shop to City Hall.

"Hey, Walter!" Tate hollered, and waved the paper out the window while turning to slip up to the curb in front of City Hall.

Just then a horn blared and brakes squealed. It was a brown UPS truck taking the same space while Tate had been looking at the mayor. He squeezed on past and pulled to the curb haphazardly in front of the truck.

"Hey, Editor!" It was Buddy Wyatt, his young neighbor from the far end of Porter Street, popping out of the UPS truck with a large box.

"Sorry I about ran into you," Tate said, "but I'm engaged!" Tate thrust the newspaper at him, and the young man peered at the front page, then slid his gaze to Tate. The boy probably thought Tate beyond such a thing as newlywed bliss; Buddy wasn't but about twenty-five, lived at home with his mother and had as a main ambition to sport the biceps of Atlas.

"Hey, that's cool, Editor. But you'd better be more careful watching where you're goin'. Don't think your fi-an-cée would be too happy should you get run over." He gave the box he carried a bit of a toss, flexing his biceps, which showed beneath the short sleeves he sported, even in the winter, and then went through the door that Mayor Upchurch held open.

Tate showed the mayor the announcement as the two of them entered the building. Walter Upchurch handed him the warm bucket of chicken and took the paper, reading the announcement aloud; he slapped Tate on the back, and together they showed all the clerks, and the mayor's wife, who stopped by, caught her husband with the greasy fried chicken and scolded him severely for setting himself up for a heart attack and leaving her a lonely widow.

Tate thanked God for giving him a partner like his Marilee and not a harpy like Kaye Upchurch.

From City Hall, he went down to the Main Street Café, where he showed everyone in there his great news and bought a round of coffee. After that he continued up and down Main Street, with its shops sporting fluttering flags of various sentiments and its sidewalks newly planted with redbud trees, for which Tate had led the fund drive. He stopped in the shops and met people on the sidewalk, and spread the news that he and Marilee were formally engaged and had set the date for their nuptials. He wanted to make certain everyone knew, and he wasn't trusting to the newspaper or gossip to get the job done.

At the Sweetie Cakes bakery, he ordered a double chocolate cake for that evening, a surprise and celebration of the official announcement. "Marilee loves her chocolate," Bonita Embree said knowingly.

"I know how to keep my girl happy," Tate said.

Bonita, laughing gaily, said, "Better than sex."

Tate ducked out on that and headed down to Grace Florist, where he ordered a mixed spring bouquet.

"It's still winter. May snow, the weatherman says," said Fred Grace.

"All the more reason for a spring-looking bouquet. Deliver it this afternoon, will ya'?"

He wrote on the card to go with the flowers: *Thank you for agreeing to be my wife…with love from the happiest man in the world.* Lay it on thick.

Why did he feel vaguely guilty? He hadn't known she was coming at the crack of dawn to make him coffee. She had hurried away, like she didn't want him to bother her. And he hadn't thought she seemed as if she wanted him to ask about her unusual actions. Marilee could get real touchy about some stuff.

Probably it was her way of celebrating this special day, and he wanted to show her that he felt the same.

Outside of the florist he ran into Norm Stidham, owner of the Texaco, married for thirty-five years and father of eight. "Well, you've been a bachelor for quite a while, Editor," Stidham said in his direct manner. "Do you know full well what you are gettin' into?"

To which Tate replied, "Yes, sir, I do. I'm more than ready to take me a wife and her children."

It was with this swelling thought that he entered Blaines' Drugstore and showed the announcement to Vella Blaine, Marilee's aunt and the most influential person in her life.

Vella was handling the soda counter by herself, it being a quiet time of day at the drugstore. She met him with her normal warm smile and reached to take the newspaper out of his hand. "Marilee called me this morning, but I was on my way to the Home Depot and haven't had time to call her back. Perry!" she shouted. "Come out and see Tate and Marilee's engagement in the paper. Tate's brought it hot off the press."

Tate watched the older woman's face as she peered through her bifocals, reading the announcement. For the first time he noted a bit of resemblance between the older woman and Marilee. It was there in the concentrated expression.

He felt a little disconcerted with the realization. Although he admired Vella's intelligence, grace and liveliness—in fact, he often encouraged Marilee to loosen up and be more lively—in that moment the thought sliced through him that if Marilee adopted some of the attitudes that Vella had of late, he would not care for it at all. Vella could get out of hand. She could be a demanding woman.

He had this thought as Perry came out from the pharmacy, smoothing his hair down as if he were about to face a judging. "What is it, Vella? I couldn't hear you." His gaze came to Tate. "'Lo, Tate, how are ya?"

With a raised voice, Tate said, "I'm an officially engaged man."

"It's Marilee's and Tate's engagement announcement in the paper," Vella told her husband. Perry had been getting progressively harder of hearing and was resisting a hearing aid. His resisting annoyed his wife, but Tate could understand the man's point of view. Some things were hard for a man to accept.

"I read it. I read the paper online this mornin'." Perry was definitely a video man; he loved his television and had recently gotten hooked up to the Internet through cable.

Vella said with aggravation, "Tate brought the paper especially to show us. You need to read the announcement printed on real paper." Vella was not a fan of television or computers.

Perry nodded and took the newspaper his wife shoved at him and began to read, while Vella asked

Tate if he wanted cold tea or hot coffee. Tate chose the coffee.

When Vella set it in front of him, she said, "Marriage to Marilee isn't goin' to be one long picnic. You'd better be ready goin' in."

He blinked. "Yes, ma'am. I don't believe any marriage is any picnic."

"You got that right. Just remember that Marilee is your gift from God and you are her gift from God. Know that deep down, and then, when disagreements come, you can stand them."

She cast Perry a glance of rare adoration, and this surprised Tate, who averted his gaze to his coffee and pondered what he and Marilee would be like at their age.

He would wear a hearing aid, he decided.

When Tate got up to leave, Perry slapped a hand on his shoulder and walked him to the door, leaning close to his ear to say, "If you decide you want any of that Vi-agra, I can give you a discount, since you'll be family. You let me know."

Tate managed to reply, "Okay...bye now," and got himself out on the sidewalk, where he stood for a few seconds in a daze, then spied Sheriff Oakes stepping of the police station next door and turning in Tate's direction.

"Hi there, Neville. Have you seen the paper yet?"

Tate waved the paper at the big man, who was a good head taller and twice as big around, and who took the newspaper and read the headline, saying, "Well, well," even as he moved the toothpick he invariably kept in his mouth from one side to the other.

Tate, watching the toothpick, reassured himself

that the big man had not, in the year that Tate had known him, come near choking.

The sliver of wood disappeared into the sheriff's mouth, where the sheriff broke it in two before he leaned to the side and spat it out. "Well," the sheriff said again, "I congratulate you, but I really think you should give this another thought. You don't know when you are well-off. Here you are at middle-age…"

Tate sort of jumped at that. Middle-age? It was true, but he didn't like the sound of it.

"…with a fancy car and a house on your own. You are set, man. She'll make you get rid of that car, and take my advice and don't be fallin' for that 'honesty in everything, so we can be closer' stuff. My wife still won't let me forget about what I told her about when I was seventeen. And just a minute ago she called to tell me she is haulin' my butt off on one of those Caribbean cruises. Says we have to relate. She gets that on *Oprah*."

The sheriff pulled out a fresh toothpick and jabbed it in the air toward Tate. "We got three kids. Wouldn't you say that's relating?"

Tate said he thought it was.

"Well, I gotta get on down to the bank and see about a loan for this romantic Caribbean getaway. Maybe go see about a vasectomy, too, because I don't want to end up with another tax deduction from this trip, either. Take my advice and don't encourage Marilee for any more children."

He headed on down the sidewalk, leaving Tate standing there, blinking and drawing in a good breath, struggling to hoist his enthusiasm back up from the ditch that had momentarily swallowed it.

This was hard work, as now his thoughts were running with questions. Surely Marilee wouldn't want any more children.

What if she did, and he couldn't provide them? He didn't know about that, not having any of his own. And he was middle-aged. Uncle Perry's voice offering the stimulating virility drug echoed in memory.

Was he up to all that was going to be required of him?

Five

A Chocolate Day...

Charlotte called and told her, "Leo, Jr.'s on his way over with five copies of the paper. That way you'll have some clippings for your mother. I know she'll want to show them around."

"Oh, yes. Thanks so much, Charlotte. I had forgotten." Marilee raked back her hair and thought how Charlotte was good at remembering these details. Charlotte took loving care of her invalid mother; she bought Mrs. Nation an ice-cream cone almost every day and fed it to her.

"I'll laminate two clippings," Charlotte said crisply. "That way you'll have one, and one for your mother. Permanent copies."

Laminate? The announcement could end up outlasting the marriage.

Replacing the receiver, she scolded herself for such negative thoughts. One could not go into a marriage with such an attitude.

Oh, maybe it was normal to have fears. Life certainly was not a secure proposition.

Of late, painful memories of the past seemed to be weighing on Marilee's shoulders. Neither herself, her sister Anita, nor their mother had thus far succeeded in what could be called a good and lasting relationship with a man. Her grandmother, her mother's mother, had had three husbands, one had embezzled and run off, one had just run off, and another had stayed while having a continual affair with a neighbor woman.

Maybe it was some disorder of the female side of the family, like something lacking in the blood, causing them not to choose well, or to drive men to drink, to dire actions, or to simply run away.

With thoughts of her own mother, Marilee opened the center drawer on her desk and took out a chocolate Hershey's Kiss. It was the last one in the little dish. She unwrapped it and popped it on her tongue. Then she sighed.

She had always felt herself to be one more disappointment in a lifetime of disappointments to her mother. Right off the bat, Marilee had been a girl instead of the boy that Norma had been set on as a first child. Her mother had counted on a son to take care of her, since she had already discovered her weak husband was not going to do that to her satisfaction. Second, Marilee had not come to be the great beauty that won the "Little Miss" contest in grade school nor the homecoming queen title in high school. A shy and studious girl, she had refused to even enter those contests, no matter how her mother had coerced, pleaded, threatened.

Then Marilee had run off to college, leaving her mother alone to cope with a failing husband and high-spirited younger daughter. Marilee had married Stuart, who was, to his credit, a semifamous and successful man, and who had proceeded to take Marilee off even further to see the world, while her mother was back home dealing with a husband who had the disgrace to choke to death while drunk and leave his wife, a victim of leftover Victorian mores, desperately seeking another man to support her.

When Marilee had returned home, she had divorced Stuart—her mother had not divorced her father, no matter what—so therefore she gave her mother a divorced daughter with an embarrassing grandchild who was disabled. Furthermore, Marilee had had an affair, which the entire town knew of, with Parker Lindsey, a very eligible bachelor and upstanding veterinarian, but had not gotten him to the altar.

That Marilee had turned down the altar because she had grown to see many errors in her ways, primarily that she and Parker were not at all a suitable match, was not how her mother saw it. In her mother's eyes, her daughter had failed to snatch up a good thing and become a well-to-do woman of society, such as it was in Valentine.

Now, at last, Marilee was doing something right in her mother's eyes. "Well, I'm so glad you are showing some sense, Marilee. I won't have to worry about your future," her mother had said upon receiving the news of the engagement.

Leo Pahdocony, Jr., riding his fancy bicycle right up the stairs to her front door, brought five copies of the newspaper. Leo, Jr. was set to join the Olympic cycle team when he went to Rice in the fall. Reggie, his mother, was set on her son *not* following in his father's footsteps and kept him on track for an education that would bring him fortune and keep him too busy to look at girls, who were obviously looking at him and his steel-hard body. Marilee didn't think Reggie needed to worry about the girls. Leo, Jr.'s first love was bikes.

"Thanks, Leo." She left off the junior out of respect that seemed his due.

"You bet." With strong arms, he flipped his bike around and rode off down the steps, going off like a rocket on the walkway.

Marilee went into the kitchen and laid the newspapers on the table. There at the bottom of the front page was her and Tate's picture.

Gosh, it looked good, it really did. Tate was handsome as all get-out. His warmth shone out. And she didn't look so bad...looked pretty, actually.

Marilee read the headline: Publisher And Associate Editor To Wed.

No matter what happened from here, *this* would please her mother.

"Mama, I have the copies of the announcement. If you're going to be home, I'll get the children from school, and we'll come up with the paper."

"What announcement?"

"The engagement announcement—it's in the *Voice* today."

"Oh, yes, dear, bring it...and will you stop and get a quart of milk, a loaf of bread and a pair of panty hose? It's turned so cold, I don't want to go out."

After ascertaining the correct color of panty hose, Marilee hung up, then went to her bedroom to put on shoes and lipstick and a comfortable old barn coat. Seeing her trench coat caused her to blush. She pushed it out of sight.

She checked her nightstand drawer for a piece of chocolate and found a lone Hershey's Kiss, which she ate, but it did not satisfy the craving that had come over her, so she checked the kitchen cabinet, where she liked to keep chocolate in various forms. There was only powdered cocoa. Her purse was empty of chocolate, too.

Taking up the copies of the *Voice*, she said, "Come on, Munro," to the dog, and headed out the door.

Driving at a rapid rate, she pulled the Cherokee into the Quick Shop and got a chocolate bar and two small packages of Hershey's Kisses. The Kisses went into her purse, while she ate the chocolate bar as she drove to school. She had to eat fast, as it was only a couple minutes' drive. Seeing Munro eyeing her, she put a small bite down for him. "You can't have any more. Chocolate can kill a dog."

At the rate she was consuming it, chocolate might kill her, too.

When she pulled into the waiting area for parents, she jammed the last of the bar into her mouth and chewed it while she wiped chocolate smears off the steering wheel with a tissue. The end-of-school bell pierced the air, and instantly children came pouring out of the building. She jerked the rearview mirror around, checked her mouth, wiped it with a tissue and applied lipstick, then tucked the chocolate-smeared tissues deep into her purse.

Should any woman with such a chocolate addiction consider herself sane enough to get married?

Getting out of the truck, she stood beside it, where Corrine and Willie Lee would be sure and see her.

They had the past days been walking home from school in the balmy weather.

Munro saw the children first and started off to meet them with his tail wagging. There was Corrine; her bright red sweater shone out. Corrine was clearly going to be willowy and beautiful, like her mother, Marilee thought with a pang. Anita had so many problems that seemed to stem from possessing a beauty that she could not manage to handle.

Willie Lee, dragging his book bag and with one tennis shoe untied, came running forward to fall on his knees and hug his dog and be kissed all over the face.

Munro was such a blessing, Marilee thought with gratefulness to God for sending the dog, one more stray that Willie Lee had attracted. It was because of the dog coming into their lives and bringing an important computer chip in his collar that Willie Lee could receive a reward and now be financially set for life. It was a miracle that even now she found hard to believe.

"I didn't know you were coming to get us." Corrine eyed Marilee in the way she had of summing up a situation.

"I think you deserve a treat today, Missy," Marilee said sweetly and hugged her niece. "And we're goin' up to Grandma's." She noted that Corrine's expression turned carefully blank.

"Hey, Ma-ma." Willie Lee grinned up at her from behind his thick glasses.

"Hey, sweetheart." She kissed him.

"You smell like choc-o-late," he told her.

It took twenty-five minutes to get to Lawton and her mother's house in a neighborhood of upscale twenty-year-old residences with sweeping lawns. Marilee pulled to a stop in the concrete driveway.

Munro had to wait in the car. A dog was not allowed in Grama's house, where there was pristine white carpeting. Willie Lee wanted to wait with Munro, but Marilee told him, "Honey, it's gotten too cold." The wind was cutting through her coat. "Munro is okay. He has a winter coat. You do not. Come on inside with me and Corrine."

She felt compelled to add to Munro, who gazed at her with sad eyes, "We won't be long."

Corrine carried the stack of newspapers, and Marilee hoisted the sack of groceries. They hurried, heads down, through the cold wind to the back door, which turned out to be locked.

Marilee pounded on the storm door.

The inside door opened. "Well, goodness knows... don't break the glass." Her mother stood back, gesturing. "Come in so we can get this door closed. You're letting in the cold."

The door got closed. Marilee took a good breath.

"Hello, Mother." She bent to kiss her mother's cheek. Her mother was a petite woman, and Marilee often felt awkward next to her.

And then she noticed her mother's chic black dress and pumps—stepping-out clothes. "You're looking pretty." Her mother was looking lovely these days, having lost weight and gotten very stylish since she had become a patron of the local *art league*.

"Oh..." Her mother smoothed her dress. "I was out at a meeting today and some shopping... but I got tired and thought I'd just not bother to get these things. But Carl likes the milk for his coffee... he just won't stop to get it."

Marilee set the bag of groceries on the counter, thinking of Carl not being inconvenienced, and how she wished she had not dragged the children into the store.

Her mother smiled brightly. "Here, you children sit at the table. I have apple juice for you." She looked questioningly at Marilee. "I didn't know if they liked this kind, but it's all I have."

"They love apple juice, thanks, Mom. Here, y'all take off your coats." Marilee helped Willie Lee, wanting to circumvent any possibility of him knocking over his apple juice.

"Marilee, this isn't the kind of panty hose I wanted." Frowning, her mother stared at the package.

"It was all they had. It's nude, like you wanted, and that's your size, right?"

"Well, yes, but I don't know if I'll like this kind." Her mother sighed. "Oh, well, I'm sure I can return them."

Marilee thought perhaps she should offer to return them.

The teakettle whistled on the stove. "I'm making us tea," her mother said, brightening. "Isn't this a day for tea? It's so seldom that you all come up to see me, and I have some exciting news."

"You do?"

"Yes. I found out just a few minutes ago, when Carl called. We're...oh dear, I don't have any Earl Grey." She raised her head from the container and looked at Marilee with doleful eyes.

"That's okay, Mom. I like regular best, anyway."

"Well, Earl Grey is my favorite...and it seems to

settle my stomach.'' She pressed a hand over her abdomen. ''I wish I had known I was out of it. I would have asked you to get some at the store.'' She stared forlornly at the teapot.

Marilee had the brief fantasy of calling Homeland and asking if they could deliver a box of Earl Grey in five minutes.

Popping to her feet, she looked in the refrigerator, thrilled to find a lemon. ''Here's a lemon, Mom. It is wonderful in tea, and good for the stomach.''

''Oh. Well, okay. Will you slice it, dear?''

As Marilee went to the counter, she glanced over to see Corrine's deep brown eyes watching her.

She cut several slices from the lemon and brought them to the table. Her mother followed with the teapot and cups on a tray, sliding the newspapers aside to make room. Marilee's gaze glided over the papers, and she asked, ''What is your exciting news, Mom?''

''Oh!'' Her mother slid into a chair and pressed her hands together. ''Carl and I are going on a cruise.''

''You are?''

Her mother and Carl, who was the owner of Cooper's Appliance Mart, had in the past year taken to traveling often to sales conventions. Her mother launched into explaining how she had just last night been telling Carl she was tired of winter, and how he had called to tell her there was a small convention of appliance salespeople taking place on a cruise out of Miami to the Caribbean.

''We can fly directly to Miami. I am so excited! Margaret Springer from the League went on a cruise last fall and said she had the best time. There's all this food and dancing…of course, Carl won't dance, but he likes to eat, and there's lots of card playing, too.''

"What is a cruuze, please?" Willie Lee asked.

Marilee, struck by a difficulty with the description, said, "It is a trip that people take sailing in a big ship on the ocean. Some trips are sailing across the ocean and some are sailing from island to island."

"They are trips for people to relax and have a good time out on the ocean," her mother said to him, speaking slowly and in the loud tone she always employed with Willie Lee, as if he were deaf. "People dress up in their prettiest clothes and talk and dance, and they can shop, too, right on the ship."

Marilee noticed Corrine tapping the stack of newspapers back toward the center of the table. Her niece regarded her pointedly.

"Oh, Mom...here's the announcement."

"The announcement?"

"The engagement announcement in the *Voice*."

Marilee passed a copy to her mother, who said, "Oh, yes," shot her a smile and then dropped her gaze to the page.

"Why, honey, this is a really good picture of you and Tate," she said with surprise. "What a couple you two make." Her tone held a warmth that Marilee felt all over. "You really look lovely here, dear, and Tate looks so handsome."

She had made her mother happy.

Then, "Oh, dear."

"What is it?" Where did the happiness go?

"Well..." Her mother's eyes came up slowly from the paper, and she gazed at Marilee with anguish. "That's the very week of our cruise."

Marilee, who distinctly remembered telling her mother the wedding date, looked at her mother, and her mother looked back with eyes just like Munro's. *People forget…people make mistakes.*

"I just can't cancel on Carl."

Marilee shifted her gaze and said, "Mother, don't worry about it. It's okay. Our wedding is just going to be small and short, not a big ceremony."

Hearing herself, she clamped her mouth shut.

"Well, my being at your wedding really isn't all that important," her mother allowed. "The important thing is Tate being there."

Marilee smiled at this truth. She was a woman grown. She did not need to impress her mother. She would never be able to impress her mother. And God knew she did not need at this late date for her mother to stand by her side.

Twenty minutes later, noticing that Willie Lee was falling asleep on Corrine, Marilee put him into his coat and lifted him into her arms. He was gaining weight; she did not know how much longer she would be able to carry him when he fell asleep. She would do it as long as she could, she thought, shifting his body, holding him so tightly that he gave a little grunt. She relaxed her hold.

At the door, her mother said, "I hope you understand about the cruise. It will be so good for Carl to get away. He stays under so much pressure."

"It's okay, Mom." She found the words came easily.

As they went out the door, she spied the package of panty hose on the counter. "Corrine, honey, get those hose. I'll return them for you, Mom."

Her mother thanked her profusely.

* * *

Willie Lee and Munro lay together on the back seat, beneath a wool throw Marilee kept in the Cherokee. The faint snoring was Munro's.

"You wanted to return the panty hose," Corrine reminded her as they went past Homeland.

"No, I don't feel like it now," said Marilee, watching the rush hour traffic. There was not such a thing as rush hour in Valentine. All the traffic made her feel a little insecure, and she felt the obligation to be alert, as her windshield kept misting over. She was always more cautious when she had the children with her.

"I'll do it for you, Aunt Marilee."

Marilee, stopped at a light, looked over to see Corrine's heart-shaped face with an eager-to-please expression. Experiencing a warm rush of emotion, she gave her niece's arm a squeeze. "You are about the sweetest thing on earth, you know that?" Corrine ducked her head, as she always did at compliments. "But I would much rather you stay warm and dry in the car. Let's just get ourselves home."

Her own home, with her children around her. There was no better place.

And in that instant, focusing her eyes on the wet pavement ahead, she knew the truest fact to be that these two children were her world. She needed them, maybe far more than they did her. It was a need that she could understand and that her heart expanded to accept.

She was not certain that she could do the same for Tate. Or any man. To allow herself to need a man made her so painfully vulnerable.

When they got home, the Grace Florist van was at the curb. Tiffany, the delivery girl, met them at the foot of the steps with an enormous bouquet of bright flowers in a basket.

"Miz James...these are for you."

"Oh! My goodness. Thank you," Marilee instinctively said, staring, stunned, at the bouquet.

"You'd better get them in out of the cold, Aunt Marilee."

Yes, indeed. Marilee stepped quickly, anxious to protect the delicate iris petals. But, oh, she had forgotten to tip Tiffany! Too late now.

She followed Corrine through the front door and received another surprise—delicious aromas and the sound of voices in the kitchen. She and Corrine looked at each other with questioning eyes.

Then through the house and the swinging door, pushing it wide to behold Tate's mother, Franny, sitting at the kitchen table, her feet propped up on another chair, paperback book in hand and a coffee cup in front of her. And there was Tate at the stove, a dish towel tucked around his waist, blue shirtsleeves rolled on his strong forearms.

Seeing his bare forearms always affected Marilee, and her gaze lingered there a long second, before Tate's holding up a wooden spoon jarred her thoughts back to the moment.

"Welcome home, sweetheart. We're havin' chicken and noodles, brussels sprouts, fresh, and tossed salad with sesame seed dressing."

All her favorites.

"I made sugared carrots for those of us who do not favor brussels sprouts." He winked at Corrine, and then his blue eyes came to Marilee's, and he gazed at her in an intense manner that caused her breath to catch in her throat.

"Look what I got on the way in," she said, finding her voice.

"Well, my golly. Do you think they're for you?" That was Tate, always kidding.

"The delivery girl said they were for a *Miz* James, but it could have been another." She set the bouquet on the table. "Hello...Franny." She was uncertain as to exactly how to address the woman.

Apparently she had chosen correctly. The woman smiled. "Hello, dear." Marilee took note again of the woman's loveliness. Surely that shade of carrot-red hair could not be natural, but no matter, it was a perfect choice.

"There's chocolate, Aunt Marilee." Corrine, at the counter, pointed to a cake.

"Well, my goodness."

Tate came toward her with a cup of something hot. Mocha, she caught by the aroma flashing past her nose.

He said, "I told you, this is a celebration. Sit and relax. I'm taking care of everything." He set the cup on the table and motioned her into a chair. "Where's Willie Lee?"

"Oh, my goodness, we left him in the car."

Marilee was instantly pushing to her feet, but Tate, pressing a hand on her shoulder, said he would get Willie Lee. "He's gettin' too heavy for you to carry around."

She sat there, with the leftover pressure of his warm hand on her shoulder, gazing after him, even after he had disappeared through the kitchen doorway. She heard the front door open and close.

Then she looked at Franny. "I don't know what I did to deserve finding such a man."

"Divine selection," the woman replied, and then motioned at the flowers, "Open the card. Is the bouquet from Tate?"

"Well, I assumed they were from him."

"Don't ever assume, dear. You can miss out on so many surprises."

Marilee, now wondering who the flowers could be from, if not from Tate, plucked the envelope out of the bouquet and opened it to pull out the card.

She immediately recognized the handwriting. "Oh, yes, they're from Tate," she said, happiness coming like little flashes of fireworks.

She read, and upon coming to *the happiest man in the world,* she burst into tears so strong that she had to put her arm around her middle, as if to hold herself together.

Corrine came over and patted her shoulder. Quite quickly in control, Marilee smiled and snatched a tissue from the box nearby and blew her nose. She hated acting so silly in front of Franny, who already must have a skewed opinion of her after that business of the morning. And heaven knew Corrine did not need to see one more emotionally confused woman.

"Flowers can do that to a woman," Franny said quite sensibly.

Marilee looked at her. "Yes...yes, they can. It's just that this is so sweet." But she couldn't show anyone. She involuntarily held the card to her chest.

"My son is quite a guy."

"Yes, he is." A sense of unworthiness flowed over her. It seemed fantastic that Tate could truly love her, Marilee.

Seeing Franny and Corrine turn their heads toward the doorway, Marilee twisted in her chair, prepared to thank Tate for the flowers. But, his expression...what had happened?

"We have a guest," he said, in a low voice because of Willie Lee's sleeping head against his chest.

A guest?

Then Tate had withdrawn and another man took the doorway.

"Hello, Marilee."

She took in the bright white shirt standing out against the growing dimness of the rooms behind him, a figure so tall that he seemed to have to duck.

"Ohmygod," she said, recognition dawning, slowly, like a foggy morning.

"Not exactly." He cocked his head and smiled.

"Stuart?" It could not be him.

"Yes. Surprise, sweetheart."

In a smooth, graceful movement, he stepped into the room and over to brush her lips with his.

Six

Lost in the Grand Canyon of life...

They had a guest, her ex-husband, who she had not heard from in almost two years, and who, having come right at suppertime, was asked to join them.

"We're havin' our engagement celebration. Please join us," Tate said to Stuart, while Marilee was still busy thinking: *ohmygod.*

She tried to regain coherent thought by busying herself with spreading the linen tablecloth on the big dining table, upon which Corrine placed the gold-trimmed china that would accommodate the down-home chicken and noodles. Tate, getting thoroughly carried away, lit candles.

Sitting with her ex-husband at her right hand, she shifted her gaze to look down the length of the candlelit table and into the handsome, smiling face of her fiancé and, returning his smile, wondered how the disconcerting situation had possibly come about.

Franny, who had brought a bottle of champagne, raised her glass and led them in a toast. "To Tate and Marilee and the vast possibilities stretching ahead of them."

Vast possibilities. It sounded like the Grand Canyon, far too wide to traverse.

Feeling Stuart's gaze on her, Marilee concentrated on getting her napkin spread in her lap, and next to seeing that dishes were passed. And keeping a smile on her lips and her eyes not lighting any one place.

Then here came Willie Lee, accompanied by Munro, padding in his sock feet from the bedroom. "I am hun-gry."

Marilee and everyone, having momentarily forgotten his existence and the ramifications, sat staring at him as he went to the chair where he normally sat at the dining table, which was at this moment occupied by Stuart.

"Who are you?" he asked Stuart in his forthright manner.

Marilee said, "Willie Lee, honey, this is your daddy. He has come to see you." Suddenly her vision was blurry. She blinked, seeing Willie Lee's eyebrows go up. "It is a surprise," she added, feeling totally inadequate to explanations.

"You are my dad-dy?" he asked Stuart.

"Yes. I am...Willie Lee."

He spoke as if uncertain of his son's name. No doubt he had forgotten the existence of a son, as well he had intended to do.

"Hel-lo," said Willie Lee and stuck out his hand for a shake, as so often he and Tate did with each other.

Stuart's eyebrows rose, and, hesitantly, he took the small hand, shaking it. "Hello."

"This is Mun-ro. He is my dog."

"Ah...hello, Munro."

"You are sit-ting in my chair, but I will sit over

here," Willie Lee said as he rounded the table to the chair beside Corrine, and at Tate's right. "You can see me from there," he added in his very literal fashion.

Marilee had the urge to grab her son to her and hug him and tell him he truly was the most magnificent soul on earth.

Stuart said, "Ah...thank you."

"I'll get your plate, honey." She started to rise, but Tate was already on his feet and reaching for a china plate and silverware.

"Here ya' go, buddy."

"Thank you." His thick glasses reflected the candlelight as he looked across at Stuart. "I like chicken and noo-dles. Do you?"

"Yes." Stuart looked down at his plate. "I haven't had it in a long time, but yes, I believe I do." His eyes came up to Marilee, and an expression crossed his face that she could not define and did not care to try.

In the midst of Stuart's telling about a trip to Scotland to photograph and report on castles, the telephone rang.

Marilee instantly threw down her napkin. "I'll get it," and she dashed through the swinging kitchen door to answer the phone on the wall.

Alone in the kitchen, thank you, God.

"Hello, Marilee. This is Parker."

Parker.

She pressed her fingers to her lips. Caught up in her inner turmoil, she had forgotten him. Guilt fell all over her. She always experienced a great deal of guilt about Parker; she always seemed to forget about him.

"Oh, Parker, I'm so glad you called. I've wanted to speak with you." Moving her palm to her cheek, she searched for words to tell the man she'd almost married some six months previously that she was about to marry another. Of course, her and Tate's engagement could not be a surprise to him.

"Well, I just got back in town yesterday," he said. "I stayed at the convention a couple of days longer...because I got married."

Marilee pressed her back against the wall. "You got married?"

"Yes. And Tate was by here today...telling me that you two are gettin' married next month."

"Yes, yes we are." Her mind was spinning. She had the sense of being in *The Twilight Zone*.

Tate had not told her he'd seen Parker, but there had not been time for Tate to tell her anything. She pressed harder against the wall, holding herself up.

"I look forward to meeting your wife." Her voice dropped. "I'd like you both to come, Parker...to our wedding."

"I'm going to be Tate's best man.... Amy and I will both be there," he said with a warmth that went to her bones.

"Oh, good." Then, "You sound happy, Parker. Really happy."

"I am." The two words rang with joy. "I'm a lucky guy, and I can't wait for you to meet Amy."

Amy, a feminine name, perfect for a woman for Parker.

"I look forward to that. And, Parker—I'm glad

for you." They had been much better friends than lovers.

"Thanks, Marilee. Me, too, you."

They bid goodbye, and she slowly replaced the receiver, standing with her hand on it. There were just too many things happening one right after another. All she could do was hang on until everything eventually stopped. Things did eventually come to an end, of some sort.

Tate was poking at a flickering fire in the fireplace. He liked to start fires, liked to have something to poke at, Marilee thought, watching him.

Franny had long gone, the children were in bed, and Marilee was ready to follow them. She was ready to crawl into bed, eat a package of Hershey's Kisses and pull the covers over her head.

She was composing phrases to ease the men out of the house when Tate, carefully setting aside the poker, asked Stuart where he was staying.

"Uh, I meant to ask if there was a hotel in town," Stuart answered, slowly uncrossing his long legs and sitting forward in the big chair.

"You passed it on your way in," said Tate. He returned to his seat on the couch, draping his arm along the back behind Marilee, his hand brushing her shoulder in a proprietary gesture. "The Goodnight, out on the west highway."

"I did? I don't remember it."

"Well, you did. Vintage place. Has small duplex cabins. Gives you privacy."

"Ah, yes, but does it provide running water?"

"I think you'd find a comfortable place up in Lawton," Marilee put in and scooted to the edge of the couch. "It has really grown since you were here. And now I'm ready to call it a night. The children will be up for school in the morning."

So much for subtlety. "We've enjoyed your visit so much, Stuart, and we look forward to seeing you tomorrow, I hope. I know Willie Lee wants to get more time with his father. We want you to visit as much as you can while you're here."

She made the best attempt she could at softening her abruptness, even as she rose and went to the door, gave him a quick hug and ushered him out.

As soon as she had shut the front door after Stuart, she turned to Tate and told him, in a manner she wished was not blunt but was, that she was too tired to talk anymore. It was as if she had come to the end of her energy and there was absolutely nothing left; she had gone bone-dry in the emotion department.

Tate responded to this by saying instantly, "Go to bed." He gave her a quick kiss, the touch of his warm lips on hers, and then, in long, totally unhesitating strides, he headed for the back door, where he paused only long enough to say, "Sleep late. I'll get the kids ready for school."

She closed the door and stood looking through the glass, watching him be swallowed up by the darkened backyard and thinking that there was nothing more a woman could want in a man than agreeability.

Then she went to the bathroom, stripped in two seconds and stood beneath the hot shower spray, letting the water pummel all thought right out of her head.

When Willie Lee heard the water running in the bathroom, he rose up, slipped from under the covers and went to the deep dark by the closet. He felt for and pushed on the closet light switch; there was enough glow through the cracks around the door for him to locate his shoes, which he put on, and then his coat and his cape.

On his knees on his bed, he pulled the string for the blinds, raising them as quietly as possible, and then lifted the window.

"What are you doin'?"

Corrine's loud whisper caused him to jump.

"I am learn-ing to fly. Go on, Mun-ro." Being a very good dog, Munro disappeared out the window.

"You're what?" Corrine came scrambling across his bed.

Willie continued on his course, sticking his feet out the window and getting himself sat down on the windowsill. He was trying to get out before the water stopped running in the bathroom. Once his mother told him not to do something, he would not be able to. So far, she had not ever told him not to go out his window.

"Willie Lee, you get back in your bed." Corrine grabbed hold of his coat.

He prepared to tell her that she was not his boss, when, quite suddenly, the running water sound stopped in the bathroom. Willie Lee looked at Corrine, and she looked back at him.

The next minute low music sounded through the wall. His mother had turned on the little radio in there. That meant she would be there a while, probably painting her toenails. His mother sometimes liked to paint her toenails and eat chocolate bars.

Also, at that same moment of hearing the radio,

Corrine relaxed her grip on his coat. Willie stuck out his hands, closed his eyes, and jumped.

He landed with a thud, falling over on his side onto the cold, wet ground.

Well, he *almost* flew.

"Willie Lee?" Corrine's head poked out the window.

"I am go-ing to my tree-house," he called up to her.

"No!"

He continued, running as best he could, following Munro, who was ahead of him.

Just then, at the corner of the house, Munro darted to the back steps, through the yellow glow cast by the porch light and disappeared into the darkness beneath the house.

Willie Lee heard hissing and snarling. Munro yelped and popped out, then ran back again into the darkness. Willie Lee followed and got down on his hands and knees, entering the dark area beneath the steps.

Light filtered through cracks in the steps. He saw a big cat and something smaller. *His kitten!* He just knew it was his kitten—and the big cat was Bubba, *Mr. Tate's big old yellow cat. Bubba was beating up his kitten!*

"No, Bub-ba!" Willie Lee reached out and shoved the big cat, but the big cat just hopped sideways, out of reach. With ears flattened and growling in his throat, he advanced against the kitten, whose small shadow could just be seen, crouching against the inside of the bottom step.

Willie Lee tried to crawl closer. "Here, kit-ty, kit-ty."

Munro darted in, but Bubba got his nose, and Munro jumped back with a yelp.

Then here came Corrine. "What are you doin'? Aunt Marilee's gonna hear."

"Bub-ba is be-ing mean to my kit-ten." He was about to pound on the door and get his mother-who-saved to come to the rescue, but he could not leave his kitten. Bubba would eat him up. "Cor-rine?"

"Oh…sheesh." Corrine picked up a dirt clod of substantial proportion and threw it at the big yellow cat, saying at the same time, "Get him, Munro." The clod hit Bubba in the side, and Munro, sufficiently supported now, made another dart. The big cat, seeing he was outnumbered, went running away into the deep dark beneath the house, or as near running as a tub of lard can go.

Despite Corrine warning him about snakes, Willie Lee scrambled forward until he could grab the kitten. It scratched his hands, but he held on, pulling it out from beneath the steps.

On his knees outside the foundation, Willie Lee cuddled the kitten close. It was shaking. "He got hit by a car this morn-ing and got dead-ed," he said, sniffing back tears, "but I picked him up, and he got okay. He needs me to take care of him."

Corrine petted the kitten. "You mean he got knocked out and woke up."

Willie Lee did not see any point in correcting Corrine. He pressed his cold nose into the kitten's warm fur. The kitten smelled like cold dirt.

"It's okay, Willie Lee. You have the kitten now."

"Why was Bub-ba so mean to him?"

"Well…" She paused, and he waited. "It is what grown boy cats do. Bubba was just bein' a boy cat and protecting his territory. But when this kitten is grown, Bubba won't do it, or this kitten will whip Bubba's tail.''

''I do not like that. I want them to be frie-ends.''

''Yeah, well, we all want a lot of things. Come on. We gotta get back in before Aunt Marilee finds out we are out, or we're gonna get it.''

Willie Lee thought that Corrine would know just how to get back inside, and he was very happy to be taking his kitten. Only he had not practiced learning to fly, and this made him sad.

Then Corrine said, ''Let's go back by the fence, where it's dark, and see if we can see the stars.''

To his great surprise, she was already dashing off across the yard, with Munro at her heels. Willie Lee, holding his kitten close to his chest, took off after them with his ever-clumsy run.

He wished so much that he could run like other boys. Feeling his cape flutter behind him, he thought, someday I will fly.

The decor of the cottage room at the Goodnight Motel contained every god-awful ugly style of the fifties, sixties and seventies, starting with the giant rose-printed curtains and going on to the green shag carpeting.

After his first look, Stuart turned off the glaring overhead light and switched on the bedside lamp, putting most of the room in shadow. Then he sank down to the edge of the mattress. He felt queasy, as he often did when exhaustion overtook him. He had been too exhausted to drive up to Lawton and a decent hotel, and determined to show Tate Holloway that he did not require pampering. It had taken almost twenty minutes to get registered by the chatty old man who was hard of hearing and was watching a television turned up to shouting level. Only one other cottage in the strip appeared occupied; it had two cars parked in front of it, indicating the probability of a tryst. The No-Tell Motel was what Stuart would have named the place.

Just then he noticed the brown metal box sitting on the bedside table. The bed had a vibrating machine.

After several long seconds of staring at the box, he dug into his slacks pocket, came up with a quarter and stuck it in the slot. The bed began to vibrate. The thing actually worked.

Stuart lay back gingerly, wondering if it would make him more nauseous. It did not. In fact, he began to relax.

His mind slipped into memories of a time he and Marilee had stayed at one of those once-modern economy motels that sported a vibrating bed, which by that time had passed the summit of popularity but were still frequently found. He recalled her youthful delight in putting in the quarters and laughing with the sensation.

And he recalled what she had felt like beneath him, giving him all she had, while the bed rocked underneath and he rocked on top.

He ached right that moment to reach back in time and touch her as she had been. To have her fill him up, as she had then, with the life of her.

Pained, he threw his forearm over his eyes. He had hardly thought of Marilee since the day he had left her, but these days the memories came repeatedly, plaguing him with a relentlessness, now that he was dying.

Damn Stuart James anyway. His showing up right at this time was no coincidence. No, sir. James professed no knowledge of the engagement, but Tate was as certain as he had spit in his mouth that the man had read about the engagement on the *Voice* Web page. He judged the man a liar and a taker. While he could admit to being on the prejudiced side, Tate had a good ability to call people as they were, and he had called this man correct, by golly.

There was no sleeping. Middle of the night, and Tate got up, got dressed in sweatpants and shirt and Nikes. Passing his mother's closed door on the landing, he saw light showing beneath. His mother never seemed to sleep, although since he did not hear a sound within, perhaps she slept with the light on.

Down the stairs with light steps, out the front door and across the porch into a cold, misty night. His big tomcat, Bubba, popped out from beneath the porch and came bouncing behind him to the street, where the animal stopped. Bubba had gotten too fat and old to even go halfway down the street.

Tate pushed himself to pick up the pace, heading along Porter and, despite good intentions, slowing to see if Marilee's bedroom light was on. Yes, it was.

He stood for a moment, gazing at the light and imagining going in her back door and into her bedroom and taking her into his arms to remind her that she was his.

Quite quickly his imagination went headlong into seeing them naked and tangled in the sheets. This picture propelled him jogging again, fast. Down Por-

ter, up First to Main and, with no letup in his steady
pace, down Main, crossing over to *The Valentine
Voice* building, where the blinds were raised, so
Charlotte was not there, at least not yet, thank
heaven. Breathing heavily, he let himself in with his
key.

The low glow of night-lights, plus streetlights
shining through the plate-glass windows, lit his way
to his office, where a poster-size print of Marilyn
Monroe in her sexy skirt-blowing pose watched over
his desk. He turned on his computer, shut the door
and spent thirty minutes surfing the Internet to find
out what he could about one Stuart James, photojournalist. With the information he found, he formed
a picture of a man who had been gung-ho on reporting on the hot situations and people of the world,
making a name for himself, until the past years, when
his pieces—all about exotic and comfortable
places—had been for slick travel magazines and *National Geographic*. Three separate pieces alone had
been about gothic estates in Switzerland, England
and Scotland, glorious photographs showing the
magnificent structures and grounds, all well within a
town that provided equally glorious accommodation.

A man gets older and doesn't want to be bedding
down in some dive or a tent or looking into the faces
of endless struggle and pain. Tate could not blame
James. He himself had given up tough stories long
ago, finding living his own life tough and painful
enough. He quit trying to make sense of life's strug-
gles, because his finite earthly brain couldn't make
sense of it.

Perhaps that was what James had discovered.

Maybe that was why he had suddenly turned up—to see what he could salvage from what he had lost.

Salvaging the results of some poor choices was exactly what had brought Tate himself to Valentine, where he was making a new life for himself.

And Tate wasn't going to let James take what he had found, either.

He shut down his computer and locked the front door after himself. Setting off jogging once again, although not as fast, he headed up Church Street toward home.

Marilee loved him. He knew this. Yet he also knew her loyalty to others in her life. It was a trait he admired greatly in her. But he did not want to see that trait come to life for Stuart James.

Seven

It's about time…

You knew about Parker getting married? You told him about our coming wedding? What did he say, how did he look, what's his new wife like? What do you think about Stuart showing up like this? What about *us?*

There had been no time to talk, of course. Tate had come in and given her a quick kiss, then out he went with the children, while she stood waving from the front door, a mother in her pink terry bathrobe sending off her family.

Closing the door, she turned and leaned against it, feeling a sense of flowing from one part of her life and ever onward to more, as her eye traveled the room, seeing all that she needed to get done.

There was an old wisdom that said life was made up of time, dirt and money. Marilee heartily agreed with that estimate, most especially when one had children. With children, one was always sweeping out dirt and wildly trying to bring in money.

At best, life was a messy affair.

She pushed herself away from the door and went through the room, picking up strewn clothes—Willie

Lee's pajamas, which, curiously, had dirt on the knees, Corrine's discarded sweater, her own socks.

Perhaps everything came down to time. Time to clean away dirt, and time to earn money, so that one could purchase soap to clean dirt. One purchased time, too, with each breath.

There was a kitten sleeping atop the clothes dryer, in a shaft of sunlight falling through the window of the back door.

"Oh, good grief, you are back." The grey kitten opened its narrow eyes a crack, yawned and closed its eyes again.

Her son's doing, of course. She looked at his pajamas with the soiled knees.

There were a lot of things she did not see her son do. Likely she was glad of that, she thought, tossing the pajamas into the nearby basket of dirty clothes.

She stroked the kitten's silky head. The kitten purred loudly. Oh, dang it anyway, but she would not put it out. She filled a small dish with milk and placed it on the floor beside the washer; it would have to do until she could get to the IGA for cat food. Picking up the kitten, she set him...yes, definitely a him...in front of the bowl. He went to licking, while she dug into the storage closet, brought out a kitty litter pan and litter, which were left over from the last feline, fixed it for the kitten and pointed at it. "There. That is for you."

Willie Lee brought them in, and she got a new pet.

Taking her precious second cup of coffee to the bedroom, she deliberately slowed her motions as she got out her clothes. She was always moving so fast. Hurry, hurry in this world. She always felt as if she could not do enough fast enough. As if she were always behind, lacking in some manner.

As she sat to work on her panty hose, Marilee thought of her front porch. She had not sat in her porch swing for at least...why, not for three weeks. She was startled at the swift passage of time. Her life was passing her by, and she hardly realized.

The telephone rang, and, thinking of Stuart, who nagged at the edges of her mind like a pesky mosquito, she paused to prepare herself.

"Hey, sweet darlin'." It was Tate. His precious drawl vibrated through her body, causing an instant smile to bloom up and out. "Kids are safe at school," he told her, "and I'm safe at the office. How's your mornin'?"

"Good. I think I shall walk to work." She quite suddenly felt grand. The result of a few extra minutes, a second cup of coffee and a warm call from a warm man. "Thank you for takin' the kids this mornin'." She mentally threw herself into his arms.

"I enjoy takin' them." She imagined he winked, as was his habit. "Well...see you when you get down here."

All sorts of thoughts flew through her mind, too quickly to grasp. There was more she wanted to say but that she could not get out. "Yes...see you in a bit."

Holding onto the receiver, she heard it click on the other end. *We have to talk, Tate. I have to share some things with you.*

Slowly she replaced the receiver into its cradle, her thoughts spinning back in time to when she had finally given in to exploring a relationship with Tate. Oh, my, how he had courted her, until she had come around. She smiled with the memory that was tucked into a sacred place in her heart.

Once she had admitted her strong attraction to him, she had relished the wonderful discovery that she could say some things to Tate that she had not ever been able to speak of to anyone else. Things about her life growing up, her difficulties with her mother and with her sister, her fear of her weaknesses, her fears for the children, and her dearest desires for them. Tate listened. He had much in common with her. What a miracle that was, finding someone who understood. And, mostly, Tate did not tell her not to have fears.

When had being able to talk to Tate changed for her?

Everything had gotten so hectic, with the Christmas holidays and many things to do for the children. They had sort of lost touch with each other, and it seemed difficult to get back together.

Perhaps she had quit being able to talk so easily when she had become fully aware of how deeply she had fallen in love with him. In the past, that had been her first big error: falling in love with a man.

Marilee walked along the sidewalk with her hands jammed into the deep pockets of her barn coat, buttons unfastened. Munro followed directly at her heels. The bright sun was warm on her head, promising a balmy day, and indeed the air was rich with the scent of verdant ground getting ready for growing things and the melody of songbirds calling to their mates.

It was what was called a moment out of time, she thought, where she could walk easy and wave to friends who drove past, such as Charlene MacCoy, who she had known just about all her life, and who waved and hollered out the window of her Suburban. "Hey, Marilee!"

"Hey, Charlene!"

Charlene perpetually drove at the pace of a woman with somewhere to go and no time to waste. The Suburban roared through the intersection of Main and Church, bouncing where the road humped.

Then, as Marilee and Munro approached the intersection, here came Aunt Vella in her new Land Rover that she had purchased in order to more conveniently haul roses, fertilizer and all the landscaping items for which she had developed a passion.

The truck stopped, and the tinted window came down. "I'm sorry I didn't get back to you yesterday. Tate came by the store and showed us the announcement. I meant to call you then, but Mrs. Andresen's dance class came in for sundaes, and last night was the first meeting of the rose club this year—I'll call you this afternoon with the report for the paper. Did you need somethin' in particular?"

Hollering from vehicle to sidewalk did not seem conducive to adequate conversation. Marilee shook her head. "I'll call you tonight."

"Okay, sugar." Aunt Vella waved, the tinted window went back up, and the Land Rover slid away, crossing the intersection and heading on north, possibly again up to Lawton and the Home Depot, where her aunt spent an inordinate amount of time perusing the wares, usually coming home to deliberate, giving her another excuse to drive up and look again.

Marilee stood on the corner, waiting for the light to change, and realized that she stood on concrete that she had traveled as a child, walking, running, riding her bicycle. Main Street stretching west and east had changed very little. When she had been a child, there had been trees along it; they had seemed big trees then, since she had been so small. When she visited from college, the trees had been gone, as the town went through a drought and a phase of modern, no-frills improvement. Five years ago the phase of returning to the original look of the town had swept through, and modern facades had been torn down to reveal the authentic rural town fronts beneath. Thanks to Tate's efforts, the trees, planted last November, had returned, as well.

Cars, head-in, lined the edges of the wide street or drove slowly up and down. Flags flew gaily from storefronts. Fred Grace was once more putting out bins of fresh flowers in front of the florist, and the Main Street Café sported a spanking new green awning. Fayrene Gardner, who had bought the café with the money she received at the death of her ex-husband, was updating the entire building. She planned to renovate the upstairs into a luxury apartment.

In that minute, Marilee experienced a soaring of her spirits. *Thank you, God, for letting me live in such a good, peaceful town.* There was absolutely nowhere else on earth she would want to live.

Full of gratitude and feeling as if she walked on sunshine, she sashayed across the street, down the sidewalk and through the *Voice* doors, where she was met by the sight of Sandy Conroy bending his long tall frame over Charlotte's shoulder, taking the opportunity to press extra close as they studied something on Charlotte's computer monitor.

"Hi, y'all."

"Hi," the two responded in unity. Charlotte automatically straightened and put on an ultraproper expression, but Sandy did not pull away from her.

"When are you going to talk this woman into marryin' you, Sandy?"

"It isn't like I don't try," Sandy said, and gave his slow, innocent grin.

Charlotte frowned, and it was the sort of painful frown that made Marilee feel a bit guilty for having brought up what she knew was a sore subject.

She headed on to her desk and dropped her portfolio and purse atop the mess of papers and files. Then, with the lingering of uplifted spirits, she strode eagerly to Tate's office. He saw her, got up from his desk, pulled her close and shoved his office door closed at the same time. She heard it slam shut as his lips took hers. Wrapping her arms around his neck, she let herself sink into the passion.

"Well..." He took a breath and eased away. "Good mornin'."

"Good morning." Was he embarrassed now? Why did he keep backing away? Oh, she was imagining all sorts of things.

The telephone rang, and he stepped quickly to the desk to answer it. "Yes, Charlotte. Oh?" His eyes met Marilee's, and she knew who it was even before he said, "Hello, Stuart. How are you?"

She turned her back, while her ears remained tuned to each word and inflection.

"You did?" A bit of surprise. "No, we haven't done a story on it, but it probably would be a good idea. Can't afford your pictures, though." Tate came up behind her and grabbed her hand. "Well, now, that's generous of you. We'd give you title credit.'' And then, ''Yes, here she is. Right here with me.'' He spoke the last very deliberately, devoid of his pleasant drawl.

He handed over the receiver, whispering, ''He stayed at the Goodnight.''

He did? ''Hello, Stuart.''

''Good morning.''

Marilee tried to phrase her questions: okay, why have you shown up now? What do you want?

''I thank you for dinner last night.'' His tone was truly appreciative.

''You're welcome. Tate said you are stayin' out at the Goodnight.'' She had trouble picturing this.

''Yes. If you stick to the bedside lamp, it isn't a bad place.''

''It reminds me of a more peaceful time.''

''Oh, yeah…so when did you stay here?'' he asked with high curiosity. She heard a clicking and remembered that Stuart used to talk on the phone and click pictures at the same time. He could never seem to pay direct attention to her. Or to others, for that matter.

''Year or so ago, when I had our house fumigated.''

''Oh. Since both you and Tate are so familiar with the place, I thought maybe you two were regulars out here.''

She understood the inference then. ''No. We're grown-ups.''

''Well, you might ask Tate. He's the one who suggested the place.''

She did not reply to this, refusing to continue the juvenile line of thought. She glanced at Tate, who perched on the corner of his desk and made no pretense whatsoever not to be listening.

"Listen." The clicking stopped. "I'd like the opportunity to return the favor of dinner last night by taking you out. Tonight, if that isn't too short notice."

She responded immediately that school nights were not available for going out. "The children have homework, and I have their clothes to get ready. There're just a lot of things to do."

Of course he didn't understand about busy school nights. He had run out on his child. She could almost taste the resentment on her tongue. It took her by surprise, and brought guilt.

"If you came to see Willie Lee, you're certainly welcome to visit him, Stuart. Why don't you come to the house again this evening, say around seven?"

Silence from Stuart's end, while Marilee, on hers, was wondering at her choice of words: *if* you came to see Willie Lee. Realizing her tight grip on the telephone receiver, she relaxed her fingers.

Stuart said, "I could pick him up from school. Him and Corrine."

"No. No, you couldn't," Marilee responded flatly. "Willie Lee and Corrine don't know you. And I don't know you." Was she being paranoid? Rather that than sorry.

Another pause, and then, "I'm hoping you will give me a chance to change that, Marilee."

She absorbed his words, his earnest tone. Stuart could always use earnestness well. "We need to talk, Stuart."

"O-kay."

That was vaguely unsatisfactory. "Would you like

to come to supper again tonight? Nothing fancy. I'll get some baked hens from the deli. We eat at six, and you can come early, around four-thirty.''

He agreed, and they bid goodbye.

"He's still here," she said to Tate, when she hung up.

"Did you think he wouldn't be?" He cast her an amused glance and then drank deeply from his coffee cup.

She felt annoyed, at what, she was uncertain. She just did not appreciate his attitude.

"I don't know exactly what I thought," she said. "He just dropped in. No advance warning. No nothin'. At least back when he left, he said he was going." Although there had not been but about an hour, time enough to pack, between him saying he was leaving and then walking out the door.

She recalled her feeling of confusion from the previous evening, the sense of powerlessness in the face of seeing Stuart standing there in the kitchen doorway. Had he not considered that he might be intruding in her life? "And you invited him to supper."

Tate's eyes widened. "*You* just invited him."

"No, I mean last night."

"What was I supposed to do? Tell him, 'Sorry, but we are about to eat and would rather you leave'?"

"Well, no, of course not." How silly of her. His inviting Stuart had been the right thing, and actually the best thing, in that Marilee and Willie Lee had not been alone to face Stuart. She realized suddenly how glad she had been for Tate's presence. Not only had she faced her ex-husband as a desirable and engaged woman, but Tate could smooth any awkward situation. He had been there for her.

"Besides," he was saying, "I thought maybe you would want to visit with him."

"Oh?" She looked at him, at his silky hair curling neatly behind his ear. What in the world was he thinking about this?

Then, before she could explore the subject further, the telephone rang and a knock sounded at the door.

Tate picked up the telephone, and Marilee opened the door.

Leo Pahdocony, Sr., their sports and agri-business reporter, who looked like a model out of one of the western wear catalogs, stuck his head in the office. "I need to see Editor a minute."

Marilee sighed deeply. "There he is," she said and left, conceding to time, which decreed an end to conversation and a moving on. With brisk steps, she returned to her desk, slipped on glasses and went to work, an exchange of time for the wherewithal to keep her life going along at a relatively clean pace.

Eight

Right out of the blue...

If Stuart had come to try to make up for what his absence—totally dropping out of their lives—had caused, a check in the mail for somewhere around $30,000, roughly figuring child support for the past four years, would have been a good starting point. Although, from the start of their divorce eight years ago, Stuart had never once paid anywhere near what had been agreed upon.

In thinking of it, Marilee supposed that since her marriage had not turned out exactly as she had expected, she should have known that her divorce would not meet her expectations, either. The trouble all began when one got carried away with expectations.

Marilee had met Stuart when she was barely twenty and attending her second year at the University of Oklahoma. At that time her expectations had settled around the idea of finding happiness by escaping her family and years of growing up invisible in a chaotic home environment with an alcoholic father and a mother who coped by pretending nothing at all was wrong.

She had thought to escape the dark chaos of her family's home life when she went away to college on a full scholarship, but she was to learn that blood and attitude followed. She continued to feel safer when invisible, until she had met Stuart, a thirty-five-year-old visiting professor. She had laid eyes on Stuart and his savoir faire, thrown away her weak glasses and fluffed her vibrant hair, and stepped out of the shadows. She could thank Stuart for that—he had drawn her out.

Miracle of miracles was Stuart noticing her, although now she understood that each of their needs had been like lock and key. She had needed Stuart's mature attention, and he had needed her naive hero worship. They had been perfect for each other.

Things had continued along thus, in such a perfect vein, for the first years, in which Marilee gave up her education and any tiny budding dreams of her own and tagged happily after Stuart, worshiping him, keeping his shirts clean, starched and ironed, no matter where they might be—crowded streets of Calcutta, thick Tennessee backwoods, concrete canyons of Chicago—as he pursued his photojournalistic career.

Then, as she gradually grew up, she began to notice that Stuart didn't so much notice her as use her for his purposes, which generally were to attend to him. He required a *lot* of clean shirts, light starch. Funny how, even today, she could still recall exactly how he liked his shirts.

As countless women before her, she thought perhaps a child would bring them fulfillment and togetherness. Also, there had been that continual ticking of her biological clock. Time again, dictating life.

One day she was pregnant. She did not think she had done it on purpose, but she sure meant to enjoy her dream of a child, a family, mommy and daddy and baby makes three, and it would all be perfect in the way it never had been when she was a child.

But Stuart had said, in his most affable fashion, "I don't want to be a father, Marilee. I don't want any part of it. I don't particularly want to be a husband."

The bald truth was that Stuart had never felt the need to pretend to be anything other than what he was, which was a man emotionally sufficient unto himself. He took her as his wife, as long as she tagged along, like an agreeable traveling companion, to give him some pleasure in bed and keep his life organized. He was exactly correct—he never had fit into the mold of husband and mate.

From the beginning, it had been Marilee's own illusions that had blinded her to who Stuart really was. In her need, she had tried to make him fit those illusions. How painful it had been when she had been forced to see that she had been the author of her own mistakes with Stuart. He had not hurt her; her own illusions had caused her pain.

But now, here he was, having shown up out of the blue, at his own pleasing, Stuart being Stuart. She felt like smacking him.

Just then she came out of her memories, blinking as she saw an enormous vase of roses floating toward her. Long-stemmed deep red roses in a tall green glass vase.

"Miz James, flower delivery for you."

"For me?"

Tiffany poked her face around the flowers. "Yes...I need to set them down, they're heavy."

Grabbing files and papers, Marilee made a space on the corner of her desk.

"Whew." Tiffany stepped back. "Got my workout for the day. There's two dozen of those beauties there."

From bottom to top, the arrangement was over three feet high, at least.

"Oh, wait a minute. Let me..." She dug into her purse and brought out enough tip money for yesterday's delivery, too.

"Thanks! I sure hope you stay popular."

Her fellow workers crowded around her desk.

"Let me get your picture with them," said Reggie, pointing her camera.

"Whoo-ee, honey, this guy has more money than sense," said Leo Sr., shaking his head.

"They look too perfect to be real," said June.

"Don't touch the petals, June. You'll bruise them." This last was Charlotte giving orders. She also plucked the envelope from its holder and passed it to Marliee.

Marilee opened the envelope. Leo was right: Tate was spending foolishly, buying her flowers as if he was a millionaire.

She pulled out the card. *For all the years gone past, my apologies. With love, Stuart.*

With love? Her first thought was that the roses might have been expensive, but they didn't make a dent in past-due child support payments, not to mention nights spent rocking a colicky baby and worrying about the future and making decisions alone.

She looked up and saw Tate staring at the bouquet.

* * *

"I'm going on. I have to run by the IGA and pick up dinner."

They met on the sidewalk. Marilee, with Munro at her heels, was just coming out the doors of the *Voice* building, and Tate was returning from a Chamber of Commerce luncheon.

"You are joinin' us for supper, aren't you?"

"I thought I would, unless you want to be alone with Stuart."

For heaven's sake. "I am seeing Stuart to talk with him before supper. That is enough. I'll plan on your mother, too, just in case. Is there anything you particularly want me to get at the store?"

"Can't think of anything." He stood at least three feet away.

"Okay. Well, we'll eat about six." She stepped toward him and went up on tiptoe to give him a quick kiss.

"Hey, here." He threw her his keys. "Take my car, and you can go past the IGA on your way home. I'll walk home later."

She opened the door for Munro to hop in; then she slipped behind the wheel and buckled up. Both hands on the steering wheel, she was gathering concentration.

She always experienced a disconcerting conflict when driving Tate's BMW. She adored driving it— sporty and powerful—but she worried about wrecking it.

With extreme care, she backed it out from its space. If she ever did wreck the car, she wanted it to be the other driver's fault. Heading down Main, keeping an eye out for some idiot who might pull out in front of her, she stopped at the light. She ran her hand over the leather steering wheel and wiggled her rear in the seat that was sun-warmed. Or was that heat lingering from Tate's rear?

Had Tate seemed unusually distant? As if he were angry at her about something. The flowers, of course, although that had not been her fault, nor anything to feel guilty over.

But she had sensed the distance earlier, in his office. That was why she had felt annoyance at him, she realized. But maybe she was imagining things.

A horn honked behind her, causing her to jump. "Oh!" The grill of an enormous truck took up the rearview mirror.

Pressing the accelerator and turning the steering wheel, she sent the BMW zipping around the corner onto First Street going north. Another glance in the rearview mirror, and she sighed with relief at being out of the gun-sight of the big truck, which had continued heading straight.

She deposited the grocery bags on the counter, then turned to gaze at the colorful bouquet of flowers Tate had given her yesterday. She liked these ever so much more than the roses, she thought as she added a bit of water to the vase. The roses were extravagant. Larger than life. This bouquet was lovely, warm and real. It fit her, and Tate knew it.

A knock sounded at the back door. Marilee opened the door to Franny, with her shiny carrot-red hair and radiant face, and wearing an ivory knit layered outfit that seemed to flow around her.

"Hi, darlin'." She gave an impish grin. "I've been shoppin' and wanted to bring over my goodies."

"Oh?"

"Yes. Are the kids home?"

"Not yet." Marilee checked the clock. "It'll be probably another ten minutes. They could make it in twenty minutes, easily, but they like to dawdle, you know."

Marilee looked curiously at the bags, and Franny said she would just have to show what she had. She could not wait.

There was an ant farm, quite an elaborate setup, for Willie Lee. "I asked the man if he had a worm farm. I understand Willie Lee likes worms, but the man didn't have a worm farm."

"Thank goodness," Marilee said, and they both laughed.

There was a set of four books of the American Girls series for Corrine, plus a young girl's journal and pen that lit up. "For writing in the dark. See." Franny demonstrated.

It was all lovely, each thing perfect for the children. How had she known?

"Oh, I just let God speak to me when I'm shopping. I got a great buy on a pair of brown leather jeans for myself. I heard distinctly to go to a certain store and down a certain aisle, and there they were, less than half price. I have wanted a pair all winter."

Leather? Marilee quickly surveyed her future mother-in-law and thought the woman could pull it off.

"And here's for you."

"Oh! Thank you." A small pink gift bag. She pulled out a small bottle of perfumed bath beads and a packet of something that looked like tea.

"Herbal," Franny told her. "My own blend. It

relaxes, opens the sinuses to air and the mind to understanding. I thought you and Stuart might enjoy it, when he comes.''

Tate must have told her.

Franny motioned. "I'll set your kitchen table for tea, and I'll keep the kids busy when they come in, so that you and Stuart can have a nice chat. You go on now and get yourself dolled up.''

"Well…''

"Darlin', your ex-husband is coming over. A woman always feels confident when she looks her best. You want to look like dynamite.''

She did. It had been her plan all along, but she had not faced what seemed a foolish, prideful notion. Now, with Franny giving it an okay, Marilee laughed aloud.

"Yes, I do.''

"Then, dear, go get to it.'' She shooed at Marilee with her graceful hands. "And choose something teal.''

Choose something teal?

Marilee got out her favorite sweater, soft teal. Franny seemed to know things.

If Stuart thought he was just going to pop back in here, just as if he had not deserted them, he might as well think again.

She peered at her image in the mirror. She didn't need very much blush, that was for sure. She applied lipstick, then carefully set the tube down, backed up and sank down on the side of the bed.

God, help me here. Surely you can help me, if you shop for Franny. I don't understand myself. And I can't imagine why, now, Stuart has to come and

make more complications. Help me to see what I'm
supposed to see. And give me understanding...
*and...*oh, this one was hard. *Please soften my heart*
to let go of the past hurt that no longer matters.

Heaven knew she had enough to understand about
today without hauling the past around with her. But
she did think that removing the resentment she felt
against Stuart was a lot bigger job than directing
someone to leather pants.

A knock sounded at the door, and Franny poked
her head in the room. "There's a problem."

Hadn't she just prayed to God for help? This did
not seem like help. He works in mysterious ways, his
wonders to perform.

A skunk. Marilee could smell the odor through the
back door.

She opened the door and looked down on Willie
Lee, a forlorn figure sitting on the bottom step. "Willie Lee, honey."

He twisted around and peered up at her, blinking
behind his thick glasses. "He need-ed me to help
him, Ma-ma."

Corrine and Munro stood far out in the middle of
the yard, looking on.

"Everyone stay right where you are. Corrine,
don't you let Munro near Willie Lee."

She closed the door again, told Franny they would
have to get Willie Lee undressed outside, and raced
away to gather a towel and blankets. On her way past
the phone, she called Parker. Valentine had a part-
time animal control officer, but she knew Parker's
mobile phone number by heart.

"Willie Lee got sprayed by a skunk in the daylight," she told him. "Corrine can show you where it is...or was."

Franny and Corrine, keeping their heads turned in a vain attempt to escape the odor, held blankets for privacy. Marilee had to be in the thick of it, in the middle of the blankets with Willie Lee, helping him with his buttons, tossing his clothes up over the blankets and out into the grass as far as possible. Munro watched from over by the fence.

"I told him not to go after that skunk," Corrine said, with disgust. "Even Munro was smart enough not to do that."

Willie Lee had begun crying now.

"A lesson actively learned sticks best," Franny said softly.

Her future mother-in-law, out on the lawn in ivory cashmere, exposed to skunk odor. Giving a big sigh, Marilee caught a heaping dose of stink and ended up coughing.

Then she was shepherding Willie Lee through the house, trailing a cloud of skunk odor, into the tub of water scented with the new bath beads. The odor changed to skunk plus sweet jasmine, with skunk odor dominating.

"He need-ed me to make him bet-ter, Mama. I tri-ied to tell him."

She gazed into her son's teary eyes. "Was the skunk sick, honey?"

Willie Lee nodded.

"How do you know?"

"He told-ed me."

Her heartbeat thudded. "Did you touch him, Willie Lee? I mean at all. Did you touch the skunk?"

Willie Lee gazed at her and shook his head. "No, Ma-ma."

Willie Lee never lied. Thank you, God, for keeping my little boy safe.

Shampoo his hair. The odor became one of skunk mixed with herbal fragrance. Skunk was still winning.

The door opened; Parker Lindsey's head appeared around it. "How is it in here?"

"He's okay. He never touched the skunk. It just sprayed him."

"I'll say." And the door closed again.

Marilee, on her knees in her best skirt and teal sweater, rinsed Willie Lee and prepared to soap him up again.

Out front, Stuart was just stepping up on Marilee's porch when the door opened and out came Corrine, followed by a man. Stuart and the man stared at each other with surprise.

Corrine said, "Hey, Mr. James...this is Parker Lindsey, our vet. Parker, this is Stuart James, Aunt Marilee's old husband."

The girl made him sound like a discarded shoe. "That's *ex*-husband," he clarified and stuck out his hand.

The man shook his hand quickly. "Hello. I'm her old boyfriend, Parker. Sorry to rush, but we're off to find a skunk."

Perplexed, Stuart watched the two go down the steps and over to the blue truck sitting in the driveway.

Stuart stepped through the door that had been left open, then closed it behind him. He was a little early.

"Marilee?" What was that smell? *We're off to find a skunk.* Was that skunk odor?

A figure came through the swinging door of the kitchen—Franny Holloway, who took time to prop open the door. "Whew, better to let the air flow. I'm afraid there is an upset to the schedule, Mr. James. Willie Lee has met with an unfortunate accident, and Marilee is occupied with bathing him. I'm making you some tea, though."

Just then Marilee appeared out of the bathroom. "Oh, Stuart. Good. Would you go to the grocery store and get some big cans of tomato juice? Three quarts, at least." With that, she disappeared back into the bathroom.

He looked at Franny Holloway, who said, "Tea will be waiting when you get back."

Turning, he went back out the front door, where he met Tate Holloway coming up the walk. There were certainly men coming and going from his ex-wife's house.

"Going for tomato juice," he told Holloway and got a kick out of the man's surprised expression. At least Holloway knew less than he did, he thought with satisfaction.

Parker and Corrine returned, and Parker, poking his head in the front door, as if in too much of a hurry to come all the way inside, told Marilee, "No sign of it anywhere. Morley Lund said he saw a skunk wandering down the ditch out back of his yard, and he got his gun, but when he came back, it was gone."

"Does it mean it's rabid, since it's wandering around in the day?"

Parker shrugged. "Could be, or it could simply have been rousted out of its hole by something. Morley says he's shot five skunks this winter. They're livin' under those old cars of his out beside his shop, and they keep eating his cats' food, gettin' into it with the cats and sprayin'."

"Well, why doesn't he move those cars?"

"Easier to shoot the skunks, I guess."

"Well, for heaven's sake."

He shrugged, gave her a quick kiss on the cheek, then left.

Marilee, standing there with the feel of his lips on her cheek, felt a smile in her heart.

Tate, who had come up behind her, said, "He's a good friend."

"Yes," she said, smiling at him. "He is." And she put her hand into his.

Everyone who needed to be gone was gone, and those who needed to be in bed were in bed. Whew.

They sat together in the porch swing, in the dark, where the beams of the streetlight did not reach. Marilee, in jeans and a thick sweater, was cocooned in a quilt. She snuggled up against Tate, who wore his suede jacket and refused to cocoon with her.

Why was it that men could not abide wrapping in a quilt? It was cozy, two wrapped together.

"Makes me feel tangled," Tate said. "If somethin' happened—the house caught on fire, or an attacker came up—I'd have to get unwrapped from the quilt before I could defend us."

And men said women had great imaginations. "Remember bundling?" she asked.

"Way before my time," he replied, and gently

rocked the swing, causing a slight squeak with each sway.

Squeak, squeak, squeak. She really needed to grease the porch swing chain.

After a moment, she said, "I believe tonight Stuart got a taste of the rigors of parenthood."

"Huh? What did he do?"

Good question. "I guess he got to observe it all. The time and energy it takes to clean up unexpected messes."

"That's about it. He observes well and gets fed in the bargain."

She thought she detected a note of deprecation in his voice and found it satisfying. No woman ever wanted her man to be patient with an old lover. It had been gratifying that he and Parker had been rivals. Their rivalry had distressed her, but it had also given her satisfaction, she thought, being totally honest with herself. Although, seeing their friendship now, she felt pleased. It was odd how feelings could change.

Probably she should be appreciative of Tate's patience in many matters, and she *was* appreciative, but at the same time his patience could get on her nerves. In her estimation, Tate could be too patient at times. For one thing, his level of patience very often showed hers to a disadvantage, and it got tiring to always be the one to lose patience first.

Squeak, squeak, squeak.

She had lost a bit of patience with the tomato juice. It had seemed to go everywhere. Willie Lee had seen her exasperation and cried, "I am sor-ry to make you mad, Ma-ma." He could never stand for her to be angry. Corrine had helped her to clean up the tomato juice. Dear, precious Corrine.

"I never, ever want to have to deal with skunk smell again," she said.

"Oh, I imagine your chances of that are slim, livin' in town. Although on the other hand, this is a rural town and in the South…and you are the mother of a growin' boy."

Her situation sounded precarious.

Squeak, squeak, squeak.

"Willie Lee said the skunk told him it was sick." She let that sit there a second and then added, "It could have rabies, Tate, and it is still out there."

"Yes, that is so," Tate agreed slowly. "But there are a lot of skunks out there, and I imagine there are a lot of skunks with rabies, and yet few people—or even dogs, for that matter—are bitten or even get around one, so I don't think we need to worry over it a whole lot." His arm tightened around her. "Willie Lee's okay, Marilee. He's safe in that bed in there. And clean, too."

Yes, her son was safe and clean. Closing her eyes, she laid her head back again on Tate's firm shoulder. She could not recall anyone she ever knew being bitten by a rabid animal. Maybe she would speak to Parker about the danger, though. This made her recall that Parker was married.

"What's Parker's wife like?"

"Amy? Oh…she's tall…. She's a vet, too. Real nice. Nice smile. Nice eyes. Real nice."

Squeak, squeak, squeak.

"She's a knockout, isn't she?"

"Yep."

Marilee wondered if she could get time tomorrow

to go see Parker to get his view on this skunk problem and her own view of his wife.

"Well, I'm glad for him." She realized with a suddenness that she was purely delighted for Parker.

"Me, too."

She sighed deeply, feeling the weight she had not even known she carried roll off her shoulders. Even though she knew she had done the right thing, there had remained a bit of guilt for calling off her marriage to Parker and leaving him in his lonely life, not to mention the mismatched colors of his home. She had felt responsible for Parker for so long that she didn't know how to stop, and now she could. Another woman had taken over the job. Quite swiftly this relief was followed by gratitude for the man in her life, and she squeezed Tate.

"Now, if we could just get Stuart settled." It pained her to see Stuart. So alone, he seemed.

"Stuart is not your responsibility to settle."

"I know that." The censure in his tone pricked her. "What I mean is that his dropping in out of the blue to—*develop* an acquaintance with Willie Lee at this late date encompasses so much more than I care to be involved with right now." How did one make up for nine years of lost fatherhood?

"So don't be involved," Tate said. "Stuart is a fairly capable sort. I think he can manage to make friends with Willie Lee, even make a stab at being a father to him, without you having much to do with it. Don't meddle in it."

"I don't think being concerned for my son's welfare is meddling," she said, and then shut her mouth, pulling away from him, if only inwardly.

His accusation hurt. And the idea of no involvement frightened her. Someone needed to see that things went along in a safe fashion and make certain Stuart didn't do something foolish with Willie Lee. What exactly this foolishness might entail, she could not have named. She only knew that she had to be involved to keep the situation from getting out of control somehow. Stuart had no idea of how to be a parent. She felt obligated to do her best to show him.

She did feel responsible for Stuart, she realized. He seemed like a lost soul, and he had once been her husband, and now here he was again, plopped down in front of her.

All of which she could not say to Tate, who more than once had voiced the opinion that she had the overwhelming tendency to mother everyone. He had been verbal in his view that her part in the relationship with Parker had been one of mothering, had even gone so far as to say she had not allowed Parker to be a man.

Well, she did not think a woman could stop a man from being a man. There was no question but that she was a mothering sort, but she thought it going too far to say that she had stopped Parker from being a man. Parker was the sort who gave himself over to be looked after and doted on and led around so that he didn't have to make decisions. Possibly he found that it took all his strength to be a veterinarian and looking after animals all the time, so he wanted a woman to look after him.

No one could stop Tate from being a man, that was for sure. Tate never let her mother him. Tate was the type who might enjoy her ministrations but never her directions.

She became aware, quite suddenly, that he was

pressing his lips to the top of her head. And that his hand was kneading her arm through the blanket.

Tate whispered, "You smell so good."

"Citrus shampoo." She had felt compelled to wash from head to toe, too.

She twisted to look up at him. Even though it was too dark to see his eyes, she knew their blueness and how he looked at her. She brought her hand free of the quilt and pressed it to the back of his neck, at the same time lifting her lips to meet his.

They kissed and kissed and kissed in a way that caused them both to gasp for breath and then go at it again. Tate claimed her lips in the thrilling manner of urgency and demand that made her pulse throb in intimate parts of her body. The passion went even higher because of their position, there on the swing, a place suitable for necking but not suitable for sex.

He kissed her until she thought she would fly to pieces with wanting.

"Oh, Tate...Tate," she whispered when his lips at last let hers go.

"Marilee..."

He trailed moist kisses down the tender skin of her neck. She put her hand into his open collar and felt the warmth of his skin.

Then, abruptly, he broke away. "I've got to go home, Marilee."

He got up so fast that she fell over.

"I'll be here in the mornin'. Same time," he said, as he hot-footed it across the yard, not looking back.

Well, for heaven's sake.

Squeak, squeak, squeak.

Marilee wrestled herself free of the quilt and strode inside, where she stripped out of her clothes, including panties quite damp, put on flannel pajamas, took three aspirin and went to bed with the pillow over her head. Even so, she thought she caught a whiff of skunk.

Nine

In the eye of the beholder…

Winston was a little disconcerted to find Mildred out of bed before sunup. Seeing the shut bathroom door, he figured she was in there, and that he could slip down and get his coffee in peace.

Unfortunately, when he came into the kitchen, there was Mildred at the table, in her orange turban and bright green print robe, with what had been a package of a dozen cinnamon rolls but was now down to six in front of her on the table.

"Leanne brought us a treat," she said. White sugar icing smudged her lips.

"If it was for us, then you might have left more."

Apparently Leanne had set the packaged sweet rolls out the night before. Winston blamed himself for not telling her that she couldn't set out things like that in front of Mildred, who had developed diabetes, the worst thing in the world for someone who was addicted to food.

"You know what the doctor said about eatin' like this, Mildred." He moved the remaining cinnamon rolls to the counter, threw a towel over them and wet a paper napkin with which he wiped Mildred's face, while she complained that the doctor didn't know how hungry she got.

"I was so hungry that I woke up," she said in a small voice.

Now she was tuning up to cry, and Winston knew it would do no good to scold her. She was growing more like a child every day, and she simply couldn't leave food alone. She had always carried it around in her purse, but now she was hiding it around the house. Yesterday he had found dried-up bacon in with the towels.

He put a hand on her shoulder, then noticed that she had not fully buttoned her robe over her humongous breasts, so he did that for her, telling her, "Why don't you have that Jell-O in the refrigerator? It ought to tide you over until we have us some breakfast." It was the artificial sugar variety, made the previous afternoon by their day help, Marie.

Mildred, brightening, got up more quickly than he would have imagined anyone of her considerable rotundness could move.

Feeling tired and annoyed at having his early morning time invaded, he turned to get himself a cup of coffee. He decided on a cinnamon roll, too, but felt guilty about eating it in front of Mildred. He gave in to the urge, keeping his back turned while he munched on it. It seemed a sad state to not be able to eat a cinnamon roll in his own home. Perhaps that was how Mildred felt, too.

Facing the window, he moved the curtain and peered out at the corral and the mare there with her filly, a pretty sight in first light. It lifted his spirits to see the horses, at the same time making him think sadly of days gone by, when his wife always had a horse or two out there. Coweta had been gone now almost four years.

Life was difficult for a man of his advancing years and still in his right mind, and not doing too poorly physically, either. It was as if people blamed him for his unusual stamina, at the same time resenting that he did not have stamina enough.

As if seeking comfort, he shifted his gaze to look across the small meadow at the Blaines' house. There was a glow in the kitchen window.

Full sadness fell over him. Days with Vella were pretty much gone, too, and he missed them. It had been pleasant to have a woman serve him morning coffee, put on lipstick for him and be capable of stimulating conversation.

But last fall, when it had gotten too cold to sit outside, he had quit having morning coffee with her. Since she had taken Perry back, Winston didn't think it fitting that he be alone with her inside the house. Not that there was anything Winston could really do of an untoward nature, but he was still a man, no matter how society discounted him as being old, and it was not proper to be alone in the company of another man's wife.

He knew he had proved a disappointment to Vella. He had kissed her one time, but the passion that erupted proved to be of a short-lived nature, with nothing whatsoever coming behind it. He himself had been pretty disappointed, although he didn't know what either of them had expected at his age. That she, a woman considerably younger than he, had actually been interested and anticipated anything else on his part had been a pleasant experience, though.

Then Perry had ended up doing enough to get

Vella to take him back, and to keep himself there. The stick-in-the-mud had actually gotten up the gumption to give that Vi-ra-grow, or whatever it was called, a try. Perry had reported considerable improvement and delight, but there was one thing Perry would never have, and that was spark. One could not get spark from a pill. At any rate, Perry's liveliness had proved as short-lived as Winston's passion, and he had returned to his dull ways and his television. Vella had turned her considerable energy to home improvement and landscaping ideas.

And Winston was alone. Again.

"'Mornin', y'all."

He turned to see Leanne, all sleepy-eyed and scratching her hair, which looked like birds had nested in it overnight. It was the going style for young women, and there was no accounting it. He had to admit, even with the hair, Leanne was a looker; she was from his wife's side of the family— Overtons, known for beautiful women.

"Good mornin'," he said.

She came over to get a mug out of the cabinet and pour her coffee. Winston watched her graceful movements. Not too many women moved like Leanne, like a lazy female cat, despite she had on men's insulated overalls with suspenders that went over a silk undershirt so thin that he could see clearly she did not bother with a bra. And she was a fully developed woman, too.

"In a little bit here, I'm gonna go feed my horses and then go up to MacCoy's for grain." She sipped her coffee. "Do either of you need me to pick up anything while I'm out?"

Mildred said, "I would like some ice cream...."

Can I have ice cream, Winston? And some chocolate pudding.''

"She needs anything low carb and sugar free," he told his niece.

He said he didn't need anything, then added, "But there is one thing I would like, and that is the courtesy of you coverin' up your body. I'm sayin' this to the both of you. I may be old and on my last leg, but I am deservin' of the respect due a man."

With that, he took his coffee and went through the house, put on his coat, tucked the flags under his arm, and went out on the front porch, with the certain attitude of sending back anyone who tried to come out with him.

As he lowered himself into the rocker, he glanced out at the street and saw a figure, a rather small woman, walking past, heading east at a smart pace, swinging her arms. He followed her with his gaze, trying to figure out if he knew her. The first golden glow of the morning sun hit her, and he saw she had copper-penny hair.

Just then the "Star Spangled Banner" blared out from a speaker at the base of Everett Northrupt's flag pole across the street. Winston jumped and sloshed his coffee.

There was Everett, coming to the edge of the porch.

Annoyed at being behind—apparently Everett had decided winter rules were off—Winston fumbled to get out the remote control, kept ready in his coat pocket, and point it through the window. He succeeded, and the strains of "Dixie" filled the air, coming from speakers up underneath the eaves, as he hurried to the pole to raise his flag. He stood as straight as possible and saluted. Then he saw that the woman in the street was standing at attention.

He liked her immediately.

And, to his immense surprise, when the last strains of the two patriotic songs died, here she came striding across his yard.

"Good mornin'," she said, sticking out her hand. "You must be Winston Valentine. I've heard so much about you from my son. I'm Franny Holloway."

Her voice was smooth and her accent in no hurry. Silver-and-bead earrings swayed from her ears, and her deep green eyes sparkled.

Winston, mesmerized, stared at her for a full three seconds before managing to gather his wits to shake her hand. *Thank you, God, I guess I'm glad to be alive after all.*

Charlotte was hanging the flags when Sandy pulled up out front. He had a small bag from the IGA deli.

"How early this morning?" he asked her, coming inside and pulling her into his arms.

"Not so early…around five." She rose slightly on tiptoe to kiss him. It was nice that she had to stretch to reach him, rather than bend down, as she had for every man in her life until Sandy, who was over six feet six inches in his boots.

The kiss revived her, as did his lean, hard body against her.

He had brought bagels this morning, and cups of rich mocha. And then he pulled something out of his pocket, a small box.

"I want you to marry me, Charlotte." His jaw

muscle worked with unusual firmness as he opened the box, revealing a beautiful diamond solitaire. "I want to marry you...for you to be my wife and for me to be your husband. I want to sleep with you. I want to be there with you. I want us to be together. Let me help you with your mother. I want to do that."

Charlotte, who never let anyone help her with anything, looked into his face. Into his dear, sweet, wholesome brown eyes. She brought her palm to touch his cheek.

"I can't." Her words came out hoarse and yet poured forth, painfully, all on the order of: I'm too old for you; you can have so much more with a woman your own age; maybe I can't have children; and I have the burden of my mother. She said all this, but not what really burned in her mind, what Sandy already knew, which was that she loved him as she had never loved any other person in her whole life. And because she loved him, she wanted the world for him. She did not want to be a burden to him; she did not want to face a day when he became sorry he had married a woman eleven years his senior.

Sandy reached for her, but, overwhelmed, she turned and ran out the front door.

She ran, in her heeled pumps, all the way, four and a half blocks, to her house. A number of people saw her, recognized Charlotte Nation, the really tall girl who worked at the *Voice,* running and wondered what might be the matter downtown. A few people called around. The telephone down at the *Voice* rang, but Sandy, still alone, was uncertain about answering. He had never answered the phone at the office before. Hardly anyone did, except Charlotte. Charlotte got a little mad if anyone else answered the phone, and especially if they didn't do it exactly right.

He stood there, with the phone ringing, trying to figure out what to do, wondering if he should go after Charlotte or let her have the time alone. He sure didn't want to press her so hard that she threw him completely out of her life.

At home, where she had thrown herself across her bed, Charlotte cried until she felt herself go almost into a faint. She had not slept but three hours the night before, and she had not had anything to eat since a small supper that hadn't set well; however, she struggled up from her state and got the telephone to call Marilee and tell her she was taking the day off. She felt terribly irresponsible taking time off and would not have been able to stand being so irresponsible as not to alert someone who could take over.

Ten

Her mother's little girl...

Miss Charlotte had a broken heart. Corrine heard Aunt Marilee on the phone to her, and saw her aunt pacing with her long strides, like she did whenever she was upset. "Honey...oh, honey," Aunt Marilee said, and when she finally hung up and saw Corrine, who never liked for her aunt Marilee to get upset, looking at her, she breathed deeply and said, "Miss Charlotte is okay. No one dies from a heartbreak." Then, as she headed for her bedroom, she added, "They just feel like they will."

It wasn't good that Miss Charlotte had called before Aunt Marilee had finished a whole cup of coffee. She never did get to finish her coffee, though, because she needed to get down to the newspaper office early to take Miss Charlotte's place, and as usual she was running about fifteen minutes late. Aunt Vella said that when it was time for Aunt Marilee to be born, they made her mama wait for the doctor, who was not yet at the hospital, for fifteen minutes, so ever since then, Aunt Marilee stayed the same course. You could set a watch by her lateness.

Aunt Marilee rushed around, telling them to hurry

up. Corrine, who was always ready early, didn't need to hurry; she focused on helping Willie Lee, who was incapable of hurrying. Aunt Marilee had forgotten that she had thrown away his skunkified shoes. Corrine dug his good Sunday shoes out of the closet.

The telephone rang. Corrine jammed the shoes at Willie Lee and called out, "I'll get it," and Aunt Marilee called back, "Bless you, honey," in the way that made Corrine know that she was a big help to her aunt.

She raced into the living room, then came to a dead stop and stared at the phone on her aunt's desk. She knew suddenly that it was her mother calling. Whenever Aunt Marilee left a message on her mother's answering machine, it was always two or three days until her mother would call. Corrine was fairly certain her mother did this on purpose. She could not have explained her reasoning, just that this was her mother's manner.

Willie Lee, who had come in the room, walked past Corrine and went to pick up the phone. "Hello?" He listened. "Yes, this is Wil-lie Lee. Hel-lo, Aunt A-ni-ta."

Corrine breathed deeply.

He giggled. "Yes, this is Wil-lie Lee, but I am grow-ing."

She realized her mother had said something funny to Willie Lee. Her mother always made an effort to make Willie Lee smile. Her mother was beautiful when she made an effort to make someone smile.

"Cor-rine is right here."

She took the receiver he held out to her. "Hello, Mama."

"Corrine? Corrine, is that my baby?" At the

sound of her mother's high-pitched tone, she pictured her mother on the other end of the line, as she was when she was in a energetic mood, walking around as she spoke, puffing on a cigarette, every part of her in motion.

"Yes."

"Well, what is it you have to tell me, honey? Your Aunt Marilee sounded like there was a surprise."

She didn't want to say it aloud. She checked and saw that Willie Lee was over on the couch, trying to get his shoes on. She cupped the receiver with her hand. "I started my period."

"What, honey? I didn't hear you."

Corrine repeated it.

Her mother let out a squeal that stabbed Corrine's ears. "You started your period? Oh my goodness!"

Corrine wished to drop through the floor. "Yes," she croaked. She wondered if her mother's boyfriend, Louis, was right there with her mother.

"I cannot believe you have started so young. Surely I am not old enough to be your mother."

Corrine experienced a stab of guilt at doing something wrong.

"Well, honey, I'm sending you a present. I'm puttin' it in the mail today."

"You are?" Sometimes her mother sent presents, but except for a jewelry box with a wind-up ballerina that she had sent at Christmas, the things were all for younger girls: pop-beads, several stuffed toys, books for young readers. Corrine had found out that it had been her mother's boyfriend, Louis, who had chosen the jewelry box.

"Don't ask me what it is. I want it to be a surprise."

"Okay." Corrine wondered if she should want to ask.

"Oh, honey, I wish I could be there with you," her mother was saying. "I miss you so much."

"I miss you, too, Mama."

Then there was silence, and Corrine had a small panic in trying to think of something more to say.

Thankfully her mother spoke. "We're thinkin' of comin' up there next month. Grama says Aunt Marilee and Tate have set the date for their weddin'."

"Yes, they have."

"Well...honey, let me talk to your aunt just a minute."

"Okay. She's gettin' dressed." She put her hand over the receiver and called out for Aunt Marilee, who was just then coming into the room. "It's Mama."

Aunt Marilee took the phone. "Hey, Anita." Then she bit her lip. "Yes she sure is growin' up," she said after a moment.

Corrine went to the couch to help Willie Lee tie his shoes. He told her to let him do it, so she just sat there on her knees, one ear tuned to her aunt's conversation. Aunt Marilee had turned her back and was mostly listening. When she spoke, it was with that clipped tone that meant something her mother was saying annoyed her, but she would not let on.

Then Aunt Marilee was holding the receiver out to her. "She wants to say goodbye."

Corrine took the phone and bid goodbye to her mother, who said, "Love you, honey," and made a smooching sound.

In answer, Corrine said, "You, too." She could

not make the smooching sound, and she felt guilty for this lapse that seemed mean.

Corrine could not tell her mother that she loved her; she could not say the words. One time on the phone her mother had pressed her.

"Don't you love your mother, sugar?"

"Yes, I do, Mama."

Thankfully her mother had let it drop, and Corrine had never had to actually say the words.

She felt guilty for not being able to say the words. She knew she loved her mother, but what confused her was how much she sometimes hated her, too. It was a secret that lay like a stain on her heart. She always felt that she needed to tell her mother she was sorry—sorry for being so mean, sorry for being a nuisance, sorry for ever being born.

Corrine knew she loved Aunt Marilee, but she never could have told her aunt with the words, either. This seemed okay, maybe because Aunt Marilee didn't say the words. Still, Corrine felt her aunt loved her. Aunt Marilee would smile at her in a way that made her feel warm and full, and sometimes Aunt Marilee would hug her right out of the blue, or would say that Corrine was sweet, or neat, or smart, or pretty as a picture. Maybe what was best was that Aunt Marilee seemed to like her to be around. Sometimes Corrine felt so grateful to her aunt Marilee, but she couldn't say that, either. She would lay her head against Aunt Marilee, hoping her aunt could feel how she felt.

Corrine was mostly grateful to Aunt Marilee for sharing Willie Lee, who was the one person Corrine knew for certain she loved totally, completely. With

Willie Lee, Corrine shared two important life factors: the lack, at least until now, of a flesh and blood father, and the sense of being different from everyone in the world.

The details Corrine's mother had told her about her father were few. At the times her mother spoke of her father, her mother would cry, sending mascara running down her cheeks, and tell her all about a man named Scott Pendley, a sweet ranch boy from some burg over near Odessa, who had been a roustabout on the oil rigs, then fallen off one and died three short weeks after they had married. But if her Scotty had only lived, he would have taken good care of her and Corrine, and they would have had everything in the world.

Her mother had described her Scotty as having blue eyes and curly blond hair, and her mother had light brown hair and green eyes. But Corrine's own eyes were the color of crude oil and her hair all but black. And why was there no picture of this man? Why were there no grandparents from her father?

Once, piecing together rumors, speculation about her parentage, she had told her mother that she did not believe her mother had ever been married. Her mother had produced a marriage certificate. "I was married. You are not a bastard child. I made sure of that."

The event that brought Corrine to live with Aunt Marilee and Willie Lee was her mother being beaten up by her latest boyfriend. Corrine did not see this violence, although it might have been better to see it than what her vivid imagination drew up when she arrived home, a small, skinny girl bearing a bag of items from the 7-Eleven at the corner, stepping through the door to find two enormous policemen questioning her mother in a living room where the television was kicked out and lamps broken, and her mother's face all cut and bruised.

Her mother went into the bathroom and had Corrine help her put little butterfly bandages on the worst of the broken skin. Later, lying awake and worrying that the violent man might return, or that something else equally horrible was about to happen at any minute, she overheard her mother on the telephone to Aunt Marilee, crying, "They'll take her away from me, Marilee."

Aunt Marilee came flying down the highway and arrived early the next morning, coming into the house with the firm strides that she employed when she meant business. She took one look at Corrine's mother draped dramatically on the couch, her face all black and blue, another at Corrine, who was frantically cleaning the house instead of in school, then looked in the refrigerator, staring for a long minute at the basic contents of a half a quart of milk, a six-pack of beer, jars of grape jelly and mayonnaise, and a package of bologna. Slamming closed the refrigerator, Aunt Marilee strode out back and looked in the trash can, and then slammed that closed, too. With each slam, Corrine's mother winced.

Aunt Marilee came marching back inside, got Corrine and took her out to the back step, pulled a Hershey chocolate bar from her purse and gave it to Corrine, saying, "Sit here." Corrine sat; no one in their right mind crossed Aunt Marilee when she meant business.

While Corrine broke off squares of the Hershey bar and put them into her mouth and looked up at the blue, blue sky and wished she were a bird that could fly away, the two women inside went at each other. Corrine wondered vaguely if some neighbor would again call the police.

Aunt Marilee screamed at Corrine's mother for being so stupid as to waste her life with booze and men. "Anita, didn't you have enough of that with Daddy and Mama? What do you want to do? Kill yourself with it, like Daddy did?"

And her mother alternately sobbed and screamed back that it was her life to do with as she pleased. "Get off your high horse, Marilee. You tried a man, and it didn't work out any better. Now you're afraid to have a life."

Gradually the women's voices subsided, and eventually Corrine was summoned back inside. Both women's eyes were red and swollen.

Her mother got down on her knees, her swollen face level with Corrine's. "I want you to go stay with your aunt Marilee for a while, honey. Just till I get a good job and can save up for a good place to live, okay? It will only be for a few months. Aunt Marilee can take care of you real well."

The few months had turned into almost two years. Her mother had visited a total of four times; the telephone calls and cards were coming more infrequently.

On the last visit, her mother had been beautiful and as happy as Corrine had ever seen her. She had brought a new boyfriend—Louis, who looked like a movie star and drove a fancy car. Corrine thought he was the nicest boyfriend her mother had ever had. That afternoon her mother had made her feel special, and Louis had actually seemed to like her. She had begun to think maybe it would be okay to go with her mother, that maybe now she would have a real mother and father and home.

But her mother and Louis had gone off to live in New Orleans, her mother promising, "I'll get us a wonderful place in New Orleans, honey, and then you can come live with me." That had been last fall.

Corrine no longer believed her mother would ever have a place for her. And she felt terribly guilty, because she no longer wanted to go live with her mother.

She had arrived at her aunt Marilee's house with all her stuff in a large plaid suitcase and four liquor boxes. Since then, Aunt Marilee had bought her a brand-new mattress and box spring, and a violet sprigged comforter and matching sheets. She had gotten Corrine all new clothes and toys, and three shelves of books. When Aunt Marilee and Mr. Tate were married, and they all moved over to Mr. Tate's house, Aunt Marilee said Corrine would have her own room, the one with an east window.

All in all, Corrine had begun to feel that her life might be okay after all. Until Willie Lee's father had shown up.

The first worry she had was that Willie Lee's father had come to take him away. That had happened to a kid—Frankie Ramundo—who had lived next door to her in Fort Worth; his father had shown up one day in a suit and shiny car and taken Frankie off with him, while Frankie's mother screamed and pulled her hair out in the driveway.

With further consideration, however, Corrine sincerely doubted anyone could take Willie Lee from

Aunt Marilee, not even a police squad breaking in with machine guns, like on television.

On Friday night Mr. Tate and Aunt Marilee and Miss Franny, who had explained, "After a certain age, dear, we women turn back to Miss again," were visiting in the kitchen, while Mr. Tate made supper. Corrine was happily reading one of her books, and Willie Lee was on the floor, observing his ant farm, all of them just like it was supposed to be, when the doorbell rang. It was Mr. James, coming in and ruining it all.

"Hello, Corrine…may I come in?"

She reluctantly stepped back. "They're in the kitchen. We're about to eat supper."

"I'm just in time, then. I brought pie and ice cream." He had bags in his hand. One was from the dairy store. Apparently he had figured out quick to bring food. She said, "We have chocolate cake."

"Well, the ice cream is vanilla and will go with that." He held out a bag for her. "And here is something for you…and something for Willie Lee."

Slowly she took the bag he offered. To not take it would be too rude. "Thank you," she remembered to add.

"You're welcome." His eyes lingered on her briefly, flitting over her face like a searchlight. She looked away to the bag she now held.

When he stepped away toward Willie Lee, she lifted her eyes and watched him. He gave Willie Lee his bag, and Willie Lee showed him the ant farm. Mr. James gave it a glance and made a comment, then strode on into the kitchen with his long legs.

Corrine sat in the big chair and peered carefully into the shopping bag, one of the fancy kind, with twine handles. She really wished Mr. James hadn't bought her anything. She felt obligated to him now. But it wasn't like a real present, not like Miss Franny's gifts.

Mr. James's present was like what her mother's boyfriends used to bring her mother, to get her to go out with them, or make up after a fight. The boyfriends brought her mother flowers and candy and jewelry, and even a microwave oven and a television. One time one of the boyfriends gave her mother a pair of diamond earrings, and the next week, when they got in a fight, he jerked them out of her ears and left. Another time, after the boyfriend was gone and they needed money, her mother pawned the microwave he had given her. "This was my invest-ment," her mother told her as they walked along the hot sidewalk to the pawnshop. "You make sure a man gives you a decent gift, so you can get some money from it when he leaves you."

Mr. James's gift was a really fancy doll. The sort you don't play with but set up somewhere to look at. A blond girl doll, with a beautiful china face. Cost bucks, she thought, examining it.

She put it back in the bag and moved to see Willie Lee's gift. It was a truck that ran on batteries.

Willie Lee, chin in his hand and eyes intently on the ant farm, said, "I can-not play with it now. I am watch-ing this ant...ev-ery-where he goes."

She went to the kitchen and through it to the laun-dry room, where she folded towels clean from the dryer. Aunt Marilee had begun giving her five dollars a week for allowance, and Corrine liked to be of help, plus at that minute she could listen and watch the adults in the kitchen, without them noticing her. She had learned long ago how to be invisible.

She continued watching the adults throughout the evening. She saw how Mr. James kept looking at Aunt Marilee. Saw how whenever he spoke, like when answering Miss Franny's questions about Scotland, he kept looking at Aunt Marilee. And when he took Willie Lee on his lap and observed the ant farm with him, he kept lifting his head to look at Aunt Marilee. It was sort of a sad look. But that did not make Corrine feel soft toward him.

Corrine had an uneasy feeling about the entire situation. In her experience, sooner or later bad was bound to happen, and it sure seemed that the arrival of Mr. James meant trouble.

"Hey, Corrine!"

It was Ricky Dale Oakes, pedaling past on his bicycle, with a black dog running alongside. Ricky Dale did a quick stop, hopped off and wheeled his bike up the walk to the porch, where Corrine and Willie Lee were playing with Willie Lee's kitten and his new battery-powered truck.

Corrine said, "Hey," but did not want to act overly interested. Ricky Dale was in her grade at school, in Mrs. Noble's class. He was the sheriff's son, but he wasn't stuck-up about it. All the girls thought he was cute, and Corrine did, too, but she wasn't about to admit it.

The next instant here came that black dog, a big puppy, running up on the porch, knocking over the truck and chasing the kitten. The kitten screeched, Willie Lee tried to grab him but missed, and Munro went after the intruding dog, while Ricky Dale and

Corrine both tried to get hold of the big canine. It was so much commotion as to cause Aunt Marilee to poke her head out the door.

"What's goin' on?"

"Just my dog went after the cat, Miz James. I'm sorry. He's just a pup."

"Well…" Aunt Marilee's eyes swept them. "Y'all look okay…. Nice to see you, Ricky Dale. How's your mama doin'?"

"Fine, I guess. She doesn't really tell me, though."

Aunt Marilee chuckled at that and went back in the house. She was working on an article and had that absentminded look she wore when trying to figure out her writing.

Ricky Dale dragged his puppy to the foot of the stairs and held on to him. Willie Lee, with his arm around Munro, sat on the top step. Corrine leaned against the post. She was glad she had on the pair of good denim overalls and a tanned turtleneck sweater that Aunt Marilee had bought her from The Gap.

"I live down Porter two blocks," Ricky Dale said, inclining his head in the direction from where he'd come.

"Oh," Corrine said. She had little experience in talking to boys, or girls, either, for that matter.

He said, "I'm goin' up to Mr. Valentine's to take care of a couple of horses."

"You are?" This from Willie Lee, whose eyes popped wide.

"When did Mr. Winston get horses?" Corrine asked. She had a disappointing moment when she wondered if Ricky Dale was just a faker.

"Oh, they ain't his. They're Leanne Overton's—

she's his niece. She moved in there a couple of weeks ago. Mr. Valentine's friend, Ms. Bell, died last Christmas, and his family thinks him and that other old lady that lives with him need somebody to kinda keep an eye on them. Miz Overton needed to separate her mare and its filly from her others out there at the MacCoys', and Mr. Valentine has that good horse place. His wife used to be a barrel racer.''

Ricky Dale seemed like he knew a lot about people and goings-on.

''Miz Overton hired me to look out for 'em. Fifteen dollars for the week, and an extra five dollars when I come on Saturdays. I'll groom and exercise 'em, just work with them, so they have people attention. That's important with baby horses, like that filly.''

Corrine wondered if he really knew this much about what he was saying, or if he liked to pretend he knew so much. She wondered if he was big enough to handle horses; he wasn't but just a bit taller than she was, maybe ten pounds heavier. Probably what he would do mostly was clean the stalls, and that wasn't exactly handling horses, but she saw no need to say this.

He continued on to say that he had been riding horses since he was three years old, that his grandfather, who used to be the sheriff for years, had taught him. He had even herded cattle with his grandfather.

''But he had to sell out his place and move into MacCoy Acres for old farts.''

Corrine wished she could think of something to say.

Willie Lee did. ''Do you have a horse?''

"No. I did have. Mason MacCoy gave me his Old Buck to ride, but he died."

Corrine could not speak to that horribly sad thing.

"I am sorry," Willie Lee said. "That is sad."

"Yeah, well, it happens. Buck was real old." He looked downward as he spoke, then lifted his head. "My grandfather's gonna help me buy another horse. A young one that I can train. I'm gonna save my money from this job."

"That will be nice," Corrine said, wishing she could come up with a better comment.

Then Ricky Dale asked, "You guys want to come up to Mr. Winston's and see the horses? You'd like the baby horse, Willie Lee."

Corrine stared at him. She was at once impressed that he spoke equally to Willie Lee and amazed at the invitation.

"Yes, I want to come," Willie Lee said instantly.

Corrine, always more cautious, said, "We have to ask Aunt Marilee."

"Okay," Ricky Dale said.

Willie Lee went racing inside. Corrine followed more slowly behind. Her mind was skimming over all sorts of reasons why going with Ricky Dale could turn out to be a bad idea. She was afraid she might do or say something stupid, and she really didn't want to find out something stupid about him.

But Willie Lee threw himself upon Aunt Marilee's lap. "Ma-ma, can we go to see hors-es up at Mr. Win-ston's with Ric...Ric-ky Dale?"

Corrine's faint hope that Aunt Marilee would disapprove was squashed when her aunt said, "Why, that sounds like a fine idea for a Saturday mornin'."

Aunt Marilee apparently considered Ricky Dale in a good light.

Mr. Winston's corral was at the rear of his deep backyard, partially shaded by large pecan trees. The mare was a black-and-white paint, a "high-dollar" kind, Ricky Dale said. Her baby, a two-month-old filly, was the same, with a large black spot on one hip and black on each ear, as if someone had painted them.

When he saw the horses, the black dog, Beau, went racing forward, barking, ducked under the fence and chased after the horses, that went all over the corral. Ricky Dale ran after him, yelling until the dog, tongue hanging out, stopped and obeyed his master's call. Corrine, standing with Willie Lee and Munro outside the corral, looking on, figured it was more that the dog had stopped to get his breath.

Ricky Dale parked Beau outside the fence and called Corrine and Willie Lee inside. Munro followed. The filly poked her head beneath the mare's neck, watching them with sharp curiosity.

In that moment of looking at the mare and her baby, looking into the deep, dark eyes, Corrine fell totally in love with another being other than Willie Lee. In that instant she was lost forever to an adoration of horses.

"Come here, Pretty Girl," Ricky Dale coaxed, then instructed Corrine and Willie Lee not to move, nor look the horse right in the eyes.

The next instant the filly was slipping beneath the mother's neck and coming forward, straight for Willie Lee. The mare moved, putting herself next to the baby, who stretched her neck and nose toward Willie Lee.

"Breathe into her nose, Willie Lee," said Ricky Dale.

Willie Lee touched his nose to the filly's nose. The filly drew back and then put her nose out again. Corrine thought it was about the neatest thing she'd ever seen, and she was glad when she got a chance to do it, too.

They all eventually got to pet the filly and the mare. Corrine decided she liked the mare best. She liked the way the mare let her lean against her and put her check against her strong shoulder. She could have stayed there with the mare forever.

But Ricky Dale had come to do a job. He found two rakes, and Corrine and Willie Lee took turns helping to clean the large stall. Corrine figured Ricky Dale wasn't a fool; he'd gotten help for the job.

Willie Lee was not much help, but Ricky Dale told him that he was.

They were putting fresh pine shavings into the stall when Ricky Dale's dog started chasing the horses again. Ricky Dale ran out into the corral. "Beau! Beau! You stop that!"

Beau looked at Ricky Dale, and the mare at that instant kicked the fire out of the dog. Kicked him hard enough to cause a loud thud and to send the dog flying backward. Corrine, watching, experienced a slice of horror and unreality. The dog got immediately up from the ground, then stood with all four legs splayed, as if for balance. Ricky Dale went toward him, and the dog started toward Ricky Dale, and then he just keeled over.

Ricky Dale reached the dog and went down on his knees. "Beau?"

Corrine, having followed after Ricky Dale, saw that the dog's eyes were closed, and its blackish tongue hung out of its mouth, but it wasn't panting. It lay still as death, a term she had heard one of the women in her old neighborhood down in Fort Worth use.

Panic rose inside her, and she looked over to the Valentine house, wondering if she should go get someone.

Then there was Willie Lee getting on his knees and pulling the dog's head onto his lap. Corrine went to tell him to stop that disgusting action of touching a dead dog, but something, some odd prickling at the back of her neck, stopped the words. Slowly she fell on her knees beside him.

"Willie Lee?"

He didn't answer. His arms were around the dog's neck, his cheek pressed against the dog's fur. His eyes were closed, and there was this strange look on his face. It was the sunlight, she thought, and looked up, seeing the beams slanting through the bare branches and shining on Willie Lee, making his pale hair glow. Corrine blinked, looking at it. She saw Munro pressed against Willie Lee; the dog's eyes were slits, as if things were bright for him, too. All was still as death.

Then she looked across at Ricky Dale, who looked at her. For whatever reason, neither of them pulled Willie Lee away.

And then Willie Lee's eyes came open, and he straightened back up. "He is o-kay."

"What?" Ricky Dale said.

Then the black dog's eyes opened up. Corrine looked harder. Yes, his eyes opened and his tongue went back in his mouth. He lifted his head.

Ricky Dale said, "Beau?"

The dog got up, sort of drunk like, and licked Ricky Dale in the face.

"Beau is bet-ter now. Right, Mun-ro?" Willie Lee smiled.

Corrine told Willie Lee to go to the backyard ahead of her. "Start feeding the rabbits, and I'll help you in a minute," she said, and hung back to say goodbye to Ricky Dale, who was getting his bike. His black dog waited a few feet away, watching with his stupid-puppy-looking expression. The kick hadn't made him any smarter.

"Thanks for takin' us along to see the horses," Corrine said.

"Yeah."

She thought he was looking at her as oddly as he had Willie Lee.

"I'm glad your Beau was just knocked out," she said, watching his face closely.

He looked down at his bike. "Yeah. Me, too." Then his eyes came up—they were very green, looked like cat's-eye marbles. "I think maybe he wasn't just knocked out, Corrine. I think maybe he was dead, and that maybe Willie Lee brought him back to life."

Corrine chose her words. "Well, I don't know about that." She regarded him with a raised eyebrow, the way Aunt Marilee could do to someone. "But I do know that if we tell that story, everyone will think we made it up. And they'll think we're crazy. Some people already look down on Willie Lee as being half-crazy.''

His shoulders dropped, and his eyes shifted, thoughtful like, to the ground.

''Don't tell anyone about what happened, Ricky Dale. Just don't tell.'' She started it as a plea, but then she added firmly, ''I won't back you up, if you tell. I'll say you're lyin'.''

She gazed at him in a way to let him know she meant business. In that moment, she felt exactly like she imagined her aunt Marilee did, which was knowing and doing whatever it took to protect Willie Lee.

Ricky Dale wet his lips, but she couldn't read his expression. Then he nodded and turned his bike toward the street. Halfway along the walk, he stopped and looked over his shoulder. ''I don't think Willie Lee is crazy.''

She didn't reply, and he got on his bike.

She turned then and went up the steps, pausing at the top to hang on to the porch post and watch Ricky Dale pedal off down the street, with the black dog running behind him.

Eleven

Off with the old, on with the new...

What was wrong? He and Marilee were to be married. They were getting along fine. No arguing. Comfortable.

The problem was the word "comfortable." *It* was not comfortable.

It was like there were questions buzzing around their heads now when they were together.

It was as if she were saying things that he could not hear.

They hadn't made love since before Christmas.

It wasn't required, he argued with himself. He had never considered sex the proof of love. Hadn't he loved Barbara Ann Jewel in senior high, and he hadn't had sex with her, simply *because* he had loved her so much. Plus, he had been terrified of the consequences, he admitted. In those days a person went straight to hell for even touching his own private parts, not to mention a woman's. Kissing was okay, but keep the tongue out of it, too, or you went to hell.

Of course, he had by the age of sixteen dared all of it, and he hadn't gone to hell. He'd gone to heaven. Well, until later, when there would be all sorts of squirmy feelings and complications. Growing up meant hard lessons, but he was far from that now. What was going on with him about this thing? He was an adult man; he should be able to understand. But that was a pitiful joke played on humankind. Did anyone ever come to understand enough?

He thought of how he had felt with Marilee in the porch swing, that last time they had been alone. Why in the world had he acted like such a fool?

He had wanted her so badly right then. Every part of him had longed and clamored to bury himself in her sweet warmth. To take succor in her rich womanliness. In fact, he swelled at this very moment with the memory and desire, as his mind quickly took off with images of their hot and sweating bodies entangled in sheets made damp by their lovemaking.

A chill swept him. The desire scared him afresh, as it had then. The wanting, the need, seemed not to have an end. It was like looking into an endless black pit that threatened to swallow him should he get one step closer.

And Marilee was backing away from him. There was no evidence in her manner of this, he argued with himself. Yet he could feel it.

Stuart James did not help matters. Not that Tate felt actually threatened by the man, but he did not at all like the way James kept looking at Marilee, as if he was about to scoop her up and run off. Tate kept having the urge to punch the man.

At least that urge he could understand, he thought with a loud sigh.

''What are you sighing about?''

His mother had come into the kitchen, quietly, in

her soft-soled ballerina slippers that she wore when doing her yoga.

"Oh, nothin'." He didn't want to resent his mother being in the house. He loved his mother. But sometimes she made him feel like a child again. Would that ever end? "I've been working on an editorial. Havin' trouble comin' up with something interesting." He hid his face in his cup, draining the last of the coffee.

"They don't all have to be Pulitzer prize winners." She put a cup of water in the microwave and pushed the buttons. "Maybe you need to skip an edition or two. You know, your readers might more appreciate your column after a bit of absence."

He frowned, not liking the thought at all. What if his readers decided they didn't miss his column? It was his paper; he wanted his name in it. Besides, use it or lose it, so the saying went.

This thought was like a splinter into his mind.

He had not done well at being a husband the first time around. And since his divorce, he had not had a long-term relationship with a woman. He could count on three fingers the number of women he had slept with in the over fifteen years since his divorce. He always wondered if men exaggerated this part of their lives.

Once again alone, he sat himself at the kitchen table and his notebook computer. Put his fingers on the keys. Writing, he knew, did not depend on inspiration. Writing came from application. Just write, and the ideas would then begin, not the other way around.

Was this the answer to his relationship with Marilee, too? And to his fears? He faced the fear of writing by the doing. Would this work with the black hole of uncertainty that sucked at him?

He wondered this as he typed out what came to mind, a garbled sentence, but within ten words, he was forming ideas and putting them on the page.

Half an hour later, as he finished up his editorial, his mother came through lugging a white plastic trash bag. She informed him that she had cleaned out the towel closet and the medicine cabinet.

The medicine cabinet? He hoped his shaving cream and razors and aspirin were not in the trash bag.

"Do you know, I found Milk of Magnesia bottles in the bathroom closet, with a fifteen-year-old date? Muriel had some definite problems with keeping house."

He had seen the blue bottles in the far back of the deep closet. He hadn't thought they were bothering anything.

With some amazement, he watched as she simply opened the back door, threw the bag out, then closed the door again, turned and immediately demanded of him: "Why have you not done anything around here?"

"I haven't even been here a full year," he said, feeling the odd need to defend himself. "And I did have a newspaper to get on its feet."

She likely didn't understand the magnitude of the job he had taken on.

"Between Marilee and the newspaper, Mom, I've been fully occupied."

His thoughts followed with: And it was easier to spend most of his time over at Marilee's. He *liked* being over at her house.

Quite suddenly he was seeing the dreary old house through his mother's eyes. The only rooms he had used at all were his bedroom, the bathroom and the kitchen. He had an aversion to the other rooms, he realized.

The big old Porter house had previously belonged to his cousin, Muriel Porter, who had also owned the paper. She had sold both to Tate and left town, and when Muriel had left town, she had carried away with her only her clothes, and no more of those than she could fit into two full-size suitcases and an overnighter. When Tate had arrived the previous spring, the closets had been crowded with clothes that looked to have belonged to at least two generations, the rooms filled with heavy furniture that possibly dated from the early part of the century, and the walls decorated with wallpaper not much newer, and aged photographs and memorabilia from a bygone era.

He realized his mother was speaking.

"There wasn't room for Muriel in this house. There was too much of her father and mother and stepmother in here. God knows they were a brooding bunch. E. G. Porter clung to every last dollar and possession of his pitiful life, until he lost it." She rubbed her shoulders and cast a disdaining eye around the kitchen.

Tate, following her gaze, saw wallpaper peeling in the corner and the dingy paint on all the woodwork.

"It is hard to breathe in this house," his mother said. "Muriel was chokin' to death here. And now all you've done since you came is bring old junk from your old life and add it all in. There is no room for new life, because of all the old dead hanging around."

His mother could get some far-out ideas.

His mother looked at him in that way she had that indicated she saw things inside him.

"I never had a house before," he said.

Maybe what he meant was that he had never made such a commitment before, not to a house, nor to creating a family life.

"Are you here to stay?"

"Yes," he said with some aggravation. "Marilee and I have talked about the house." Yes, they had. "There are lots of changes we'll be making. We're goin' to have another bathroom installed down here under the stairs, get everything painted."

He left off, unable to recall what exactly they had spoken of. Their discussions had been the sort of talk people indulge in when they're dreaming out loud.

"Life is a flow, Tate. When you hang on to things, you dam up the flow. Discard what is no longer used...what no longer *suits*," she said in an emphatic manner, "and you make way for the new and better and perfectly suitable to enter. Do you really need an antique refrigerator?" she asked, putting her hand on the old Kelvinator.

Without waiting for an answer, which Tate was trying to come up with, she came toward him and touched his arm.

"Let go of the old life and start with the new, Tate. Simply begin."

After several long seconds, he said, "Yes, you're right," and bent and kissed her cheek.

He started out of the room, then paused at the doorway. "What will I do when you are gone?" he asked her, struck suddenly to the core with the horrendous thought.

"What makes you think I'm goin' first?" she snapped at him, adding her saucy grin.

He shook his head and walked out, his eyes misting over, thinking about the foolish assumption that there came a day a man got too old to listen to his mother. He had not reached that stage. Maybe because his mother kept one step ahead of him at all times. One step ahead of just about everybody, really.

In his bedroom, from the top drawer of his dresser, he brought out the black velvet ring box. He opened it and looked at the band inside that matched the diamond ring on Marilee's finger.

With this ring, I thee wed. That was what he had thought when he slipped the engagement ring on her finger. He had, somewhere in the past days, forgotten that. He had made his commitment to her, and then gotten sidetracked.

Possibly commitments had to be reconfirmed each day.

Replacing the ring in the drawer, he stood looking around for a full minute, assessing the situation with the eye of a man of renewed conviction.

Then, moving in long strides, he went to the bedside table and pulled out a well-worn leather address book, flipping through it until he found the number for the travel agent he used most often. Guy, down in Houston. He dialed, and when Guy came on the line, he told him to put together a vacation at Disney World for two adults and two children. "The best rooms, the best wine, the best…well, you get it. This is a trip for a lifetime," he told the young man. He was already in debt; going deeper didn't seem a problem.

As he said goodbye, his eye dropped down the short page of the worn address book and stopped on his ex-wife's address and number. He had not used it in some ten years. Yesterday, dead and gone. He ripped out the address and tore it into small pieces, then tossed it into the trash basket.

Again he surveyed the room. Somewhere he had read that the bedroom set the tone for the marriage. Should start off on the right foot—make this an incredible room, since he hoped what went on in here would be pretty incredible. A room for lovers.

A room for his fair love, for the heart of his heart, for the wife he would love as he loved himself.

But, and here was a daunting dilemma, he had no idea how to bring about such a room, or quite what Marilee would find suitable for incredible happenings.

A knock sounded at the door, and his mother poked her head inside. "Here, dear. I knew I saved this card for a reason. It's the card of an interior decorator in Dallas. I used to go to yoga class with her mother. Delightful lady. Liked colors. I imagine her daughter will be equally adept at colors and such."

"I was just thinking about a decorator," Tate said, slowly taking the card.

"Oh, I'm sure you were. The memory of that card just popped into my mind." She glanced around the room. "God knows we need some help here." She swept out in her usual sweeping manner.

The name printed on the card, in iridescent turquoise, was Honey Moon. "Specializing in personal expression and harmony in environments."

Sounded really New Age.

Taking a deep breath, he picked up the telephone. Never let it be said that he wasn't ready to move right along with the modern era.

He went through several assistants, but stuck to his guns in his intention to go to the top and speak to Honey Moon herself. If nothing else, he wanted to know what a woman with such a name sounded like.

"Yes, this is Honey Moon." Her tone made him think of moonlit nights in the bayou, just the type of interior decorator he suspected he needed.

He explained his need, and, much to his surprise, she told him she could do all the work from Dallas. "I have clients all over the country. I will have everything delivered and set up by emissaries."

Emissaries? Sounded expensive. He had good credit, thus far.

She said, "I will e-mail you a questionnaire. Fill it out, skip no questions. Make a drawing of your bedroom, and include the directions north, south, etcetera. Send that and a picture of you and your intended bride. Don't fax those. Send them FedEx."

He didn't think he would have been surprised if she had requested a lock of Marilee's hair.

A shrill buzzing split the air, followed by what sounded and felt like a wrecking ball slamming into the house.

Marilee, reacting in the fashion of someone deeply in thought, as she was with the article she was writing about rabies in the state, jumped and let out a "Yaaa!"

Abandoning her chair, she raced into the laundry room, where the washer was halfway across the floor and into takeoff position. She threw herself atop it in an attempt to hold it down, while pulling out the knob. It halted abruptly, as if shot dead.

Whew. Catching her breath, she glared at the machine, wondering how it could barely wash clothes but could manage to walk a good two feet.

It probably was due to the strength of the quilt from Willie Lee's bed. She should have taken it to the laundry but had not wanted to take the time, so she had stuffed it into her large-capacity, but not large enough for quilts, fifteen-year-old model that she had purchased from her neighbor Leon Purvis when, in an effort to bribe his wife into not leaving him, he had bought her a brand-new and sparkling Kenmore washer and dryer set. His wife had been appeased—indeed, had sang Leon's praises for about a year—but eventually she had left him anyway to become a cross-country truck driver who apparently never had to bother doing her own laundry but used drop-off service.

She thought longingly of the washer she had seen in the latest *Better Homes and Gardens* magazine. It loaded from the front, like a commercial washer, and handled quilts and bedspreads with ease, so the advertising stated. It cost a mint.

She could buy one when she married Tate, came the whisper into her mind, followed closely by the question: Would Tate mind her spending so much money on a washer?

Was she marrying Tate for a washer?

This dismaying and guilty thought sliced through her and was followed immediately by another: Would marrying him be in vain, if he wouldn't let her buy a washer?

She did not like to think of herself as a woman who married for appliances. Of course that wasn't why she was marrying Tate.

Although she would have to concede that it was a hard world, and women had married for less convenience than an appliance, she thought, just as the children burst in the back door, Willie Lee saying, "We are back from Mis-ter Win-ston's, Ma-ma."

"I can see that. Did you have a good time?"

"Yes."

"Take your shoes off, Willie Lee," said Corrine, always neat. "We fed the rabbits and cleaned their cages before we came in."

"You two have been busy this mornin'." Marilee shoved at the washer, and Corrine, familiar with the machine's idiosyncrasies, stepped beside her to help move it back into proper position. Marilee jumping on one corner was required to get it level again.

"Hors-es have long necks," Willie Lee said. "I pet-ted the baby. She lik-ed me. The mo-ther lik-ed me, too, but not too much."

Marilee repositioned the quilt and started the washer; it wobbled like a chair that had lost a leg, but it ran okay. She went to make the children peanut butter and jelly sandwiches and to listen to tales of their experience with the horses. Talking of horses made her think of what Parker had told her about there being more cases of rabies in horses and cattle than in dogs or cats. She couldn't find a pencil to jot down the thought.

"It's in your hair," said Corrine, the ever-helpful.

She jotted the thought on a napkin, stuck the pencil back in her hair for future notations and went back to being a mother, passing bread to the children. "Go on. What else?"

Willie Lee cocked his head and said, "They smell-ed like sun-shine. They poop a lot, but it does not stink so much like dog poop. And the mo-ther is grumpy."

"She is?" She thought proudly that Willie Lee was doing good these days spreading his peanut butter on the bread.

"Yes. She kick-ed Beau. Hard."

"She did? Who's Beau? Is he hurt?" Becoming alarmed, she looked to Corrine for explanation.

"Just Ricky Dale's dog…stupid puppy. He was annoyin' the mare. He's okay."

"Oh, well, good." She had the distressing thought that perhaps she had been negligent in allowing the children to go alone to see the horses. Some horses could be dangerous, and she had not even considered this, being preoccupied with laundry and writing to earn a living.

"He got dead-ed, but he is o-kay."

He got deaded?

The doorbell rang. "Hey…anyone home?"

It was Stuart's voice. He came into the kitchen at the same instant the washer had another fit. Marilee and Corrine raced into the laundry room and threw themselves on the washer to hold it down, Marilee fumbling to turn it off.

Into the resulting quiet came Stuart's voice. "What's wrong with it?"

"Overload," Marilee said.

She doubted that the man had ever operated a washing machine in his life. At least not a private one.

There he stood, her debonair ex-husband, with his hands casually slipped into the pockets of his slacks, not a hair out of place, and wearing a perfectly starched cotton shirt and sharply creased chinos, done up at some hot, steamy laundry out of his view. He could have stepped out of a glossy catalog for high-priced travel clothes, while she, leaning desperately on a washer, with sweat curling her hair that she was not certain she had combed that morning, and wearing a worn T-shirt and jogging pants, felt she could be cited as justification as to why men ran off with their secretaries.

The pencil fell out of her hair and clattered to the floor.

Stuart bent to retrieve it. She saw the silky, shiny silver hairs at the top of his head as he did so. As he handed her the pencil, he chuckled and suggested that she was no match for a washing machine. This comment and accompanying laugh struck her in a fateful, wounded place.

She said, "I'm going to take a hot bath. Children, you can take naps or watch television. Stuart…" She grabbed the basket filled with clean clothes and jammed it at him. "You can fold clothes. And when I get out of my bath, we're going to have a talk."

She strode past him, leaving the fumes of her anger in the passing, and leaving Stuart, thoroughly bewildered as to what he had said wrong, holding the basket.

He looked into it. There were lacy panties on the top. And bras. How did one fold a bra? He did not do his own laundry, except for washing out underwear and a shirt now and again while on a shoot in some wild yonder, and it had been years since he had been out in the wild yonder.

He looked down to see the girl, Corrine, staring up at him. He often found her watching him with her eyes deep and dark as those of the old witchy-women back in the Cajun bayou where he had spent his childhood, then escaped. Gave him the willies.

"How about I give you, say—" he checked his pocket "—three bucks, and you fold these things?"

He thought for a surprising instant that she was going to refuse, but then she said, "Okay," and reached to take the basket. It was a load for her, but she seemed adept. She took it to the kitchen table, then turned to him and held out her hand.

"You fold them first."

She shook her head and kept the hand out. He put dollar bills in it. "Smart girl."

Some minutes later he had sat himself on the couch, idly watching cartoon figures that Willie Lee liked on television and wondering exactly what he should reveal to Marilee when they talked. He had hoped to make better inroads into her good graces before he had to reveal the state of his health. Or ill health, as was the case.

He had sent her roses, but she hadn't brought them home from the office. He had been trying for a romantic candlelit dinner for two, but he couldn't seem to get her away from a crowd of people. He had begun to think of a picnic, which was to have been his proposal this afternoon.

Then her voice echoed in his thoughts: "We're going to have a talk."

He began to feel a little panicked. He wasn't ready for any deep, calling-to-account conversation. He just wanted to make up to her, somehow, to have things okay between them, so that she would feel kindly toward him when he told her the truth of his situation.

The girl appeared in front of him, stuck an opened magazine toward him and tapped it with her finger. "Aunt Marilee would like one of these."

He stared at her a moment, then took the magazine and looked at what she showed him, an advertisement for a washing machine. "This one?"

"Yes. And you might want to get the dryer, too."

Although Corrine could not name the desire that drove her, she felt a longing to take care of her aunt Marilee, if she could possibly do so, in the same manner that she looked after Willie Lee. In some general way she had the idea that they would all be better, no matter what happened, to get a washing machine while the getting was good.

She was pleased when Mr. James poked his head in the kitchen, where she folded clothes at the table, and said in a very rushed manner, "Tell your aunt Marilee that I'll be back later." He winked. "I'm going to get her a surprise."

Marilee slathered on her best face lotion, blew her hair dry and billowy, and whipped on her makeup, doing the full job. Lastly she chose Sahara Sunset Red lipstick. With all this, she was putting on every bit of confidence she could rake up. She had a few things to say to Mr. Stuart James, and she would do best to look competent when she spoke.

Dashing in her robe from the bathroom to her bedroom, she slipped into soft jeans and a deep blue sweater with a draping boat-neck neckline. Sultry, but not too much. She spritzed White Shoulders on her neck and remembered how Tate always told her she smelled delicious when she wore it.

What was she trying to do?

She looked at her reflection in the mirror. She did not want to be a woman a man left, as Stuart had left her. She could not abide appearing like that.

That was yesterday. Let go of the resentment. Deal with today.

She tried, as if heaving an enormous rock from the middle of her soul. The feeling would not budge. And *today* she still did not want to be the sort of woman a man ran from. She did not want to be ashamed.

Straightening her shoulders, she stepped out into the living room, where she found Willie Lee and Munro asleep upon the rug in front of the television, and Corrine slouched in the big chair, reading.

"Where's Stuart?" she asked, casting a glance toward the kitchen.

"Oh, he left for a little bit," Corrine told her. "But he said to tell you that he'd be back later."

"How much later?"

"He didn't say. But I think he went to get you something."

"What? What did he say?"

"Oh, I don't know. He just said he was going out to get you a surprise."

Stuart had never once given her what she needed, Marilee thought, which was his undivided attention.

Twelve

Of love, women and washing machines...

Aunt Vella called. "Is now a good time to come over? I have some bridal magazines for you, and I want to talk to you." Vella had learned, most especially in the last year, to say things straight out.

"I guess so. What do you want to talk about?"

Holding the telephone between her shoulder and her chin, Marilee dipped a peppermint tea bag into a cup of steaming water. She could only stomach herb tea when the lowest of moods came on her. Those moods were beyond even the ministrations of chocolate. Stuart's inclination to keep leaving her, which had gone on throughout their entire marriage, when he had frequently left her places—stranded at hotels waiting for him; stranded out at back-country groceries, waiting for him; and even once stranded at an airport overnight, waiting for him—until one day he told her he was going and would not return, so there was no need to wait, seemed to overwhelm her, as fresh as when she had been married to him.

"Well, about Stuart being here, for one thing. I had to hear about that from Julia J.T., who also told

me that Tate's mother has come up from Texas.''
Her aunt's voice betrayed hurt.

"We've all been busy," Marilee said, then
thought to ask, "Who's Julia J.T.?"

"Our postmistress and self-appointed society reporter, Julia Jenkins-Tinsley. I get so tired of saying
that entire name. Why doesn't she pick one or the
other and stick with it? Julia says Frank Goode told
her Stuart has paid for a month out at the Goodnight.''

"He has?" So there was a strong possibility that
he truly would be back. The knowledge, curiously,
did not lighten her mood.

"You didn't know?"

"He hasn't said. We haven't had time to talk, either." The peppermint tea burned her tongue.

"Well, that's what Julia says, and Julia is usually
accurate. I'll be there in five minutes."

Marilee hung up and wondered if she ought to go
ask Julia just where Stuart had gone that afternoon,
and when he would return.

Vella Blaine had seen her niece only a scant few
brief times in the past month, as they had both been
very involved with their own business. Vella's business had constituted what she thought of as getting
a life. This endeavor had begun last summer, when
she had thrown her husband Perry out of the house.
Since their reuniting had not proved fulfilling, she
had worked to accept the marriage as it was and gone
on to make a life she could possibly stand to live,
while remaining as Perry's wife. She could not bear
to throw him out again. That was too much upheaval
for both of them, having been married for forty-six

years. The guilt was too much for her to bear, because she recognized her fault in causing Perry to become dependent on her in the ways of everyday living. He had no idea what to do on his own, couldn't even keep his clothes clean. And she did love him. That remained, despite being bored to death by him.

Yet living with him and having so little in common, most especially no sexual relations at all, was killing her. She sought expression for the more lively side of her nature in the venue of classes in gardening and landscape design, researching healthy cooking, and encouraging herself into the new woman she longed to be.

That was why, when Marilee saw her, her eyes widened. "You got your hair cut."

"Oh, yes. Like it?" Vella touched the back of her smoky-colored hair. Always short, it was now very, very short and enhanced with hair gel in the modern manner. And today she wore painter's jeans and a large cotton sweater. Being a big-boned woman, she had rarely ever worn pants. She always felt too prominent in them. But she decided it was okay to be prominent, and she liked the loose jeans.

Her niece was gazing at her, taking it all in. "Yes. It looks wonderful on you...but I'm glad you didn't dye it," she said of the hair. In fact, Marilee thought she might not be able to stand it if her aunt showed up with bright black or orange hair.

"Oh, no...I don't have time for that stuff. Here are the bridal magazines. Belinda snatched them from the magazine deliveryman." She liked to point out whenever her daughter did something thoughtful for someone, as usually Belinda did not stir herself on anyone's account but her own. "He regularly only leaves two different ones at the store, but she got you all he carried on his truck—five in all. There ought to be some good ideas in them."

As she spoke, Vella sat herself down. She observed her niece and saw the tea bag in the saucer. "Are you drinking herb tea?" Her observation turned sharper; things were deep if Marilee was past chocolate.

"Yes," Marilee answered in a tired voice.

"What's wrong?" Vella knew her niece well; she had been more of a mother to Marilee than her own mother. Heaven knew her sister-in-law had tried, but, as a mother, Norma Cooper had always been a square peg trying to fit into a round hole. She had never grown up herself. Some people simply were not cut out for parenthood, and it was too bad those people could not figure that out before they had children.

"Oh, nothing."

Vella sat there.

Marilee's gaze came up and met Vella's. "Stuart comin' back seems to have dredged up some annoying old feelings."

"That's usually the way of it."

"Well, it's silly. I got past this years ago. I was a little surprised when he showed up. Here I had not had a word from him in almost two years, and he shows up. Now, of all times."

"A bit rude to be so startling," Vella put in. "What if you hadn't been at home? What if it had been your wedding day, or you were off on your honeymoon?"

"I don't imagine that would have bothered him. And I wish I *had* been gone. Then I would not have to go through this now.'' Anger vibrated in her voice, and she lowered her eyes. "You know, I am wantin' him to have regrets for what he gave up...wanting him to want me now that I don't want him and he can't have me, and I'm feeling the hurt of him leaving me all over again, and worryin' that he needs somethin' from me...and I don't have it to give. It is just plain nuts," Marilee added emphatically.

"But it *is* human." Vella had grown to the age where she was generally surprised when human beings *did* make sense. "Feelings are feelings, sugar. They are not good or bad or rational, they just *are*. And they are indicators of things going on within us that need to be dealt with."

Marilee sighed. "I know."

Vella didn't think her niece did know. People were all the time saying they knew, when they really didn't.

"It is wearing. I do not have time for this." Marilee raked her hand through her hair with agitation.

Vella observed her, then asked, "Where's Tate today?" and glanced at the door, as if he might appear any minute. In fact, Tate Holloway had been in this house most times whenever Vella had stopped by in the past months. He had pursued Marilee with an uncommon single-mindedness possessed by few men when it came to a woman.

"He was working when he called this mornin'. We both were. I don't know about this afternoon." She turned her eyes to the clock. "I suppose he and Franny will call about supper. I have no idea what to have for supper."

"Franny—that's his mother, right? I guess she

came up to get a look at you. Julia says she is from Texas and is very artsy."

"She is…and quite pretty, and very nice."

Vella noted the warmth in her niece's voice and experienced a prick of pique, which she found highly annoying. She was a grown woman, and certainly too adult to be touched by such a shallow thing as jealousy of another woman.

She said, "I'll have to meet her. I heard she had coffee with Winston the other mornin'." Ah, there was the needle poking again, just with the telling. But Vella's relationship with Winston was over…over before it had become anything, because it never could.

"Oh, really?"

Vella changed the subject. "What about Stuart?"

Marilee played with the earring in her lobe in an absent manner. "He hasn't changed all that much. He's thinner. Older. But it's sort of like time has not touched him."

"Hmm…that sounds like Stuart." Vella had never thought there was much inside Stuart that time could touch. "How'd it go between him and Tate?"

Marilee shrugged. "Tate was cordial. You know Tate."

"No one can be as cordial as Tate when he makes up his mind to be. Sometimes it's annoying. He makes everyone else look petty." And it made Tate appear untouchable at times, she thought. "Nothing like a good foolish blowup to make a person be real and alive."

Marilee didn't appear to be listening. They each fell silent for some moments.

Then Vella asked about how arrangements were

going for the wedding. She noted that Marilee looked almost surprised at the question.

"Well...we have an appointment with Pastor Smith on—" her gaze went to the calendar hanging by the telephone "—oh, tomorrow afternoon. I'd forgotten. Do you suppose you could baby-sit? Maybe Franny could stay with the kids."

Her niece was definitely distracted about the matter, Vella thought.

"I have an appointment," Vella said, feeling vaguely guilty, but not guilty enough to call off her appointment—the tall, thick-shouldered image of a man filled her mind—about which she did not intend to elaborate, but Marilee didn't ask, anyway.

"What about the invitations?" she asked. "I'll be glad to help you address them."

"I haven't gotten them yet."

Vella did not think this adequate. "Have you made a list of those you want to invite?"

"Well...there isn't a long list. You and Uncle Perry. The kids, of course. Everyone at the paper. Charlotte's going to stand up with me, and Parker is Tate's best man. Mama and Carl are going to be out of town—"

"They are?" Vella cut in.

Marilee nodded. "They're goin' on a Caribbean cruise. It's all set."

Vella didn't think she should criticize Marilee's mother to her face, and, in fact, she didn't think Norma would add all that much but demands if she did attend the wedding.

"Oh. And where are you and Tate plannin' on goin' for your honeymoon?"

"I don't know. We haven't decided."

There was simply too much undecided to suit Vella. She wondered if she should point out that Marilee was not giving this wedding anywhere near sufficient attention. It was going to be an important milestone in her life—entering a second marriage, the second chance of a lifetime, and she wasn't likely to get another at her age, not to mention that half the town would be coming to the ceremony, formally invited or not. Tate had been going around inviting people at the same time he had been showing off the engagement announcement. This was Tate's manner. And so many people loved Tate and Marilee and would want to celebrate with them. Marilee could not see this. Marilee rarely saw how beloved she was by many people, who remembered her from childhood, and who had read her writings in the newspaper each week for years and thought of her as their very own Marilee.

The next instant Vella realized she herself had not been giving sufficient attention to the moment, when Marilee's expression crumbled like a clay figurine shot with a BB gun, and she dropped her head to her arms on the table and sobbed.

Vella quickly pushed the swinging door closed, not wanting to awaken Willie Lee and Corrine, who had fallen asleep with her book on her chest. She filled a glass of water for Marilee, then on second thought she drank it herself and ran another for her niece.

Her niece cried for quite an amazing amount of time. When she seemed to be drying up, Vella said, "Here, sugar, have a glass of water and a tissue, and tell me what this is all about."

Marilee blew her nose fully. "Oh, my mascara is

probably all over my face." She got up and looked in the mirror and moaned.

"Marilee," Vella said firmly, "quit worryin' about your looks and tell me what is going on with you. You are about to be married to a wonderful man and start a wonderful new life, and here you haven't made one arrangement and you're cryin' your head off."

Her niece sighed and sat down heavily, dropping her hands between her legs. "I don't know where to begin with this wedding. Stuart and I were married by a justice of the peace. I have never been involved with a wedding."

"That is easily solved. I will help you. Most of it we can contract out." Vella's time at landscaping classes had her using terms like contract out. "What else is the matter?"

Then Marilee shook her head. "I'm so angry at Stuart. I hate feeling so angry. It was all so long ago. It's just stupid, and Tate and I..." She shook her head. "Oh, I don't know what's wrong. Just nerves, I guess."

Vella regarded her with an expectant eye. "Nerves, you guess?"

Her niece shook her head and bit her bottom lip, looking teary again.

It came out from her then, haltingly and in great confusion, something about how Tate didn't seem interested in making love, or they didn't have time, but as far as Vella could gather, Marilee was very interested. Or maybe not. Vella got so annoyed at the confusion of messages she was getting that she said, "Which is it? You want sex, or you don't?"

Her tone was rather sharp, and she instantly regretted it. She herself knew very well what confusion a person could get into over the many facets of a relationship with a man.

Marilee looked startled. "Oh, I do." Her gaze wandered again. "I want Tate badly, but...well, we *are* busy, and Tate doesn't seem all that interested. Well, if he were, wouldn't he insist on us finding time? Of course the children...and then, well, Stuart has shown up."

There were too many wells in there to suit Vella. "You are having jitters, Marilee. And questions. It is to be expected in your situation."

"Yes, I am afraid, and I should have learned something from the past."

Vella saw they were at last getting to the heart of the matter.

"What if I'm makin' another mistake?" her niece wanted to know. "What if I'm not a person who can be married? I am quite good as a mother, but I just seem to mess up with tryin' to be a wife...a lover to a man. Why, I can't even attract my own ex-husband to stay and have a conversation with me."

"Stuart is not attracted to anything other than his own desires. Did Tate seem dissatisfied with you, when you have made love?"

Marilee reddened. "Well, no. But that was months ago. And it isn't the same as being married to a person. He just seems, well, far too accommodating without sex."

Vella, who noted the well, had her own experiences with and without sex; either could be trying and confusing.

She laid her hand atop that of her niece. "Sugar, you need to talk this all over with Tate. You are afraid because of old fears. Get them out where you can look at them, and they won't seem nearly so daunting."

Marilee's gaze slipped sideways.

Vella shifted in her chair, getting a firmer seat. This matter required conviction of attitude. "I have learned that one thing paramount in this life is to accept your feelings and speak them honestly aloud. Feelings are given to us by God. There's no need for shame over a one of them, not a one. Don't let them pile up inside, but deal with them as they come. Take them to God and confess them to Him, and you'll feel better immediately. Then deal with them with this man with whom you intend to spend the rest of your life. Start out straight and honest with exactly who you are.

"This is important, Marilee. Don't form the habit of hiding yourself from Tate, because you think what you feel is wrong, or because you don't want to hurt him. It isn't that you don't want to hurt him so much as you are afraid of yourself."

Marilee's eyes came up then, sparking. Vella was encouraged.

"Talk to Tate," she said again.

Marilee breathed deeply. "Yes, I will."

"Ohhh!"

Marilee had been rather listlessly going through the bridal magazines with her aunt, who was making a schedule of what they would need to accomplish, and when, for the wedding, when her eyes lit on a dress that caused that certain leap inside of her that happens when a woman recognizes the perfect outfit.

It was a wedding dress with a wide sweep of a

neckline, cutting across the shoulders, much in the manner of the sweater she wore at that minute. Marilee adored tops that showed her shoulders, which she thought were one of her better features. The sleeves of the dress were long and slim, and the dress skimmed the body, then fell in a soft swirl just above the ankles.

"Now that's a dress for a *woman.*" Aunt Vella's eyes shone with approval. "It is perfect for you."

"But not in white." Marilee had certain convictions about her wedding. "How do you think it would look in…" Eyes glued on the image, she tried various colors. "Dusty blue?"

"Hmmm…" Aunt Vella looked at Marilee, then looked at the photograph on the page. "Apricot. Deep, warm apricot."

"Oh, yes." Certainty and pleasure washed over her.

"And we'll take this picture down the street to Margaret Wyatt and get her to make it up. Doesn't look too hard."

"I didn't know she made gowns."

"Uh-huh…Margaret made the costumes for the senior play this year, and the gowns for each of Ramona Stidham's daughters' weddings. She is excellent. Then we will be able to tell Fred Grace that we want all apricot roses. He'll handle that."

Marilee studied the dress on the glossy page, picturing her hair done up and herself wearing the dress, in apricot. Her heartbeat picked up a delighted tempo as it does in any woman who sees herself happily beautiful in a dress, all saucy and swirling around her ankles that swept up from strappy heels, smiling and gracious, and indeed capable of any endeavor required of her.

At that particular moment there came a rapping at the back door, and it opened, with Tate poking his head inside. "Hello...is my bride-to-be home?" He came inside, followed by Franny.

Marilee, still affected by seeing herself in the beautiful dress, went instantly to Tate, totally oblivious to Franny, and wrapped her arms around his neck and kissed him. She had meant it to be a simple kiss, but he held her fast and went all out.

"Well, don't mind us," said Franny, who went forward to Vella to hold out her hand and introduce herself.

Marilee, coming back to earth, pushed away from Tate, wondering what in the world had gotten into her.

There was no time to recover or smooth over, because just then the kitchen door swung inward, with Corrine following and announcing in a breathless manner, "There's a big truck comin' in the driveway!"

En masse, like a tidal flow, they all exited the kitchen and went through to the front windows to see what Corrine was talking about. It was a truck, the side emblazoned with Cooper's Appliances, the appliance store owned by Marilee's stepfather. Stuart was there speaking to the driver.

Marilee went to the door Tate had already opened and followed him out onto the porch to greet Stuart, who said quite grandly, "Make way for the new washing machine."

Well, mercy.

* * *

"It's the latest technology," James said to Tate. "Loads from the front. Won't go off balance. Can handle blankets and quilts."

"I see that," said Tate, who stood beside him, looking on from a safe distance so as to avoid being mowed over by female enthusiasm. The women were oohing and aahing and swarming over the washer and dryer like bees feeding on ripe honeysuckle.

"Marilee had her heart set on it," the man said of the washer. He was clearly pleased with himself.

Tate kept his mouth shut and his arms folded in front of him, although he was fairly certain that no one would condemn him for socking the guy who was attempting to seduce his fiancée with appliances.

"I can fit," Willie Lee said. He had crawled into the washing machine.

"Oh, you wild boy," Vella said. "Get out of there. What if it started?"

"I would get wet."

"It can't start without pushin' these buttons," said Corrine, who indicated the buttons, then put her face back into the instruction manual.

"Why don't you try it out, Marilee, while the appliance men are still here?" proposed his mother, who Tate would have thought would not have been in there, getting carried away. He considered his mother's enthusiasm very near betrayal.

"Good idea. Let's rewash Willie Lee's quilt."

Watching the women, Tate was put in mind of hens clucking over a new baby chick. He wished he could have gotten something back from Guy about the honeymoon arrangements. Surely a grand honeymoon would top a washer and dryer, although, observing the excitement, he wasn't certain that even carte blanche to Walt Disney World and breakfast in bed for a week could top this deal.

Marilee, her face glowing with pure rapture—yes, it was rapture, Tate saw—whirled around. "Oh, Stuart." This was her fourth *Oh, Stuart,* at least. "I've been wanting this very washer. How did you know?"

"A little bird told me," Stuart answered and winked at Corrine, whose expression also showed traces of admiration.

Stuart, who had little experience in buying presents, was thoroughly glad he'd gone all out with the washer and the matching dryer, too. Apparently two dozen long-stemmed roses didn't cut ice here in this country of motherhood and home-ownership.

He had a sense of a glimpse into a foreign world and was reminded of how Marilee had been during her first trip to Europe with him. She had looked at everything from the giant plane to the first-class accommodations to every bit of the foreign land with great wonder, and upon Stuart as a prince among men for giving her the world.

He had forgotten how it felt to be a prince among men, he realized. Each time Marilee's eyes lit on him, he experienced a sort of expansion of his entire being.

She kept saying, "Oh, Stuart," and regarding him with wonder and delight, and he kept expanding. He had the thought that maybe he had found the cure for his illness, that maybe he had gone into instant healing. At the very least, in that moment his sickness held no meaning for him at all.

When Tate announced, "I'm takin' everyone out to celebrate the new washer and dryer," Marilee instantly came out of her ecstasy over the new washing machine and realized the situation.

Tate was jealous. Always a man who liked to shine, he had stood back this entire time, while she had neglected him in her thrill over the washing machine. She felt immediately ashamed that an inanimate object could have gotten her so off track as to make her forget him, one of the most thoughtful men in the world and one who certainly didn't deserve being forgotten for a washing machine, no matter how wonderful.

She went to him, and quick thinking came to her aid, when she said the perfect thing. "Oh, thank you, sweetheart. What a wonderful idea. That way we can go out and celebrate this lovely wedding present Stuart has given us."

She beamed at Stuart, and he blinked.

Tate, instantly jumping onto Marilee's train of thought, said, "That's right. A present like this needs celebrating. Let us show our thanks, Stuart. Valentine's choice of restaurants certainly won't come up to those you've enjoyed throughout the world, but the Main Street Café does the best it can."

The idea met with enthusiasm from Aunt Vella and Franny, who appeared to have become friends on first sight. The friendship was stimulated by both women discovering they each liked onion burgers.

"I'll drive," Aunt Vella said, and directed everyone where to sit.

Willie Lee and Munro went back into the cargo area, while Corrine sat between Franny and Vella up front, and Marilee found herself crammed between Tate and Stuart in the back seat. Tate put his hand around her shoulders, while he leaned forward and tossed comments to Stuart, and Stuart batted them back, about like a tennis match going on in front of her face.

"So, how long are you goin' to be able to stay, Stuart?"

"I don't really have any schedule."

Marilee thought of what Aunt Vella had said about him paying for a month at the Goodnight. She didn't want to get into that, though.

"No assignment waiting?" Tate asked.

"No…I am working on the one about vintage motels. When I get enough together, I'll let you see if you want bits on ones in this area."

"I know we will. Maybe you'll want to stretch your stay until next month and come to our wedding."

Marilee listened carefully.

"I might be here."

In her robe and slippers, Marilee went through the dimly lit rooms, checking the front door, putting final dirty dishes into the dishwasher, checking the back door, all the while savoring the quiet of the house. Just her and the children, sleeping now, alone, at last.

If she was this relieved to be alone with the children, how would she manage when she married and Tate was present all the time? The thought was disturbing.

They would be over at his house, she thought, with an instinctive glance through the back door window glass, in the direction of the big Porter-Holloway house, which could not be seen through the rows of cedars.

Which was it—she could hear Aunt Vella's voice—Porter or Holloway?

Holloway, she thought firmly, and tried the name on for size: Marilee Holloway.

The girl, Marilee Justus, had been left so far behind that she sometimes could barely remember her. Marilee James, who had been married to Stuart, no longer existed, so it was right that the name passed on. It seemed there ought to have been a name between Marilee James and Marilee Holloway. Perhaps it was the right time, after all, for Stuart's visit, in order that she might, in a manner of speaking, hand him back his name.

Just then her gaze fell on the new washer and dryer. Smiling with pleasure, she ran her hand along the cool, smooth enamel surface of the washer, and remembered Stuart and how happy he had seemed at giving her this present.

She was deeply touched. Surely this was his attempt to make amends for his past neglect.

It would take a lot more than a washer and dryer to make up for nine years of abandonment.

Perhaps there was no way to make up for the hurt. Perhaps there was only moving past it. With forgiveness.

Thirteen

Where love comes great, so comes fear...

"Your mother has a date with Winston?"

Tate nodded. "They're attending a play up at the senior center in Lawton."

"A play? What is it?"

"*Kiss Me Kate,* I believe."

She tried to picture this. Yes, she could see it, wigs, costumes and big bosoms.

Tate added, "And afterward they're havin' dinner at Christopher's. Mom was dolled up for the occasion. Wore her diamond earrings."

"Your mother seems to me to always be dolled up. She's drivin', I take it?" This would be nice for Winston, who wasn't allowed to drive himself anymore. Then she pictured Franny's sports car. "The MG?"

"I lent her the BMW. It's easier on Winston...who looked like a cool cat, too. His best Stetson, dark coat and string tie. Looked ten years younger."

Aunt Vella was busy, and Franny was off on her date. This meant the children would have to go with them to their consultation with Pastor Smith.

"What about Jenny?" Tate asked. Jenny was the teenager who had baby-sat for the children on a number of occasions.

"It's too short notice to call her," Marilee said.

There was a question in Tate's expression. She could almost hear him thinking: Why hadn't she reserved Jenny days earlier? Why had she not prepared for this meeting? In that annoying instant of clarity that one gets when facing oneself, she knew she had kept putting off any plans concerning this meeting with Pastor Smith.

"Where's Stuart?" Tate asked. "He's been here every day, and now he's not? Why don't we call him to come stay with the kids?"

Marilee didn't like the idea.

"Why not?" Tate observed her. "He's Willie Lee's father, Marilee. And if he was going to *abscond* with Willie Lee, I imagine he would have done so before now."

Marilee did not care for the sarcasm in his voice.

Before she could whip out a reply, however, Willie Lee appeared in the kitchen doorway. "What is ab-ab-s-con-d?"

"Tate was just teasing, honey. Ab-scond. It means to carry away. Now, sugar, go get your jacket. We are all goin' to see Pastor Smith...yes, Munro, too, but he'll have to wait outside."

She shot Tate a pointedly raised eyebrow while waiting for Willie Lee to be out of earshot, after which she said, "No, I don't think Stuart wants to take off with Willie Lee, but neither do I feel confident that he could handle any crisis that might arise. Crises do arise at the most inopportune times, like when mothers are absent.

"And I am not telephoning him—" she spoke with careful diction, enunciating every one of her *g*'s, as was her habit when seeking to make a point "—because I do not consider him at my beck and call for baby-sitting...and because I cannot tell you of the countless times during our marriage when I would be waiting for him and would telephone him to find out where he was and when he was going to come, only to get no answer, or to have him say one thing and do another. I had not heard a word from him in two years before he decided to drop in. I am not calling him now."

Tate was staring at her, his eyes widening as her feelings tumbled out, unchecked, like so much water breaking a dam.

Immediately she turned her back, awash with self-consciousness. She had not known she felt any of it and was quite dismayed to have to look at her anger fresh, as if her intentions of forgiveness last night had never been.

"Come here," Tate said in a gruff manner, and then he had grabbed her arm, turned her and was hauling her against him. "The man should be horse-whipped," he said, his tone and words a soothing balm to her wounded spirit. And then he was kissing her in a way that caused her to slip her arms around his neck and kiss him ardently in return.

She gasped for breath when they broke apart, and her head spun, and she blinked back silly tears.

Tate whispered, "I am not such a fool as to ever set you aside, Marilee. I love you, and I won't ever let you doubt it."

"Oh, Tate."

She looked into his eyes, which were intent upon

her, so dear and blue and hot as a day in midsummer. Words tumbled over themselves and jammed in her throat. She pressed her hand to his cheek.

Then a movement, a footfall, some motion, drew their attention to the doorway. Stuart stood there.

"Sorry to interrupt."

There he was, her ex-husband dropping in at will again.

Stuart's eyes moved from Marilee to Tate and back again. "Willie Lee asked me—if I understood him correctly—if I was going to abscond with him." He paused, gazing directly at Marilee. "I told him I hadn't planned on it."

Tate said promptly, "Well, good. Would you stay with the kids while we go to see the pastor about the wedding plans? Make yourself at home. There's a fresh pitcher of ice tea in the refrigerator."

Marilee found Stuart's reply of, "Uh...okay," far from reassuring.

"That's great," Tate said. "Thanks a lot, buddy. We won't be but an hour or so." He had hold of Marilee's hand and was leading her toward the door.

Tugging away, she insisted on jotting down the phone numbers for the parsonage and Tate's cell phone. "Just in case anything should happen."

Tate appeared with her coat, and as she slipped into it, she thought Stuart's expression was still a little hesitant and uncertain. He actually looked a little ill.

But then Corrine was there and saying, "I know Tate's cell phone number by heart, Aunt Marilee," with a logic and confidence that caused Marilee to smile and bend over to kiss her niece's cheek.

Tate took her hand again and hurried her through

the living room, saying as they went out the door, "It's a beautiful day. Let's walk." He entwined his fingers in hers and smiled a smile that touched deep into her middle. What a bug she was for her moodiness of late. She so wished she could get a handle on that.

Corrine, who had followed, hung on the porch post and watched her aunt and Tate walk down the brick path to the sidewalk. Her gaze lingered on the adults, seeing Aunt Marilee's soft wool coat swing jauntily with her steps and how her aunt leaned her head briefly against Mr. Tate's shoulder. A great sense of satisfaction engulfed her. Somehow, whenever her aunt seemed happy, Corrine felt happy.

For another full minute she clung to the porch post, listening to birds chirp, looking up through the bare tree branches to the cloudless sky and feeling the warmth that promised spring was just around the corner. She went over and sat herself in the porch swing, at the edge, so that her feet would touch the floor; she pushed back and forth and prayed that she would never have to leave her aunt and Willie Lee.

Her imagination, given rare rein to visit the positive side, formed lovely pictures of life for all of them together, with Aunt Marilee as her mother and Mr. Tate as her daddy, and Willie Lee there needing her to look after him, flowers on the breakfast table, saying grace at meals. And having her own room, with a four-poster bed, like the one she had seen in *Southern Living* magazine.

Maybe she could even have a horse. Maybe they would move to a house out in the country. She pictured moving Mr. Tate's big house out in the country, and there was a red barn and a wooden corral, and inside it a horse for her, a painted pony, and a littler one for Willie Lee. And big trees surrounding the house, hovering over it as if stalwart protectors. It was all so beautiful and filled her heart so much that her breathing was squeezed.

Just then, a sound—a bicycle rattle—popped her eyes open. Here came Ricky Dale Oakes, speeding into the driveway, veering from the rear bumper of Mr. James's car and coming across the grass, braking at the foot of the porch steps. Corrine felt a flash of delight.

The way he said, "Hey, Corrine," in a hushed voice, like he had a secret, caused her wonder what was up. He parked his bike and took the steps two at a time. "I got—"

His words were cut off when his stupid black puppy, tongue lolling out of the side of his mouth, came pushing up past him and over to slobber on Corrine.

"Eww…get away from me, dog."

"Oh…here, hold this." Ricky Dale pulled a box from inside his jacket and shoved it at her. It was a big matchbox. Then he took his rowdy dog by the collar and led him off the porch, making him lie down at the foot of the steps.

Corrine looked at the matchbox. There was something inside, and it did not feel like matches.

Ricky Dale hopped back up on the porch and took the box, saying, "Look at this."

He pushed open the box. Why, there was a little bird inside. Its head came popping up.

"It's just a baby," Ricky Dale said in a hushed tone.

Corrine looked more closely. The little bird

blinked its eyes and shook its little self, then fell over.

"I found it over at Mr. Winston's. I think it's wing is broken."

"Oh," Corrine said sadly. Then, "Why are you whisperin'?"

"Look, get Willie Lee out here and see if he can fix it."

Corrine stared at him. Then she shook her head. "No."

"Come on, Corrine. Let's just see what happens. Maybe it was coincidence that Beau got up after bein' kicked…but maybe Willie Lee did do somethin'. Let's just see what happens. I won't tell. I promise I won't."

She glared at him. She didn't think she could like him now, and this made her really mad at him, because she had begun to count on liking him and having him for a friend.

"Don't you want to see if Willie Lee can do it?" Ricky Dale said pointedly.

Her gaze, which had dropped again to the little bird in the box, flew upward to his eyes. They were the cat's-eye marbles again.

"We need to see, Corrine."

She did want to see, although she could not say that, so she just said, "Okay. You go on around back. I'll bring him out there." The backyard seemed a lot more private.

She slipped quietly through the front door. Willie Lee, with Munro lying against him, was watching his ant farm, over on the rug in front of the television. The action of explosions on the television arrested her briefly. It was a movie. On Pay-for-View. They almost never got to watch movies on Pay-for-View. Aunt Marilee considered most of them unfit for children's consumption. Apparently Mr. James found them fit for him.

But he wasn't in sight, and she wondered where he was. She pushed the front door closed and went to look in the kitchen, but upon passing the hall, she saw that the bathroom door was shut. Maybe she could get Willie Lee before he came out.

She raced on tiptoe over to Willie Lee, who she saw wore his red cape. "Willie Lee—" she knelt down and spoke in a hushed voice "—come on outside a minute."

"I am watch-ing my ants."

"I know, but you can come back and watch 'em. Come outside a minute. Ricky Dale has somethin' he wants to show you." She tugged at his cape.

"O-kaayy. Come on, Mun-ro."

They had reached the kitchen doorway when Mr. James's voice came from behind them. "Where are you kids goin'?"

Corrine turned to see him wiping his face with a washcloth, which struck her as curious, although her mind went on quickly to thinking up what to say. "Just out in the backyard. One of our friends is here."

"Well, don't be goin' off. I don't think Marilee would want you going anywhere when she isn't here."

"We aren't." Corrine had Willie Lee by the hand and pulled him on through the kitchen and out the back door.

Ricky Dale, sitting on the bottom step, hopped up. "Hey, Willie Lee."

"Hel-lo."

Corrine saw with a little worry that Ricky Dale had closed the big matchbox again; she hoped the little bird wasn't smothered or squished.

This worry was relieved when Ricky Dale opened the matchbox, and the little creature fluffed itself up. It was amazing how much smaller the already small thing could become.

"A bird." Willie Lee said with delight, blinking rapidly behind his glasses.

The bird fluttered and fell over.

Ricky Dale said, "I think it has a broken wing. Can you fix it, Willie Lee?"

Willie Lee tilted his head, and his eyes went from Ricky Dale to Corrine. Then he looked back at the bird.

"Maayy-be."

Corrine noticed how small her cousin's hands were when they gently took the little bird. He showed it to Munro. "Lo-ok, Mun-ro, a lit-tle bird. Oh, it is ok-ay lit-tle bird-y. Do not be a-fraid. Mun-ro won't hurt you. He likes birds."

Corrine had a sudden worry about disease. She had heard that birds could spread disease, by lice or something. She hoped Willie Lee didn't catch something. It would be all her fault, if he did.

Willie Lee, holding the small creature in one hand, stroked its head with one of his fingers. Corrine watched his hand and finger, but then she noticed it seemed like the sun was shining on him. She looked upward. The sky was clear, but she couldn't see any particular shafts of sunlight.

She looked again at Willie Lee, and her skin prickled as she saw that his pale hair seemed so bright, and that his glasses had glare on them.

Just then Ricky Dale's stupid puppy let out a woof and lunged up on Ricky Dale, knocking him off-kilter. Munro, who obviously didn't want any excess woofing around Willie Lee, turned on the bigger dog and growled his displeasure.

"Be quiet, Beau. Sit!" Ricky Dale ordered, but the dog had already lain down.

Corrine, who had been distracted by Ricky Dale and his dog, found Willie Lee was opening his hand and giggling.

"It tick-les," he said. "Mun-ro, it tickles."

The bird was fluffing in Willie Lee's lightly cupped hands.

"Can it fly?" Ricky Dale asked breathlessly.

"I think so. Maayy-be."

Willie Lee opened his hands and lifted them. The bird fluttered, and then the wing that had before been bent, came out to match the other, once, twice, and then the little bird flew up in the air. Corrine, her heart in her throat, watched it fly, little wings batting the air as it made a short trip to the clothesline pole, where it perched, tilting its little head back and forth at them.

Munro gave a yip at the bird.

"It flew," Ricky Dale said.

Corrine breathed deeply and gazed at the bird. Then a movement, something, caused her to glance at the back door, and she thought she caught sight of what could have been Mr. James's white shirt.

They had formed the basic plan for the wedding ceremony and were at a lull when Marilee felt the hair on the back of her neck prickle. It was the sensation she had whenever she sensed, usually correctly, that her children were up to something or needed her aid. She told herself to not react foolishly, as her gaze went to the telephone on the pastor's walnut desk. The telephone, however, picked that fateful moment to ring.

Marilee jumped and looked expectantly at the pastor, who said nonchalantly, "Naomi will get it," and shifted in his chair, leaning forward with his forearms on his thighs.

Marilee, who had sufficient experience with synchronicity, had to restrain herself from snatching up the phone when it rang a second time.

Pastor Smith continued, "Well, then, now that we've got the actual wedding itself ironed out, I want to talk to you both about marriage in general." He held up his hands. "Now, I know that you two are adults well experienced with life and the problems that can come up. You both probably know far more than I do about living, but I don't see that as an excuse to give you two a cut-rate job." He grinned in a hopeful manner.

Marilee thought of how he was younger than herself by four years; he did seem happily married, however, with normally happy children. Five of them. How did he stay sane? Maybe he wasn't.

A knock at the door, and Naomi poked her head inside. "You need to take this call, dear."

Marilee watched the small, compact man go out, rather than take the phone right there at his desk, and, like a fast train south, her mind went from approving his forward thinking about the possible need for privacy to anticipating that the call concerned her children, that possibly something dire had happened.

Her thoughts were jerked from this vein by Tate, rising from beside her on the love seat and stepping over to the large potted fern at the window, where he poured the contents of his china cup. This action, which she had only seen on comedies, astounded her.

"Naomi makes the worst coffee I have ever tasted," he said in a hushed voice, returning beside her on the couch and setting his cup back in its saucer. "I don't like to disappoint her, though. She always seems so eager to please."

"I know. If she gives a choice, I usually ask for a cold drink." She gazed at her own half-finished cup and was considering getting up and tossing it in the fern, too, although there was the question of possibly killing the plant. She had waited too long, though, because Pastor Smith appeared back through the door.

At his smile, Marilee, remembering her concern for the children minutes before, felt reassured.

"Sorry for that interruption." Easing his khaki trousers, he resumed his seat in the chair across the coffee table from them. He gestured at their cups. "Would you two like more coffee?"

"Oh, no, one cup is just fine for me," Tate said instantly. "Keeps me awake."

The pastor regarded them. "Well, now, where was I?"

"Something about marriage," Marilee prompted. She had begun to feel the need to move things along in order to get done and get back to the children.

"Oh, yes. I thought I'd go over some of the points I like to make to couples getting married. Probably this is old hat to you both, like I said, but I like to do my job." He rubbed his hands together, as if warming himself up to the task. "Let me begin with the trickiest subject." A brief pause. "Sex."

Tate said, "Well, sir, that's always an attention-getter."

Marilee hoped she wasn't about to learn something about Pastor Smith that she would find either annoying or distasteful.

"Yes, it is...my point exactly," said the pastor, clearly satisfied that his point was appreciated. "Sex," he said, and rather loudly, his gaze moving from her to Tate, "has proven a good barometer for the state of a marital union. Falling in love is thrilling, but staying in love can be tiresome, and it requires attention. This is what commitment is about—paying attention.

The pastor was a man who talked with his hands, and now he swept the air with one. "Pay attention, and commitment naturally follows. If two people are interested in their sex life, paying attention to it, then likely the marriage is a happy one, based on honesty and openness with each other in all areas. If not, then the trouble is not in the bedroom, it just appears there, and it generally appears there earlier than people recognize, starting with inattention."

He took a breath and pointed with his finger. "Think about this, when either of you let yourselves get too distracted to pay open attention to each other, or quit being honest about your feelings. Don't deny your feelings, pay attention to them and speak of them."

Marilee experienced this curious crawling sensation up her spine at the word feelings.

"If you will pay attention and be totally honest in this one area of your life, likely you will be honest in all other things. It is sort of like me speaking of it first. Now that we've spoken of sex, I've got your attention, and we can go on much more easily to other things, can't we?"

Marilee, who realized that she had been anticipating some real revelations that hadn't materialized on the sex subject, found herself preoccupied with ideas of a sensual nature. She wondered what other subjects could successfully follow that of sex and still be heard. She caught more about honesty of feelings, and experienced that crawling sensation again, and the admonition to make actions match words, and about how marriage could on occasion be a grind...something in there about wheat kernels being ground to useable soft flour.

He ended by saying, "Read Psalm four. It's a good one. Now, let's have a word of prayer."

He put Marilee's and Tate's right hands together between his own and said, "God, bless these two hearts in union, and carry them through the next hectic weeks of bringing together a wedding. Amen."

What everyone appreciated about Pastor Smith's prayers was that he got to the point.

Fourteen

A picture is worth a thousand words....

They had visited with Pastor Smith for barely an hour, but when she stepped out the front door of the parsonage, it almost seemed like another day to Marilee. The sky had become hazy, and a breeze had come up. She pulled the collar of her coat closed. Tate put his arm around her shoulders and gave her a squeeze. He looked like he was about to speak, but he did not.

She wished he would speak whatever was on his mind. That she couldn't seem to speak her own thoughts did not keep her from blaming him for not speaking his.

Oh, Lord, keep me from shrewishness.

They crossed the street in front of the church, and suddenly Marilee said, "Let's go inside."

The double doors of the sanctuary were unlocked. Marilee thought Pastor Smith unlocked them each morning and locked up each night. He had started the practice of opening the sanctuary every day shortly after he had gone away to a pastoral retreat and returned with a beard and to introduce guitar music into the services. The beard was short-lived, but the guitar music and open welcome to the sanctuary had remained.

Once a hobo had been found living in the sanctuary; he had been there for three days in the middle of the week. He had been extremely neat. Upon discovery, he said that he had come in for a retreat and felt much refreshed. The congregation had rallied to provide the man with assistance and a place to live, but the man, Hot-foot John, he called himself, said he was not a vagrant but a hobo and wanted to be on his way. The congregation outfitted him with brand-new clothes, a top-of-the-line backpack, food and fifty dollars in cash. After he had left, there had been discussion of keeping the sanctuary locked, but Pastor Smith had stood firm.

Marilee told Tate all this standing there in the vestibule, gazing into the sanctuary that was bathed in ethereal sepia tones from the hazy afternoon light coming through the tall, gold glass at the top of the pictorial windows. When she had finished her tale, she realized she had not said as much to him in weeks. Maybe she had never told him such a lengthy narrative, and she could not imagine why she had done so now. He gazed at her, as if questioning this, too.

Turning from him, she went into the sanctuary. He followed. Their feet made no sound on the thick carpeting. She slipped into the back pew, their regular place on Sunday. Tate slipped in beside her.

Her gaze was drawn to the front and the dark wood of the altar. Everything was peaceful, empty of voices and movement.

"It's beautiful," she said.

"Yes."

They sat in silence for some minutes in which Tate began to bounce his knee.

"Tate," she began, then stopped.

He took her hand in his and squeezed it.

Finally Marilee said, "I'm scared." She paused to search for a complete and understandable explanation of her feelings, in order to share them as the pastor, and even Aunt Vella, had advised.

Before she could come up with this explanation, however, Tate broke in, saying, "Well, me, too. I think only a numbskull would *not* be scared. I've been a bachelor for most of my life, and here I am, marryin' a woman who is ten years younger than myself."

Marilee, who had experienced a slice of annoyance at being interrupted, was surprised. "I don't even think about our age difference."

She realized she had held the expectation that Tate would soothe her fears, and here he was putting more out there. She was irritated with him for doing this, and irritated at herself for being irritated at him. She also thought his concern a little petty.

"Ten years is not a great age difference," she said. "Lots of people are ten years apart. Once people get to a certain age, a few years don't mean anything."

"I don't want you to look around one day and realize that you're married to an old man."

"I will be."

His eyebrows shot up.

"You will be old, Tate. Someday. And so will I. We can only hope this proves the case, anyway."

Tate's expression turned reflective. "I believe you're right there."

Marilee's mind moved on to the fact that she was actually eleven years younger than Tate. Odd how he took it as ten. Maybe, being honest, she was somewhat glad to be a number of years younger, although speaking of this did not seem uplifting, so she let it go.

"I don't face being old very well," he said.

"I don't think any of us do, but I don't see the need to get all worked up over how things will be twenty years from now. Today is enough to handle."

Marilee spoke more sharply than she had intended, and her conscience pricked. She should apologize, but she did not, and sat there staring at the altar far in the front. Be honest with your feelings, the pastor had said. She would be—if she wasn't so confused about them.

"I want to marry you, Tate, and I'm scared to death, too." She turned to face him, and having said that much, continued to push the words from her mouth. "And I need contact with you, Tate. But whenever I've initiated contact with you, you always have to run off somewhere."

He blinked twice, as if he had no clue about this. She wondered how in the world he could not have a clue.

"We hardly have a minute to ourselves, Marilee," he said.

His frown bothered her. "We had quite a few minutes the other night in the swing, and you just up and ran off. The term is 'running.' That is what you did."

"We couldn't do anything in the swing. I thought it best not to let things get out of hand. There's no sense in gettin' tied in a knot."

"There's a lot people can do in a swing, underneath a blanket," Marilee said, surprising herself. Her cheeks burned. But she thought of what Pastor Smith had said about honesty. She wanted to be honest about what she thought. This thing needed attention.

"You simply didn't want to be...well, intimate with me. You wouldn't even get wrapped in the blanket with me. And before that, there was Wednesday morning in your car. You could have come in. We had the house to ourselves."

"I had things waiting for me at the paper...and you had work, too. You said that. You said you wanted to work."

"Don't you want to make love with me? Maybe we already have the intimacy problem the pastor was talking about. It is already showing up in the bedroom."

"We don't have a bedroom."

"We could have gone to your house...before your mother came. We could go off to a motel—to the Goodnight."

"Would you do that? Do you want it like that? Sneaking around?"

"Well, maybe not...I don't know." She could not nail down the difference between sneaking time alone in her house or sneaking it at the Goodnight but somehow there *was* a difference. She did not like the basic idea of sneaking.

"I don't care if we decide not to do anything about it, but I would like you to suggest sex, at least. To show me that you want me. If you wanted me, I think you would make certain that you showed me. I think every moment you got me alone, you would be kissing my socks off.''

There. It was out. And she felt quite silly. But she did feel honest, and the honesty seemed to ride a wave of courage.

"You know what I've always liked about you, Tate? That you are a man who takes initiative. I don't want you to command me, but there are some things that I feel are important for you to do, and one of those things is for you to take the initiative in this situation.'' Fair or not, that was what she thought.

He gazed at her. She couldn't read his expression. The next instant, however, he took her face in his hands, saying in a husky voice, "So you want some kissin' that will knock your socks off?''

She saw the raw intent in his eyes just before he kissed her.

It was a thoroughly alluring kiss that turned red-hot in an instant. They broke for air and then went back for more, all greedy and devouring.

"Marilee…" His voice was hoarse and breathless when he lifted his head. There was pain and yearning so profound in his blue eyes that she could hardly bear it.

"Oh, Tate.'' She touched the side of his face. His dear face.

"Marilee…Marilee, I…''

Her flinging her arms around his neck and kissing him yet again stopped his voice but not the words that echoed in her mind. It was more than his words, it was the love and raw desire pouring out of his eyes and through his lips and eager tongue that kissed a hot, tantalizing trail down her neck.

Eyes squeezed against tears, she pressed her cheek to his.

"Oh, Marilee, I've felt so far away."

"Oh, Tate, so have I. I just didn't know how to get past it all and get back to you…. Tate…"

Then he was kissing her again, her mouth, her cheeks, her eyes, eating her up with his lips and his hands that pressed her to him, heating her body until the hard, cold knot that had been inside gave way in a sudden burst, and love, like sweet heated honey, poured throughout her being. She savored the taste and scent of him, the sense of love swirling around them like a dust devil on a hot day, a magic blessing not to be missed.

"Marilee, I want you. I do." His voice was ragged and breathless in a manner that made her feel like a woman blessed and powerful, as he trailed kisses down the other side of her neck. "Oh, Marilee…"

"Tate…Tate, my darling." She kissed him, his lips, his cheeks, his neck, wanting to soak him up, all of him.

"Daddy, there's someone in the church."

The young voice echoed through the tall-ceilinged sanctuary and seemed to flow down upon them, like cold rain.

Ohmygod.

She and Tate sprang apart. Straightening her spine, and her clothing, trying as best she could to appear sane, although she felt far too shaky to be doing a very good job of it. Thank goodness for Tate's supporting hand on her elbow.

Pastor Smith appeared, and right beside him were his three sons. "Ah…I'm sorry to interrupt, ah, your prayer together." He grinned a knowing grin. "Good thing to start, too, right at the very first." His grin widened. "We came over to get ready for Sunday night services. The children make certain the sanctuary's straightened up for me."

"We're done with our time alone...after your powerful sharin' with us, we needed to contemplate it together," Tate said, giving way to his tendency for exposition as he and Marilee edged toward the front door.

"Well, good. Start out right. And come back for tonight's services. We'll be glad to see you!"

The pastor's voice rang out behind them as they raced hand in hand and choking back laughter, out the vestibule and down the wide concrete steps and along the sidewalk, like children fleeing their mischief, flying on exuberance. The cool air on her hot, damp skin felt sensual and delicious. She saw the damp hair that fell across Tate's forehead, his merry eyes and bright teeth as he laughed.

Oh, he was so handsome!

Just past the church parking lot and beneath the still-bare branches of a crepe myrtle arching over the sidewalk, they fell together in laughter.

Brushing back her hair with his fingers, Tate cupped the side of her head. "Ah, Marilee...I do want you, darlin'...I do."

He kissed her tenderly, and then, for the barest touch, they pressed their foreheads together. The feelings that ran through her were profound, real and true and precious, like the first sight of a brand-new morning.

He put his arm around her shoulders, squeezed her against him, and they began the stroll homeward.

Hugging close to him, her arm around his waist,

Marilee felt joy almost too much to contain. She realized that the fears of only moments ago were gone. She had gotten them out into the light, and had seen how distorted and unreal they really were. In an instant of clarity, she looked into her feelings, like Willie Lee looking into his ant farm, and saw that she had not wanted sex so much as this that she now experienced with Tate. This feeling—it was everything—a sense of being with him totally, having his total attention and giving him hers.

"I'm not very good at expressing my feelings," she said, in that moment of understanding. "Most of the time it seems easier not to pay them any attention."

"Hmmm."

"I can't very well express them, when so often I don't know what they are." She regarded him earnestly. This seemed an important revelation.

He nodded in a most gratifying manner. "I'm not too good with speakin' of feelings, either," he said. "I haven't had much experience with it," he added, and she thought this a splendid effort on his part.

"Well, we have that in common." She again nestled into his shoulder, thinking of this, delighted to remain connected to him.

After a moment, Tate said, "We'll just have to learn, won't we?"

"Yes. Yes, we will." What a dear, rare man he was.

She laughed, and he laughed, and then, right there in plain sight, he kissed her socks off again.

When a carload of teens went past and blew their horn, they jumped apart.

"We're gonna get arrested before we get home," Marilee said.

"It'll be worth it…. We'll get the sheriff to put us in the same cell." He cast her a lascivious grin as again his arm went around her shoulder, and they fell into a comfortable stroll.

"In the Valentine jail, we would be in plain view of everyone…and you know who Pastor Smith reminds me of? A short version of Andy Griffith."

"Yeah, he does. Especially his accent when he was yelling for us to come back tonight. I expected to hear him say, 'Y'all come on back now, y'hear?'"

They laughed again, and Marilee thought what she appreciated most in Tate was his sense of humor about everything, from the smallest to the largest incidents. She told him this, and he said what he admired in her was that she encouraged everyone to have humor.

They walked along, casting smiles at each other, their hearts communicating without words. The fears, unacknowledged and unspoken, had built a wall, Marilee thought.

"We will need to remember times like this," she said.

"Yes." And after a minute, he said, "Let's have a secret signal to remind us."

"A signal?"

"Yes, maybe a tug on the ear, like this."

"You do that all the time anyway, when you're thinking."

"I do?"

"Yes, you do. How 'bout wetting the lips." She showed him.

"I don't know. Other women might think I'm comin' on to them."

"Then...tongue in cheek."

He shook his head. "Here, wiggle the eyebrows. Just a bit."

She tried it. "Okay. I can do that."

"That's it, then. Our private secret signal to remind us we are connected."

Oh, it was lovely. Lovely walking home with his arm around her and the warm, sparkling feelings in her heart.

Then, at the corner of Porter Street, Tate said suddenly, "We need to talk a little bit more," and glancing around, he then started across the street, tugging her along.

"Where...?"

"Here."

Marilee was startled. "Buddy's Mustang?"

"He won't mind," Tate said, rounding the front of the red Mustang that sat parked in its usual place at the curb in front of the white house on the corner where Buddy Wyatt, the young UPS deliveryman, lived with his mother, Margaret.

Opening the passenger door, Tate helped her into the seat, slammed the door, then went back around and got in on the driver side.

Marilee admired Tate's audacity—surely no one could be as charmingly audacious as Tate, and this always attracted her—yet she was concerned about overstepping respectable behavior by making themselves at home in another person's private vehicle.

"Oh, Buddy and I are friends," Tate said, when she brought up the concern. "I showed him our engagement picture in the paper the other day, and he wished us well. Besides, he isn't usin' his car right now.''

True enough.

Tate twisted to face her. "Let's make a pact right now. We will be honest with each other from here on out.''

"I didn't know I wasn't being honest about my feelings, Tate. Did you? Did you deliberately not tell me that you were worried about your age, or about not having time alone?'' She wasn't certain he had admitted to being worried about not having time alone with her, but she believed he had indicated this.

He blinked. "Well, no. I didn't deliberately not talk about it, but I was reluctant to talk of it, and I knew this. I somehow thought…well, that things would just work themselves out, but now I know that is not necessarily so, and that the best policy is to bring things out into the open. Even if I feel I might be misunderstood, it is best to speak what's on my mind.''

"Did you think I wouldn't understand you?'' She had always considered herself a rather understanding person.

"Of course not.'' Tate stared at her, then tugged on his ear. "But some things are hard to speak of, Marilee, and that may be the clue to the need to do just that.''

"Yes, now we know. But we didn't before, so that was not dishonesty. That was lack of knowledge.'' This was distinctly different to her, and she wanted that understood.

Tate opened his mouth, closed it, then said, "Okay, let's make a pact to talk out our fears. From right here and now, for the rest of our lives. We'll talk each night before bed. Or any time we need to. We won't hold back. We'll speak any concerns, honestly and openly.''

"I agree. Let's shake on it."

They did, and kissed on it, too. Then Marilee was startled by a tapping at her window glass. It was Buddy Wyatt, hands in his tight jeans pockets. She rolled down the window.

"Hi, Buddy," Marilee said, a little embarrassed.

Tate leaned across the console. "We needed a place to talk privately. I didn't think you'd mind."

"Oh, no. I don't mind, Editor...but are you two about finished? I have a date. You can use my mom's car under the carport, if you want. She's busy watchin' *The African Queen* on the television."

They thanked the young man, declining his kind offer, got out of the car and headed on home to Marilee's house, again hand in hand.

Stuart was in the kitchen, gazing out the window. "The kids have a wild bird," he told them.

Marilee and Tate went out to the tree house to get the details.

Yes, they were told, Willie Lee had tamed a wild bird. Corrine explained something about it being pushed out of its own nest over at Mr. Winston's, and that Ricky Dale had brought it to Willie Lee.

"Of course," Marilee said.

Willie Lee jutted his arm over the tree house railing, displaying a small bird perched on his finger. The small bird took off in a fluttering manner, flying over to the clothesline pole. Tate said it was a titmouse and generally not afraid of humans.

"I was a Boy Scout for a brief time," Tate explained, at her raised eyebrow.

"Where did you get the birdhouse?" Marilee asked, returning her attention upward to Corrine and Ricky Dale, who were fastening a basket birdhouse to a thick branch in the tree.

"Mr. James made it," Corrine said.

For heaven's sake. Marilee squinted, trying to get a better view of the birdhouse.

Corrine said, "I found the basket in the laundry closet, Aunt Marilee. I didn't think you would mind."

"No, honey, of course I don't mind." She saw that Stuart had cut and rewoven the basket quite neatly.

Stuart, still watching from the kitchen window, saw Marilee turn and look his way. No doubt she was surprised about him making the birdhouse. He had surprised himself in the action.

He watched the bird fly back to the tree house and land on a branch very near his son's head. He recalled seeing the bird in his son's hand.

Then his gaze passed over Marilee standing beside Tate, who slung his arm easily over her shoulder. Holloway said something, and Marilee and the kids laughed. He felt left out. Totally alone.

Turning from the window, Stuart walked slowly to the kitchen table, where he sank down into a chair. He was so tired. Dread, like a stormy sea, washed over him. He saw stretched in front of him the great horror of his life all alone, and his heart squeezed with such intensity, he felt as if he could not get his breath. If he could change many decisions from his past, maybe he would now. But he could not.

A tremor went through him. He couldn't face his future alone. He just didn't think he could.

Raising his head, he looked through the open kitchen door, through the living room to the big front door, in his mind getting up and walking out, getting in his car and driving away. He had no idea where he would go. Likely there wasn't one person on earth who would miss him. Who would look one minute for him.

He could not seem to make himself move.

Just then the back door opened. Instinctively Stuart straightened his spine, gathering himself and what dignity he could muster. In came Willie Lee, running in his clumsy gait, straight to Stuart and saying the most amazing thing.

"Fa-ther…Fa-ther, come and see."

Hearing the boy call him Father was startling enough, and then Willie Lee threw himself onto Stuart's thigh, where Stuart had to grab him to keep him from falling.

"My bird went in the nest you made. He likes it. Come see." The boy's eyes were large behind his thick glasses. He tilted his head, regarding Stuart in a disconcertingly probing fashion.

Then there was Marilee in the doorway. She regarded him, and he regarded her. "Go on and see the result of your handiwork. I'm going to make us some sandwiches."

Her tone was warm, and so was her smile.

Stuart, a lump coming into his throat, nodded. "Okay, kid," he said to Willie Lee. "Let's go see this bird of yours in his house."

Willie Lee surprised him by taking his hand. "I will show you."

Marilee watched them go out; then she peered through the window, seeing her small son leading the tall man across the yard.

The sight of Stuart, sitting all alone at the table when they entered, the stark loneliness she had glimpsed on his features, cut deep into her heart.

Willie Lee scrambled up into bed, and Marilee tucked him in. Kissing his cheek, she was reminded by the fresh-washed scent of him of the horrible encounter with the skunk. Give thanks for small blessings, she thought.

"Ma-ma?"

"What, sugar?"

"I think my fa-ther is sick."

She paused in smoothing his blankets. "Why do you think that?"

"I just do."

"Well...maybe he just isn't feeling well today. Maybe tomorrow he will feel fine."

Her son's expression cleared. "Okay." And he turned over, snuggling into the covers, where he would be asleep in seconds.

Marilee kissed his unruly hair and whispered, "God bless and keep Willie Lee."

Fifteen

Age is only a matter of mind....

There he was, Winston Valentine, sitting at a candlelit table with a beautiful woman, in a fancy-schmancy restaurant, eating a piece of chocolate cake rich enough to provoke an instant heart attack in a man of his age.

"I'll be poppin' Tums after this," he said, gazing at the lovely face across from him.

"But it's worth it, isn't it?" she said, as sultry as any woman could possibly be.

Winston wondered at what had come into his life in the form of Franny Holloway.

She had said, "Winston, I believe we need to go out. How 'bout it?" Tongues would be wagging over this, her sitting on the front porch with him, and then showing up, dressed in what looked like a whole bunch of silk scarves, with a neckline that dipped to show the creamy flesh of her small breasts.

She took hold of his arm when they walked, too, and she looked at him when he spoke. She listened to him as if what he said was of great interest. She seemed especially interested in what Valentine was like in the early days, and he delighted in telling her about how the train used to stop there, and the way the town filled up on Saturday nights in the summer, and the long lines of cotton wagons in the fall. Where she had grown up in Texas had been much the same.

And she didn't laugh or even look mildly bored when he told her about the visits, that first year, from his dead wife, Coweta.

"The flesh is temporary, but the spirit lives on," she said with warm understanding. "I've seen a number of dead people—any that I had a close attachment to. I loved my daddy dearly, and I saw him shortly after he died from a kick in the head by a mule. Only one time. He went right on to the other side, and I never saw him again. My mother told me I imagined it and gave me a teaspoon of cod liver oil. Believe you me, I certainly was not quick to tell her when I saw my aunt get up out of her casket and go looking at everyone. I never saw Mama, but then Mama liked my sister best."

Winston, who at first was relieved to know she had some experience in seeing spirits, began to feel uneasy. He sure hoped she wasn't a nut. Although, what other type of woman who looked like her would go out to a restaurant like this with him?

"You must have loved your wife very much, and she you," she said.

Something struck him hard. He nodded, averting his eyes. "We had ups and downs...some humdingers, too...but we both saw it through. I miss her."

Franny stretched out her arm and laid her hand on his. "You were very blessed, Winston. Better to have known the love, even with the hurt, than not to know it at all."

He felt the need to ask her about her life, but he

shied from this. What if she told him secret feelings? That would just wear him out.

She said then, "Excuse me, darlin'," and slid back her chair. "I need to go powder my nose, and I think I'll call Tate to let him know we're all right. No tellin' when we might show up at home." She winked.

Yep, that Franny was something, Winston thought. He felt a little regret at his cowardice in not asking about her husband. He knew she was a widow. She had said that much. Maybe he could bring himself around to asking when she came back.

He took several deep breaths and stretched his shoulders. He sure didn't want to be some old man who fell asleep in his chair in a public restaurant. It wasn't yet seven o'clock, either.

Glancing around, checking out the other occupants of the restaurant, he felt his spirit sink. He was the oldest in the place by far. He got tired of being the oldest.

Just then he recognized the woman at a table across the room.

Vella?

Naw. That wasn't Perry across from her. It was some guy with dark, steely-colored hair. Wore a turtleneck with his sport coat. Fashion plate.

He looked again at the woman. Sure looked like Vella. That was Vella's exact new haircut.

Certainty hit him hard. It *was* Vella.

Just then, he watched the man reach over and take Vella's hand.

And, possibly because he was staring at her, Vella's head came around, and she saw him. She looked surprised. He wished he had looked away earlier, but since he had not, he gave her a nod.

It might not be at all what it looked like, he told himself, taking a sip from his water glass to give himself something to do. And even if it was, it wasn't any of his business. But Vella had to be a durn fool if she thought just because she was up here in Lawton, someone from Valentine wouldn't see her. He sure wished it hadn't been him.

He had drunk half his glass of water before he realized.

Franny returned. "Tate must be at Marilee's.... I left a message. No need to disturb them. Those two don't hardly get a minute to themselves. Would you mind if we took time for coffee? I hardly ever drink it, but I do like this mocha."

He said fine. He was trying not to look in Vella's direction.

But then here she came, making a bead on their table. She came head-on in that long stride of hers, with her escort coming right behind her.

Winston stared at her when she stopped and said, "Hello, Winston...Franny." Then she proceeded to introduce the man as a Lawrence Somebody—Winston didn't clearly catch the last name. "Lawrence is landscaping my backyard. I'm havin' raised beds, a flagstone patio with a pergola, and a pond."

"That sounds right grand, Vella," Winston said, while observing that the Lawrence fella had his hand on Vella's elbow, like she was his. He wasn't a day over fifty-five, either.

That Vella and Franny were apparently quite good friends surprised Winston, who understood that Franny had only been in town since Tuesday night.

She and Vella chatted a bit about the new washer and dryer that Marilee had received from her ex-husband. The ex-husband being around was news to Winston, who began to feel he was missing a whole lot. That was what happened when a man got old. He either missed things, or people overlooked telling him.

When Vella and her man friend left, Winston said, "Vella's married."

"I gathered that," Franny said, and smiled blandly. "One would think you are jealous, Winston."

Startled, he found himself gazing into her twinkling green eyes. "No, ma'am. I'm enjoyin' the company of a beautiful woman right this minute, and I'm smart enough to know when I'm in tall cotton."

She laughed gaily and asked if he would like to go home by way of the lake, which she had heard about. "Perhaps you could direct me, darlin'?"

Good heavens, she was flirting with him.

Eighty-eight years old, but he wasn't dead yet. And if he got excited so much by Franny that he had a heart attack, he would die happy.

The headlights of Lawrence's Cadillac spotlighted Vella's Land Rover, which was parked in the black-topped lot outside his shop.

"Thank you for a lovely evening, Lawrence," she said, even as she opened the door to slide out of the seat. She had to hold herself back from running to her vehicle, jumping in and racing off. She was acting like a fool.

But Lawrence got out quickly and walked her to

the Land Rover, took the keys from her hand and opened the door. He was such a gentleman.

"I thank *you* for your company tonight, Vella."

Before she knew what he was about, he bent and brushed her lips with his.

"Oh." She started to duck into her vehicle, then paused and turned back to him. There were moments in the life of a woman her age that weren't likely to come around again.

She lifted her lips, and his met hers. It was a full, deep kiss, and when they parted, her eyes opened reluctantly and she swayed just ever so slightly.

Placing a steadying hand on his chest, she leaned over and whispered her age into his ear.

His acceptance of the knowledge with such equanimity—a mere soft smile and murmur that she was a very attractive woman—caused Vella to wonder if he was actually that unconcerned, or if she looked every inch her age, so he had not been fooled from the beginning.

Trembling, she quickly averted her face and slipped behind the wheel of her vehicle.

"I'll be down in the afternoon. Two o'clock," Lawrence said, before shutting the door firmly.

Allowing herself only the barest glance at him out of the corner of her eye, she drove the Land Rover out of his parking lot and back to Valentine, driving with both hands on the steering wheel, praying with fervor, although her prayer came out something like: ohmygod, ohmygod.

Thinking that she had to speak to someone, she drove to Marilee's house. It wasn't very late, barely eight-thirty. She could always talk to her niece. Marilee had been there for her last year, when she had gotten all messed up and left Perry flat. She did not want anyone to solve the confusion for her, but she just wanted to talk to Marilee. Probably Marilee would be shocked. Maybe she shouldn't tell Marilee about a possible lover. Leaving Perry was mild compared to the thought of getting into an affair. Marilee could really be strict about such things.

No, she could not tell her, Vella decided, as she pulled to a stop in front of Marilee's cottage, where warm light glowed from the front windows.

She gazed at the house for some moments, debating about going in at all. Loneliness fell over her like the darkness outside, and she thought of how simply touching Marilee always brought comfort. It always had, she reflected, hooking the strap of her patent leather purse over her arm and striding up the walkway. Perhaps that was why so many people seemed to come to Marilee and lean on her. And now here she, Vella, the elder and usually strong one, was coming to do the same thing.

Jerking her shoulders up straight, she told herself sternly that she would simply have tea and discuss the wedding arrangements some more. That would give her time to get her emotions straight before she had to go home and sleep beside Perry.

Then, just as her hand went to the knob, something—some sound, some change in light—arrested the action. She looked left and saw the light from the window had dropped. Faint strains of music... sultry...George Strait singing a love song... reached her.

She stepped to the window and peered through the glass to see Tate and Marilee at the far end of the room, silhouettes lit from behind by light falling through the kitchen doorway. They danced, moving slowly, intimately.

They kissed.

Vella stared for a long moment, her throat growing thick and her chest filling with longing. Once upon a time, so many years ago, she had done the same with Perry.

And dear God, she longed for such a time with a man again, she thought as she turned from the window.

Would this longing never end? She had tried to have a relationship with Perry, but he had locked most of himself away for forty-five years and could not open up to her. She understood this and did not blame him, yet she so wanted a man with whom to share her heart...her being.

She would not intrude on Tate and Marilee's precious time. This was the sort of times a couple needed to have and to build on in order to open themselves to each other. If she had understood that reality forty years ago—even thirty years ago—and acted upon it, maybe she would have something with Perry now.

Or maybe not. Perry was such a lump, she thought, without rancor, as she went quietly down the porch steps.

Just then, here came a black Cadillac pulling into the driveway, swinging in wildly, stopping short behind Marilee's Cherokee. Norma Cooper, her small head sticking up behind the steering wheel.

Vella knew instantly that some crisis had befallen Marilee's mother; Norma never came down, and most definitely not at night, unless she needed something from Marilee.

Stepping out with determination, Vella headed for the Cadillac and met Norma struggling to get out of the seat.

"Marilee is busy right now, Norma. She and Tate are finally havin' some time alone." Vella was tall enough to look down at the top of her ex-sister-in-law's head.

"I need to talk to my daughter." Norma slammed the car door.

Vella, who noted with a bit of surprise that Norma appeared very stylishly dressed, blocked the woman's path. "Your daughter is busy with her husband-to-be. Don't go in there and interrupt them with whatever you have on your plate this time. Is it Carl?" No wild guess; Norma's problems always revolved around Carl.

The petite woman stretched herself as tall as possible, looking up at Vella. "It is none of your business. This is something I need to discuss with Marilee."

She moved to step around Vella, who sidestepped and blocked her way.

"Norma, if you go in there and bother them, I will tell Marilee about all the men you slept with after her daddy killed himself. I will tell her of the clarinet player you ran off to Dallas with."

She saw this was not fully getting the effect she wished. In fact, Norma said, "What have you been drinkin' Vella? You are nuts. Get out of my way."

The woman shot out a hand to push Vella aside. Vella held her ground as hard as any lineman. "I'll tell Carl about your private account in the Citizens Community Bank. I believe it's up to fifteen thousand dollars now. At least it was last month. Where did you get all that?''

Norma stopped, her mouth flying open. "How do you know about that?"

"Oh, Norma, nothin' in Valentine is secret."

Norma reached a hand out to the Cadillac fender. "I've got to talk to Marilee. Carl got arrested for public drunkeness. I don't know how to get him out. Marilee always helps me with this." Her voice broke.

Vella, experiencing only the slightest twinge of pity at the woman's distress, nevertheless closed her mouth against the initial comment that as many times as Carl had been bailed out of jail for drunkenness, Norma ought to have the procedure down pat. Instead she looked at the facts—Norma never had been able to do a darn thing for herself; it was too much to expect miracles now.

"I'll help you, Norma. All we have to do is call a bail bondsman. Come on. I'll follow you up to your house, and we can make the call from there."

She made certain Norma was in her car and headed in the right direction before getting into the Land Rover and following. Once more on the road, both hands on the wheel, it occurred to Vella that she had taken a rather distorted tack about being so protective of Marilee.

It had been about herself, she realized. In that moment of looking in the window at Marilee, she had looked back at herself and seen clearly all her mistakes and regrets at things left undone. It did not seem the wrong things done that caused such regret, but more the opportunities and desires that had gone *un*done.

She had no right to criticize Norma for her silliness, she decided, keeping her eyes focused on the red taillights of the black Cadillac. First get the beam out of her own eye.

Vella, always confident about handling details, took care of securing Carl Cooper's release all by telephone from his own kitchen. "He'll be out and headed home in half an hour," she told Norma when she replaced the receiver.

"Will it be in the newspaper report?"

"Carl is not some state senator or somethin'. There's no way to stop him being listed along with all the others."

"Oh."

Wearily Vella took up her patent leather purse once more, wondering at how, only a few short hours earlier, she had been dining with a most handsome and charming gentleman who was not her husband. A woman of her age. She felt every inch her years right at that moment.

"Well…" Norma rubbed her arms, trying to bring herself to say thank you to this woman, her dead husband's sister, who had always been a royal pain in her side. Amenities were required. And when it came to the choice of humbling herself to either her daughter or Vella, she found it easier with Vella, who had, after all, blackmailed her into this, so Vella owed her the effort to get Carl released.

Norma opened the back door and said the required, "I appreciate your efforts, Vella." She wanted Vella gone now. She just wanted everything to be over.

Unfortunately, in that instant, Vella took note of Norma's tone of voice, which was not at all thankful. She looked at Norma and had a vague recollection that she could not name, but that prompted her to say, "Norma, you have treated Marilee as if she were responsible for you from the day she was born, as if you were the child instead of the mother. Stop it. Let her have her life now, with Tate."

"Well, I never…"

"I know you haven't, and it is time you did. Grow up."

Leaving the woman looking as if she wanted to hit her, Vella walked out into the night, to her invincible Land Rover, which always gave her a sense of power to drive. In fact, for an instant, when she turned on the headlights and saw Norma's Cadillac in front of her, she had to resist the strong urge to drive right over the black car.

What had happened to her, Lord? Why had she turned so mean? She tried to feel remorse and ask forgiveness, but did not succeed. She might regret speaking frankly to Norma in the morning, but she thought not.

She sighed deeply, having the inner knowing that this confrontation with Norma had not come on suddenly. She had wanted to say what she had to the woman for at least thirty years, ever since she saw Marilee living an uncertain childhood.

Then a deeper knowing came on her. Norma had reminded her of her own mother. Vella had been mother to her own mother, to her brothers and sisters, onward to two daughters, one who had not left home until the age of thirty, when Vella had pushed her out, and even then, Belinda had gone only as far as the apartment over the drugstore.

And, somehow, to her own husband, Perry, God love him, she had also become mother, rather than wife. After forty-five years, this was ingrained and unchangeable, leaving her feeling a hole in her being, where a full woman should be.

Maybe some things needed to be said, she decided. Maybe hard things had to be said by tough people. She could not change things for herself, but maybe what she said would help Marilee…and Norma, too.

At home, Vella found Perry asleep in his recliner in front of the television. She regarded him and felt a sense of tenderness, for which she was very glad.

She touched his shoulder gently. "Perry…come on up to bed. You'll get a backache if you sleep here. Here, sugar, let me help you up…there you go."

There was nothing like realizing one was not perfect to bring on the peace of true humbleness. Vella spent a long time that night, propped against her rose-print covered pillows, watching the moonlight make a pattern on the walls, listening to Perry snore beside her and apologizing for her sins.

She was not, however, one bit sorry for what she had said to Norma Cooper.

Sixteen

State of grace...

Marilee awoke with traces of a lingering dream that she could not fully remember, but that reignited her desire to surprise Tate by appearing in his kitchen, in the Victoria's Secret nightgown, first thing in the morning.

She had regretted ever since the previous week her botched intentions in this endeavor and kept feeling the urge to give it another try. It was an inner struggle, one voice urging her to open wide and risk, the other voice advising her to keep to the narrow way of caution.

This moment the voice of daring dominated, however, and she flung back the covers with a sense of purpose. She needed to follow romantic desires, she thought, in order to practice being a romantic woman. She really felt she would forever regret it if she did not follow through.

Quite quickly, she splashed water on her face, brushed her teeth, creamed up, added a dash of lipstick and pinned up her hair in an alluring disarrayed manner.

As she was getting into the nightgown, the roar of

her neighbor's truck blasted through the early-morning silence.

If the roar awoke her children, then that would be an indication from God that her endeavor was foolhardy, she thought, as she tiptoed past the children's door—although what good was it to tiptoe, after that roaring blast that was still fading down the street?

Munro and the new kitten were curled on Willie Lee's bed. Neither moved, nor did the lumps beneath the covers of the two beds, for the long seconds that Marilee watched.

Fully encouraged, she went back to her bedroom, slipped quickly into her trench coat and tall cowboy boots, and, as an afterthought, hung long silver earrings at her lobes. Long dangling earrings always made her feel sexy. A cautionary voice hissed in her mind, and she shoved it in a closet and glided through the house and out the back door, then across the yard to the gate that seemed to open magically with her first touch. In fact, it swung open with such ease and quietness that she had to wonder about it and looked around her for evidence of angel beings.

Perhaps the gate had been affected by her confidence, her new thrill and delight at allowing a self deeply denied and buried to come out and shine forth.

If Franny were in the kitchen, she thought, she would simply say, "Excuse me, I've come to make Tate's coffee and entice him a little bit." Or something equally as bold.

Tate's kitchen was empty. She was relieved.

She listened. No sounds. She went to the cabinet, located the tin of coffee, and prepared the coffee-maker. As it gurgled, she again listened closely to hear if someone might be stirring upstairs. All was silent.

This was perturbing. Her gaze located the clock on the wall; it was old and yellowed, displaying the time as ten after six.

She couldn't stay here long, waiting for Tate to appear. Her motherly instincts were beginning to tug, haranguing her for having left the children unattended and coming up with all sorts of dire predictions of what could happen should she not be her normal vigilant self.

The coffeemaker gurgled its final gurgle. Marilee prepared Tate a cup with cream and sugar, as he liked it, took a deep breath and started down the hallway and up the steps, heading for Tate's bedroom. Each step in her boots seemed to echo on the oak flooring.

She paused at the top of the steps, again cocking her head. All the doors were closed; the hall landing was shadowy, lit only by the first light of dawn coming in the window at the end. She thought she caught a sound, and she walked on tiptoe, stopping at the bathroom door to listen.

Just then the sound of water running on the other side of the door caused her to jump slightly. Tate, or his mother?

Knowing the bathroom also had a door into the master bedroom, she continued on to Tate's bedroom, which she had seen only twice ever—and thinking of this, she felt firmer determination to become familiar with the house of the man she would be marrying, so she walked more firmly.

At the closed door, however, she did not burst in but slowly opened it and peeked around. "Tate?"

The lamp on the nightstand was on, showing the empty, rumpled bed. The door to the bathroom was ajar, light spilling through.

Shy about seeing him naked, and curious at the same time, she at first averted her head as she stepped into the center of the room. It went totally against her nature to come into a person's privacy like this.

She was going to marry this man, for heaven's sake.

She had been single so long that sharing someone's privacy and giving of her own seemed exceedingly foreign to her.

As she thought this, she leaned over to see exactly what she could see through the crack. A virile figure, bare skin, plaid pajama pants.

The sight caused a pleasant throbbing deep inside of her.

Just then the door swung open, and Tate, wiping a towel over his face, stepped out.

Marilee jerked up straight, sloshing the coffee, and Tate jumped back upon sight of her, sending the towel flying.

And then he was laughing. "You scared me."

She held out the cup and saucer. "I brought your mornin' coffee."

"You did?" Surprise was quickly followed by delight. "Well, thank you."

She smiled as she handed it to him, and then she opened wide her coat, saying in as sexy a voice as she could find, "I also brought you a sight to stir your senses."

His eyebrows arched upward on a grand scale, and he stared at her, his mouth parting in a manner that Marilee found quite satisfying. Watching expressions pass over his face, she experienced her power as a woman. It came over her with such force as to amaze her.

Thus encouraged, and still holding the coat wide, she sauntered forward until her face was inches from his, her eyes locked on his. "Good mornin', Editor." She lifted her lips to kiss him.

Tate broke away. "Oh, lady…let me set this coffee down."

Almost in one movement, he set the cup and saucer on the nearby chest of drawers, then took her to him and kissed her in a manner so thoroughly consuming as to leave Marilee breathless and panting.

"Tate…I…have to go back…. The children are alone."

"Hmmm…" He kissed her again, moving his hands beneath her coat and caressing the bare flesh of her back.

She sighed against him, with passion flowing in delicious waves over her body as she felt his warm, hard skin, and his scent filled her nostrils. She had the thought that perhaps she was more surprised than he.

More firmly, she got hold of herself. "I really do have to go back. I just wanted to practice gettin' into the habit of being a lover."

"Well, I like it, lady. You goin' to do this every mornin'?" He grinned wickedly.

"If you're good…very, very good."

He reached for her, and, giggling, she eluded him and raced on tiptoe out the door, wrapping her coat closed, mindful of running into Franny.

He came after her, down the length of landing, and

HOW TO GET YOUR
2 FREE BOOKS AND FREE GIFT

1. Peel off the 2 FREE BOOKS seal from the front cover. Place it in the space provided at right. This automatically entitles you to receive two free books and an exciting surprise gift.

2. Send back this card and you'll get 2 "The Best of the Best™" novels. These books have a combined cover price of $11.98 or more in the U.S. and $13.98 or more in Canada, but they are yours to keep absolutely FREE!

3. There's <u>no</u> catch. You're under <u>no</u> obligation to buy anything. We charge nothing – ZERO – for your first shipment. And you don't have to make any minimum number of purchases – not even one!

4. We call this line "The Best of the Best" because each month you'll receive the best books by some of today's most popular authors. These authors show up time and time again on all the major bestseller lists and their books sell out as soon as they hit the stores. You'll like the convenience of getting them delivered to your home at our discount prices…and you'll love your *Heart to Heart* subscriber newsletter featuring author news, horoscopes, recipes, book reviews and much more!

5. We hope that after receiving your free books you'll want to remain a subscriber. But the choice is yours – to continue or cancel, anytime at all! So why not take us up on our invitation, with no risk of any kind. You'll be glad you did!

6. And remember…we'll send you a surprise gift ABSOLUTELY FREE just for giving "The Best of the Best" a try!

MIRA

SPECIAL FREE GIFT!

We'll send you a fabulous surprise gift, absolutely FREE, simply for accepting our no-risk offer!

Visit us online at
www.mirabooks.com

® and TM are trademarks of Harlequin Enterprises Limited. © 1998 MIRA BOOKS

Books FREE!

DETACH AND MAIL CARD TODAY!

HURRY! Return this card promptly to get 2 FREE Books and a FREE Gift!

The Best of the Best ™

YES! Please send me the 2 FREE "The Best of the Best" novels and FREE gift for which I qualify. I understand that I am under no obligation to purchase anything further, as explained on the back and opposite page.

Affix peel-off 2 FREE BOOKS sticker here.

385 MDL DH5U   185 MDL DH5V

FIRST NAME   LAST NAME

ADDRESS

APT.#   CITY

STATE/PROV.   ZIP/POSTAL CODE

BB1-02

The Best of the Best™—Here's How it Works

Accepting your 2 free books and gift places you under no obligation to buy anything. You may keep the books and gift and return the shipping statement marked "cancel." If you do not cancel, about a month later we will send you 4 additional novels and bill you just $4.74 each in the U.S., or $5.24 each in Canada, plus 25¢ shipping & handling per book and applicable sales tax, if any.* That's the complete price, and — compared to cover prices of $5.99 or more each in the U.S. and $6.99 or more each in Canada — it's quite a bargain! You may cancel at any time, but if you choose to continue, every month we'll send you 4 more books, which you may either purchase at the discount price...or return to us and cancel your subscription.

*Terms and prices subject to change without notice. Sales tax applicable in N.Y. Canadian residents will be charged applicable provincial taxes and GST.

If offer card is missing write to: The Best of the Best, 3010 Walden Ave., P.O. Box 1867, Buffalo, NY 14240-1867

BUSINESS REPLY MAIL

FIRST-CLASS MAIL   PERMIT NO. 717-003   BUFFALO NY

POSTAGE WILL BE PAID BY ADDRESSEE

THE BEST OF THE BEST
3010 WALDEN AVE
PO BOX 1867
BUFFALO NY 14240-9952

NO POSTAGE
NECESSARY
IF MAILED
IN THE
UNITED STATES

caught her at the top of the stairs, pushing her up against the wall as both of them laughed breathlessly.

"Tate...your mother will hear."

"So? I need to kiss your socks off."

And he did.

When he broke away, she cupped the sides of his head and gazed into his dear, luminous eyes only inches from her own. "I didn't know," she said in a breathless whisper of wonder. "I thought it was sex I wanted. Oh, and I do...but it really is this that I wanted. This closeness with you."

It was a miracle to her, and she took in the virile scent of him, the salty taste of him on her tongue, the warm, erotic glaze in his eyes.

He said, "I know." And she saw the truth of his understanding in his eyes.

She nodded, biting her bottom lip, then bringing forth, "Let's wait...for sex. I don't want it to be something sandwiched in...something grabbed without thought. There's so much, with the wedding, Stuart here, the children. Let's wait until our wedding night."

Would he understand? Where were her words to say that she rather liked this precious getting to know each other?

He regarded her, then pushed himself against her, pinning her to the wall and rubbing her pelvis with his groin, which was clearly aroused, and the realization caused an immediate reaction inside of her.

"I think that's a fine idea, Miz James," he drawled in a tone that rippled through her body. "I can practice kissin' your socks off—" he kissed her eyes, then bent and kissed the bare skin at the swell of her breasts, sending tremors down her legs "—and anticipate making love to my wife. Anticipation is sweet, don't you think?''

"Yes…yes, I…think." Actually she could not think at all.

"Ah-hem."

At the sound of the voice, she and Tate first froze, looked wide-eyed at each other, and then turned of one accord and looked down the stairs to see Franny standing at the foot.

"I am sorry to interrupt. I really am. But I need to go to the bathroom, Tate, and there is only one of those in this old house, so excuse me."

She came sweeping up the stairs as she spoke, in her flowing dress, throwing her scarf over her shoulders. Her pumps dangled from two fingers.

"Are you just gettin' in?" Tate asked, incredulous.

"Yes, dear. I had a wonderful night. Simply lovely."

"And Winston is still alive, I hope?"

"Oh, yes, dear, quite. Old people don't sleep as much and are used to odd hours," she tossed over her shoulder as she passed by and headed for the bathroom.

Just as she opened the door, she turned to them and said, "You know, the sexiest organ in the body is the mind. Winston still has all his mental capacities."

Then she disappeared.

Marilee and Tate stared at each other, and then burst out laughing. "Go," Marilee said, pushing him toward his bedroom. "Have the coffee before it is stone-cold…and don't you jog in the mornings?"

She hurried down the stairs, and he called over the

railing to her, "You bet I'm joggin'. I've got to work this frustration off somehow."

"Tate Holloway!" She was mortified to think of his mother hearing him.

She raced out of the house and across their backyards, and when, halfway, she threw back her head, a joyous laugh erupted from her lips.

How had she been so blind as to not understand what she was truly seeking? How had she been so blind as not to know about this beautiful, magnificent sense of oneness with a man?

She was in love. She really was. Did she glow? She looked at her arms and body as she fairly floated through the gate in the magical dreamy state of grace of a woman in love.

"Good morn-ing, Ma-ma."

Startled, she pressed a hand to her chest and jerked her head upward. "Willie Lee, what are you doin'?"

"I am in my tree house," he said in his usual factual fashion.

"I see that, honey. *What* are you doing in your tree house so early in the morning?" She hoped he didn't ask her what she was doing in the yard so early in the morning.

"I am teach-ing Whis-kers to like Bir-dy." He lifted the kitten to show her.

Only Willie Lee could do such things.

She allowed him his freedom, saying only that she would call him when breakfast was ready.

Pausing at the back door, she looked back into the big elm tree and the small basket birdhouse there, remembering Stuart and what Willie Lee had said about him being sick.

Willie Lee was only a little boy, she reminded herself. Not burdened with intellect, he had a unique way of seeing the truth of things, however; he was still only a little boy who could misinterpret what he saw in his literal take on things. He might have picked up some sense of distress on Stuart's part, but it likely meant that Stuart had suffered a headache and had been tired of his lengthy and unaccustomed exposure to the children.

Tate came out whistling and paused at the edge of the porch to inhale deeply. By golly, he could smell the sweet freshness of spring!

Again whistling, he jogged down the steps and broke into a run, whizzing past the twiggy lilac bush that was beginning to swell with leaf buds. The orange cat, Bubba, jumped out and followed him down the street but gave up after several yards and plopped down near the curb to clean his fat belly.

As Tate came to the Wyatt house on the corner, Buddy, who was doing his morning pull-ups on the porch beam, called, "You sure are full of energy this morning, Editor!"

"Yes, indeed," Tate called back. Passion did not belong only to young men with biceps, he thought.

He made it around to Main and was still going at a good clip. Being ten minutes earlier than usual, he found the street quiet. Bonita Embree of Sweetie Cakes Bakery had not yet opened up, nor had Grace Florist. Charlotte's car was the only one on the street, parked out front of the *Voice,* and the flags fluttered on either side of the door, further indication of her presence.

Tate was relieved. Charlotte's absence on Friday had given him great appreciation for the scope of her work at the paper. She virtually ran the place, although he wouldn't want to admit that to her. She already had an exalted sense of importance. In fact, she could overwhelm him.

Maybe he should go over and tell her how much he appreciated her, he thought, slowing his stride. Holding on to his pride so often got him into trouble.

Just then, however, the door of the *Voice* opened, and a tall man strode out. Sandy, walking with swift, angry strides to the corner, where he vehemently tossed a brown bag into the green mesh trash can. Then he headed on across Church Street and beyond, in the direction of his apartment.

Watching the young man, Tate's spirit took a nosedive. This seemed a definitely disheartening sign that Sandy and Charlotte had not made up. He came to a full stop, gazing across the street to the *Voice* windows, which were still covered by the closed blinds. He sighed, considered going to talk to Charlotte, but a certain trepidation at facing the woman, plus the desire to hold to the joy filling his life right that minute, propelled him once more into a jog. This morning was too special and precious to get weighed down by things that by rights were not any of his business.

Spirit rising once more, he hit the corner and turned up the hill of Church Street at an energetic stride.

Then here came Parker down the hill, approaching the intersection from the opposite direction.

"Looks like you are tryin' to wear yourself out," the younger man said with a knowing grin.

"Yep," Tate said, grinning broadly.

Life was good.

* * *

Vella, dressed smartly and sensibly for an active day, went to the kitchen phone and dialed the private office number for Waller Landscaping. Lawrence's voice, his recorded voice mail, came over the line, as she had expected at this early hour.

"Lawrence, this is Vella Blaine," she said in a businesslike tone. "I will not be home this afternoon. I am occupied with producing a wedding, however, I leave the backyard in your capable hands. I will be in touch."

And that was the end of that, she thought, giving, upon returning the receiver to its hook, a large, deep sigh, which was a mixture of regret and relief.

She had made her choice to direct her considerable energies into the preparations for Marilee's wedding, rather than get lost in an impossible affair. She had distinctly heard a direction from God to get out of herself and her carnal desires and focus on helping see that Marilee got married. Since she had developed such a strong controlling streak over the years, she might as well put it to good use.

Just as the sun became a fiery ball on the horizon, she stepped out her front door, carrying a notebook that bulged with magazine articles and lists of things to do. She backed her Land Rover out of the driveway in a purposeful manner and headed down the street.

Everett Northrup was out in his yard, standing at attention and saluting his flags. "The Star Spangled Banner" was blaring from his house. Vella's gaze shifted over to the Valentine house. But there was no sign of Winston, not in his yard nor on his porch.

Tapping the brake pedal, she slowed the Land

Rover, her eyes searching the porch. No, no stooped figure bringing himself to attention.

She slammed on her brakes in the middle of the road between the two houses and their flagpoles, lowered the passenger window and cocked her head. She did not hear "Dixie" playing. The house was silent.

Ohmygod, he's died!

In a state of shock, she veered over to the curb, jammed the gearshift into Park and hopped out just as the strains of "The Star Spangled Banner" faded away. A man did not raise a flag for all these years, every morning that the sun came up, and suddenly quit. The only time Winston had missed was when he'd had his stroke. She looked again at Winston's yard and front porch, thinking her eyes must have failed her. She had known this day would come, only she could not bear it now. She simply could not.

She looked across to Everett, who did not seem as concerned as he should be. "Where's Winston?"

She was already heading around the front of the Land Rover when Everett said, "He's in bed."

"What?" She stopped. Had he said in bed or dead?

"He's in bed. Doris saw him come in just about thirty minutes ago. That fancy woman—the Editor's mother—brought him. Looked like they'd been out *allll* night."

All night?

The image of Winston and Franny and their intimate camaraderie at the restaurant passed across Vella memory, coming like a blow to her chest.

Everett shook his head. "Gonna kill himself, but I guess no one wants to live forever."

Vella slowly walked back around to get into her Land Rover, automatically shifting it into gear and pressing the accelerator, heading along the street in something of a numb state.

Winston wasn't dead. He hadn't had another stroke. Thank you, God.

Oh, she missed Winston. She squeezed the steering wheel with fervor.

But she was a married woman, and Franny was not. She was not jealous, and this surprised her. She would not, after all, change her decision to remain married to Perry. She had once thought maybe she would, but she would not. She was growing to accept her life, and with this acceptance, she could see her many blessings. Her heart filled with gladness for Winston, a dear old friend, and for Franny, a promising new friend.

Just then she realized that she had come to a stop at the intersection of Porter and Church. She noticed an early blooming forsythia on the opposite corner. The weather was warming early this year. The forsythia blossoms would be perfect for Marilee's wedding. If they were done blooming around Valentine before the wedding, she could drive north and still get some.

The wedding was only three weeks away!

Seventeen

Destiny of a small, intimate wedding…

Vella, toting a heavy-looking notebook, came blowing into his office. "Marilee has okayed this invitation style, but she wants your okay on it."

"She called me earlier. I was told to be at your disposal." Tate had not known he had been concerned about the wedding preparations until Marilee had told him that Vella was taking charge. With Vella in charge, things would go smoothly.

She whipped out the card and held it before him.

"Okay." He was quite pleased to have accommodated her.

She sat herself in the chair next to his desk, saying as she put on her reading glasses, "Now, let me have your invitation list. I'm just gettin' a head-count now. I'll get addresses later." She unfolded a notepad and poised a pencil.

"Well…everyone here at the paper, of course. That'll be fifteen. Here's a list, and the addresses, too," he said, pulling two sheets of paper out of a desk drawer and passing them to her. "Parker Lindsey's my best man—that's Mr. and Mrs. now. His wife's name is Amy."

"They came in the store the other day. She got prenatal vitamins, said she was planning for the future. I need to tell Marilee."

Tate found this startling. It made him think of his own position, as a soon-to-be new husband. And it seemed life was moving on at too quick a pace.

Vella prodded him to continue with his list.

"Okay...there's Sheriff Oakes and his family, and everyone over there at the sheriff's office. I guess we should invite the mayor and everyone on the City Council...and their families, too, of course."

"That's just one invitation per family, though." Vella was writing furiously.

"Put Fayrene Gardner down. I think I've already invited her. And Norm Stidham and Ramona. Fred Grace and his family, of course."

Vella lowered her pad and gazed at him. "How about if I just invite everyone who is a member of the Chamber of Commerce?"

He nodded. "That will probably cover it. And you'd better get an extra ten invitations, at least, to allow for those we think of at the last minute."

"You know, Tate, this *is* about the last minute."

Marilee was finishing up the final edits on her piece on rabies and her "Voices of Valentine" column, both of which she would proudly be turning in by the deadline time of noon, when the telephone rang at the edge of her desk.

It was her mother. "Hello, dear...I won't bother you but a minute."

"You aren't botherin' me, Mom. What is it?" Marilee tucked the receiver in her neck and proceeded to save her documents to a separate disk.

Her mother was saying, "Well, it won't take me but a few minutes. I know you are busy. Vella called up here this morning to get my list of people to invite to the wedding."

Vella had called her mother? Oh dear. Marilee stopped her endeavors with the computer and took hold of the receiver.

She had not thought about Vella possibly contacting her mother. Not that she had meant to hide the fact that her aunt Vella was organizing the wedding; she just hadn't intended to purposely tell her mother. Marilee experienced a panic, having the sudden vision of her mother and Aunt Vella vying over control of the wedding plans, something along the lines of World War III breaking out between the women. This scenario included yelling, spitting and hair-pulling.

"Vella told me she was helping you with the wedding." That sat there.

"Yes." She couldn't think of anything else to say.

The line hummed for some seconds. "Well, I told her to be sure and invite the Mathesons and Cora Smith, who I used to live next door to down there. And my pastor and his wife, and of course everyone from Carl's store."

Marilee closed her eyes. "We're just having a small wedding, Mom. Just immediate family and close friends."

"Betty Matheson has been my best friend for fifteen years now. And I've known Cora Smith since I was ten years old. She knew Mama. She'll be hurt if she doesn't get an invitation. There are manners, Marilee. Probably hardly anyone from the store will come, but it's rude not to invite them. It would make

Carl look bad. And Vella did ask me. I tell you what, that is my list, just do what you want to.''

"We'll be keeping it down, Mom, but I'll make sure and invite the Mathesons, and Cora.''

"You can't invite the Mathesons and not Pastor Ames. The Mathesons are members of our church. And Carl will feel badly if you don't invite the people from his store. I guess if you want to not invite people, don't invite Cora and the Mathesons, but do include Pastor Ames. And you have to invite Carl's manager, Roger Gaither.

"No, on second thought, Invite the Mathesons, Roger Gaither, and Cora and Pastor, but you know Cora won't come—she hardly gets out anymore—so you'll still have only the others.''

Marilee swallowed. "We'll invite them all, Mom. We'll need you to provide addresses, though.''

"I told Vella I'd have them to her by tomorrow. I wish she would have told me earlier.''

Marilee wondered if she and Tate could elope. They had considered it briefly. Maybe they should reconsider.

"Well, the other thing I wanted to speak to you about is your wedding present,'' her mother said in a more forceful tone.

"What about my wedding present?'' was all she could think to ask. It seemed a little greedy to expect a present, and a little ungrateful to say she did not want one. Oh, this wedding was becoming a thorough nuisance. She had experience with being engaged and calling it off, but no experience with weddings.

"Carl and I have decided we want to pay for your wedding.''

Marilee sucked in a breath. "Pay for the wedding? Oh, Mom, I don't think that is necessary."

"Of course it isn't necessary, Marilee. This is what we *want* to do. And this way you don't have to worry about expenses or trying so hard to keep it small."

"It isn't the money, Mom. I want a small, intimate wedding." Crowds had always made her nervous.

"How much did you plan on spending?"

"I don't know." She felt silly, not having thought this through. "I'm having Margaret Wyatt make my dress, and then Corrine will have to have a dress, and Willie Lee a suit." Quite suddenly she began to see that she did need to make a budget. She grabbed a pad and began making notes to consult with Vella.

"What about your bridesmaids' dresses?"

"I'm just having one—Charlotte is standing up with me." But maybe it was required that Marilee purchase a dress for Charlotte.

Her mother answered that. "Dear, it is the bride's part to pay for the dress of her attendant…and there are invitations, and the flowers and the photographer."

Yikes! Marilee hadn't thought at all of the photographer. Maybe Reggie would do it as a favor.

"There's the reception hall," said her mother. "And you could really enjoy a live band. Betty's daughter had a band at her wedding. It really adds to everything."

"A band?" Good heavens. "No, Mom, we aren't having that elaborate an affair. Just cake and punch. It's going to be simple and small, like I said, and we're havin' the whole thing at the church. We are using china and crystal, though," she added, knowing her mother would appreciate that.

"How about if you just send me your bills?"

"Oh, no. No, I can't do that." She imagined her mother poring over every receipt and shaking her head. "How about if you pay for my dress? I'd really like that, Mom."

At that particular moment, Vella breezed in the front door. Marilee waved at her, while trying to keep her mind on the conversation with her mother, who was saying maybe she would have her bank simply transfer money into Marilee's account.

"Mother, you don't need to do that. My dress is not terribly fancy. The material is a little expensive, but there isn't any beading or anything. I'll find out a cost on it and let you know."

"Marilee," her mother said with unaccustomed firmness, "I *want* to pay for the entire wedding, just like Vella wants to help you with all she is doing. I want to help, and this is my way. It is what I can do."

Her words and tone struck deep into Marilee, who, after a minute got out, "Okay, Mom. I would appreciate it very much."

"Good." She heard the pleasure in her mother's voice. "I think, then, dear, since you say it will be small, I will have the bank transfer five thousand into your account. That is our present to you. Use it how you will, and if you go over, I'll send down another two thousand."

Marilee sucked in a breath. "Mom, that is way too much."

Vella was hovering. "How much?"

There was a pause on the line, and then, "Dear, I

want to do this. Please let me do this for my daughter."

Her mother's sincere tone brought tears to her eyes. "Thank you, Mom."

"You're very welcome." Her mother was happy again. "And get lots of pictures for me to see when I come back from the cruise."

"I will."

The two made their goodbyes, and, breathing deeply, Marilee hung up.

Vella, who had plopped herself on the end of the couch and was kicking off her shoes, said, "However much she is giving you, she can afford it. So how much is it?"

Marilee, who was considering exactly what to reveal to Vella about her mother's rivalry, told her.

"Oh, good. Now we can get a live band."

Marilee looked at her.

"It was your mother's idea, and I told her that would be a little costly. Isn't it nice that she took the hint?"

"Vella!"

"Marilee, your mother wanted instantly to help, and her way is to give you money. You can use it. Let her do this."

Aunt Vella eyed her. "It makes her feel good about herself, sugar. You hardly let your mother do anything for you. You hardly ever let *anyone* do for you. That is false pride. It is how you keep people from getting close to you."

Marilee gazed at her aunt, whose eyes did not waver.

"Now lay that pride aside. Take this gift from your mother graciously, thank her heartily, and enjoy it. You will be giving her the gift of a part in your life...of being helpful to you for a change.''

The wedding preparations were well and truly under way. Marilee took twenty minutes to confer with Vella at the kitchen table.

"Margaret is set to do the dress and will search out the fabric and bring us samples. I gave Fred Grace a bare-bones idea of what we wanted in the way of vases and flowers, and he's working up an estimate. Bonita Embree will do the cake—white, with chocolate chips," Vella said.

"Tate okayed the invitations, and I've ordered them," she went on. "They will be ready on Thursday. I'm going to ask Belinda to address the envelopes. She has beautiful handwriting." She tapped her pencil on her lips. "We've got to get them in the mail before the end of the week. On second thought, you and I will have to do the addressing. Belinda is too slow."

"How many people did Tate come up with?"

"Oh, with couples, I figure about fifty-five or sixty, give or take a few."

Marilee stared at her.

"With your mother's list, that brings us to seventy-five, give or take a few. And you do know it is the custom to invite the entire church? We don't have to send out invitations, though. We simply have an announcement put in the bulletin."

Vella made a note on her pad, then looked up to see Marilee staring at her.

"Sugar, don't worry. Only about half of these people will actually show up. And these will be the ones who love you."

Leaning forward, she laid her hand over Marilee's. "I think you should realize that you and Tate do have a certain standing in the town. And these people really care about you. They are happy for you and want to rejoice with you, sugar.

"You have never let yourself be fully happy. Do so now. Let yourself be happy and celebrate this time, Marilee."

It was sprinkling, so she drove to the paper, and just as she pulled into a space at the front sidewalk, it became a downpour. Impatient and determined to make the noon deadline—Marilee was habitually late and frequently taken to task for this by Charlotte—she raced through the rain and in the door, calling out to Charlotte, "I am on time this Monday."

Ever since Vella had spoken about allowing herself to be fully happy, she had been trying to see what that felt like. She smiled at Charlotte and produced her computer disk, as well as the folder with the paper copies. She could have sent the files directly from her computer, but she was not as yet comfortable with this. She always had an odd feeling, as if her articles were going off into outer space. She preferred to hand them personally to Charlotte and Tate.

Charlotte did not look up from her computer monitor.

"I'm on time," Marilee repeated as she laid the file folder and disk on the counter in front of Charlotte's desk.

"Yep," Charlotte said. That was all.

"How are you today, Charlotte?"

Charlotte glanced at her over her glasses. "In a hurry. It is deadline day."

"Yes, it is. I'll take these on into Tate." Marilee picked up the disk and folder again, then hurried off to Tate's office.

"I brought my pieces." She went to put the disk on his desk, which she saw was covered with black-and-white photographs. Before she could see what they were, however, he was up, shutting the door, taking her into his arms and kissing her.

Afterward, she laid her head on his chest. Just for a few seconds. She felt a thorough happiness for those seconds, too. Maybe that was how happiness came, in seconds, and one had to take note or one missed them.

She looked down to the photographs again. Stuart's, she thought, her eyes falling on a shot of the Goodnight's neon sign.

There were shots of the local motel's exterior and interior, and pictures of three other motels that appeared to date from the forties and fifties and were still in operation over on State Highway 81, Tate told her. Each had the explanatory text in Stuart's precise printing.

"He's captured the lingering glory under the shabbiness," Tate said, admiration in his voice. "He's good at what he does."

"He always was."

"He's lettin' us have these for nothing, except his byline."

"That's generous of him."

"Well, it isn't likely that printing them in a small local paper will keep one of the big magazines from buying his complete article. He's going down to get some shots from some places in Texas. He's decided to concentrate on towns along Highway 81—the Meridian Highway. Route 66 has been done to death.

"Oh, by the way, he wanted me to tell you that he's goin' down to Texas for the next couple of days, so don't look for him."

"He's left town?" She was surprised.

"Yes. He said he'll be back Wednesday evening." Tate studied her, and she averted her gaze downward again, at the photographs.

Why hadn't Stuart called her himself? She opened her mouth to ask Tate, but closed it. There was no need to question Tate about her ex-husband's motives. Of course, there was no particular reason for Stuart to speak directly to her, no need for her to be overly sensitive. Likely he would return, and in any case, it wouldn't matter if he did not.

"When are you going to print these?" she asked of the photographs.

"Starting them on Sunday. Gonna run a series of three. Put them in their own pullout insert," he said, eager and proud as a boy with a new toy.

It came as something of a surprise to experience a quiet evening. The children were in bed early, and she and Tate were alone. There was nothing like a good rain to slow things down. There came a pleasant pattering on the windows and roof, while they sat together on the sofa in front of a crackling fire.

Tate, kneeling and poking at the fire, said, "Do you realize we've barely been alone since my mother and your ex-husband arrived last week?"

"Yes. So don't waste time frittering with that fire,

when you can sit here and fritter with me.'' She was really becoming bold in her honesty.

His smile thrilled her. He positioned himself next to her and pulled her into the curve of his shoulder.

''Oh, this is so nice,'' she said, sighing deeply and nestling close.

He nuzzled her ear and whispered, ''Mmm, yes, ma'am, it is.''

After a few minutes, she said, ''What do you think of eloping?'' She twisted and looked at him.

''Eloping?'' His eyebrows went up, and the firelight reflected in his wide eyes.

''Yes. We could elope and not bother with a wedding.'' She again laid her head on his shoulder. He wore a cotton flannel shirt that was worn soft and carried his scent.

''I will do whatever you want to do, Marilee. The wedding will be nice, but it isn't essential. But we would have to face Vella, and now your mother.'' She had told him about her mother's gift of the wedding costs. ''I don't know about that. I guess it depends on how badly you want to elope.''

She sighed and thought of Corrine's face that evening, when told she would be the flower girl, which was Vella's idea.

''I just want it to be peaceful, like right now. This wedding—'' she twisted to look at him ''—there's more to it than I had imagined. It's like when a woman buys a dress. A new dress means one must have new shoes, and the new shoes have to have a bag to match, and sometimes one must have a sweater or coat to match all that. It all just grows.

''We should have just eloped the day we decided to get married.'' She flopped back against him.

He said, "We could elope, get it over with and still have the wedding."

"What would that accomplish? We would still be having the wedding."

They fell quiet.

"Maybe I should tell you," he said.

"Tell me what?"

"No, I don't think I should tell you. Spoil the surprise."

"You have to tell me now." Again she twisted to look at him.

"No, I don't."

"Yes, you do."

"Nah...you can wait."

"I won't leave you alone unless you tell me." She began nibbling on his ear and slipping her hand seductively inside his shirt.

"I can take it," he said, smiling broadly and showing how much he enjoyed her caresses.

"Oh, tell me, Tate. There, now I've begged."

He grinned. "Okay. I have a honeymoon booked at Walt Disney World. I don't have everything finalized, but we're gonna have the luxury suite, with the kids right across the sitting room from us, and a room for the nanny."

"A nanny?"

"Yes, ma'am. Fully qualified, with references. It's sleeping late, breakfast in bed, champagne with dinner. Top of the line all the way...if that is agreeable with you. It is all contingent on you accepting the idea, too."

"Oh, Tate." She stared at him. "You planned for the children to come on our honeymoon?" What manner of man was she about to marry?

"I want their mother's undivided attention. I'm no fool. And since we're startin' this thing out as a family, we might as well get used to the concept."

She laughed and hugged him so hard that he had to caution her not to break his neck or wake up the children with her excitement.

"Boy, I sure wish the wedding date would hurry up and get here." She was ready to get on with the honeymoon.

"Anticipation, remember?" he said, with a wicked gleam in his eye, as he pulled her across his lap.

A while later they broke apart, both breathless and perspiring, gazing longingly at each other.

"I do want the wedding," she said in a soft voice, as if hesitant at admitting too great a desire. "I do," she said more firmly and daringly. "I want to celebrate this that we've found, Tate."

She could not express what she felt she had found. The single word, love, seemed not to cover it. It was so precious, so far beyond her understanding.

"I want to honor our marriage, and to share the joy with our friends." She had wanted this all along but had been afraid to speak of it, as if, once spoken, the powers that were always ready to snatch away dreams would surely snatch this one.

"We'll do it," he said with conviction.

She sighed and laid her head against him, staring into the fire. Why did she always feel the other shoe was about to fall? Why could she not simply accept the happiness, without feeling guilty or anxious, and that she was in some way going to have to pay dearly for it?

Eighteen

Change begets change....

It was warmer in Dallas than it had been up in Valentine. Stuart felt the morning sun through the pale blue shirt he wore. Even sheltered by sunglasses, his eyes squinted slightly in the glare from all the sunbright concrete of the hospital complex.

Having always traveled, he was adept at confidently finding his way to where he wanted to go in an unfamiliar setting. There was the sign: Cancer Center. All one had to do when going anywhere, he mused, was follow the signs. It would have been better if there were such direct signs on the journey through life. Turn here for the Walk of Fame...take this road for Relationship Success.

Although he could not say that he would have done things differently, he did so much wish things had turned out different. Wished that he had formed true friendships. But he had always found them binding in some way and had simply not been able to do so. That was the fact. No need to wish for what was not. No need to let it hurt.

Standing just outside the automatic doors was a frail-looking woman wearing a green turban, with oxygen tubes attached to her nose. Her husband—or a man Stuart took to be her husband—stood beside her, his hand on the handle of the wheeled oxygen bottle.

Stuart turned his eyes from the pair and focused on the darkly tinted doors as they slid open.

Just inside the doors, his gaze fell on a boy in a wheelchair. The boy's pallor and shaved head bore witness to sickness. Stuart's gaze slid sideways and fell on a woman, probably the boy's mother, who stood nearby, conferring with a hospital person, identified by a pleasant blue smock and a name tag bearing the hospital insignia. Hospital personnel were like soldiers, he thought.

He skirted the information booth, went around a corner and then turned, taking the camera he more often than not carried slung over his shoulder, unsnapping the case and checking the light. Quickly, in one motion and all on instinct, not a designed purpose, he stepped out from the corner, focused on the boy in the wheelchair and clicked. Then he pressed his back against the wall and snapped the cover in place.

He remained pressed against the wall for several seconds, feeling a little dizzy and out of breath. When that settled, he went back to the information booth, where he was given directions to the lab by a woman far too perky to be appreciated in such a place.

He went down the hall and made the turns, passing hospital personnel chatting, an elderly man being wheeled by an equally elderly woman—he held the double doors open for them—and a big man with his head bandaged, who seemed disoriented and had to be led along by his wife and a male nurse.

At the window of the lab, he was directed to fill out some papers by a pleasant woman who appeared so young as to give him an urge to ask for her ID. He refrained from the joke, which she might find in poor taste. Besides, he wanted it all done, with as little chatting as possible.

He knew the routine, had provided everything beforehand by the miracle of fax and computer, but they needed the information again, the young woman told him in a patient manner. He was reminded of how everyone in Texas always seemed rather happy and never in a hurry, except when driving on the interstate—where vehicles flew rather than drove.

He filled out the form and returned it to the young woman, who told him to have a seat.

Several minutes later the double doors swung open, and through them came a man in a wheelchair. Stuart took him in—he could have been anywhere from fifty to eighty, pale complexion, shoulders slumped, eyes vacant, being pushed by a burly male nurse, who said, "Wait right here for a minute, Mr. W—"

Stuart did not catch the man's name, and he quickly overted his attention and gaze to the wall, where a big print of three Navaho women hung. It was a semi-abstract. He thought of his father, dead now some forty-three years. Where had the years gone? He never liked to think about his father and felt a foolish anger at the old man in the wheelchair for reminding him.

Another turn of his head and he saw his faint reflection in a glass partition. He jerked his gaze away, looking at magazines on a nearby table but not having the inclination to browse. He'd seen most of them already anyway.

Ten minutes ticked by, and no one came for the man in the wheelchair. Stuart, who glanced surreptitiously at the man, began to worry, as it looked as if the man was listing to one side. Another five minutes, and still no one came.

Stuart, who was checking his watch every minute or so by then, began to hope his name was not called for the lab tests, because he wanted to make certain someone came for the sick man, who was definitely listing to one side. He began to worry all sorts of worries about the man's needs that no one was seeing to. What if the man had been forgotten, overlooked? What if he sat there and died, and no one knew? Stuart kept glancing at the woman at the desk, to see if she paid any attention; he debated speaking to her about the sick man.

A glance around the waiting room, but he saw no one else who seemed concerned. They were all either talking or had their nose in a magazine, or simply stared at their shoes. Mostly definitely no one looked at each other, as if they could not bear to see more sickness.

In an automatic manner born of his lifetime's work, Stuart unsnapped his camera cover and quickly focused, snapping the man's picture without anyone in the waiting room knowing what he did. And then he took another of the room of people.

"Stuart James?" A young woman in the hospital uniform and holding an official-looking clipboard stood at the double doors.

He got up and followed her, leaving the sick old

man still sitting in his wheelchair. He was about to ask the young woman about the man when she directed him through another door, leaving him standing alone, awaiting further instruction.

When his tests where done, he returned to the waiting room to find that the sick man in the wheelchair was gone. He was greatly relieved.

Although the appliance store—his future wife's stepfather's store—agreed, for a handsome extra fee, to same-day delivery, they absolutely refused to haul away the old appliances. "Not our job. We deliver. That's it."

Tate thought this was pretty tacky, considering the small fortune he had just dropped in their store. Stuart James wasn't the only one who could splurge on the latest in home technology.

Asking for help had always been difficult for him. He mentally went through the list of men who might be willing to lend a hand. Short list. Finally he sucked up his pride and put in a call to Parker Lindsey. "Hey, does a best man help move out old appliances?"

Lindsey said he didn't know about best man rules, but he would help. He could come over around noon in his old pickup truck that he kept for those times he might have to haul around a hog or dogs or equipment. The man's ready willingness made it easier for Tate to breathe.

They tackled the old curved-top Kelvinator first. They wrestled it out the door and onto the top step and then across onto the opened tailgate of Lindsey's old pickup. Next they hauled out the stove, vintage seventies' gold, and then the dishwasher from around the same time period. Part of the floor came up with the dishwasher.

"Watch it, don't drop that corner on your toe."

"Just yank it up."

"If we scoot it around this way, it'll go through the door."

"In your dreams."

"Be careful...don't... You okay?"

It was work from which friendships grew.

"Thanks, buddy. I'll do the same for you sometime," he told Lindsey, puffing a little when they closed the pickup tailgate.

It was a new experience for him, having a friend to help him like this. He grabbed Lindsey's hand and shook it with feeling.

Lindsey grinned. "You'll be following up on that payback sooner than you realize. Amy is makin' her plans to redo my whole house. You know, you might have wanted to let Marilee do this herself. Women are a little funny about gettin' things in the house how they want them."

"Oh, I intend to leave her plenty to work on, but I didn't want her to have to put up with too much old stuff right off. Don't want to frighten her away."

He waved Lindsey off and watched the truck head out into the street, carrying the old appliances away to join all the other decades of used up and discarded appliances at the landfill. One day the planet would likely be made of such things, he thought.

The delivery truck arrived. He raced outside and directed it through the portico and around the back. It would be more convenient to bring the things through the back door, plus he didn't want to take any chances of Marilee spotting the truck. He thought it might be too much to hope that his neighbor across the street wasn't keeping a watch out her window.

Two bulky young men did the job of bringing in the appliances and setting them in place. Tate stood back and watched. Young muscles and experience made bringing the new in seem a lot easier than it had been taking the old out.

"You don't have a hookup for the ice maker," the young man told him, looking a little perplexed at not finding a water hose connection.

"Is that a requirement for the refrigerator to work?" Tate asked, feeling definitely behind the times.

"Oh...no. But your ice delivery in the door won't work...and neither will the cold water. It's inconvenient," he added, still holding the perplexed expression.

"I'll have a pipe put in." Tate made a note on an index card to locate a plumber.

In came the stove. The trim at the end of the counter had to be broken off for the stove to fit. Tate had mismeasured. He made another notation for a carpenter. After getting the gas pipe hooked up, the young man told him very seriously that he needed to have a new gas pipe run. "I did the best I could, but this here hookup is old, and it's leaking. Smell it?"

"I don't smell anything."

"Then you're the one in a hundred who can't smell it. I'd have a repairman come, if I was you. You might wake up dead one mornin'."

"I can smell it," said his mother, who came over sniffing. She added, "I'm one of the few who is able to smell carbon dioxide, too." The young man gave her a respectful look.

The dishwasher fit exactly. "Can't stop this water leak, though," the young man told him. "You'll have to get the repairman. You need a new connection. I think you might need a whole new pipe comin' in here. And some floorin'.."

Tate made more notes on the index card. He wondered if he was going to end up having the entire house replumbed and rewired. He might have to sell the house in order to raise the money for all the remodeling that was going to be required.

Then he remembered the look on Marilee's face when she had received her washer and dryer. It was worth any amount of money to see her face when she beheld these new appliances. He had topped Stuart James, yes, sir.

It sure brought a man high to be able to please his woman, he thought, waving off the appliance deliverymen.

He went back inside and saw his mother caressing the new stove with great reverence. "I'll make some fresh bread," she said with enthusiasm. "We must make certain it works correctly."

"Don't tell Marilee," he cautioned her, afraid she would get carried away and let the cat out of the bag.

He glanced around the room and thought that he'd better have painters in, too, at least for the kitchen. The gleaming brand-new appliances made the walls and cabinets look twice as shabby. Knock out the wall to the old laundry-storage room and do it up right with new linoleum and refinished woodwork. Maybe even new windows.

It was like Marilee had said, get one thing, and

then another was required, and another and another. Change begat change, he thought, and found that revelation as disconcerting as it was exciting.

As fate would have it, Honey Moon, his decorator with the outlandish name, telephoned him that very afternoon to say that her emissaries were set to come the following day to begin work on the bedroom walls.

"We are doing a texture on the walls. Apricot sunset."

"O-kay." Tate tried to let go the urge to question and direct.

"You'll love it," the woman told him in her sultry voice. "Trust me."

He almost asked her if she could handle repainting the kitchen, then decided that he needed some control somewhere. He would find his own painters and choose his own colors, too. White. Basic white appeared to be back in favor.

"By the way," said Honey Moon, "you'll have to move out of the bedroom."

Even though it was cool and breezy, Aunt Marilee wasn't there after school to pick them up, and they got to walk home. When they reached the corner of their block, Corrine saw Aunt Vella's Land Rover parked out front. Ricky Dale, who had walked with them, pushing his bicycle, got on it and pedaled on home, calling to her, "I'll be back pretty quick."

While Willie Lee rolled around with Munro in the yard, Corrine raced up on the porch. She pulled over the little stool, stood on it, stuck her hand in the

mailbox on the wall and fished around inside, bringing out three envelopes and an IGA flyer.

Her spirit drooped with disappointment. There was
no package from her mother. It was awfully early for
the present her mother had promised to come. Her
mother would put off mailing things for days. She
might even forget she had said she would send a
surprise, Corrine reminded herself. There was no
need to keep hoping, because she might be disappointed.

She went on inside, where Aunt Marilee, Aunt
Vella and a woman she recognized as living in the
house on the corner were sitting at the dining-room
table.

"Come here, honey," Aunt Marilee said, "We
need you to choose a dress for the wedding. Mrs.
Wyatt is going to make it."

On her way across the room, Corrine dropped her
backpack on the sofa and placed the mail on her
aunt's desk. Then her aunt introduced her to Mrs.
Wyatt, who was a pleasant-looking woman. Corrine
stayed plastered to Aunt Marilee's side.

Her aunt showed her two patterns. "Do you like
either of these?"

Corrine studied the drawings, tilting her head this
way and that, trying to imagine. "This one, I think."
She watched her aunt carefully.

She knew she had chosen correctly when Aunt
Marilee smiled. "That's the one Vella and I like best,
too." Corrine felt relieved.

It took Mrs. Wyatt only about three minutes to
measure Corrine, who did her best to be still. Then,
finally, it seemed okay for her to leave. She slipped
away to change her clothes and was just tying her

play sneakers when she heard the front door open and close, and Willie Lee call out, "I'll get her."

"Well, hello, Ricky Dale," said Aunt Marilee.

Corrine, coming out of the bedroom, almost ran into Willie Lee. "Ric-ky Dale is here. He wants us to come with him to see his grand-moth-er."

Corrine went into the living room and heard Ricky Dale saying, "It won't take long, Miz James. After I see my grama, then we can go to take care of the horses. I'll take real good care of Willie Lee."

"I know you will, Ricky Dale," Aunt Marilee said. She had a thorough liking for Ricky Dale. "At five o'clock you come on home," she said to Corrine. "I'll be expectin' you by five-fifteen."

"Yes, ma'am."

"And you all mind that horses kick."

"Yes, we will." Corrine saw that her aunt was getting that worried expression and feared she might change her mind about allowing them to go, so she edged toward the door, tugging Willie Lee along.

Then Aunt Vella asked, "How is Minnie doin', Ricky Dale? Is her eye still giving her trouble?"

"Yeah. She still has to wear a patch."

Corrine had the door open and implored him with eyes.

"You tell Minnie I said hello, and I'll stop by tomorrow," Aunt Vella called as they slipped out the door.

Corrine closed the door and whispered to Ricky Dale: "What's this about your grandmother?" She wanted to get over to see the horses and didn't appreciate being dragged around the neighborhood.

Ricky Dale motioned for them to come off the porch. His stupid dog, Beau, was on the walkway acting goofy, and Munro growled at him. Beau sat and panted.

"My grama found out today that her old cat has liver disease. It's been sick for months, and Doc Lindsey told her he has done all he can." Ricky Dale looked from Corrine to Willie Lee. "My grama really loves this cat, and Mama is afraid she is goin' to give up livin' when the cat dies."

Corrine looked at Willie Lee, who looked back at them.

"Grama has to rest her eye at this time of day, so she's layin' down listenin' to *Lake Woebegone* on the radio. We can go in the back door, Willie Lee can touch the cat, and no one will know."

Ricky Dale's grandmother, Minnie, lived over on First Street, two houses before the pastor's house.

"How are you gonna get the cat?" Corrine wanted to know as they went down the side yard to the back. "You're gonna have to find it. What if your grama hears you?"

They came to the back door, and Corrine stopped, waiting for an answer to this question before she would move another inch. She took hold of Willie Lee's hand and held him, too. She liked to have a plan.

Ricky Dale had to come back to them. "She isn't gonna hear me, but if she does, I'll just tell her that I'm showin' Willie Lee the cat."

"Why would you show Willie Lee a sick cat?"

"Who cares? You guys wait here, and I'll bring it out."

He went up the brick steps, opened the screen door and then the big door without hardly a sound, and disappeared inside. Willie Lee sat himself on the bottom brick step, and Munro sat beside him. Corrine stood with her arms crossed, and Ricky Dale's black dog lay beside her feet, thankfully quiet for once. Perhaps Munro was training him.

A few minutes later Ricky Dale came out, quickly and quietly, with a big old grey fluffy cat. A Persian. He handed the cat to Willie Lee. Fur went everywhere.

"It's losin' its hair," Ricky Dale whispered. Indeed, it did seem like it was getting patchy, Corrine thought. Other than that, it was just an old cat.

Ricky Dale took hold of Beau, who wanted to sniff the cat. Munro pressed up close to Willie Lee, who said hello to the cat and then showed the cat to Munro. The cat seemed too sick to be worried about the dogs. He just lay in Willie Lee's arms. Ricky Dale said it hadn't eaten in two days.

Corrine watched her cousin pet the animal. Willie Lee's eyes looked closed, but she wasn't certain. She looked carefully to see if he glowed, but the sun was very bright, and she thought it might just be the sun shining on him.

"Are you done, Willie Lee?" Ricky Dale asked after what seemed a long time, and Willie Lee was still petting the cat.

"O-kay," Willie Lee said, looking upward with a smile. "He is a nice cat."

"Did you make him better?" Ricky Dale asked.

"May-be." Willie Lee shrugged.

Ricky Dale took the cat back inside, and then they went over to Mr. Winston's to see the horses. Ricky Dale led the way on a path that cut through yards. Corrine had a daring feeling, as if she were entering

a new part of her life, beginning to learn about the
neighborhood, where she had lived for over two
years and yet had not before ventured beyond her
aunt's and Mr. Tate's houses.

Taking hold of Willie Lee's hand, she told Ricky
Dale to take the other, and they began to run, lifting
Willie Lee, who giggled in delight, off the ground.
They ran until they fell, all at once in a heap and
laughing, then got up, lifted Willie Lee, and ran
again.

When her gaze lit on the horses, Corrine hurried
on ahead of the boys, forgetting about Willie Lee in
a rare moment of rapture. The mare came slowly
forward, put down her nose, and Corrine exchanged
breaths with her.

The recent rain had caused the three-sided stall to
be overly wet. Totally disgusting to Corrine, who did
not like messy, and she would not have had anything
to do with it, but Ricky Dale was her friend. Loyalty,
which Corrine possessed in abundance, compelled
her to help.

They worked side by side, shoveling the old urine-
and rain-soaked shavings and manure into a wheel-
barrow, which Ricky Dale, the biceps of his skinny
arms bulging, would then push outside to a compost
pile. He was thorough and intent on pleasing his em-
ployer, whom he said was very particular about her
horses having a clean stall with fresh pine shavings.
Corrine wanted to please both the horses and her
innate desire for neatness.

Just then, hearing Willie Lee's laugh, she looked
up to see him atop the mare. Her heart leaped in her

throat. Throwing down her manure rake, she hurried forward, but Ricky Dale grabbed her arm.

"He's okay. Let him be. Don't scare the mare."

She held her breath as she watched. If anything happened to Willie Lee, Aunt Marilee would die. Corrine was supposed to look out for him. She would die, too, if anything happened to him.

Her eyes fastened on to Willie Lee, she watched him be carried around by the mare, who walked in a lazy manner, while Willie Lee gripped her mane and grinned happily. The filly, prancing, followed at the mare's hip.

Willie Lee looked over and saw them. "Look at me," he said, proud as could be.

Winston, inside at the kitchen sink, glanced out the window and saw the small boy atop the big paint mare. "I thought you said that mare was barely green broke," he said to his niece, who was at the table, painting her fingernails.

"She is. She's only been ridden maybe twice."

"Well, it's three times now." Winston watched Willie Lee in the act of getting the mare to move over beside the rail fence, while Corrine climbed up to get on behind him.

"Ohmygod! She'll kill them," said Leanne, who had come to peer beside him. "I told Ricky Dale...I told him not to try to ride her."

"Well, apparently no one told Willie Lee," Winston said. Seeing the stricken expression on his niece's face, he added, "Honey, there ain't nothin' you can do but trust God right this minute. And it looks like it's all okay," he added, returning his gaze to the corral and watching the two figures, the small boy and the taller girl, be carried around by the big horse in a perfectly gentle manner. He was not so amazed as Leanne, who, he noticed, stood there with a baffled expression, still carefully holding her fingernails out, as if doing some sort of Chinese Kung Fu stance. He was older and had seen his dead wife reappear, so he didn't think anything could surprise him.

"That mare might want to throw *you* off," he told her, "but she knows those are kids. She'll take care of 'em. Kids and animals are closer together. They're closer to the Lord in their innocence."

Still watching the children in the sunlight, he remembered back in time to his own children, who had ridden in that same corral. "Not much prettier than kids and horses, is there?" he said.

He didn't think Leanne heard him, though, as she was through the back door before he finished. He watched her stride toward the corral, checking her pace as she neared, mindful of not scaring the mare.

"Corrine!" Aunt Marilee called. "Telephone for you. It's Ricky Dale." She raised an amused eyebrow.

Corrine took the telephone. "Hello." She had never spoken to a friend on the phone. And Ricky Dale was a boy.

"I wanted to tell you that my grama just called and said that her ol' cat ate half a can of food tonight. Grama's real excited."

"Well, good." She breathed easier because her aunt Marilee moved away.

"Maybe it will live."

"Maybe. I hope so," she added, wanting to let

him know that she hoped the best for his grandmother and her cat.

"Well, guess that's it. Tell Willie Lee."

"Okay."

"See you tomorrow at school. Want to do the
horses with me again?"

"Oh, yes. If I can."

They said goodbye, and Corrine happily replaced
the receiver.

When Aunt Marilee tucked them into bed, Willie
Lee said, "I ride-ed a horse to-day."

Corrine held her breath. Thus far, in telling the
story of his ride, Willie Lee had not slipped up and
revealed that they had ridden without permission, and
that Leanne Overton had forbidden them to ride anymore. Likely her aunt would worry and not let them
go to the corral.

"Yes, you did," her aunt said with a smile and
kissed Willie Lee.

"I guess I can-not fly, but I can ride a horse."

"That's right, honey. A boy cannot fly, but a boy
can ride a horse."

Thankfully Willie Lee just said, "I am glad I am
a boy," and turned over.

Aunt Marilee said she was glad Willie Lee was
her boy, kissed him, and then came over to hear Corrine's prayers. She said, tucking the covers around
Corrine, "A girl can ride, too."

Corrine nodded, careful not to say anything. That
was the best way not to slip up with a wrong word.

Her aunt turned out the light and left the room.
Corrine listened to her aunt's footsteps go away into
the kitchen, then she whispered a fresh caution to

Willie Lee not to talk a bunch about riding the horse. "Aunt Marilee won't let us go over there if she finds out we rode the mare without askin'."

After a minute Willie Lee whispered back, "I rid-ed, Cor-rine, just like a nor-mal boy."

Corrine blinked and knotted her hand in the covers. "You sure did. You were good, too."

A rage took hold deep inside of her. People thought because Willie Lee was a little backward that he couldn't understand that they made fun of him. That he didn't hurt like everyone else. Anytime Willie Lee suffered, she did, too, because of her immense desire to protect him and her frustration at not being able to do so. She wanted to beat up the entire mean world.

Nineteen

Family ties…

Moving out of the bedroom was not too hard. Presuming he could leave his clothes in the closet, he took himself off to sleep in the third bedroom down the hall. The bed was old and lumpy but would suffice. His mother brought him the Pledge and a dust rag, both of which he used on the nightstand, leaving everything else untouched.

Tate's definite dilemma, however, was how to keep Marilee away from his house and from seeing the work being done. He didn't want her to see anything until it was finished. He wanted it to be a great surprise. What if she decided to repeat her fanciful effort of bringing him morning coffee?

There was nothing else to do but head off all possibility of her coming to him by going to her first. Just before daybreak, he went hotfooting it across the backyards, bearing two bags from Juice's bakery at the IGA, where he had gotten the best French roast coffee and sweet rolls.

He crept in the back door and was instantly met by Munro, who blocked his way into the dimly lit kitchen. "It's me, Munro."

The dog wagged his stub of a tail.

Tate got Marilee's favorite mug and one for himself from the cabinet, and emptied the steaming contents of the foam cups into them. He arranged the sweet rolls on two plates.

Seeing Munro sitting there, gazing up at him, Tate broke off a bit from one roll and gave it to the dog.

He left one plate of sweet rolls on the table for the kids, put the other on a tray, along with the coffee, and headed through to Marilee's room. Outside it was growing lighter at a rapid rate. There was enough light coming in the windows for him to clearly see Marilee's tousled dark head of hair on her pale pillow. She did a little wuffling snore.

Standing there, gazing down at her creamy cheek, Tate's heart swelled with so much feeling as to bring a lump to his throat and cause him to forget himself and begin to sit on the side of the bed.

Just in time, he froze in midsit, as he remembered that Marilee didn't much care for mornings. He feared she would get aggravated at him for waking her.

Looking around, he quickly reviewed his options, which seemed few. Simply leaving his offerings might not keep her away from his house.

He decided to sit in the small chair and wait a few minutes. Maybe he would be lucky, and she would wake up on her own, he thought. He took a chance to edge the tray onto the table underneath the window, the tabletop already crowded with photographs, fancy glass bottles, books, and other odds and ends. He just about knocked over a bottle but caught it before it clattered.

Setting the bottle on the floor seemed the best choice.

Marilee snored loudly, and he practically jumped.

He had to move some clothes draped on the chair in order to sit. He looked over the room, seeing the dresser top crowded with paraphernalia. Clothes, on hangers and off, hung over the closet door, and shoes were scattered about.

It was instructive, looking over her bedroom. He noted that rose was a repeated color. He would have to tell that to Honey Moon.

He was a neat person about clothes. He liked to put all his shirts of one color together in the closet. His mother had shaken her head at this. He said it was easier to get dressed with his clothes in such order. He wondered what Marilee would think of this habit. Separate closets appeared a must, another thing to mention to Honey Moon.

This room was all woman. It was frilly. It even smelled like a woman.

He liked the smell.

His gaze returned to Marilee. She was doing that little wuffling sound again.

He leaned back in the little chair, carefully, because it seemed dainty and perhaps could collapse under his weight. He watched the steam spiral up from the cups in the fresh light falling through the open window blinds.

Tate did not realize he had fallen asleep until he opened his eyes and saw three pairs of eyes staring at him.

"Good mornin', Tate," Marilee said, a slow, sultry smile playing across her lips. Sitting cross-legged on the bed, she sipped coffee and ate a sweet roll.

"Mis-ter Tate, you snore." Willie Lee was peering right at Tate's nose.

"So does your mother." He took up his coffee, which was no longer steaming, rose and went around the bed and climbed in, positioning himself against the propped up pillow.

Marilee and Corrine were staring at him as if he were some apparition.

"I do not snore," Marilee said.

"Yes, you do, and sweetly, too."

"You snore a little bit, Aunt Marilee," Corrine said, and then, apparently deciding retreat was in order, headed for the door, saying, "I'm goin' to get us some milk, Willie Lee."

They all ate together in the bed.

"I can get used to this," Tate said happily.

Marilee gazed at him, as if wondering if he told the truth.

Tate ushered the children out the door to his BMW, leaving Marilee gathering her purse, keys and tote, as usual.

"Look, can you kids keep a secret?"

Corrine nodded, and Willie Lee said, "Mun-ro will, too."

"Okay. I need your help. I'm havin' a bunch of work done over at my house as a surprise for Marilee, for her wedding present. I don't want her to see any of it until it's done. Now, I need you two to either head her off or call me, if you find out she's about to come over to my house. Just for the next couple of weeks or so. Do you think you can help me out here?"

Corrine, bottom lip caught between her teeth, nodded eagerly, her dark eyes holding a rare sparkle.

"I will try, Mis-ter Tate," Willie Lee said in an elaborate whisper.

"How about you just callin' me Tate? Would that be all right with you?" This did not seem quite right, but it was all he could think of.

The boy blinked his eyes behind his thick glasses. "Yes. That is all right."

Then, as they got into the car and Marilee was joining them, Willie Lee asked from the back seat, "Ta-ate, you are go-ing to mar-ry my mo-ther, right?"

"Yep."

"But you will not be my fa-ther."

"No, son. Stuart is your father." Tate looked at Willie Lee in the rearview mirror, then glanced at Marilee. He felt on uncertain ground.

"Tate will be like your father, though, honey," Marilee said. "You will have two fathers. Why don't you call Mr. Tate Pa?" She seemed quite happy, as if having been very clever to think of this.

Tate wasn't certain he liked the sound of Pa. It seemed like that was a name for an old man.

Corrine piped up to ask, "What am I going to call you?"

What indeed?

"Why don't you call him Pa, too?" Marilee suggested. She was definitely pleased.

He glanced in the rearview mirror and saw Corrine's mouth moving, practicing the word. They were all going to sound like a family from the backwoods addressing their grandfather.

"How about Papa Tate," he said. It was marginally better, somehow. As he repeated it to himself, he found it had a certain ring to it, rather reminiscent of Papa Hemingway.

The discussion of the morning of what to call Tate got Marilee to thinking. She was Willie Lee's mother, but aunt to Corrine. Tate would be Willie Lee's stepfather but Corrine's...what? Stepuncle? Neither title carried any legal responsibilities.

Corrine, she thought, was like a little raft, adrift, having neither father nor mother. Certainly Marilee had no legal standing at all. This concern had passed across her mind so many times since the day she had brought Corrine home from Anita's. Not having a solid idea of how to cope with the fact, she kept putting off doing anything at all.

In an instant her mind had drawn up the distressing picture of having to bar the front door of the bungalow, holding off state officials with chiseled faces, but knowing she was doomed because the state, total strangers, had more rights than she did. The next instant, she saw the bungalow empty, lifeless, because she had moved away to Tate's big house and Corrine had been taken away.

The hard facts remained, as true today as the day Anita had given her Corrine's care—Anita could come at any time and take Corrine away, or they could be faced with a health catastrophe, because Corrine, not being Marilee's legal daughter, was not covered under Marilee's health insurance, and Anita did not have any health insurance at all.

When Marilee married Tate, likely she would go under his health insurance policy, as his wife, but this left Corrine and Willie Lee, no legal relations at all, out, drifting on their little raft.

Something had to be done.

"No, I won't accept your resignation."

Tate's loud voice jerked Marilee out of her troubling thoughts. She looked over to see him standing in the doorway of his office and shaking a paper at Charlotte, who strode to her desk.

"You can quit," he said, "but I won't accept it."

Marilee had never heard Tate yell. She had heard him annoyed with Charlotte and arguing with her, but never yelling.

Tate disappeared back into his office. There came a somewhat familiar clanging sound. He had kicked his trash can. Tate did not yell, until now, and he did not slam doors, but he had been known to kick his trash can.

Marilee's gaze swung over to Charlotte, sitting at her desk in the bright light falling through the plate-glass window.

Charlotte quitting? She had been with the *Voice* longer than any of them, for fifteen years, since she finished junior college and decided she liked working at the paper more than anything else and would not go on to higher education.

Marilee pushed up from her chair and hurried forward to her friend's desk. "You aren't quitting the paper?"

"Yes." Charlotte's mouth was an implacable line. "I'm going to head Molly Hayes's office. She's expanding her tax service."

"Charlotte." She stared at her friend, who finally raised her eyes. They were red-rimmed, Marilee saw. "Oh, Charlotte, don't do this."

"I have to," Charlotte said in a faint voice.

"No," Marilee said, quite suddenly angry. "You *choose* to."

Just then, as she walked away, she saw Sandy turning from the doorway of his glass cubicle. He was slumped as if someone had shot him.

They went to lunch at the Main Street Café.

"I'm not all that hungry," Tate said, as they slipped into one of the newly covered green vinyl booths.

Fayrene Gardner, with the passion of new ownership, was updating the café, and green was her favorite color. She had gone with a breezy and soothing fern-leaf-sprigged paper for the walls.

"I'm starved," Marilee said. She felt a little piqued over Tate's poor humor. She felt responsible for lifting him up, only she didn't know what to do for him.

She gazed across the table at him, and sympathy, and quite a bit of curiosity swept her. She had never seen him so angry. He was clearly wrought. This was gratifying, as it illuminated the fact that he was as human and shakable as the rest of them.

Perhaps she did recognize the scowl, she thought, remembering having seen it when she had been adamant about not entering into a relationship with him. He had reacted in the same fashion, she remembered. Feelings from that time, when she had so badly wanted to give in to her own desires for him and yet kept holding herself away out of fear, came flowing over her. She had treated him quite ruthlessly in her fear, and now here Charlotte was doing the same. How senselessly humans behaved.

Swamped with the urge to wipe away his hurt, she put her hand atop his. He gave her a smile, but it did not reach his eyes.

Fayrene, thoroughly familiar with serving them, came with glasses of ice tea. "Meat loaf is good today, Editor."

Marilee thought that it was a good thing she did not mind being second banana to Tate.

"Okay," he said, then withdrew his hand from Marilee's and rubbed his knuckles.

"I'll have a BLT," Marilee ordered. "And a piece of chocolate cake," she added, feeling in need of bolstering.

"Uh-huh." Fayrene jotted on her pad, gave them a speculative eye, then went away with their orders.

"I couldn't get her to see reason," Tate said, still rubbing his knuckles.

"There's no gettin' Charlotte to do anything she doesn't want to."

"I offered her a raise."

"It isn't the money, darlin'."

"I know that. It's her stupid pride. She thinks she's God. That she has to take care of her mother and make Sandy's decisions for him. That's what I told her, too."

Marilee nodded. She was dumping sugar into her ice tea and realized that she likely had enough.

"You've got to try and talk her out of it. We can't operate without her." His gaze was intense.

"Tate, when has anyone ever been able to talk Charlotte into or out of anything?" Even as she said this, she was mentally composing what she could say to Charlotte; all of it was angry, so better left unsaid. Why in the world was she so angry at Charlotte?

Didn't the woman have a right to do whatever she wished? None of it was Marilee's problem.

Just then Franny came in, and, spying them, she swept over and slid in beside Marilee, who scooted over to make room. "We may have a band for the wedding," she said with some excitement.

Marilee gazed at her with surprise, and Franny explained that she had been alerted by Vella as to the need for a band.

"And then there I was at the post office, gettin' a post office box, and somehow out of my mouth came the information that we were lookin' for a band for your wedding, and Julia Jenkins-Tinsley told me about her brother's band."

Marilee wondered about Franny getting a post office box, but this question went unasked, because Franny continued to explain that the band was called the Swing Boys, and that they played both country swing and jazz.

This seemed a curious stretch of ability.

"Now, I haven't heard them, so I'm going on Julia Jenkins-Tinsley's opinion right now, and she is related to the band leader. They are playin' this Friday night over at the VFW club, so Winston and I are goin' over there to check them out."

Marilee regarded her, imagining her and Winston out on the dance floor. She wondered if she should add a word of caution.

Fayrene brought Tate's and Marilee's orders, and, assuming rightly, an ice tea for Franny, who ordered a large serving of guacamole and chips, based on Winston's recommendation that Fayrene's cook made the best guacamole in the state.

Then Franny wanted to know what was wrong,

because Tate had the volcano expression. Tate eyed his mother, and Marilee explained about the crisis with Charlotte quitting, and all the whys and wherefores. By the time she finished, she had begun to worry that possibly this meant Charlotte would not be her bridesmaid.

"She probably won't want to have anything to do with a wedding. And Sandy will be there. We can't not invite him, especially since he'll still be workin' for the paper."

Thinking of Charlotte not working for the paper, she got overwhelmed and started in eating her chocolate cake before she finished all of her sandwich. In fact, she held the sandwich in one hand, while she forked the cake with the other.

"She is caught up in 'should living,'" Franny said. "Bless her heart. Oh, my, this guacomole looks wonderful!"

Realizing she had food in both hands, Marilee decided to go with the cake and laid the remaining bit of sandwich back on the plate.

Out on the bright sidewalk, heading back to the *Voice* offices, Marilee said, "Tate, we need to talk about some legalities with Willie Lee and Corrine."

"What legalities?" He appeared still preoccupied.

"We will need to consider where we stand in regards to legal guardianship. We have to do that for health insurance, and if anything else should come up where the children need a legal guardian. Like, what if something were to happen to me? Willie Lee wouldn't legally be your son, and Stuart could take him off to who knows where, and Corrine would be left hanging, too."

Actually, this disconcerting thought had just come to her.

"We have to discuss all this, Tate, and get straight what all we need to do to see that the children are secure."

"You're right," he said, glancing at his watch. "But I can't do it right this minute, because I have a meeting with the Downtown Improvement Alliance this afternoon, and before that I need to consult with Monahan about the insert for Sunday's edition." He opened the door to the building.

"How about tonight?" She was mentally checking what she had to do that evening. Stuart might show up. She probably should not begin a discussion with him until she and Tate had ironed things out.

Tate shook his head. "I'm coverin' the County Republican Party monthly meeting. The state chairman is gonna be there. In fact, it's a dinner meetin'."

"Tate, we have to get this straight." All sorts of concerns about the children were racing through her mind.

"I know, darlin'. We'll do it Thursday. How's that look for you?"

She thought it was okay.

"We'll take off in the afternoon, if we can, and spend some time together." He wiggled his eyebrows in their secret sign, kissed her cheek and headed away to his office, passing Charlotte's reception desk like a bullet.

Marilee looked at Charlotte, who kept her gaze on her computer monitor. She went on to her own desk, where she plopped down and opened her planner, seeing the notation for the following evening—invitations.

She sat there for some minutes, listening to time marching on.

Twenty

Letting go of yesterday...

In the late afternoon, with several windows thrown wide to the warming spring, and the radio playing country music, Marilee went searching through bureau drawers and closets for the topaz earrings that she and Anita had bought years ago at an antique shop in Dallas. She wanted them to go with the something new, which would be the dress, and the something borrowed, which would be her aunt Vella's vintage hair comb, and something blue, the garter, of course, to wear for her wedding.

In the course of the search, Marilee began dragging out long forgotten items, so many things that she had started to clean out the previous year, when she had been about to marry Parker. Then she had aborted both her marriage to Parker and the cleaning out, as well.

One of the things that she dragged out now was the ridiculous velvet robe with the fur collar that her mother had given her as a present. Evidence of her mother's love.

She slipped it on, surveyed herself in the mirror, laughed, and strode over to the table beneath the window to get her glass of ice tea, doing an impersonation of Bette Davis, letting the length of robe sweep grandly behind her.

That was how Stuart found her. "I knocked, but no one answered. I thought I heard the radio, and the door was unlocked." He was chuckling.

He had come back. He had said he would return, and he had followed through.

"Drama Queen at your disposal," she said grandly, presenting the back of her hand.

He strode forward, kissed her hand and whipped a bright bouquet of flowers from behind his back. "For my queen," he said.

"Oh, Stuart."

A lump formed in her throat. These were not roses. These were evidence of his thinking of her at an odd and tender moment. The gladness she felt amazed her, and, feeling the need to hide her emotions, she buried her face in the flowers, as if to inhale their fragrance.

Then she saw him whipping forth his camera.

"Oh, no, Stuart!" Seeing that she could not jerk the robe off in time, she then posed there in the fuzzy light falling through the screened windows.

"Enough." She removed the robe, even as he kept clicking shots.

Trying to ignore his action, and making faces into the camera at the same time, she strode to the kitchen to put the flowers into a vase, telling him along the way that the children were over helping a friend— "Ricky Dale, you remember him, don't you?"— look after some horses.

"Would you like to go see them?" she asked then, seizing the idea quite suddenly. "You should see

Willie Lee, Stuart. He's so excited over the horses. They're just a little over a block away, an easy walk.''

Struck with the idea of encouraging him to get to know his son, as well as the excuse to cut short their time alone, she barely gave him the opportunity to decline, plunked the flowers into a quart mason jar, and was leading the way out the back door, taking a shortcut across Tate's backyard, all the while chatting about Willie Lee's and Corrine's newfound love of horses.

To her own amazement, she brought forth an idea that had been percolating in the back of her mind that a horse might be a particularly good learning tool for Willie Lee, to help build his sense of self-confidence, as well as something that could be employed in the specialty classes for the learning disabled children that she helped develop for the local school.

Stuart walked along beside her, ducking under several low-hanging tree branches, his hands easy in the pockets of his slacks, his head tilted in a manner that indicated he was actually listening intently.

''The mare ain't gonna come over this way, 'cause y'all are strangers,'' Ricky Dale informed them. He stood there at the fence with them, the short sleeves of his T-shirt rolled up on his skinny arms in the manner of thirteen going on seventeen, while they watched Willie Lee and Corrine pet the big horse and her baby.

Stuart clicked shot after shot with his camera.

There was a curious intensity to his expression. Marilee supposed that he had always been intense with his photography, and that this quality had simply grown stronger with his age.

Willie Lee demonstrated how he could call the filly, and Ricky Dale said, as if he were proud, "That filly'll follow Willie Lee anywhere."

Marilee and Stuart applauded, while Willie Lee beamed and said, "She likes me."

"Well, of course," said Marilee, with motherly pride.

"We can-not ride the mare. Miss-uss Over-ton said not to," Willie Lee told them.

"She did?" Marilee said, puzzled.

"She wants to be here with us," Corrine said. "Can we bring them carrots tomorrow, Aunt Marilee? They like carrots and apples."

As they walked back through the yard, Winston came outside and visited with them for a few minutes. He shook first Stuart's hand and then Willie Lee's, in the familiar way the two had developed long ago. He bragged on the children's care of the horses in a way that was good for children to hear.

Then they walked home, by way of the sidewalk this time. At one point Willie Lee took hold of Stuart's hand. Impatient with the slower elders, Corrine and Ricky Dale began a game of tag and enticed Willie Lee to join in with them, adapting themselves to his slower movements.

Watching, Marilee gave thanks at being able to provide a carefree sort of childhood for Willie Lee and Corrine.

"We don't appreciate our childhood until we're far beyond it," Stuart said, apparently having some of Marilee's same thoughts. "At least I didn't."

Marilee nodded. She often felt she'd never had a childhood, but let this thought go unspoken.

Stuart took several shots of the children, and then said, "I didn't appreciate what I had with you, either, until it was gone. My excuse is that it took me a long time to grow up. I guess a person has to get beyond some things to really see what they were. I regret that, Marilee. Please accept my apology."

She stared at him, speechless, searching his face for sincerity. "I accept," she said, and swallowed. "It was a long time ago. It's water under the bridge now."

Feelings that she didn't want to deal with tumbled over her.

After another minute, as she watched the children running and laughing in the street, she added, "I apologize for ever blaming you, Stuart. And you know, I do believe that everything works out for the best. It's been best for me on my own. I had a lot of growing up to do, too. And I've had a good life here, and so has Willie Lee."

Looking at Stuart then, she saw him nod and avert his gaze downward. He looks so old, she thought suddenly. And tired, and sad. She was struck deeply.

"Today is what matters, Stuart. I'm glad you've come." She took his hand and squeezed it.

His response was surprise, then a smile. Marilee hoped he didn't misinterpret her overture and think she wanted more than she did. But she was glad for what she had said. It was as if a burden had been lifted from her shoulders.

When they reached the front porch, Stuart asked, "Where's Tate this evening?"

"He has to cover a political meeting."

He nodded.

"Are you stayin' for supper?" She very much wanted him to.

"I can, Miz James," Ricky Dale put in. "But I gotta call my mom."

"Then do so...but your dog cannot come in the house." Chuckling, she looked at Stuart with a raised eyebrow.

"Are you making spaghetti?" he asked, and she was relieved to see his playful humor had returned. "I always liked your spaghetti."

"You did? I didn't know that."

"I did," he said adamantly, and as they all went into the house, he told the children how Marilee had managed to make spaghetti on a hot plate in a number of hotels.

Although she had not fully discussed things with Tate, the quiet evening with Stuart seemed the golden opportunity to broach the matter of Willie Lee's present precarious legal situation and the possibility of Tate adopting him. Surely Stuart would not take offense, but would see that the best interest of his son was at stake.

Help me, God. Give me the words.

All through the meal, the conversation carried mostly by the children, she watched her ex-husband

and mentally composed ways of opening the subject
of Willie Lee.

She came out from tucking the children into bed
to find Stuart had made coffee and brought the pot
and mugs on a tray into the living room. He had the
stereo playing soft music.

"May I have this dance?" he said in a grand manner.

She went loosely into his arms, keeping a proper
distance as they waltzed around the room. Stuart had
always possessed a litheness and grace that made
dancing with him a special experience.

Inhaling his scent, feeling the crisp cotton of his
shirt beneath her fingertips, feeling the movements
of their bodies to the music and his hand warm on
her back, it occurred to Marilee that the three men
she had loved each had a certain grace and smooth-
ness about them. Educated men, all, and lovers of
fine things, even fine moments.

She looked into his face then. He smiled at her,
that winsome, endearing smile.

The music ended, and Stuart released her, saying,
"Shall we have our coffee before it gets cold?"

He sat on the sofa. She picked up her mug and,
feeling the need of distance, sat in the big armchair,
kicking off her shoes and curling one leg beneath her.
She felt uncertain of the intimacy between them, and
glad for it, too.

"Your coffee is very good," she told him, breaking the silence.

"I learned on my own." Again that self-deprecating smile.

There was another silence, and then Stuart said, "You've done a really good job with Willie Lee."

She chuckled. "I think Willie Lee is the one who does a good job with everyone else."

They fell quite naturally to speaking about their son then. She got up, retrieved Willie Lee's baby book from the shelf and brought it to the couch, where she sat beside him and showed him the pages with some eagerness to share with him what he had mistakenly given up.

Closing the book, she sat with it on her knees. "Stuart…"

He gazed at her with a raised eyebrow.

"I have been thinking that it would be best if Tate adopted Willie Lee. He never intends to take your place with Willie Lee, but there are legal considerations, such as insurance, and to have Willie Lee provided for if anything should happen to me."

Stuart looked down at his hands.

"Willie Lee will always need care. He'll always need to be provided for. These are things that must be planned for long-term."

Stuart nodded in a manner that allowed Marilee to quit holding her breath. He leaned forward, his forearms on his thighs. "I think…" His voice was hoarse, and he cleared his throat. "It is the prudent course. I have no objections."

"Thank you, Stuart." She was so grateful she had not given in to her spiteful feelings of days before.

She had misjudged him, and was glad not to have revealed it.

"I want to help provide for Willie Lee," he said. "I know I haven't done anything regular. And I'm pretty ashamed of the amount of money I've gone through. But I do have some savings and some stock investments. I want to turn it all over to him."

Marilee didn't think it would be very nice to say that Willie Lee had money. She reached over and took his hand. "Be here in his life, Stuart, whenever you can. We welcome you."

Stuart looked at her, and then stared at the floor. "I guess that's still the one thing I can't do, any more than I ever could. You see, I don't have long to live."

Marilee wondered if she had heard correctly. Surely not.

He was looking at her.

"What?" She drew her hand from his.

"I'm dying, Marilee. I have maybe six weeks to three months."

He gazed at her for some moments, in which she stared at him, having no idea of what to say; in fact, a certain roaring began in the back of her brain and spread to her ears, so that she heard his voice just above it, as he told her that he had an incurable cancer, already spread to his liver and other places, and that even if he could have been offered treatment, he wouldn't have taken it, because what sort of life would he be given?

Of all the things he might have said to her, of all the things she had imagined, such as him walking out without a word and not returning, or him going crazy and running off with Willie Lee—only she had never really believed this, simply thought it up in angry moments—or getting a phone call to tell her he had dropped dead out on some photo-shoot in the far reaches of Tibet or glitzy Monaco, this was one thing she had not imagined.

So why had he come back? She listened as he told her, in a roundabout fashion. She listened, and she looked at the coffeepot and cups on the tray he had brought in, and she thought of the colorful bouquet that sat now on the kitchen table, and the brand-new washer and dryer, which she was using almost maniacally, and the giant vase of roses. And the way he had danced with her.

Thinking of all these things, the roaring grew louder in her ears and her hands knotted into fists in her lap.

"My father died of cancer," he told her, his face drawn and his eyes on the coffee table. "In a nursing home. I went to see him. He was in a bed pushed against a wall."

He looked at her. "I didn't understand anything then. I didn't understand that the way I lived was the same way he had lived, not forming any attachments, and that then in the end, there isn't anyone. I don't know how I'll face that. I don't know how I'll face any of this."

So he had come to her. And brought presents.

He gazed at the coffee table.

"What do you want from me?" said Marilee, who

sat with her spine ramrod straight, her hands in fists in her lap.

His head came up. He frowned and ran a hand over his face. "I don't know. I just thought that I wanted to see you...and Willie Lee."

He looked at her, at her hands. "I know I don't deserve anything from you, Marilee. God knows, I know I'm asking a lot, but...I was hoping to just be with you, as much as I can."

"You are hoping to be with me."

An uncertain expression passed over his features.

"I am getting married, Stuart. In one month."

He nodded, again looking pitiful. "I know," he said in a hoarse, low tone. Then he chuckled. "If I could have, I would have had better timing."

She counted to ten, but the words came out anyway. "We are divorced, Stuart. We have been divorced for nine years. I am marrying another man. I am going to be his wife. I don't quite know how I can say to him, 'Oh, by the way, my ex-husband needs me to be with him for the first months of our marriage.'"

It was sarcasm, and it cut like a knife. She saw him wince, as if from a blow. She hated herself for allowing her anger to have control. Compassion fought for a place, but so did the urge to lift the sofa cushion and beat the living daylights out of him.

"I have Willie Lee and Tate and Corrine to think of. And my own life, Stuart. I'm not putting all of us aside for you. I'm not doing it."

She was on her feet and speaking loudly with the last of it. Totally at a loss, she turned and strode around the couch and into her bedroom, where she managed to keep herself from slamming the door, at the last minute thinking of the children.

She plopped down on the bed; then after a minute, she got up and checked the drawer of her bedside table for some chocolate. Finding none, she slammed the drawer closed.

She paced for some minutes; then, turning out the light, she lay back on the bed and stared up at the ceiling. She thought she heard the front door open and close, but she wasn't certain, and wasn't about to open the door and look and possibly have to face him again. She felt imprisoned in her own bedroom. She felt as if she could hardly breathe, and as if she, too, were fighting for her life.

She tossed and turned and cried into the pillow. She reached for the phone half a dozen times but did not call Tate. She didn't want to wake him. She wondered at him not calling when he came in, but likely he had come in late, figured she would be asleep and decided not to wake her.

Her not calling him was more than not wanting to wake him. It was shame at her attitude. Shame at showing her anger at a dying man. Surely Tate would think her heartless. Or else he would be outraged at Stuart, and she couldn't bear that.

Stuart did not mean that he wanted to be with her. What he meant was that he didn't want to be alone. He had come to her to take care of him, as he had always done. To use her. And his presents had been bribes, not presents at all.

He was dying.

What concern was it of hers? She was getting married. She had a new life ahead of her with a wonderful man who didn't deserve to be put second.

But Stuart was the father of her son. He was a fellow human who needed help in a horrible trial. He had no one else.

What about Tate and Willie Lee and Corrine? What about their lives? Was everyone simply to put their own lives on hold for this man who had never cared about anyone or anything but himself?

What about my own life?

The pillowcase and bed sheet were damp with her tears and sweat. She dragged herself up and slid down on her knees beside the bed. Folding her hands together, she rested her forehead on them and prayed, "Help me, God. Help me to know what to do, and to do it."

Crawling on hands and knees, she got back into the bed and slept at last.

Twenty-One

Life lessons...

She awoke and lay there for timeless moments, staring at the grey first light filtering through the window blinds. Then, like one awakening from the dead, she drew herself up from the warm bed, turned on the bedside lamp, and slid her feet into slippers and her body into her robe. She looked at her reflection in the mirror over the dresser. Even in the dim light she could see that her eyes looked like slits in a cantaloupe.

She was at the kitchen table, sitting with a steaming mug of coffee in two hands, when Tate came in the back door. He stopped in the laundry room doorway, regarding her with surprise.

"You're up."

"Yes," Marilee croaked in a hoarse voice. She had to admire that Tate was made of stern stuff to smile at her, with her looking like the wrath of God.

He came over, bringing with him the aromas of mocha and sweet rolls—two bags from the IGA deli. Setting the bags on the table, he kissed her quickly. "I can't stay. I've got the Methodist men's breakfast meeting this mornin'. I forgot all about it, until Pastor Smith called me to remind me that I was speakin'."

She nodded. She caught the warm, adoring light in his eyes and had to look away.

"I'll see you down at the paper later," he said, in a gently lowered voice, as if respectful that she was not fully awake. He knew her well. He tenderly kissed her forehead and left, closing the back door softly behind him.

In her mind, she raced to the door to call him back and to pour out her situation to him. In reality, she sat, knowing, for one thing, that she was incapable of fast movement.

Oh, she wished she had been able to tell him about Stuart. At the same time, she was relieved not to have to speak of it just yet.

Such thinking was too much for so early in the morning. She tossed the rest of her coffee down the sink, poured the mocha from the deli's foam cup into her blue earthenware one and carried the sweet brew into the bath.

She ate a Hershey's Kiss and opened another while she looked up the number for the Goodnight Motel and dialed. A craggy voice answered.

"May I have Stuart James's room, please?" She had no idea at all of what she would say to him. Some sort of apology seemed in order, although she was feeling a rising urge to beat him with the telephone receiver.

"Whats'zat?"

She raised her voice. "Stuart James's room, please."

"Wait a minute."

She waited.

A woman's voice came on the line. "Can I help you?"

"I'd like to speak to Stuart James's room, please." That sounded silly. She wanted him, not the room. She really didn't want him. Possibly she wouldn't get him.

"I'm sorry, he's not here."

She gripped the receiver. "Do you know when he'll be back? Can I leave a message for him?"

"He isn't comin' back. He checked out this mornin'."

"Oh. Did he leave a forwarding address…a number where he can be reached?" Speaking to him had become imperative to her.

"No. There's no reason for him to do that, I don't guess. Is this Marilee James?"

"Yes."

"Well, honey, your ex's done gone. I'm sorry. But I want to tell you how much we enjoy your pieces in the paper. That series you did on detention centers was real interestin'. Our nephew is out here in this one that just opened. He goes home on the weekends."

"Thank you…thank you very much." Just as she replaced the receiver, she realized the woman had still been talking. She felt so rude.

She only realized she had been sitting for some moments at her desk when Corrine came up beside her and said in a small voice, "Are you all right, Aunt Marilee?"

She saw that Corrine had the anxious expression she had so often worn during the first months upon coming to live with them, and which could on occasion still crop up. No child should have so much nameless anxiety.

"I'm just fine, honey." She put her arm around Corrine and hugged her. Then, knowing security came only from honesty, she said, "I have a problem, but it isn't anything you can help with, sweetheart, and it is not life-threatening."

She saw the anxiety ease on the child's heart-shaped face. "Is it one of those life-lessons, like Aunt Vella sometimes says?"

"Yes, dear…yes, it is." Marilee chuckled.

"Maybe you should let God handle it," Corrine said in a helpful manner.

Marilee hugged the dear child again. "I'm trying, honey. I'm tryin'."

Being with the children always made her feel stronger. Perhaps this was because she determined to appear courageous and not worry them; she was, she thought, as she rounded up children, backpacks, purse, keys and cheerfulness for the drive to school, a good enough actress to win an Oscar.

The children were deposited at school, and that left Marilee alone with her own thoughts, which quickly generated regrets and fears. As she drove to the newspaper, her spirits sank to her toes.

She had been cruel to Stuart. Oh, not in her decision that she could not change her life to suit his, but in her much less than sympathetic response. An angry response, understandable, but not acceptable.

She *had* to speak to him. The urge came over her so strongly that she realized her eyes kept searching for him along her way, as if she could find him right there on the corner of the IGA parking lot. *Oh, God, please let me have the opportunity to make things right.* Just how she would accomplish this feat, she wasn't certain. She only knew that she had to speak to him. To show him that she did care. To right a wrong she had committed.

The hopeful idea popped into her mind as she approached the *Voice* building that Stuart might have left a message there. She zipped into a space head-in to the curb and strode inside, on the short walk from her Cherokee having come by the absolute certainty that she would find a message from him, because this made perfect sense. Surely he would leave her a message and not just run out on her again.

Now why would she think that? He'd run out before. Running was what he did.

It was earlier than she ever arrived, and Charlotte was the only one present.

"Do I have messages?" Marilee stopped in front of the reception desk.

Charlotte, without a word, handed Marilee one slip of paper. The message was from yesterday afternoon, from Iris out at the MacCoy Green Acres Senior Living Center, who said she would fax in the upcoming report for the March activities.

"Stuart didn't call this morning?"

Charlotte looked up and blinked. "No." She looked curious. "What's the matter?"

Marilee, starting to speak, felt tears well into her eyes, and the lump in her throat choked any words. This amazed her, even as she saw Charlotte's eyes pop wide. Marilee James never cried, at least not in public.

With Charlotte staring at her, Marilee blinked and swallowed and tried to get herself together.

Then Charlotte was on her feet, saying, "Marilee,

I have to quit…. I just can't stay here around Sandy. I just *can't*." With the last, Charlotte's face crumpled, and she went into tears, too.

The mention of Charlotte quitting, combined with the sadness over Stuart, caused Marilee's mind to produce a heavy dark blanket of sadness about the entire state of life on earth, and she burst into full-fledged sobbing. Words came then, on the order of, "Oh, Char-looottte…"

She started around the reception desk, where Charlotte met her, and the two women fell together, sobbing.

Sheriff Neville was coming out of the Main Street Café just as Tate parked head-in to the sidewalk, right beside Marilee's Cherokee.

"Hey, Editor. How-you this mornin'?" Sheriff Neville shifted the toothpick sticking out from his lips from one corner of his mouth to the other.

"Too good," said Tate, whatching the toothpick. "I'm a man gettin' married—weddin' is still on for March 21."

"Well, we'll see." The sheriff grinned, and the toothpick stayed right in the corner of his lips. "Maybe you'll come to your senses."

"Any news for the paper?"

The sheriff shook his head. "Things are right quiet. Oh, tell Marilee that Morley Lund got those skunks cleaned out around his place. We had to go over there yesterd'y and get him to stop usin' his firearm in the city limits. He misaimed and shot out his neighbor's garage window and like to have got the man in the behind, too. But before we got there, Morley had sent those skunks runnin', two of 'em straight to heaven. The vet's new wife came with humane traps and said she'd see to roundin' up any more that happened along. She got Mrs. Lund's prize Pekingese right off the bat.''

By the time he finished, the sheriff, who enjoyed playing the small-town hick to the hilt, was grinning widely.

"Have you ever considered writing up these tales, Neville?"

"I believe that's your job...but maybe I could help you out on occasion." Giving a wink, he added, "Adios," and headed on along the sidewalk, while Tate strode into the *Voice,* his steps quickened by the sudden, gleaming idea of writing a book based on characters drawn from Valentine. In a flash he had imagined the book and its outstanding cover, and seen himself autographing it for lines miles long. The networks would even come to cover the event.

The fantasy vanished from his mind in the manner of being shot clean to smithereens, however, when he stepped through the glass door and saw Marilee and Charlotte, clinging to each other and crying to beat the band.

The sight of any two women in such behavior would be startling, but with these two usually reserved females, it was immensely unnerving. All sorts of horrible scenarios required to work up this emotional display passed through his imagination.

God, don't let it be any of the children. The thought caused a weakening in his knees.

Tate closed the door with enough force to get the women's attention.

Upon seeing him, they made visible efforts to get

hold of themselves. When he finally spoke, he asked in a careful tone, "This isn't about something happenin' with one of the children...or your mother, Charlotte?" Better Charlotte's mother than the children, truth be known; he was a practical man.

Both women shook their heads. Marilee, sniffing, said, "It's...it's...oh..." She got two tissues from the box on Charlotte's desk, handing one to Charlotte.

Feeling a firm hand was needed, he said, "Let's go into my office and have some coffee." He took Marilee's elbow. She was shaking.

Charlotte hung back, so he said, "Charlotte, how about you, too?"

Thankfully she did not argue. Perhaps she was too worn-out from crying.

Tate got three cups of coffee from the pot that Charlotte had already brewed. He was surprised that his hands shook. It was a heck of a note that these women had been able to upset him so much—he, a seasoned journalist who had covered and dealt with all manner of crises, from murders and fatal accidents and riots.

Although, on his own, in his solitary life, he had never been as vulnerable as he was now, as a man who loved a woman and children and friends. Love and connection made a man vulnerable.

He returned to his office. The women sat on each end of the leather couch, dabbing at their eyes with a tissue. As he passed them their coffee, he heard voices entering the City Room. Stepping to his door, he saw June, Imperia and Reggie coming in the rear entrance from the alley. He called to Reggie to please handle the reception desk and phone. "Charlotte's in conference in here. I don't want to be disturbed."

Reggie's eyes widened, and then she nodded. He shut his door and pulled the visitor chair around to face the couch.

"Now, let's talk out what is goin' on here," he said. "Marilee, why don't you go first?" He was closer with Marilee and felt he could respond to her easier. He would have to work up to Miss Charlotte.

"Stuart is dying," Marilee said.

"What?" said Tate, feeling hit out of left field.

"What?" said Charlotte, clearly feeling the same. Apparently her crying was not about the same thing that Marilee's was.

"Stuart told me last night that he is dying." She began tearing up and took deep breaths. "I was so thoughtless in how I responded, and then I came in here and looked at Charlotte, and thought about her leaving..." She looked down at the tissue in her hand and began tearing it to pieces. "I haven't done well in either circumstance. I haven't said straight to Charlotte that I don't want her to leave."

She leaned toward Charlotte. "I haven't been there for you. I'm so sorry, Charlotte. I have been so caught up in my own life. I've been racin' around, trying to avoid so many feelings and doubts, that I simply couldn't be there for you. I haven't been there for you to talk things over, like a friend does for another. I should have been willing to step in and speak to you about this situation with Sandy and your mother, and to say that I understand—but you do need to open your mind to other options," she added, more like the normal Marilee.

"I have not seen any of this. I have just felt like

I had more than I could handle, dealing with my-self,'' she went on. Her shoulders and her tone dropped, and she pressed the shredded tissue to her breast. ''And then last night Stuart told me about…his situation, and I saw how he needed me, and I was so awful to him. I was angry at him for needing me.''

She began to tear up again as she turned to Tate. ''Oh, Tate, we have to find him.''

Tate's mind was still trying to catch up to all she had been saying. This was one of those horrible times in life when reality seemed totally unreal.

''Stuart told you he is dying?'' Maybe he had mis-understood.

But Marilee nodded. ''Yes.'' She swallowed and breathed deeply. ''He told me that he has cancer of a fast and consuming variety, nontreatable. He prob-ably has only a couple more months. That's why he came here. Because he has nowhere else to go, and he doesn't want to be alone.''

It was sinking into Tate with the full force of a sledgehammer. All the pieces being pounded into place.

He watched Marilee's magnificent struggle to keep from sobbing. ''He wants me to be there for him,'' she said, reaching over and squeezing Charlotte's hand. ''Like Charlotte is for her mother.''

A cold shiver of understanding went down Tate's back.

Then Marilee added, her voice rising, ''But now he's gone off, and I can't let him leave like that. I have to speak to him.''

''Stuart's gone off?'' His mind was now separat-ing and dissecting the matter.

"Yes. I called the Goodnight earlier, and they said he had checked out. He's just run off again, like he always does."

Tate was somewhat glad to see her flash of anger. "We have to find him, Tate. We have to."

Tate and Charlotte looked at each other in a moment of coming together as one mind, knowing what must be done.

"We'll find him, Marilee." Then, to Charlotte, he said, "He was drivin' a Hertz rental car. You take that end, and I'll make some calls."

Instantly Charlotte was on her feet and striding out the door on her long, purposeful legs.

Tate went to his desk and took up the phone, punching in the numbers for the sheriff's office. He looked over at Marilee.

"We'll find him," he said, thinking about how he had wanted to beat out the guy with all his new appliances, and all the time the guy was dying. *Maybe.* Maybe the guy was working another angle. Tate didn't think he should overlook that possibility until he knew for sure.

Marilee came over, put her arms around his waist and laid her head on his shoulder. He held her against him, feeling the need now to hold on tight to keep her from slipping away.

"The rental car has not been turned back in to Hertz," Charlotte reported to him an hour later.

"It's early yet. He hasn't had time to get back down to Dallas…if that was where he was goin'." He mused that James could take the rental car anywhere. Still, Dallas seemed the best bet. He did not think James would go very far from good comfort, whether truly dying or not.

"I'll check back with them in a couple of hours," Charlotte said. "I don't want to wait for another shift. I told the girl I was from the sheriff's office. She bought it, so I want to try to get her again."

He breathed deeply. "Well, Sheriff Neville has made some calls to request friends to keep a lookout, but he won't put out any all-points. James has only been gone a few hours and hasn't committed any crime. We'll just have to wait and see what turns up. I called a buddy down in Houston who knows how to find people."

Charlotte began going through a stack of papers and files on the corner of his desk.

"What are you looking for?"

"My resignation. I'm retracting it."

Waa-hoo!

"I tore it up," he admitted.

"You tore up my resignation?" She regarded him with indignant eyes from behind her dark-rimmed glasses.

He felt mildly ashamed. "Yes," he said, falling back on the strength of honesty. "I told you I would not accept it."

She turned on her heel and strode away, saying, "A person does not get the respect due around here."

He jumped up from his chair and hurried after her, catching up with her just before she got to her desk and grabbing her to him in a big hug.

"How's that for respect? I'm darn glad you've changed your mind, Miss Charlotte.... So glad that I'm willin' to make a fool of myself and get slapped for it. This paper can't run without you. That's it, plain and simple. I'm indebted to you for stayin'.'' There, he couldn't be more humble than that.

Applause came from the other desks in the big room, getting louder and louder, until Charlotte's co-workers were on their feet. Sandy Conroy's long, tall frame came out from his glass cubicle and into the middle of the big room, where, clapping, he called out, "Yee-ha!"

Charlotte, her face flushed, swept her gaze from Tate to everyone, then primly sat herself at her desk and went to work on her computer.

"Charlotte!"

Marilee ran to catch up to the tall woman, who was walking home to check on her mother during her lunch hour. The two walked together along the older sidewalks that led into the neighborhood of small clapboard boxlike houses dating from a brief boom in the fifties. Most were painted white, many needing repainting. Some had been fortunate not only to have been kept up, but to have received improvements along the lines of vinyl siding, picture windows and enclosed porches. The limbs of great elm trees stretched above yards where one was neatly tended and daffodils poked forth, and another had worn patches in the grass and was littered with plastic toys.

"Thank you for trying to find Stuart," Marilee said, annoyed at herself for finding conversation so difficult.

"Mmm." Charlotte nodded.

They walked in silence for a long minute, while Marilee formed what she wanted to say.

Finally she came out with, "I don't have many friends. Oh, I know a lot of people, but I don't think of them as friends. I just never have been able to open up and let other people into my life much."

She found understanding on Charlotte's face.

"I think of you as about my best friend, and I'm so glad you aren't leaving the paper. Thank you for being there for all of us. I don't think you know what you do, but everyone there relies on you. And I really want you to stand up for me at my wedding. It means a lot to me."

Despite feeling that she sounded a little incoherent, Marilee felt a sense of freedom coming over her at the effort to speak her heart.

"I think of you as my only real friend," Charlotte said slowly, without looking at Marilee. "And I'm looking forward to being your bridesmaid. I have never been a bridesmaid."

They smiled at each other, shyly, and then they began to speak of the wedding, deciding to have a shopping spree for choosing a new dress for Charlotte. Marilee, who had never in her life been shopping with a woman friend, wondered what the experience would be like. She dared to say as much, and Charlotte replied that she, too, had not ever been shopping with another woman, besides her mother. "And that was years ago," she added.

"We have led inhibited lives," Marilee observed.

Charlotte chuckled at that. "I've been having an affair with a younger man. That does not seem so inhibited...but you are right," she added, breathing a deep breath. "My life has been quite inhibited. I don't know how it happened. Just one day I woke up and here I was in this place, thirty-five, having tended Mama for nigh on ten years, and with day following day of always saying, 'tomorrow.'''

Marilee nodded. "I know what you mean."

At that, for some reason, Charlotte laughed more gaily than Marilee had heard her laugh in a long time.

Charlotte's house had not undergone any grand remodeling from its original state, but it was kept nicely, a small white cottage with a climbing rose-bush, bare yet, but promising to climb up a trellis onto the porch. It was a picture out of a children's book, thoroughly feminine, having been inhabited only by Charlotte and her mother for some twenty years.

The inside continued with the same cottage atmosphere, with chintz curtains and flouncy pillows, everything in shades of pink, mauve and blue. The decor seemed too cute for Charlotte, not to mention long, tall Sandy. It was the reflection of Mrs. Nation, who was as small as Charlotte was tall. Obviously Charlotte took after her father, who, it was reported, had been tall and robust and had run off when Charlotte had been in grade school.

Marilee said hello to Mrs. Nation from the bedroom door; the tiny room was so crowded with frills as to discourage entering. In any case, Mrs. Nation, a shrunken figure in the hospital bed, simply looked at her with rather vacant eyes. Although she nodded, it was the day nurse who said brightly, "Mrs. Nation is havin' a good day today."

Marilee followed Charlotte with her gaze, watched her friend tenderly kiss her mother's pasty cheek, fluff the pillow upon which she reclined, touch her lifeless hand, all very quickly, one motion and seeming to go ever faster, so that she was in the room and then out of it again and on into the kitchen, where she made Marilee and herself glasses of ice tea with sprigs of mint from a pot on the sill.

The thought sprang into Marilee's mind: run through life, busy, busy, busy, and then we don't have to stop and face the hungry lions.

"Tate and I can come and sit with your mother sometimes," she said, taken by impulse. "I don't really have experience, but I think Tate and I together can handle it. Tate is quite good at such things. You should see him with the children."

Gazing at Charlotte, who did not sit down, but stood at the kitchen sink, one arm across her middle and the other clutching her glass of cold tea, Marilee felt shame in not offering months ago. She, like everyone, considered Charlotte able to handle everything. Just as everyone had always thought about Marilee herself. Both of them hid their weaknesses quite well.

Charlotte observed her.

"Let Sandy help you, Charlotte. I'm learning how much Tate can help me. I'm always amazed, how much he wants to do. I simply never knew there were such men." The faint shadow of her distant father crossed her heart. "It isn't often a woman finds a man who's willing to help with things like mothers and children. Don't let this opportunity pass you by just because of a silly few years' difference in your ages. Tate was worried about growing old the other day. I told him we had enough worries to think about today, without projecting so far into the future."

She thought of Stuart and how he would not grow old. He only had today.

Charlotte said only, "If you're ready, we should head back," and set her glass in the sink.

Twenty-Two

Smoothing the knots in the skein of time...

When they came home from school, Willie Lee headed straight around the house to the backyard, to see his bird. Corrine went up on the front porch, drew over the stool and climbed up to stick her hand in the mailbox and fish around.

She brought out a phone bill, a sale postcard for JCPenny's, and a Victoria's Secret catalog. There was no small box addressed to herself. Likely her mother was not going to send the present. Likely she had forgotten. There had not been a card from her in weeks.

Corrine went over to sit on the swing for some minutes, not wanting to face her aunt or anyone when she felt so close to tears. What was wrong with her? Why did her mother not care about her?

Then her gaze was diverted by the Victoria's Secret catalog and the almost naked woman on the front cover. The women in the catalog fascinated her. Corrine had lately been examining her chest and finding she had breasts growing. She wasn't sure she wanted them. She always wondered how the women in the catalog got shaped as they were, since she had never seen any women like them in real life. She would have asked Aunt Marilee about this, but she was too embarrassed to speak of such private things as the shape of a body.

Maybe she *would* ask, she thought, feeling a flicker of daring as she gathered up the mail and her and Willie Lee's backpacks and went inside.

She was a little surprised to find Aunt Marilee and Mr. Tate—Papa Tate—sitting close together on the couch. They turned and looked at her, quite suddenly smiling at her in that way grown-ups smiled when wanting to hide their discussion.

"Hey, pumpkin, how was school?" said Mr. Tate.

"Okay, Papa Tate," Corrine replied. She had been making an effort to try out the new name, to see how everything set with it.

Mr. Tate seemed pleased.

All evening, Corrine did her best to please while she listened carefully to the adults and caught snatches of whispers but not what was going on that they did not want to talk about in front of her and Willie Lee. Aunt Vella came after supper, and she and Aunt Marilee and Papa Tate—the name was growing on Corrine—sat at the dining-room table and wrote out the invitations. Aunt Vella was told whatever was going on. Corrine caught Aunt Vella saying Stuart's name on several occasions, and she decided whatever it was, was something to do with him. She came to the conclusion that he was not there, and he was supposed to be there.

She was a little relieved to be satisfied that whatever the trouble was, her mother had not caused it, for once.

And she had known Mr. James would be the cause

of trouble. She took it as a good sign that her aunt
Marilee was making out the wedding invitations;
surely this meant the marriage was to take place.
Still, Corrine had learned a long time ago not to
count on something too much, or it would not come
about.

She thought Papa Tate looked especially worried,
even if he did still smile a lot like normal. She
brought him a glass of fresh ice tea, hoping to make
it all better.

Stuart checked out of the hotel room he had only
hours before checked into. He went down the elevator and out into the starlit night. The wind coming
off the plain and whipping around the tall buildings
of the city tugged at his hair, and he shivered in the
falling temperatures. Halfway across the narrow lot,
he dropped his duffel bag, his grip seeming to give
way. In the process of trying to pick it up, he dropped
one of his camera cases. A man coming from a
pickup truck helped him pick up his bags.

"Thanks."

"You bet."

Stuart went on to his rental car, threw the bags
inside, got behind the wheel and headed off, directing
the vehicle west on the interstate, heading back to
Valentine.

Marilee and his son were the only loose ends of
his life, one carefully lived without ties. Now, suddenly, he didn't want to be without ties. It would be
as if he had never lived at all, and that was too hard
to take. Somehow, some way, he wanted to tie up
the loose ends, so there would be a knot on the skein
of time with the name of Stuart James written on it.

The only way to do that was not to run out on Marilee in the end. It was now the single purpose for him.

Charlotte debated about telephoning Sandy all evening. She actually picked up the telephone twice but did not dial.

Then, like a gift from heaven, she heard his TransAm pull up out front. Instantly she flew to the front door and out of it into the soft, cool night. She stood on the edge of the porch and watched him round the hood of his powerful car. He carried a bouquet of flowers. He walked head down, as usual, and did not see her standing there until he was halfway up the walk.

The streetlight fell on his face, showing his surprise, which was followed quickly by determination in the quickening of his long strides.

"I brought you these." He jutted the flowers at her, as if daring her to refuse.

She found his unusual sense of firmness very attractive. "Thank you, Sandy," she said softly, reaching for the flowers.

"Can we just start seein' each other again?" he asked. She had always appreciated how simply he spoke.

"Come inside. The night nurse will be here in another hour, and then we can go off and talk." She took his hand. It was warm and moist in her own.

Just before entering, there in the deep darkness of the porch, she paused and kissed him, and was rewarded by his answering passion.

She led him into the kitchen, where she put the flowers into a vase. He stood over by the refrigerator, watching and definitely ill at ease, a long, tall hunk of a man in a dainty kitchen.

"Do you still want to marry me?" she asked, pausing to look at him.

He swallowed and tucked his hands up under his armpits. "Yes, I do."

She arranged the flowers in the vase.

"I don't have much money," he said, "but I think together we could rent a house big enough to accommodate you, me and your mother. I've looked at several."

He had been looking at houses!

She finished getting the flowers correct to please her and brought the vase to set in the middle of the table. "There. They sure are pretty."

She looked across at him. He was a patient man, never rushing her to hurry up and speak.

"I have saved, in the bank and investments, about one hundred thousand dollars. How about if we buy a house?" She was very good at investing.

His eyes went round as saucers, and his mouth fell open.

Then he began shaking his head and saying, "No...no, I can't be lettin' you buy our home. I..."

She went to him, enjoying as always being able to look slightly upward into his eyes. "Darlin', if I can bear with being eleven years older than you, I believe you can bear with using my money for a house."

And then he kissed her just as she wanted.

Vella had gone, the children were in bed, and Tate was alone with Marilee at last. He dimmed the lights, put a George Strait CD into the stereo and turned the volume low, then pulled her into his arms. Feet slid-

ing over the smooth oak floor in the wide area behind
the couch, his thighs pushed on hers, his belly to her
belly, her breasts against his chest. She laid her head
on his shoulder and gave a pleasurable sigh as he
caressed her back.

He wanted her right then, and he knew she wanted
him, and it felt good, the wanting to bond together.
It was the specter of death that propelled them, he
knew. It was death making them aware of how precious were their lives together.

The question before them all evening had been of
Stuart James. They could not disregard him by saying he was not their problem.

"He's Willie Lee's father," Marilee said.

"Yes, he is."

"He was once my husband. He isn't anymore...but he is someone to me."

"Yes, he is."

At last she believed that he was in full agreement,
that he was going to stand there with her.

"I'm asking so much of you, I know," she said.

"I am to be your husband. We'll get through it
together," he said.

And in their dancing, bodies and hearts touched
and melded together. It was stimulating and heady.
He swept her one way and then another, and he savored the motions, the scent of her, the feel of her
skin that already belonged to him, and which he
could at any moment, he knew, take for his own.

Marilee raised her head and looked at him. "I
don't want this to change our plans. We've made our
plans, everything perfect for us. It's important, this
time for us to anticipate our coming together as one.
I don't want to give it up. I want all we've planned,

Tate. This time will never come again. We don't want to let it pass by.''

Even in the dimness, he saw the heat in her eyes and plain on her face.

He kissed her neck and heard her sharp intake of breath.

''We won't let it,'' he whispered into her ear, kissing her lobe and then down her neck, feeling her tremble against him.

Then he kissed her, and she kissed him.

''Oh, Tate.''

She breathed the words against his neck. He held her tight against him, cherishing her more than he had ever cherished anything in his life.

They danced for some time, necking as they did and not daring to sit down, until both were hot and forced to break apart. They giggled like teens. It was heady, like some sort of drug, Tate thought, calming himself as Marilee went to get them coffee.

They sat long on the couch, talking about options for when they did find Stuart.

''You know, Marilee, we can make all these plans, but Stuart may not want any of them.''

She said she knew that, but he didn't think she did.

Willie Lee didn't think his mother would hear him. She and Papa Tate had music playing in the living room. He tucked his pillows under his covers, then got behind his blinds and got the window open without Corrine hearing.

Munro hopped out, and Willie Lee positioned himself on the windowsill. He did not wear his cape, because he knew now that he could not fly. But he could jump, and it felt like flying.

He put his hands out and jumped.

He landed with a hard thump and went rolling on the damp, moist ground. Munro licked his face, and then Willie Lee was pushing to his feet and adjusting his glasses. He had not bothered with coat and shoes, and his feet felt really cold. It was very dark, but he could follow the wall of the house to the backyard, where he and Munro ran to where they could clearly see the stars.

He loved this time, when he could simply be. It was okay if he could not fly. He didn't have to. There were many other things he could learn to do.

Tate felt it safe to sleep in an extra half hour on Saturday morning, yet he still got up anxious to head off the possibility of Marilee coming over to his house and finding all the remodeling going on.

Finished shaving, he threw aside his towel, opened the bathroom door and saw his passage blocked by an enormous oak bedstead passing by. A man on the back end—one of Honey Moon's three emissaries—said, "'Mornin'."

He was followed by another emissary, who said, "Your mother let us in. She's made prune muffins." He held one up in his callused hand.

It wasn't yet seven o'clock in the morning. His mother had been out with Winston until the small hours of the morning—and now she was up and baking?

Tate followed the men and what turned out to be the oak headboard of the bed Honey Moon had sent up from Dallas. The men propped it against the wall in the master bedroom. Tate went over to examine it.

A sleigh bed! He loved a sleigh bed!

"Like it?" asked the emissary who was in charge of the crew.

"Yes...yes, I do," Tate said, running a hand over the smooth rolled wood.

"Honey knew you would."

Tate's confidence that Honey Moon knew her stuff was rising. He glanced around at the walls. The dreary wallpaper was gone, replaced by something Honey Moon called texturing. Paint with sand thrown in it, Tate thought, but he liked the effect. The color was Sahara, so the head emissary had told him. It did give a warm glow. Intimate.

He was quite pleasantly surprised, as he had been preparing himself for something on the order of purples and leopard prints from Honey Moon.

Remembering then that he didn't want Marilee happening over to see any of this, he hotfooted down the stairs, with the intent of getting over to the IGA and the mocha machine. Sweet bread aroma mixed with the faint odor of paint met him, leading him into the kitchen, where he just about tripped on a tarp still spread on the floor.

There didn't seem to be enough painting being done in the kitchen to justify a tarp, he thought. Not only was the crew he had hired slower than molasses in January, but they kept coming across rotted wooden places that had to be replaced. Tate regretted that he had not turned the kitchen job over to Honey Moon, as well, rather than Joe's Paint Job crew. He had been misled by so reliable-sounding a name.

"Good mornin'," his mother said. She looked as

fresh as if she had slept ten hours and had a leisurely bath.

"You didn't come in until almost two o'clock," he said, not really knowing why he had to speak of it.

"Winston and I had a grand time. And the band is booked." She handed him a basket. "Here, take these to Marilee this mornin'. So many of those commercial bakery items are not good for anyone. And here's your mocha, too."

Mocha, too?

At his obviously amazed expression, his mother said, "I bought you and Marilee a new coffee machine. Does all this fancy stuff...see? You needed it for your new kitchen. I saw a toaster I really liked, too. They're makin' them like back in the fifties again, and they are so cute. I'm going to get it, and if Marilee doesn't like it, I'll keep it with me. I think I'm going to move in with Winston."

"Oh."

He watched her filling foam cups with the steaming brew.

"You mean you're goin' to stay up here in Valentine?"

"Yes. I want to be around my son and his family."

He digested that. "I'm glad, Mom."

They smiled at each other.

Then he looked around. They had new appliances, but the kitchen where they were seemed more to be coming apart than together.

"I'll get these boys goin' on this kitchen today," his mother said, as if reading his mind. "I'm goin' to ride them until they'd rather finish than deal with

me. You take care of Marilee and finding Stuart.''
She handed him the cups set in a small box.

Finding Stuart.

Tate thought of this problem on his way out the
back door. He had a sense of wanting to yell at the
world. He felt a little guilty about the part of the
motive he had held to upstage Stuart. For one thing,
the endeavor was both petty and fruitless, especially
considering that Stuart was dying. *If* he was dying,
and more guilt came on him because he had doubts.

The point to all he was doing, though, was to
please the woman he loved. Yes, by golly, that was
the heart of his intentions, and those were good. Only
good could come from a good motive. He wanted to
give pleasure to Marilee and make all their lives easier in the bargain. Winners all the way around!

He would do well to keep his focus on heading
toward the wedding. He wasn't letting anything stop
it.

Tate found Corrine in the kitchen, standing on a
chair and preparing the coffeemaker. Her tiny toenails were red on her bare feet. Such a little fragile
doll, she was. He wanted to protect her from all the
life that lay ahead. A sense of futility swept him; then
he bolstered himself and said brightly, ''You're up
early, pumpkin. Is your aunt Marilee awake yet?''

''She's on the phone with my mama,'' Corrine
said, as she carefully measured the coffee into the
basket.

''Oh.'' He watched her get down from the chair
to go over to the sink to fill the glass pot with water.
''I brought your aunt a cup of mocha, but she'll want
coffee, too. Would you like me to help you with

that?'' He indicated the pot of water that seemed a lot for her skinny arms and wrists.

''No.''

''Okay.'' He backed off, emptied the foam cups of mocha his mother had provided into stoneware cups and fixed a plate of three muffins, telling Corrine that his mother had made them and to help herself.

He put the cups and plate on a tray and carried it all into Marilee's bedroom, where he found her sitting on the edge of the bed with the telephone pressed to her ear. She gave him a glance and a wave, but she was definitely distracted. Marilee always got distracted when talking to her sister.

He set the tray on the table by the window, easing it onto the edge, then sat beside her and kissed the silky skin of her bare shoulder where her nightgown strap had slipped away. He was instantly aroused to the point of forgetting himself and began slipping his hand to her breasts.

Marilee was so intent on speaking to her sister, who had alarmed her with the information that she was going out of town on Monday, to Buenos Aires with Louis for a week, that she pushed Tate's caresses aside. She needed all her attention focused on the conversation at hand. Marilee decided that with Anita going out of the country, now was the imperative time to speak to her sister about the question of Corrine's security.

''Anita, we need to talk about Corrine's medical insurance. There are things to consider.'' She might have added: now that you've pretty much left your daughter, but she bit her tongue on that bit of factual criticism.

"I'm not offered any insurance, Marilee," Anita said. "I'm still only workin' at Louis's firm part-time."

"Honey…" She reached for Tate's hand and hung on to him while she searched for as gentle a choice of words as possible. "Corrine needs health insurance. She isn't my daughter, so I can't put her on my policy."

"Corrine's young. If she has to go to the doctor, I'll send you some money. Louis has plenty, and he adored Corrine when he met her."

Louis had met Corrine once, the previous summer, when he and Anita had come up for a visit before moving off to New Orleans. Anita had not seen her daughter since, and the cards and calls were becoming less frequent. How did Marilee address all this? She felt as if she were walking through a minefield. What if she angered Anita? She could crush her sister with what she felt needed to be done.

She said, "Corrine could get something serious that required hospitalization. I don't know what all, Anita, but we have to look at the situation." Deep breath. "We need to make me and Tate her legal guardians. If Tate and I adopt her, she can have full medical benefits and anything else she needs."

There, she had said it.

The line hummed for long seconds. "You always wanted this, didn't you, Marilee?" Anita began to cry. "You've always wanted to take my baby from me."

"Anita, that's not how I mean it. I'm thinking of Corrine's security. She needs health insurance, and she needs to be provided for if anything should happen to me…or to you. Do you want her only living relatives to be Mama and Carl? She'd end up with them, if something happened to me. Or the state could come in here and put her in a foster home.''

"I'll come get her," Anita said after a moment. "Give me a few weeks, and I'll come get her."

She had known this was coming. "Can you do that? Can you provide for her, with only a part-time job and no insurance?" Marilee toughened her heart. "I won't let you take her, Anita, unless you can provide for her better than you have in the past."

Anita screamed into the phone, "You can't do this! You can't!" And then she began to sob.

"Honey…honey, listen to me. I am not trying to hurt you. I love you. I don't want to hurt you, but we need to do what is best for Corrine. You'll always be her mother. I'm not taking that away. She knows who her mother is and always will."

Anita cried some more, and Marilee sat there squeezing Tate's hand and wondering what else to say.

Then Anita said, "I just can't talk about this anymore right now. I'll call you back later."

The line clicked dead.

Twenty-Three

Hallelujah! Shopping day...

Destination: the biggest shopping mall in Oklahoma City. Marilee drove, stopping to pick up Charlotte, who came running out of her house like a young girl.

Windows down! An oldies' station playing on the radio! Happy hopes of shopping till they dropped!

"I want to get somethin' to get Winston's blood pumping," Franny said.

Charlotte cast a look of alarm over the seat. "I imagine you are doin' that already, Franny. You might kill him if you increase it."

"Yes, well...good way to go," the older woman answered smartly.

"You *are* joking, right Granny Franny?" Corrine asked, wanting to smile, but not quite certain.

"Yes, dear. It is a truth that is so true it is funny. And I love you, darlin'." Franny kissed Corrine, whose eyes showed both pleasure and uncertainty of someone who could say I love you so easily.

They arrived at the turnoff for the mall, and then there it was before them: shopping Mecca. All in the car, small-town girls used to small-town stores, stared and gaped like hicks from the backwoods, all except Franny, who was never overly impressed by anything.

There was a host of angels singing in the heavens, Marilee thought, gripping the steering wheel and having a sense of seeing something on the order of the great pyramids, the structure being sandy in color and standing brightly against the clear blue sky. And being Saturday, the traffic, which surrounded them on all sides, flowed toward the enormous structure like the flow of pilgrims to their holy place.

Walking across the parking lot, they were all so excited with the shopping potential that awaited them, they forgot Corrine and her shorter legs. Marilee looked around and saw Corrine craning her neck upward, lost in wonder. "Y'all slow up!" she said to the others and raced back to take Corrine's hand. Quite suddenly she recognized possible dangers. "Help me keep an eye on her," she whispered to Charlotte and Franny.

From store to store, rack to rack.

"Oh, look at this!"

"Aunt Marilee, can I try this on?"

"Oh, that is perfect for you!"

"Not your color, Marilee."

"Ohmygosh, who would possibly wear this?"

"Well, I would, darlin'."

"Does this make my behind look big?"

"Sugar, don't look at that." Hands over Corrine's eyes.

"Oh! In this dress, my ship will come in!"

"A ship? Honey, you'll bring in the entire fleet with that."

* * *

Marilee came upon Corrine gazing at a mannequin wearing a hot pink T-shirt and fashionably faded jeans. *Oh, dear Lord, she is growing up so fast.*

"Would you like to try that outfit on, sugar?"

Corrine looked at her with wide eyes, then nodded.

They went into the store for teens—flashing lights that caused Marilee's eyes to squint—and chose the proper sizes. Corrine disappeared into the dressing room, and when she reappeared, Franny and Charlotte had joined Marilee.

"Perfect for you!" Franny said instantly.

"You are not a little girl anymore," Charlotte said.

"You are so lovely," Marilee said, and kissed her niece's cheek. Then, "I'll go see if they have that shirt in yellow, too."

"Oh, thank you, Aunt Marilee!"

Three hours later, tired bones lugged shopping bags to the food court and plopped into chairs at one of the few vacant tables.

"We should have paced ourselves," observed Charlotte, who removed her shoes.

"I never realized shopping could be such hard work," said Marilee, who had not yet found an outfit for wearing on the flight to the fabulous Walt Disney World honeymoon.

"There's just too many people around here for me," said Corrine in a rare, candid moment.

"Perk up, y'all," said Franny, who looked as fresh as she had at the beginning. "We have just gotten started. Charlotte doesn't have her bridesmaid dress, and Corrine still needs a swimsuit. Marilee, you must get more than bras, and I have to find my drop-dead gorgeous dress.''

"You have found three drop-dead gorgeous dresses.''

"Yes, but not *the* dress.''

With all they had purchased, none of it was what they had come after.

Marilee said, "Franny, sometimes perky doesn't sit well.''

"Oh, darlin', I love you.'' Franny gave her a hug, then went off to order a pita-bread sandwich.

The three others looked at each other.

Then Marilee, dragging herself off the chair, said, "Begin with action and the spirit will follow. Come on, y'all.''

The three of them slumped over to join Franny in purchasing food, and quite quickly, upon eating and a bit of rest, hopeful shopping spirits soared once more.

They split up: Corrine and Franny went to several stores on the lower level, and Charlotte and Marilee went to several on the second level.

"Let's focus on gettin' you a bridesmaid dress first,'' Marilee said. "I sure don't want to go home without the main thing we came for.''

"I'm keeping an eye out for a wedding dress, too,'' Charlotte said. "What do you think about this one?''

Marilee observed the dress, then realized what Charlotte had said. "A wedding dress, as in you and Sandy have decided to get married?''

"Yes,'' Charlotte said in a breezy manner.

"Ohmygosh!'' Marilee let out a whoop, and several ladies gave her an eye. "This is wonderful, Charlotte."

"So while we're at it," Charlotte said, "you'd better get a bridesmaid dress for my wedding. Something in blue. That's going to be my theme color."

Marilee hauled off and hugged the taller woman, an action that somewhat surprised her and definitely surprised Charlotte. Self-conscious, Marilee went to draw back, but then Charlotte gave her a quick hug in return.

"We shouldn't have waited so long," Marilee said, the words popping from her mouth as tears blurred her vision.

Charlotte cast her a quizzical look.

"To be friends," Marilee said. "I'm so glad for being friends."

"Me, too." A smile quivered on Charlotte's lips, and then she quickly averted her eyes, taking dresses off the rack and slinging them over her arm. "It would have been nice if you were a little taller, though, so we could share clothes."

Marilee burst out laughing.

On the drive home, Marilee's thoughts turned to Stuart. Maybe there would be a message waiting at home from him. She started to use the cell phone to call and ask Tate, then decided doing that would not make her get home any sooner.

The streetlights had come on when Marilee pulled the Cherokee into her own driveway, having dropped Charlotte at her house first. She turned off the key, then looked around into the back seat to see Franny and Corrine leaning together, asleep. She gazed at them for long seconds.

Now, she thought, relief falling over her, Corrine will have another woman to help her along, to teach her things. Franny could teach Corrine so much that Marilee herself did not know.

Thank you, God...for today, for Franny, for my dear friend Charlotte.

And then here came Tate, stepping off the porch. On sight of him, her heart jumped, and she slipped out of the Cherokee and raced through the cool, moist night to fling herself into his arms.

His response was to lift her clear off the ground. "Ah, woman, home from the hunt."

"Oh, Tate." She hugged him fiercely and then kissed him, and all the while her heart was singing, *Oh, Tate...thank God for you...for all of the beloved people in my life.*

He set her down. "I take it you had fun and success in bagging the proper new outfits and baubles for the occasions ahead."

Only Tate would talk in such a grand manner!

"Yes, we had a delightful time. So much so that you might need to carry your mother into the house."

His eyes went wide, and then he bent to peer into the back seat. "Let's wait and see if she wakes up," he said, as if he had taken her words quite literally.

"Has there been any news?" she asked then.

He looked confused.

"About Stuart?" His expression had already told her what she needed to know, and her spirit dipped as he shook his head.

"We will find him, Marilee. It's only been a few days. He's gonna turn up any minute."

She nodded and moved to the rear of the Cherokee. He followed and helped her to unload, trooping behind her like a bellman lugging packages into the house. Her heart warmed to step into the cheery glow of home, where Willie Lee was already put to bed and coffee awaited in the kitchen.

She dropped her bags and turned to throw her arms around Tate again and to kiss him passionately.

"Hey, let's go out and come back in again," he said, continuing to hold her tightly.

The telephone rang, and Marilee moved quickly from his embrace to answer, her thoughts running straight to Stuart.

Tate put a hand on her arm. "Your sister called about an hour ago. She was pretty drunk."

Marilee looked at the telephone, ringing a second time. She went to her desk in the living room and checked the caller ID. "It's Mother." She lifted the receiver; it felt very heavy.

"Marilee?"

Her mother spoke in a sharp tone. Marilee instantly wished she had not answered. "Yes, Mother?" She met Tate's gaze, finding strength there. He moved to massage her shoulders.

"Anita just called here. She is all upset. She says you are taking Corrine from her, that you and Tate are going to adopt her away from Anita."

Marilee breathed deeply. "Yes, I have approached Anita with the idea. We need to take care of Corrine, Mom. We need to get her some health insurance and to make certain to safeguard her future. She needs to be provided for, and Anita can't do that."

As she said the last, the front door opened, and Franny and Corrine came straggling inside.

"Well, you have upset her no end. You are sayin' she isn't a fit mother. You can't do this to her. She is out of her mind about it. There is no telling what she might do.''

Marilee breathed deeply and moved into her bedroom for privacy. ''I am not doing anything to Anita. I am trying to take care of Corrine. And Anita *is* out of her mind. She is an alcoholic.''

Marilee could not believe she had said the word flat-out to her mother.

Her mother gasped, then said, ''Anita is not an alcoholic. She has a bit of a drinking problem, but she is not like your daddy.''

Marilee had no words for this.

''You are drivin' her to this drinking, too,'' her mother added. ''You have gotten her so upset.''

''I can't talk to you about this now, Mother. I am tired, and I have to get Corrine to bed. And I don't want her to hear any of this conversation. I'll call you about this soon. Goodbye.''

Well, she didn't think she would get points in heaven for hanging up on her mother, but she believed she would be understood.

She went out and plopped herself in the big armchair, where Corrine came and cuddled against her, and Tate brought a cup of coffee thick with sugar and cream for her, and a cup of hot chocolate for Corrine. Then he sat himself on the coffee table and listened to the female ''shop-till-they-dropped'' tales, nodding and laughing at all the right places.

Marilee watched the way his eyes crinkled, the way he winked at Corrine, the way his sleeves were rolled up on his forearms.

She watched Corrine, who described the wondrous shopping mall and even went to dig out the clothes she had gotten and show them to Tate, holding them up with her tired skinny little arms.

Anita's image swept her mind, and her chest squeezed. She never had been able to help Anita. God knew she had tried—and failed. But she could take care of this child and help her to have a good childhood. The sort of childhood she and Anita had missed.

She got into bed and reclined there on the cool pillows for a few minutes, gazing at nothing. Finally she turned out the light and slipped down beneath the warm covers. The temperature had fallen drastically into the thirties.

Extremes of spring trying to come and winter still holding on with strong fingers, she thought.

That was how she felt, too. She was both extremely happy and extremely sad. Tears welled in her eyes, as she thought of the wonderful day she had experienced with loved ones, and the dear, wonderful man she was to marry in a wedding for which she longed with all her heart. She thought of her mother's distress, of her sister's self-destruction, and of Stuart. She felt she had failed them all, and yet, what else could she have done?

She wished she had spoken more kindly. She wished she had had answers for everyone.

The tears ran down her cheeks, and she felt hardly able to breathe. She slipped out of bed, to her knees, folding her hands in prayer. Thank you, God, for the wonderful day we all enjoyed...for finding that perfect dress to wear on the plane...that Corrine was so happy with the things she bought...that Charlotte is saying yes to love. Thank you for Tate.

Precious gratitude washed over her, like a healing potion.

Help me to give whatever I can to Tate, my gift of a partner that you have given me. Look after my mother…and my dear sister, Anita…and Stuart, wherever he is. I give them to You. I know I can't handle all their needs. Thank you for watching over all of us.

She climbed back into bed and cuddled beneath the comforter. The next instant she was startled by a plop on her bed.

Oh, it was Munro. He came up and pressed close to her side.

"How did you know?" she whispered, putting out a hand to pet his fur. She had become accustomed to Munro appearing at certain key times.

"Thank you, Munro." Curling around him, she drifted off to sleep.

Tate was enjoying a Sunday afternoon siesta on his porch when the call came from his detective friend. Stuart James had been located. "In the hospital. Police brought him in. He'd collapsed at a gas station Thursday night. Word is that he's due to be released tomorrow morning."

"They found Stuart?" asked his mother, who had appeared in the doorway.

"Yes." Tate got to his feet, then stood there a moment, gathering his breath in preparation for telling Marilee. He didn't quite understand the great reluctance that came over him.

"You don't have to tell her," his mother said, watching him closely.

That had occurred to him. What if he didn't tell

Marilee where Stuart was? There was a big chance this would mean no more Stuart James in their lives. Problem gone.

"Yes, I do," he said.

"Yes, you do," his mother agreed with a gentle smile. "But let her decide for herself what she wants to do."

He knew that, he thought impatiently, as he went down the porch steps and across the backyards and through Marilee's back door, calling out her name.

"Just a minute!" came her answer, in a curiously panicked tone.

Corrine appeared, barring the swinging door. "You can't come in here. Aunt Marilee is in her weddin' dress.... She's havin' alterations."

Here was a perfect excuse to just turn around and walk back home. Perhaps during a delay in telling her, James would disappear again.

He went to the refrigerator and drew out a pitcher of cold tea, pouring himself a glass, keeping his back to the swinging door and thinking of walking out the back door.

A minute later he heard the swinging door open. He slowly turned to see Marilee tying her robe around her. She asked the instant their eyes met, "Has Stuart been found?"

He felt a flash of anger at the dying man.

"He's in a hospital down in Wichita Falls." And he had better really be dying, or Tate might kill him.

Twenty-Four

Getting through to new beginnings...

At the last minute, before heading out the door with Tate, it occurred to Marilee that she had to explain to the children about Stuart. She sat with them on the porch, on the top step.

"I have to tell you two something about Willie Lee's father."

Two pairs of eyes regarded her. Corrine's dark eyes were wary; Willie Lee's were soft and wide. *Give me the right words, Lord.*

Willie Lee said, "My fa-ther is sick."

Marilee, more relieved than surprised, nodded. "Yes, he is. And he needs somewhere to stay where he isn't alone...where people can take care of him, so Tate and I are going to go get him and bring him here to stay with us.

"Well, with you and Tate," she said, her gaze moving from Willie Lee to Corrine. "Corrine and I are going to move over to Papa Tate's house, and he will move over here, with Willie Lee and his daddy. That way your daddy can have my room."

The two pairs of eyes blinked.

"This house will be for the guys." With the

thought of leaving Willie Lee at night, she reached over to touch him. "And Papa Tate's house will be for the girls. Just until the wedding. After that we'll all live together over at Mr....Papa Tate's house, and Stuart can have this house, so we can still be nearby to take care of him."

That about covered it, as much as she felt she needed to cover it. If the children had questions, they kept them to themselves, and Marilee wasn't going to encourage the asking. She left them with instructions to go inside and help Aunt Vella and Franny get things ready.

Tate drove, and as he backed out of the driveway, Marilee said, "I don't know how I will leave Willie Lee at night."

Tate said, "I'll be with him, Marilee. I promise."

"I know…. I trust that, or I'd never do this."

"I forgot to tell Franny where the sheets for my bed are kept." It was the third thing to pop into her mind that she had forgotten.

"Corrine will show her."

"I don't know if Corrine knows. And my mattress requires those deep pocket sheets."

"Corrine knows everything, and besides, your house isn't that big. I'm sure they'll find them."

She nodded, blinking back sudden tears. "I love your mother, Tate." She was overwhelmed at the situation, and her heart seemed raw with feelings rushing through it at incredible speeds. "What would we have done had she not come up?" She was still amazed at how things seem to fit; Franny had hospice training and experience, and Stuart needed someone to take care of him.

Tate reached over and took her hand. "All this is right up Mom's alley. And she was planning on stayin' anyway.... I forgot to tell you. She told me she was movin' in with Winston."

Marilee took that in, and guilt fell over her. "Oh, I'm sorry we have waylaid her plans."

"Postponed. She doesn't mind. She just wants to be up here with us now." He rubbed her hand with his thumb, as if trying to impart strength.

"Well, I'm sure glad of that. She's so good for Corrine...good for all of us."

They had reached the outskirts of Wichita Falls. She took up the paper with the sketched directions to the hospital that she'd gotten when she had called to make certain a Stuart James was still a patient there.

"Marilee...you know that Stuart may not fall in with the idea of comin' back with us. Just because you've decided this, doesn't mean that he will."

"I know."

She squeezed Tate's hand and imagined him in Corrine's narrow bed. He had assured her it would be fine, although he would appreciate just blankets and not the floral bedspread.

The floor station was busy. Finally a nurse responded to their inquiry. "Yes, let's see...Mr. Stuart James...he's to be released in the morning." She pointed down the hall. "Third door on the right. It's a double room, but he's in there alone."

Marilee looked at Tate.

"I'll wait there," he said, indicating a nearby alcove with chairs and a sofa.

They kissed quickly, and she turned and left him,

walking along the hallway alone, experiencing the rising urge to tiptoe. The door to Stuart's room was ajar. Was it the right one? Mistakes were made in hospitals. Yes, there was his name in one of the two slots beside the door. The other slot was empty.

The door was ajar, and there came the sound of the television. She peered inside through the narrow opening. The first bed was unoccupied, and the dividing curtain hid most of the bed on the far side next to the window.

All she could see was feet beneath the white covers. She stared at them. She could not ever recall Stuart lying in bed; he had always gotten up first thing upon opening his eyes and never gotten back in bed until he was ready for sleep at night.

She hoped she didn't give him a heart attack, appearing like this.

Knocking lightly, she went in. His eyes popped wide when he saw her. Words escaped her. She went to him and flung her arms around him.

He shook his head as she talked. "I don't need your pity."

"Oh, yes, you do," she said, startling him. "Stuart, don't be a martyr. Do what is good for all of us...for Willie Lee, for me—and for yourself."

He looked at her. "Let me get dressed. I can't discuss this wearing a hospital gown."

When she did not move from the side of the bed, he motioned with his hand, as if sweeping her off. She was heartened to see that he appeared stronger than when she had first laid eyes on him.

She got up, went to the edge of the curtain and stood with her back turned, continuing to explain the perfection of the plan, speaking all the while she heard drawers opened and closed, and throughout her assistance in getting his shirt and slacks from the closet on the wall.

Stuart's discharge from the hospital was obtained that very afternoon. The nurse appeared quite relieved that the patient had a family to go to, and that the hospital would not be responsible for letting him go driving off by himself.

Marilee, feeling her job for the moment was done upon getting him to go along with them, encouraged him into the front seat and left him and Tate to each other. Men, being men, they talked immediately of sports and vehicles and the journalism they both so loved, leaving Marilee to relax in the back seat, where she observed the two males. Both were in a hard place and handling it amazingly well.

Whatever lay ahead, they would all get through. *You always have gotten through, haven't you?* she heard in a whisper from the recesses of her brain.

The next thing she knew, they were driving down Main Street. She knew it was Main because she opened her eyes and saw the neon Blaines' Drugstore sign.

"Marilee...honey, we're almost home." Tate's voice.

She sat up. It was twilight. Streetlights had not yet come on. The buildings and trees and bushes were bathed in the ethereal glow of a sun now set but casting light upward. It had grown cold.

Stuart pressed the button to lower his window. He did it automatically, his hand moving there as if avoiding the door handle and the wild impulse that came over him to open the door and throw himself out before reaching Marilee's house, where he didn't think he could bear to walk inside. Somehow he had been confident and comfortable on the drive—he was, after all, most at home while traveling.

But now the trip was ending. He was reaching his destination, and suddenly he did not want to reach it. Trips he understood. Trips were in between times, when there were no expectations, nothing much required of him but to be carried along.

That was why he had always traveled, he saw in an instant of clarity. To avoid destinations, or to at least keep them to a minimum. There were things one had to do, accomplish, complete, upon reaching one's destination. Destinations always involved some sort of commitment.

The car came to a stop in Marilee's driveway, and when the engine died, Stuart felt like his energy did, too. He forced himself to move and get out, however, determined to keep his shoulders straight. The pity he was certain he would receive would be bad enough without his appearing pitiful. He wished angrily that he had never considered the idea of coming back here. It was a stupid idea. He didn't think he could take it.

He went to the rear of the vehicle to load himself with his own bags, camera cases around his neck, small duffel bag on one shoulder, a big one in hand. Tate took the other; he would look foolish to protest.

He was following Marilee up the walk—thank goodness she wasn't talking, saying something soothing—when he looked up and saw Willie Lee coming to meet him. He wondered what Marilee had told the boy about him.

"Hel-lo, Fa-ther." Willie Lee lifted a hand and took Stuart's and walked along beside him into the house, stepping across the threshold into his destination.

It was warm, inviting, comfortable. He was surprised, and relieved. For just then, he would let himself rest. He could think of facts later. For right now, he would be grateful to have come to a place that wasn't a hospital and where he wasn't alone.

Franny and Corrine had cooked a pot roast, vegetables, rolls and apple pie, and they ate the meal in the dining room beneath the warm glow of the hanging lamp, in the manner of a family, as indeed they were, Marilee reminded herself.

Afterward Tate said, "Well, Marilee, let me take you over and show you my surprise."

"A surprise?"

"Come on...no questions, just come along."

She ran her gaze around all the faces at the table, wondering if anyone knew what Tate was talking about. Franny and Corrine's expressions showed that they did.

Tate, having rounded the table, took her hand, drawing her up after him, leading her through the kitchen and out the back door into the night. She told him they probably should have gotten coats. Were they going far? Excitement washed over her at the anticipation of a surprise.

"Not far." Tate led her through the back gate and over to his house, where he paused at the top of the back step to tell her to close her eyes.

She obliged. Her heart had begun to beat hard, and she held tight to Tate's hand, a little fearful of tripping over the threshold. She thought she smelled a familiar odor. Paint?

"Wait until I tell you to open your eyes." The light was flipped on. "Okay, you can open them now."

Marilee opened her eyes.

Where was she? Tate's kitchen? Yes, but it was different. It was painted, although the doors were off the cabinets and sitting against the wall, and the countertop was partially ripped off.

"It isn't all finished." Tate said. "But we've begun."

"Oh, Tate." There was a new refrigerator, a new dishwasher, a new stove, and a new sink, too. He watched her look at all of it, and she did her best at oohing and aahing. She was impressed, but mostly she wanted to make certain her admiration matched his expectations.

He had done it for her. Tears filled her eyes.

"Don't go tearing up yet." He took her hand and led her through the house, up the stairs and down the landing to his bedroom, stopping in front of the closed door.

"You cannot go in this room until our wedding night," he told her. "You cannot open the door. In the next week, you will see men coming and going from this room, but you cannot go in there."

Men would be coming and going?

"Not even a peek?" she asked.

"Not even a peek, unless you want to spoil your surprise."

"I don't want to do that." She knew that if she spoiled her surprise, it would spoil it more for him.

"Good."

She threw her arms around his neck and brought her lips to his in a fierce and ardent kiss, until they both were out of breath. When she could speak, her voice came in a husky whisper.

"Tate Holloway, there is no other man like you on earth. I shall love you till the day I die."

When the telephone rang, Corrine was drying a pan and keeping an eye out the back window for Aunt Marilee and Papa Tate. She moved to the phone on the wall and answered, her mind immediately anticipating either her mother or her grandmother, and in either case she was wary.

"Hey, Corrine. It's me—Ricky Dale."

Her eyes popped wide. She looked over at Granny Franny, who seemed intent on cramming leftovers into the refrigerator. "Hey," she said.

There were long seconds of silence in which Corrine figured Ricky Dale had called her, so it was up to him to carry the conversation.

"Look, I got somethin' bad to tell you."

"You do?" She gripped the receiver.

"My grama's cat died."

"Oh." Then she thought to say, "I'm sorry, Ricky Dale. Is your grama real upset?"

"Mom says she's not. Mom just got back from over there. She said Grama seemed to be accepting everything now. She said Grama said the cat had ate real good, and then the next thing Grama found it dead. No sufferin'," he added.

"Well…good."

"I guess Willie Lee didn't cure it."

"Guess not."

Silence again.

"Are you gonna tell him...about my grama's cat?"

"Yeah, I'd better, or one of us might slip up, and then he'll find out anyway." She was a little irritated at Ricky Dale for letting the job fall to her.

Ricky Dale said, "Do you think it was just coincidence with Beau and the bird?"

"I don't know." She did not think it was coincidence with the dog and the bird, but she settled for saying, "Maybe he just can't do it all the time."

"Yeah, maybe."

Another silence.

Then Corrine said, "Hey, I'm movin' over to Tate's with Aunt Marilee. It's because Willie Lee's dad is goin' to live here for a while. He's sick and needs to be looked out for. You can call me over there, if I'm not here."

That sounded a little confusing, but Ricky Dale said, "Okay. My dad's got the number written right here on the wall."

After Corrine had hung up, she wondered if he had meant Tate's number was written on a piece of paper or actually on the wall. She could never bring herself to write on a wall.

She thought that maybe Willie Lee would be asleep. He had gotten his bath before supper. If he was asleep, she could wait to tell him about the cat. If he was asleep, she wasn't supposed to tell him, was the way she figured it.

But he wasn't asleep. He was on his bed, looking at his picture book of dogs, with Munro.

Corrine stopped in the doorway and looked across into her aunt Marilee's room. The light was on in there, where Mr. James was puttering around, putting away his things. Curious as to what the room looked like with him in it, she stepped back and peered cautiously. Mr. James was sitting on the end of the bed now. Just sitting there. Corrine didn't think the man was only sick. She thought he was dying, but no one wanted to say that.

Going on into her and Willie Lee's room, she quietly closed the door. Then she went over to his bed and told Willie Lee about the cat.

Willie Lee's bottom lip quivered, but he didn't cry. "It was a real-ly old cat," he said. "Real-ly, real-ly old."

"Yeah." Corrine chewed her bottom lip, then said, "Is that why you couldn't fix it, Willie Lee? Because it was so old?"

"May-be. I do not know. Mun-ro just told me may-be."

"Oh. Well, it was nice of you to try. Ricky Dale said his grandmother was not too upset."

She got up and retrieved her book bag, shoving favorite books into it, and her mother's picture, then looked around to see if there was anything else she wanted to make sure to take with her this first night.

Her gaze lit on Willie Lee. She wished she could take him. She didn't like leaving him over here, out of her sight. Willie Lee had hardly been out of her sight since she had come. The more she thought of this, the more she disliked leaving him.

"Willie Lee, don't go out the window while I'm over there at Papa Tate's house, okay?"

He looked at her and blinked.

"Promise me, Willie Lee."

"I am one of the guys now, Cor-rine. I am a boy and can do some things."

"I know that, but I'm still your *older* cousin, and I'm supposed to look out for you. Just don't go out the window. You'll probably get Papa Tate all upset if you go out the window."

Willie Lee's eyebrows went together for a thoughtful moment, and then he told her in a factual manner, "No. Pa-pa Tate does not get up-set."

Sometimes Willie Lee could be really smart.

Twenty-Five

Moving on...

March, which had come "sneaking in," as Tate put it, showed its true colors and began to roar in its first full week. The temperature bounced back and forth from cold to warm, sometimes changing twenty degrees in one day. Storms rolled from the high plains, bringing tornado conditions, winds that whipped tree branches beginning to bud with leaves, and a total of almost three inches of rain. This was quite normal for the season in Oklahoma, so no one was overly shaken up. The tornado sirens went off twice, which sent more people outside to watch the sky than to take shelter.

Tate, Stuart, Willie Lee and Munro were among these sky watchers all the way out in the yard, near the curb, for the best view, while Marilee went back and forth from the television reports to the front door, trying to keep an eye on both the TV and her loved ones, anticipating when she would have to run out there and grab Willie Lee to race him to shelter. The men were on their own. Franny and Corrine, and Vella when she was there, stood in between, on the porch.

Marilee caught sight of yellow forsythia bushes that had burst into bloom, and she began to be concerned that none would be found still blooming by her wedding date. She watched each bush she found, telling herself that forsythia bushes surely were not a life-and-death matter.

Marilee's mother, who took the tack of brushing off Marilee's attempt to talk about the situation concerning Corrine and Anita, pretending, as she always had, that there was no problem, assured Marilee that she had a friend who lived half an hour farther north and who had plenty of forsythia that should bloom at exactly the correct time. "I will cut them for you," her mother said, quite amazing Marilee, who wondered how her mother would be able to accomplish this task at the same time as being on her Caribbean cruise but decided not to pursue this question and to accept the generous offer in the spirit in which it was given.

"Thank you, Mother. I would so appreciate it."

Why was it, when there were so many true worries she could think of—wedding preparations, Stuart's sickness, Anita's self-destructiveness, mothering children, becoming a wife, setting up a new household—that she had to dwell on insignificant things like the availability of forsythia?

Thinking of forsythia was so much easier, she decided; all the rest of her concerns could be, and very often were, overwhelming.

Despite a constant sense that she might be overlooking something, the wedding preparations appeared to be thoroughly on track, complete with the country-swing band of which Winston and Franny—and Vella, too, who had accompanied them to the

VFW hall—approved. The three older people had become something of a trio.

Margaret Wyatt was making the final nips and tucks on Marilee's and Corrine's dresses, and Tate's and Parker's suits were approved.

"We don't have to wear tuxedos, do we?" Tate had asked anxiously at the beginning of planning. "I'd really rather not."

"No, dear, we'll keep to an informal wedding. Your grey suit will be perfect. You look so handsome in it. And Parker has a sharp-looking blue one he bought for his mother's wedding a couple of years ago."

"It's pretty convenient that you are familiar with Parker's wardrobe," Tate observed.

A little uncertain as to the exact nature of Tate's attitude, Marilee responded forthrightly, "It does make life easier, doesn't it?"

She had wanted a cozy, informal wedding, and she would get the informal, but cozy was another matter. The replies were coming in for the reception; it appeared everyone they had invited intended to come, even just about all the employees of Cooper's Appliances. The refreshment order had been increased twice. Marilee was adamant, though, on using china serving dishes. She was not going paper-plate informal.

Franny and Vella were industriously making bows for the pews and reception table and anywhere else they could think to put them; anyone who passed by during a critical bow-making procedure was asked to be of assistance and put forth his or her finger. Once Marilee came upon the surprising sight of Stuart with one index finger toward Franny and the other toward

Vella. He looked quite disconcerted, a man who had managed to avoid intimate ties finally all tied up.

It appeared, very much to Marilee's amazement, that Stuart coming into their midst was proving to be a success in ways no one had imagined. A path began to be worn across the backyards, with all the coming and going from early morning into the night between Tate's and Marilee's houses.

There was constantly something forgotten in one house that was necessary in the other. Within the first two days of Stuart's arrival, Marilee's closet was empty of her many things and Stuart's belongings had taken their place. All the clutter on the table beneath her bedroom window and the nightstands was now in the bedroom she used at the big old house, as well as being scattered about other rooms there. In this gentle fashion Marilee's and Corrine's clothes and personal items, their very lives, were eased over to the big Holloway house.

To keep his things at his own house and not be hauling them back and forth, Tate returned home for major showering and dressing. He liked seeing Marilee's things living beside his own. He got excited when he saw her brush on the bathroom vanity. Once he stopped on the landing and inhaled deeply. His mother coming out of her room asked what he was doing.

''I'm soakin' up Marilee's essence,'' he said.

Because of the ever-increasing remodeling and repairs proceeding in the kitchen of the big house—and now a new bathroom begun beneath the stairway—meals were either cooked at Marilee's house and eaten in her dining area, or brought from the Main Street Café or the IGA delicatessen.

Franny discovered that Stuart liked espresso, so she bought an espresso machine and took up drinking it with him along about midmorning, when Stuart would arise. Within two days of this, Winston and Vella joined them, coming down Church Street and cutting through the backyards, adding to the traffic on the path.

On her second morning in Tate's house, Marilee stepped out of the bathroom and encountered three strange men passing by on the landing. Each said a polite, "Hello, ma'am," slipped into the master bedroom and shut the door. Down in the kitchen, where Tate joined her with mocha and rolls from the IGA, she could hear faint thuds from the master bedroom.

She gazed at Tate, looked at the ceiling and again at Tate, who smiled and said, "Don't spoil your surprise."

When she came back from getting the children to school, two men were working in the kitchen, and Franny was checking out their progress. Two of the bedroom workmen came through the back door, bringing a large king-size mattress. Marilee thought it big enough to accommodate their entire family.

The next day, as she was clearing out worn and faded towels from the bathroom closet, she caught the sound of hammering in the bedroom on the other side of the door. She pressed her ear against the door, then carefully laid her hand on the knob.

Drawing herself up straight, she let go of the knob and firmly left the room.

Tuesday afternoon, at her own home, when Corrine brought her the mail, Marilee found two envelopes addressed to Stuart. They were fan letters from the first part of his photo article on fifties' motels that had run in the Sunday edition of *The Valentine Voice*. Both had been sent to the *Voice* offices, but Julia Jenkins-Tinsley had forwarded them to Marilee's house. That explained how word of Stuart's presence and situation got around town so quickly.

Friends and neighbors, both sympathetic and curious, began to drop by to visit, often bringing food, and since there was so much food, people felt comfortable to stay quite a long time. A bridge game started up one afternoon, in which Stuart did not participate but took pictures with the aim of doing a study on the face of vanishing small-town America.

He began to take pictures all over the place. It seemed as if every time she turned around, Marilee heard the clicking of a camera shutter. Stuart took up going for walks around town and taking pictures that Tate began planning to run in special Sunday edition inserts. Charlotte searched the files for old photographs, which Tate paired with Stuart's new ones, resulting in the first insert to be entitled: "Valentine Then and Now."

"Small-town America isn't vanishing," stated Mayor Upchurch, who dropped by one evening and sat on the front porch with everyone. "It's just changing. Life moves on here, same as anywhere, except maybe a little slower."

As soon as the words came out of his mouth, the mayor had the idea of a brand-new slogan for the town, that it was time to leave behind their current slogan of Flag Town of America—people were letting their flags get ragged and not replacing them—and become the Small Town on the Move.

The debate about town then became: small town on the move to where? Everyone had different ideas.

Tate did an editorial on the subject and invited people to drop by the offices to give their opinions, which he would then publish in the paper.

Charlotte, who hated this practice of open invitation to all and sundry, put up a sign in front of her desk that read: For All Opinions, See The Editor. Beneath it was an arrow pointing to Tate's office. She told Tate not to even think of asking her to get anyone coffee.

"I wouldn't think of it, Miss Charlotte," he said.

There was something else that went on in the town that Marilee, after hearing of the third occurrence, realized was a result of the situation with Stuart.

The first occurrence was Fayrene Gardner down at the Main Street Café telling Marilee that she had telephoned her mother, from whom she had been estranged for fifteen years.

Fayrene said, "I did not want to drop dead, like my Dave did last year, and meet St. Peter and have to explain to him why I was not speakin' to my mother." She added, "It was bad enough that Dave and I didn't get back together when we had the chance. We kept puttin' it off. It doesn't pay to put off."

The next, and quite amazing, thing to happen was Leo Pahdocony, Sr. booking a trip to Cancún for his and Reggie's upcoming twentieth anniversary. When Reggie found out that her husband had not only come up with the idea but had himself done the entire work of making the arrangements and all she had to do was pack her bags, she had gone white as a sheet and sunk into her chair. Charlotte, always alert, had made her put her head between her legs.

While Reggie was down there, she whispered to

Charlotte, "He must have a lover…or maybe some horrible disease."

Charlotte said with all practicality, "So what if it's both? Take the chance for this celebration while you have it, Reg."

The third happening Marilee heard about was the return of her neighbor's wife. Julia Jenkins-Tinsley told the tale when Marilee went into the post office to pick up a parcel for Franny.

"Oh, hey, Marilee." Julia was hanging up the phone. "I was just talkin' to your cousin Belinda. I was tellin' her about your neighbor Leon Purvis and his wife gettin' back together. Did you know that Stella's come home?"

Julia leaned on the counter and told all about how Leon Purvis had located his wife on her trucking route and begged her to come home to try their marriage again. Stella Purvis admitted that part of it had been Leon suffering a backache, but that on the telephone he had cried and said he didn't want to die with regret about their marriage. Stella had gotten home within six hours and said she was tired of the open road anyway.

"Stella was in here this mornin' fillin' out change of address forms and told me all about it herself," said Julia. "She started cryin', even."

Marilee had found the parcel slip in her purse and handed it across the counter. Julia picked it up but didn't quit talking.

"I asked her if Leon had told her about your Stuart, and she said no, so I told her about how you've taken in your sick ex-husband, right into your home. I tell you, hon, I am so touched, and so are a lot of other people. It is sure makin' people do some thinking. I'll bet that whole thing is why Leon called Stella. Did you hear about Fayrene and her mother?''

"That Fayrene called her mother over in Childress?''

"Yep. Her mother's comin' over here at the end of the month. She didn't even come last year when Fayrene had that setback about her ex-husband, but she is comin' now.

"I think you are a saint for takin' in your ex, but there's some around that can't imagine how you could have brought him into your house after all this time and how he treated you and Willie Lee. And there's a few sayin' it all has to do with Stuart being a big-time journalist and leaving you and Willie Lee a lot of money.'' She cast Marilee a curious glance.

"Would you get Franny's parcel? I need to go get the children from school.''

"Oh, yes. It's right here.'' Julia stepped aside, looking over some shelves, then reached in and pulled out a large padded envelope that she passed across the counter. "Well, you are a rare woman, Marilee. Tate and Stuart are lucky men.'' She gestured at the parcel. "It's from Frederick's of Hollywood. How old is Tate's mother?''

"Old enough to shop where she wants,'' said Marilee. "Thanks, Julia.''

She turned and went out into the muggy air of a spring day and started down the sidewalk. She got out of sight of the post office window before checking the package for verification that it really was from Frederick's of Hollywood.

It was. Well. So many things were not what they appeared.

Take her own life, for instance. For her part, Marilee knew there was a lot of talk around town about the situation with her and Tate and Stuart, and there of course was a lot of rehashing as to how she had been engaged the previous fall to Parker.

My goodness, how could she end up looking like a vamp, when she had hardly had any love life for her entire existence?

She herself did not quite understand her own actions concerning Stuart. She was neither a saint nor a sinner, and the idea that some people would consider her in either light made her uncomfortable.

She knew she had simply done what she must. It was tied up in her desire to give Willie Lee every chance to know his father, and his father a chance at knowing his son. And yet, it was more than that. She knew that to not do what she could to help Stuart, who truly was all alone, somehow denied herself, who and what she was. She believed, rightly or wrongly, that she would want someone to help her if the situation were reversed. Certainly, truth be told, she was benefiting from Stuart's presence as much as was everyone else, and it had not cost her anything out of her life but a little time and a house that would have been going empty anyway.

It was, too, as if something needed finishing, and this was the way to do it.

Still, Marilee had a little difficulty with how smoothly everything was going. She had expected more problems concerning Stuart, and she felt uneasy about the wedding preparations seemingly going on without a hitch. In her experience, when life ran this smoothly, something dire was about to happen. Fully aware that this was a negative attitude, she tried to shake it but did not quite succeed.

The truth that came floating up in her mind at that moment was her concern over the possibility that Stuart might drop dead right on the eve of the wedding.

There, she had admitted it. So much for her supposed altruism.

She had, in fact, been observing her ex-husband closely, trying to gauge his waning energy. It didn't seem to be particularly waning. Yes, he took an hour or two's nap in the evening, but this could be attributed to his walking all over town each day. He had even gotten a bit of a tan. He'd always been skinny, so his current gauntness was not any particular indication of a lack of health. Tate reported that he and Stuart—*her ex-husband,* she seemed to have to remind her intended—sat up nights talking about the ever-expanding photo article on Valentine and small-town America in general. Stuart had contacted two national magazines, and both were interested in his photographs and the concept.

Marilee hoped very much that he would live at least until after the wedding and honeymoon. She really hoped they did not get a nasty surprise and find him dead on the eve of the wedding…or maybe *during* the wedding.

God knew she was doing the best she could. She would trust God to handle everything and know all would work out for the best, no matter what happened, and she would take it as it came. Yes, she would.

Whatever else was there to do?

Franny showed Marilee and Corrine what she had ordered from Frederick's of Hollywood—a bright

floral kimono robe and a padded girdle. Inspecting
the girdle quite thoroughly, Corrine said, "Granny
Franny, why does it have these little pillowy
things?" The pillowy things were the padding on the
derriere.

"Because I have a bony behind, and I wanted to
see if this would make sitting on the church pews
more comfortable."

When Marilee pointed out that the church pews
were padded, Franny promptly replied, "Not
enough."

Then she brought forward one more thing she had
purchased from Frederick's—a shimmering white
stretch satin and lace strapless teddy, a gift for Marilee.

When Marilee eyed it uncertainly, Franny said, "It
is just the thing for underneath your wedding dress.
It is for you alone, no one else will see, and wearing
it will make you feel one-hundred-percent woman.
Remember that, Corrine," she told the young girl.
"God made you a woman, and that is something to
respect and honor."

The way Franny put it, it would be sacrilegious
not to wear the sexy thing.

Marilee donned the teddy. It was amazingly comfortable. And it did make her feel very much of a
woman. "I didn't know I could look like this," she
said, beholding herself and her breasts, which had
become voluptuous, in the mirror on the chifforobe.

"Honey, those catalog models don't have all their
endowments naturally, you know," said Franny quite
practically. "They simply know how to make the
best of what they have by squeezin' it all around."

Marilee slipped into her wedding dress. It felt

wonderful on her skin. Seeing her reflection in the mirror, she drew in a breath.

"You look beautiful, Aunt Marilee."

Corrine's tone reflected the awe Marilee felt. She touched her bare skin above the scooped neckline, then smoothed the soft, flowing skirt that fell to just above her ankles.

"You will do my son and your mother proud," said Franny.

"I would like to move my desk to your house." She handed Tate his morning coffee. "To the alcove in your living room. It's so perfect. It's so much bigger than my living room. And I just love the area, with the windows. I was thinking that maybe we could move your small desk from the dining room and have ours side by side."

"In the living room...well, okay. What do we do about the stuff that's already there?"

"I called Albert's Antiques out on the highway. They'll buy them, if you are agreeable."

His eyebrows went up. "Oh." The eyebrows went down. "Fine. Then your desk is the first thing we'll move." He leaned over and kissed her, as he always did when seeking to please.

"I'd like to do it today."

"You would? Today?"

She nodded. "We could ask Parker to help, to bring his old pickup truck."

"Are we in a hurry?"

She felt a little silly and had to get courage to speak honestly. "Not a hurry, but I want it done. It just seems that moving my desk over to your house will make certain that the wedding will happen on schedule. Like putting a firm nail into the plan.'' She felt more confident; it all made sense to her. ''Like believing and acting on the belief.''

''Okay, darlin','' he said instantly. ''You got it.''

Early that afternoon, Parker came with his old pickup truck, and he and Tate hauled over the desk, while Marilee, Stuart, Franny and the children came along the path with the computer, lamp, pictures and whatnots. Marilee had chairs and tables moved from the alcove and directed the placing of her desk, then the moving of Tate's desk from where it was stuck in the dining-room corner. It was a small desk, but he said he liked it.

''Didn't I give you this?'' asked Stuart, picking up a blue china vase and regarding it closely.

''Yes...and I love it.'' She took it and placed it correctly.

''I gave her this,'' Parker piped up, waving a letter opener.

''I gave her the living-room nook,'' said Tate quite happily.

The antique chairs and crooked walnut table now sitting in the middle of the living room were carried out the front door and loaded into Parker's truck, which sat at the foot of the steps.

Marilee stood on the front porch of the big old house and watched the truck drive away, in the front seat all four of the important men in her life: Tate, Parker, Stuart, and Willie Lee, who had said, ''I am one of the gu-uys,'' and climbed in on top of Stuart's lap.

Franny came up beside her. ''There go the men who have contributed to the woman you are. You are blessed.''

"Yes," Marilee said, her vision blurring as a surge of gratitude flooded her heart. "Yes, I am."

All the hurts from her past were fading away, she realized. Life flowing on like a river, always. Pain and joy mingling. Now was a time of healing. Now was a time of forgiveness. Now was a time for letting go of the past and moving on with her new life.

She wondered why, although she felt herself moving on, she also felt a foot dragging.

Twenty-Six

Unexpected surprises…

Papa Tate was given a surprise bachelor party, and Aunt Marilee was given a surprise wedding shower, and each knew about the other's party but not about their own.

In fact, Aunt Marilee had told everyone that she didn't want a party, but Aunt Vella said, "That's not acceptable on her part. She'll have to bear up," and Granny Franny and Charlotte agreed; the three of them got both parties going, putting Parker and Mr. James in charge of Papa Tate's party, but pretty much telling them everything to do.

There was one thing Corrine noticed that Mr. James did all on his own, or at least started all on his own, and that was to fix up a poster of pictures of Aunt Marilee from when she was a kid on through the time of their marriage to display for Papa Tate. Aunt Vella jumped in to help him, and searched through albums belonging to Aunt Marilee in order to get some of the pictures; even though he was a photographer, he didn't have but a couple of pictures of Marilee. Corrine had seen him take one out of his wallet and put on the poster board, right in the middle.

Granny Franny liked the idea, so she gave Mr. James pictures of Papa Tate and had him make up a second poster board. It was decided that the poster of Papa Tate would go to Aunt Marilee's party, and the poster of Aunt Marilee would go to Papa Tate's party.

Corrine and Willie Lee were included on all the secret plans and admonished half a dozen times not to tell. Corrine knew neither she nor Willie Lee would tell, but she wasn't so certain about all the grown-ups, especially Aunt Vella's daughter, Belinda. She heard Aunt Vella tell Granny Franny that she wasn't inviting Julia Jenkins-Tinsley until Friday evening, to minimize the possibility of Julia letting everything slip.

It was decided to have Aunt Marilee's party down at Aunt Vella's house, where she had a big front porch and her flagstone patio was now finished, even if the landscaper had fallen off on a quality job— Aunt Vella's description—and the party could flow inside and out, if the weather was really nice.

Papa Tate's party would be at his own house, where he would least expect it. Aunt Vella said that men didn't care about a house being partially torn up for renovation.

After church, Papa Tate and Aunt Marilee took each other to the IGA. Each one thought they were keeping the other busy. As a further diversion, Granny Franny gave them a list of groceries she herself wanted, saying that she and Winston were giving the rose club a little party on Tuesday.

Willie Lee, when Granny Franny tried to take him

down to Aunt Vella's, insisted on staying at Papa Tate's house for the bachelor party. "Me and Munro are gu-uys," he said, standing firm, with arms crossed, Munro right beside him.

Corrine regarded her cousin with concern. She felt caught between taking up for him against the adults and leaving him at a place that she found questionable. She had seen Parker bring in a case of beer, and this did not set well with her. She did not know what went on at bachelor parties, but she had caught snatches of comments that led her to suspect them. Ricky Dale had told her that his older brother had described to him a bachelor party, and that such a party entailed a lot of drinking, nude women and pornographic movies. This sounded like what had gone on at a house down the street from Corrine in Fort Worth, which had been filled with unsavory characters and to which the police had often been called. Corrine, who could not imagine Papa Tate drunk or with a nude woman, had told Ricky Dale that she figured Papa Tate's party would be the NASCAR race that he liked to watch on Sundays, and talking about sports and what those nuts up in Washington were doing. Privately, though, she was not completely certain of this assessment.

Then Mr. James said, "Of course Willie Lee stays with us. I'll watch out for him."

As far as Corrine had seen, Mr. James had never watched out for Willie Lee, but there he stood, with his hand on Willie Lee's shoulder. She eyed him and recalled him placing the picture of Aunt Marilee from his wallet so very carefully in the middle of the poster.

Granny Franny agreed to letting Willie Lee stay.

Corrine slowly followed the older woman out to the little MG, with the top down, and slipped into the passenger seat, where Granny Franny set the cake from Sweetie Cakes bakery—a big sheet of double chocolate, with white icing—into her lap, and they headed off to Aunt Vella's house up the hill.

The guys did not have cake, but submarine sandwiches and pickles and chips and jalapeño dip, and stuff like that that went with beer and Coke and root beer and ice tea. And farting, Ricky Dale said.

This was the first ladies' party Corrine, who had only school experience with parties, anyway, had ever been to. She slipped into being invisible and passed around the crystal dishes of mints and refreshed cups of punch, while taking in all the expressions and actions and comments made by the ladies. She was amazed by how Reggie Pahdocony jumped up in front of all the ladies and pretended to sing into a spoon, sounding just like Reba McEntire. Tammy Crawford liked to say, "I don't think so," in a smart way, and she wasn't careful where she put her sweaty tea glass. She set it right on Aunt Vella's polished mahogancy end table, but Corrine wiped the water up quickly. The general consensus was great surprise that Zona Porter came. The small grey woman sat quietly in a corner with a smile on her face. Miss Charlene—Papa Tate always called her Miss Charlene—was unusually vivacious. Corrine heard her grama Norma use this word. Miss Charlene hugged just everyone; she smelled of fresh perfume that Corrine liked.

Aunt Marilee's face was flushed, and she was smiling very big and laughing with delight each time

she opened a gift. A few of the gifts were very lacy
bras and panties. Corrine couldn't wait to get a closer
view of these; she was beginning to understand that
those women in the Victoria's Secret catalog weren't
shaped like they seemed at all, but made themselves
that way with underwear. This seemed a lot of trouble and silliness to Corrine. She didn't ever intend to
do it but to wear jeans and T-shirts all her life.

"Little girl, could you get me some more mints?"
Miss Mildred, the old lady who lived with Mr. Winston, held one of the crystal dishes toward Corrine.

"Yes, ma'am," said Corrine, who eyed the dish
with some amazement, then looked at the big purse
the older woman clutched on her lap. Corrine did not
think it her place to be rude and question.

She went through the dining room, passing Grama
Norma, who was speaking to Charlotte. "I wish
Anita was here for this. It has been forever since I
had my girls together. Did Vella call her, do you
know?"

"Vella tried to reach Anita all week, Norma," said
Charlotte. "She left messages, but Anita hasn't re-
turned them. Marilee told me she'd tried to call
Anita, too."

"Well, she might not be back from South America
yet. Her boyfriend, Louis, has a lot of business down
in South America, you know."

Corrine moved on through to the kitchen, where
Aunt Vella and Granny Franny were cutting the cake
and putting the pieces on Aunt Vella's fine china.

"It's good for Willie Lee to be with the men,"
Granny Franny was saying.

"Stuart really is a surprise with this, isn't he?"
Aunt Vella said.

And Granny replied, "People can rise to occasions when given the chance."

Corrine filled the dish with mints, and, laying an eye on her as if seeing her for the first time, Granny Franny asked her to start handing out the cake.

"I'll be back.... I'm takin' these mints to Miss Mildred. She wanted some more."

"Oh, no! We don't do that!" said Aunt Vella, throwing up her hands. "Mildred is filling her purse.... She can't have this much candy. Just take her this bitty piece of cake. Thank you, sugar."

As Corrine passed back through the rooms, she heard that Reggie Pahdocony thought she might be going into early menopause, and Julia Jenkins-Tinsley had an overactive thyroid, and Imperia Brown whispered something about an overactive mouth.

Miss Mildred, upon sight of the cake, seemed not to remember she had asked for the mints. "Oh, thank you, little girl."

Corrine stepped aside, casting furtive looks at the older woman, wondering if she would stuff the cake into her purse, but she sat and ate it with a smile.

Someone asked Aunt Marilee what something old she would be wearing for the wedding, and Aunt Marilee replied that she would wear earrings that she and Anita had bought down in Fort Worth a long time ago. Corrine saw a shadow pass across Aunt Marilee's face. Probably no one else noticed it, but Corrine did.

"Honey, why don't you wear my pearl necklace and earrings?" Grama Norma said. "They would be lovely."

"I want to wear the earrings Anita and I bought," Aunt Marilee said.

Grama Norma wasn't going to let it go, though, and kept saying how she thought the pearls would be more refined than costume jewelry. Corrine saw how her aunt got the straight back and small but determined smile, and all of a sudden for some reason she was thinking of her mother with great longing.

She had tried and tried to hold the feelings off, but now, because everyone had mentioned her mother's name, the feelings were coming over her in a flood. She could imagine her aunt Marilee and her mother buying the earrings. Her mother loved dangling earrings.

Corrine slipped unnoticed back into the kitchen and out the back door. She sat on the steps. Aunt Vella didn't have a back porch.

Corrine could see down to the corrals behind Mr. Winston's house. The horses stood at the wooden fence, swishing their tails.

A tiny fly lit on her arm; it was the first one that year to plague her. She noticed then how still and heavy the air had become. She gazed up at the sky that was covered by solid grey cloud. It was almost the same color as the stones in Aunt Vella's new flagstone patio.

Then she was lost in her imagination as she saw the image of her mother sweeping along toward her, smiling in the beautiful manner she did whenever she was having a good day. Oh, Corrine loved those days when her mother was having a good day! In her imagination, she hopped up and ran to her mother, who hugged her, and then produced a gold box with a gold ribbon and said to Corrine, "Oh, honey, I didn't forget you. I just had to find the exact right thing, and then the exact right box to put it in, and to bring it to you myself."

Corrine, whose eyes had filled with tears, was brought out of the daydream by a blaring noise. Puzzled, she listened to the sound. A siren, she realized at the same moment of noticing a rising breeze.

The tornado siren!

Instantly on her feet and filled with panic, she tried to get in the back door, but couldn't get the knob to turn. Behind her, the screen door banged against her back. Then, at last, she burst into the kitchen. It was empty.

"Corrine! Corrine!" That was Aunt Marilee.

"I'm here!" she called, even as she raced through the dining room, where women were on their feet and peering out the north windows and jabbering so that the siren could hardly be heard.

In the living room, Aunt Marilee took hold of her and headed for the front door.

Aunt Vella, standing at the door, stopped them and barked orders. "You can't go down there now. Those men will take care of Willie Lee. You see to Corrine. You two get in the cellar."

Corrine saw the hesitation on Aunt Marilee's face.

"It's comin' out of the west, right at us," said Reggie, who had turned on the television for the weather warning.

Then Aunt Marilee said to Corrine, "Come on. We're gettin' in the shelter."

"There's only room for six in the shelter," Aunt Vella said, raising her voice to everyone. "Four of you follow Marilee and Corrine, and you others come over here and help me make room in the closet under the stairs. Mildred, sugar, you come over here with me.''

As Aunt Marilee jerked her along, Corrine caught sight of Miss Mildred crying and waddling toward Aunt Vella.

The wind was high out the back door. Granny Franny was there ahead of them and trying to get the cellar door open, but her tiny size was no match for the door in the wind that jerked it out of her hands. Corrine and Aunt Marilee took hold to help, and then Aunt Marilee was stuffing Corrine down into a cinderblock cubbyhole in the ground. Corrine looked back up for Aunt Marilee, but there was Reggie Pahdocony coming in.

''Aunt Marilee!'' Corrine screamed.

''Shush…she's comin' honey,'' Reggie told her, pulling her back to the rear of the cubbyhole, where Corrine waited with a thumping heart, until she could maneuver herself to sit beside Aunt Marilee, after her aunt had closed the cellar door.

She found herself surrounded by five other women, all of them squished together and panting hard and smelling like perfume and fear. Aunt Marilee, who had miraculously produced a flashlight, pointed the beam downward, and it sent an eerie glow on their faces.

Granny Franny had not come down, Corrine saw with distress.

''Good Lord, just listen to that wind,'' said Imperia Brown.

They all listened. Corrine sure hoped Granny Franny wasn't blowing away. She wasn't very big. Corrine imagined Granny Franny flying through the sky, like the witch in the movie *The Wizard of Oz,* only Granny Franny was pretty and would be smiling.

"It might be just a good windstorm," Grama Norma said. "Might not have been a tornado at all."

"It's a tornado," Charlene said.

Aunt Marilee took hold of Corrine's right hand, smoothed it out of a fist and held it in her own.

Just then something thunked against the cellar doors, causing them all to jump, and Belinda to let out a little scream.

Twenty-Seven

When the going gets tough...

Marilee, her heart pumping with both trepidation and curiosity, first peeked out, then led the way up out of the cellar.

Well, for heaven's sake.

She stood there, blinking in the remarkable bright light shafting through thick dark clouds, and looking around at a quite normal world. The stone patio was wet from a heavy downpour, and water trickled from the eaves, but the rain fell softly now. The rain and the few limbs scattered about gave proof of a storm, and here a roof shingle, there quite a big limb, and over yonder what looked like a twisted piece of siding. But the house stood right there, seemingly undamaged.

The world was intact, the trees, Aunt Vella's rose garden, the concrete benches on the new stone patio. Perhaps it *had* been nothing more than a strong windstorm.

The other women came snaking around her, led by her mother making a beeline inside the back door. Marilee, being brought back to the present, took Corrine's hand and followed, her thoughts now racing to

Willie Lee and Tate and finding out what had happened.

In the living room, women were gathering their purses and streaming out the door, although Granny Franny was at the door and telling everyone to please stay for a bit, for safety's sake. All wrought up, no one listened. They just went running out to their vehicles, while Aunt Vella, on the porch, yelled warnings about possible downed electric lines. Although scattered with small limbs, the street looked clear to Marilee. She pointed this out.

"Well, we don't know what the other streets are like," replied Aunt Vella.

"Do you think it was a tornado?" Marilee asked. She still had hold of Corrine, she realized, and she didn't let go.

"It was a good windstorm," Aunt Vella said, striding back into the house. "We don't have any electricity, so something's down somewhere."

Mildred Covington had two plates of half-eaten pieces of cake balanced on her knees and was eating out of both.

Marilee's mother was on the couch. She looked as white as a sheet and was breathing deeply.

"Mother, are you all right?"

"Well…I'm shaken up."

Marilee hoped her mother was okay, because Marilee needed to leave her and get down to Tate and Willie Lee. Phone, perhaps she could phone, she thought, wishing that she had Tate's cell phone, but then he wouldn't have one. It might be quicker just to run down the street; it would only take a few minutes. While her mind was going a mile a minute in this distorted fashion, she turned to find that Belinda was at the telephone ahead of her.

"It's dead," Belinda said, dropping the receiver into the cradle.

"Aunt Vella, don't you have a cell phone?" Marilee finally let go of Corrine. Corrine stayed close beside her.

"Well, yes," said Aunt Vella in a manner as if just then thinking of it. She had to find her purse and dig into it. "Now let's see. Oh, dear, the battery's low, but it should still work." She punched in the number for the drugstore. "It's ringing," she told Marilee, who stood watching her aunt impatiently.

"No answer," Aunt Vella said after a long minute. Her eyes were round and worried as she passed the little phone to Marilee.

"Oh, Mama, Daddy's probably still sittin' there watchin' a war picture on TBS," said Belinda.

"There isn't any electricity, Belinda."

"Not here, but we don't know about Main Street," Belinda pointed out.

During this exchange, Marilee dialed Tate's house and listened first to a long silence and finally to ringing…and ringing. "No answer," she said.

"The phones could be out, but they'll still ring," Belinda said.

Marilee thought to try Tate's cell phone, but for the life of her, she couldn't remember the number. Her brain had gone into a spin, picturing the rest of the town, which they could not see, wiped off the face of the map.

Her gaze fell on her mother as she considered her options; she would have to leave her mother, who sat on Aunt Vella's couch, fanning herself with a magazine.

"Mom, I have to go check on Tate and Willie Lee. You sit here and rest." She grabbed Corrine's hand, giving only passing thought to leaving the child in her mother's care. She knew it would be Corrine taking care of her mother, not the other way around, and besides, the child was stuck to Marilee like glue.

"Be careful, dear," her mother called after her.

She realized she had not driven, that Tate had brought her.

"I don't think we should take the cars...we might get cars stuck all over," said Franny, who came beside them as they started down the front porch steps.

"I sure hope Perry had sense enough to get in the closet," said Aunt Vella, who followed.

Just then Dixie Love came out her door across the street. She hollered that she had no damage, and Aunt Vella hollered back, asking if she had electricity. Dixie said no.

The rain had stopped. Marilee, Corrine beside her, hopped over the water running thinly down the gutter, while the street was already showing dry patches.

"Nothing looks damaged around here," Marilee said, finding the fact of all the houses intact extremely reassuring.

"Mr. Winston's flags are tore up...so's Mr. Northrupt's," Corrine said, pointing.

Just as they passed the Northrupt house, Mr. Northrupt came out his front door and hailed them. "We're okay here!"

"Good!" Marilee called back.

She broke into a jog as they came around the curve going downhill. There was a big elm split right in two, and the part that lay out in the road blocked the view of Tate's house. Corrine went surging ahead.

"Oh, Aunt Marilee!" she called back over her shoulder in a way that sent alarm racing through Marilee.

Then she got her first sight of Tate's house.

Her stride faltered. The roof and half the top floor were gone. The bedroom that had been Franny's was totally exposed; the bedspread flopped in the breeze. The wonderful old magnolia that had stood beside the house was broken off over the portico, under which the tail-end of the BMW could be seen.

"Oh my God," Marilee said.

"Yes, Father, help us bear up," Franny said.

Corrine was running ahead. "Come around the front!" she hollered back to them.

Marilee and Franny headed for the house, and Aunt Vella called that she was going on to the drugstore. Marilee hesitated, looking at her dear aunt, who was running faster than was wise for a woman of her age.

"Be careful, Aunt Vella!" Then Marilee followed Franny, and both of them started calling, "Tate! Willie Lee! Is everyone okay?"

Every dark thought that could be raced through Marilee's mind, and she saw pictures of Willie Lee, Tate and Stuart being sucked up and swirling in a tornado, and the telephone and Munro, too.

Then, just as she reached the bottom of the front steps, she looked, and there was Tate coming out the front door, with Willie Lee beside him, and Stuart's taller frame coming behind.

Oh, thank God.

Corrine reached them first and threw her arms around Willie Lee.

Marilee stood there staring, then sank down to the steps because her legs gave out.

Word of the general safety of the town and just what had happened came by way of Sheriff Oakes and Deputy Lyle Midgett, who drove past in their canvas of the town, and various neighbors living near the corner of Porter and Church Streets, who came to see the damage to the Editor's house, commiserate and tell their own stories.

The tornado had been small and had come in from the west like a bouncing ball gone astray. It had bounced its way along what used to be an alleyway running behind the houses on Porter Street, a distance of some three long blocks, snapping power lines along the way. The passage of the tornado behind their house had been witnessed by Leon and Stella Purvis, who saw it all from the window of their kitchen; the two had been working on Leon's hot rod truck and had not heard the siren because of the roar of the engine.

"Stella said that the light looked funny, and I turned off the truck engine and heard the siren about the same time I caught the roar of the dad-blamed tornado," said Leon, who had hotfooted it over to the big house to see if anyone had been injured.

Stella, who had come with him and who was puffing hard on a cigarette, said, "We saw it from our kitchen window. There wasn't any time to take shelter anywhere else—Leon had the closet so full of stuff, it could have killed us. That thing snaked down to the alleyway right behind the yard. Looked like somethin' out of the movies. Just like some animation, I swear. It danced back upward past Marilee's yard and then just disappeared into the trees behind your house, Editor. Then stuff was flyin' ever' which'er way through the sky. I knew the house'd been hit.''

It was theorized that the big Holloway house had been what turned the tornado off course and sent it angling southeast. This was surely a blessing, or it might have gone right on down and demolished the school.

The way Marilee saw it, the school would not have been occupied, and Tate's house was, so that had not been much of a blessing, although she did not think she should complain, since her dear family was safe, as, it appeared, were all those in the surrounding neighborhood. From all of the early reports, it seemed that the big Holloway house was the only house in Valentine that had been touched.

The tornado had gone on across the street, taken a lick at the Fletchers' garage, then stayed on the ground for several hundred yards, where it demolished a doghouse—vacant—fences, bushes and trees, and a telephone connector box, explaining the lack of telephones all the way down Church Street. When it went into the back part of Winston's deep yard, it apparently lifted off, destroying one of the big elms in the process. As if thus satisfied, the tornado had disappeared into the clouds.

''I don't think it would have dared touch Coweta's roses,'' Winston said. He did not go immediately to look at his place, because he had to sit down and catch his breath from all the excitement, but Everett Northrup had come down to tell him that his house was still there. Everett was a little miffed at not having been invited to the bachelor party.

Marilee remembered Aunt Vella. She asked for Tate's cell phone, and he told her it was in his car, which was now underneath the portico that was underneath the magnolia. He had the idea to try the telephone in the living room, which Marilee did not think for a minute could be working.

"I called down here from Aunt Vella's cell phone, but no one answered."

"Oh, I thought I heard it ring, but we were busy with everyone leavin' in such a hurry. We didn't even think about the phone."

He dialed the number for the drugstore, while Marilee waited for him to tell her the phone wasn't working, but then he surprised her by talking to Aunt Vella. She had to contain herself to keep from snatching the phone out of his hands.

"They're okay." He handed the phone to Marilee.

"Aunt Vella?"

"Yes, sugar, we are fine…just fine."

At the precious sound of Aunt Vella's voice, Marilee squeezed her eyes closed. It seemed odd to be speaking on the telephone in a room where everything was perfectly intact and to know that above her head the house was blown away. Opening her eyes, she saw Tate mounting the stairs. Going up to see the great wound to the house.

Aunt Vella was saying, "Your uncle Perry thought to get in the pharmacy closet. If that tornado had hit, he would have been pilled to death. I told him that's what he would have gotten for being so wedded to this place and television that he wasn't up there at Tate's party, the old stick in the mud." Profound affection echoed in her voice. "Anyway, it doesn't look like any real damage on Main Street, except for a couple of forgotten flags, and Fayrene's pretty new green awnings over at the café and her apartment are ripped to shreds. Bless her heart. She's awfully upset about it. Already asked Perry for a sedative. Oh, and our electric's out…. Funny the phones are working, but Perry says the wires are mostly underground."

Aunt Vella said she and Uncle Perry would be coming back quickly in Perry's car, since the roads were open, and they hung up.

Marilee stood there with her hand on the phone, thinking of Tate upstairs, but knowing she had to call Charlotte first.

Charlotte picked up on the second ring. Yes, her friend had found her mother and house all fine. Some wind had come through, but not damaging, although they, too, were without electricity.

"Isn't it funny we have a phone?" she said.

Marilee started to tell her about the wires being in the ground, but Charlotte said Sandy had just driven up, she had to go, bye.

Marilee stood there with her hand on the receiver, going through a mental list of who she needed to check on.

Just then the phone rang, causing her to jump.

"Marilee?" It was Parker. "You and everyone else over there okay?"

Parker had left before she and Corrine had gotten to the house. She told him they were fine and asked about his house. She knew Amy was okay, because she was down in Dallas visiting her sister, who had a new baby.

"There wasn't any damage here at all," he told

her. "All the animals made it through, and I even have electricity. I'm headin' out west of town now, though. Fella out that way has a couple of cows cut up from flying debris. Heard a radio report that said there were a couple of little tornadoes sighted touching down."

Marilee reminded him to call Amy first and let her know he was okay. He had not even thought of that, of course. As she hung up, she scolded herself; she really needed to quit trying to take care of Parker. Let his wife do the job.

Closing her eyes, she gave thanks that those nearest and dearest, and even those she didn't even know, were all safe from the storm. What did damaged houses matter? she thought, and she headed for the stairs.

Glancing through the opened front door, she saw Stuart sitting on the front porch, his head resting back, eyes closed. Willie Lee lay leaning against him, and had fallen asleep, and next to him, Munro had curled. Corrine and Franny sat on the steps with Winston, speaking with Leon and Stella. All safe.

Quite suddenly Marilee needed to be with Tate and to touch him. She went rapidly to the steps, paused a moment with her hand on the newel post, then started up.

Hearing the creaking of the stairs, Tate looked over the landing. "Don't come up...the stairs may be weakened."

He didn't want her to come upstairs. He worried about the stability of the house, and he just didn't want her to come up,

But Marilee responded with all logic, "You're up

there,'' and kept on coming. "Is my wedding dress okay?''

He told her it was fine, that her room had not been touched, hoping that might stop her, which was a useless hope, of course. She kept on up the stairs and went straight to the back bedroom she had been using, to the closet to check her dress.

He turned again to walk back into what was left of the bedroom he had intended to share with her, her voice, filled with relief and delight, floating after him. "Oh, yes, it's fine. Thank you, God!''

Tate was thankful, but he was also angry. Standing there in the midst of the wreckage, the anger was winning.

Marilee appeared behind his shoulder, wrapping her arms around his waist from the back. He supposed it didn't matter now that she saw the room; it was all ruined, his surprise, his hope for starting out on the right foot.

"Oh, Tate, the bed is beautiful!'' Marilee said, then hurried over to it, hopping over fallen roof joists to get there. "My gosh, where did you get such a bed?'' She gazed at him with wonderment.

"The bedroom is gone,'' he said, just in case she had not noticed.

With sudden, painful clarity, he realized that he had wanted to be the big man in giving her this room. He didn't want to look at that notion, and he tried to push it away, but the knowledge washed over him again, and he knew that he had wanted to be to her all that Stuart had not been, just to make sure that he proved to be a better husband.

"You planned a skylight for us,'' she said, sitting

down on the plaster- and debris-covered mattress and looking upward.

He stared at her, at her calm face. Her positive outlook was salt in his wound. He wanted her to be as hurt and outraged as he was.

Unable to speak of his anger, he kicked a board, and it clattered, but not enough.

She said, "We're all okay, Tate. If we're together, that's all we need."

He did not need her censure, he thought, even as the truth of her words seeped into him.

He had to tell her. God knew that he could hardly face himself, much less her, but he had to tell her.

"Marilee, the house isn't insured."

Her eyes rested on him.

"I put everything into getting the paper off the ground. I've been balancin' money all over, trying to get the *Voice* goin' good, and the house insurance has come last. I let it lapse."

He had been a fool, and now she would know. She would know he was irresponsible, like Stuart, not taking care of their home. She would be disappointed in him. He was disappointed in himself. He had been reaching further than he could truly and safely reach. Trying to appear bigger and smarter than he was. How could he have let something like this go? He had thought he could gamble for six months, that everything would be fine.

Suddenly he was so tired. He'd been working and planning and balancing to get his newspaper off the ground, to keep all the staff employed and receiving paychecks, and he could no longer keep up the juggling pace.

Then she was there in front of him, attempting to

put her arms around him. That made him angrier. He didn't want her pity or consolation.

"We don't have a house to move to after the wedding."

"So what?" she shot back at him.

He shook his head. "We will probably need to postpone the wedding until I can get us a place to live."

Her eyebrow arched. "Until *you* can find us a place? I thought we were together?"

"Okay, until *we* can find a place." He closed his mouth against the anger that wanted to spew out.

"We can rent somewhere, Tate. We can pitch a tent in your backyard and cook in your kitchen, if nothing else."

He thought her attitude far from realistic. "Be serious. This is Valentine, Marilee.... Empty houses aren't just waitin' around, even for rent, and I'm pretty well flat broke."

The last echoed inside of him. He had credit, which was already so stretched it was likely to snap back at him. He wanted to knock his head against a wall. He wanted to hit something.

"I have some money set back. Enough to rent something for a month or so. We'll find a place. There is no reason to postpone the wedding just because things are not perfect." She spoke in that reasonable tone again, and he couldn't stand it.

"I'm not usin' your money."

"Why not?"

"I'm just not. And you're not touchin' Willie Lee's money."

"I would never in this world think of touchin'

Willie Lee's money. And don't you point that finger at me, Tate Holloway.''

He drew back the offending finger and raked a hand through his hair, finally bringing himself to say, ''I'm sorry, Marilee. I'm angry at myself, not you. I'm just tryin' to figure out what in the hell we're gonna do, since I've screwed up so badly.''

Now she did that chuckling thing and looked at him as if he were a child. She reached for him, taking his face in her hands and gazing into his eyes with her own the pure blue of a clear summer sky.

''Honey,'' she said, speaking slowly, ''we're goin' to do the best we can. That's what we're goin' to do.''

He felt himself melting into her eyes.

''My dearest darlin','' she said with sweet lips turning upward, ''sometimes we humans make choices that don't quite work out as we planned, because life interferes. I'm sorry to tell you, Mr. Editor, but you are as human as the rest of us. And you are the human man I love. It is not this house I love, but you. I love you and Willie Lee and Corrine, and we are all okay. It is you I want to marry, and you who Willie Lee and Corrine need for a father. We could all live in a tent. Where has your good sense gone to?''

She loved him. He heard it in her voice, felt it in her hands on his face and saw it in her eyes. It washed over him like a warm wave.

He wrapped his arms around her then, holding her as if his life depended on it. It seemed to, in that minute. ''Oh, lady, you are always a surprise to me,'' he said, when he could speak.

She drew back and looked him in the eye. "I am repeating back to you what you have taught me."

And, although it seemed a little egotistical, he knew that was the truth. He chuckled and kissed her neck, savoring the feel and scent of her, and knowing that the biggest mistake he had made in the past minutes was in overlooking that she was on this earth and with him.

She pushed back and arched an eyebrow. "Is the bed paid for?"

"No," he said sadly. "On credit."

"Well, let's try to pay for it before anything else."

He threw back his head and laughed hard, and the next instant the skies above opened up and rain poured down.

Startled, he looked at Marilee, and she looked at him. Her eyes were as lights from her face, shining out through rain that dribbled onto her eyelashes and down her cheeks. He felt it sliding down his face, too.

There seemed only one thing to do.

Giving her a courtly bow, then taking her loosely in his arms, he waltzed her around the small space in which they stood, atop the crumbled plaster and between the collapsed boards, to music that only he and Marilee could hear, together.

Twenty-Eight

Wonders never cease...

The rain was short-lived, and sunlight sliced through billowing purple clouds. To the west the dry line was approaching, showing blue sky.

As the phone at Aunt Vella's house was out, Marilee and Tate were preparing to walk up to tell her mother the roads were clear and everything was all right. Marilee had begun to worry about her mother, who she thought could have had a heart attack or something because of being so upset by the storm.

But then here came her mother's car, Belinda at the wheel, pulling to a halt at the curb. At the same time, from the opposite direction, Aunt Vella and Uncle Perry arrived in Uncle Perry's big black Cadillac.

Belinda got out of the car, slammed the door and came across the yard, leaving Marilee's mother to help Mildred out of the back seat. Marilee hurried out to assist both women. Her mother had on heels that sank in the rain-soaked lawn.

"Marilee, I've got to have some ibuprofen...extra strength," said her mother, rubbing her head. "I can't drive home like this. Perry, you do not have any ibuprofen in your cabinets. You don't hardly have anything at all at your house, and here you are a pharmacist.''

Perry, whose arms were full with three tubs of ice cream, responded, ''I have aspirin. It's a good medicine.''

''She was wantin' a Valium,'' Belinda said under her breath. ''I could use one.'' She took one of the gallons of ice cream from her father and proceeded straight into the house.

''We have ice cream for everyone,'' said Aunt Vella, putting forth two shopping bags full of gallon tubs. ''I called the electric company but couldn't get an answer. There's no need to let this ice cream ruin. Let's have a celebration that we're all still here!''

Marilee, Aunt Vella and Franny took the ice cream to the kitchen to dish up. Belinda was at the table, eating straight from the container. Looked like Rocky Road.

The kitchen, too, was as if nothing at all had occurred upstairs or in the neighborhood, except for the lack of electricity. Marilee kept switching on the light switches by habit, which illustrated how dependent she was upon light. Aunt Vella told how when she was a girl, they used only daylight in the houses, because their form of lighting was the kerosene lamp, and no one would be using that during the day. Franny echoed the same sentiments and tales.

Listening to the women's voices, Marilee again felt gratitude fill her heart. She hoped that when everything got back to normal, she would not forget the lesson of what was truly important in this world, although, she probably would from time to time, and have to be reminded. She sure hoped that it wouldn't take a crisis to remind her, though, Lord. Just a gentle whisper would be fine.

"Here, Mama...I thought strawberry was your favorite," she said when she returned to the porch, handing her mother the bowl.

Her mother's eyes jumped, and for a moment their eyes met. "Why, yes, thank you, dear," said her mother, who sat a little straighter in the porch chair and smiled.

She handed Stuart a bowl of the vanilla and raised a questioning eyebrow.

He gave her a wink. "Still my favorite," he said and their eyes held each other's for a brief instant.

"Do you want a pillow?" she asked, concerned about his bony body sitting on the porch floor.

"Don't baby me, Marilee," he said, averting his eyes and spooning the softening ice cream.

As she headed back through the screen door, she heard her mother say, "My, this just hits the spot, Vella. Thank you for bringing this ice cream. The best thing in a crisis is to do something very normal and even festive."

Wonders never cease, Marilee thought, so startled by her mother's compliment to her aunt that she paused in midstride. A tornado did a lot of damage to material things, but perhaps it unleashed true good feelings inside people.

In the kitchen, Belinda was still sitting with her gallon of ice cream, and she had found the chocolate syrup in the cabinet. She offered some to Marilee. "I imagine you could use this," she said.

Marilee was overcome with tender feelings and

hugged Belinda, saying, "I'm so glad we're all here."

"Me, too," Belinda said, holding the syrup can up to Marilee.

"I am here."

Marilee turned to see her son, with Munro beside him, gazing at her with sleepy eyes. She scooped him up, something she had not done in a long time, as he was growing so heavy, and danced around the room until he giggled. "Yes, you are here, and I am so glad," she said.

"We want ice cream," he said. "I want cher-ry, and Mun-ro wants van-i-lla, please."

"And you shall have it, my prince."

She sent him back out to the porch with a dish of cherry for himself and a dish of vanilla for Munro. Then she proceeded to spoon Rocky Road for herself from Belinda's container, and to spoon the syrup in hefty measure over it.

"Come join us outside, Belinda."

Belinda looked startled at the invitation, then came along.

The voices of those gathered on the porch floated to her as she walked the length of the hallway. It was a comforting sound. She wondered vaguely where she would sleep that night, but the fact did not seem very important. Nothing seemed too important next to seeing Tate's eyes meet hers and Willie Lee's head bent over his ice cream and Corrine licking her spoon.

Just then she heard a young voice calling, "Willie Lee! Willie Lee!"

It was Ricky Dale, pedaling hard on his bike, up

the curb and across the yard, with his black dog bounding behind him.

He stopped on the walkway and beheld everyone sitting around the front porch and on the steps. "Willie Lee, you...got t' come." That was all he could get out, because he was gasping for breath.

Observing him, his wide eyes and tear-streaked face, Marilee panicked, thinking perhaps the boy's entire family had been killed in the tornado and this tragedy was just now coming to light.

"What is it, Ricky Dale?" asked Tate in a calm voice.

"The horses...the...the baby is hurt." His eyes shifted to Willie Lee. "She's cut bad.... You gotta come, Willie Lee."

Tate was on his feet. "We need to get Parker over there."

"Parker's out on a call," Marilee said, setting her bowl of ice cream on the porch rail, watching Willie Lee and Munro head down the steps, and Corrine go right behind them.

"Willie Lee?" Tate said with puzzlement.

"Is Leanne over there?" Winston asked, but the children were heading across the yard. Marilee watched, her mind going ninety miles an hour: the horse is hurt, Ricky Dale thinks Willie Lee can do something. What is going on? Should I stop them? I'll go, too.

She was already heading down the steps, slipping past Tate and Leon Purvis and seeing Ricky Dale hit the street, his legs pumping the pedals of his bicycle. Corrine had hold of Willie Lee's hand, and they were running as fast as Willie Lee was capable. Marilee broke into a jog to catch up with them and took Willie Lee's other hand.

They were halfway up the hill when a black car slid alongside—Uncle Perry's car, with Aunt Vella at the wheel. Tate, in the back seat, said through the opened window, "Get in. We'll drive you."

He already had the back door open and was reaching for Willie Lee. Munro and Corrine scrambled into the car behind him, and Marilee threw herself inside, coming to rest against Franny and Corrine, as Aunt Vella punched the accelerator.

"Vella, don't kill us," said Uncle Perry who sat squished in the middle of the front seat, with Winston next to him.

Marilee had to take hold of the door to keep from being flung atop Tate and Willie Lee as Aunt Vella turned into the driveway of the Valentine home. Up ahead, Ricky Dale disappeared around the garage, following the overgrown gravel track that led to the rear of the acreage.

Aunt Vella followed, scraping against green budding lilac branches. Thankfully she slowed and negotiated neatly around the limbs of the demolished elm tree, coming to a stop behind Leanne's pickup truck at the corral.

The tornado had taken out not only the big elm nearby but had torn and twisted the tin horse shed, and splintered a section of the wooden corral. Pieces of tin and split boards were scattered about.

On the far side of the corral, the mare was tied to a fence post. Nearby Leanne and Ricky Dale were crouched beside the filly on the ground.

Marilee opened the car door and was hurried along in getting out by Willie Lee pushing from behind.

Willie Lee tried to run and stumbled. Corrine reached him first and helped him up, then they ran on.

A noise made Marilee look over her shoulder to see the dismaying sight of her mother's car coming up the driveway, and then she hurried on with the others toward Leanne and Ricky Dale, who was urging, "Come on, Willie Lee."

At the first sight of Leanne, Marilee instinctively reached for Tate's hand. The woman had so much blood all over her that she looked like she'd been through a battle. The explanation for this lay on the ground in front of the young woman, who had her hands wrapped around a towel that was wrapped around the filly's ankle.

"Flyin' tin got her. I can't get the bleeding stopped," Leanne said, her voice so desperate that Marilee immediately went down on a knee and put her hand to the young woman's back, as if to hold her up.

"Leanne, honey…" This was Winston, coming up on her other side.

Then Willie Lee was on his knees and scooting close to the filly's head. Her eyes were glazed. Marilee started to speak a word of caution to her son, but then she saw Munro pressed close, and Corrine and Ricky Dale right behind him. Something stopped the words in her mouth.

"Help her, Willie Lee…please help her," Ricky Dale sobbed.

Marilee kept her eyes on her son's face. No one

else said anything. Willie Lee caressed the filly and laid his head down on her. All seemed quiet.

Don't let this horse die, God, Marilee prayed, but all of a sudden she experienced a great fear for her son. She moved to reach for him, but Tate held her back and whispered, "Shush," in her ear.

She leaned against his hard chest, gripped his strong hand and watched her son's pale head.

After what seemed a long minute, Willie Lee rose off the horse and looked at them all from behind his thick glasses. "I think she will be bet-ter now."

Everyone looked at the filly.

She blinked, and blinked again. Her eyes had cleared.

Next she moved, making an effort to get up.

"No...no, Baby Girl, lie there," Leanne said. "Ricky Dale hold her head."

This time, though, it was Corrine who took the animal's head and caressed her neck, speaking soothingly.

"There, pon-y...lay still," said Willie Lee, who patted her neck. The filly relaxed against Corrine.

Marilee became aware of a clicking sound. She looked over to see Stuart taking a picture. He had obviously already taken several, moving even then to a different angle.

"Stuart," she said in a low tone.

He either did not hear or ignored her.

Then Aunt Vella was there with a towel she handed to Leanne. "Here's a fresh one. It's clean enough."

Leanne slowly and carefully unwrapped the bloody towel. "Ohmygod, the bleeding's stopped," she said in a breathless tone.

"Praise God," Winston and Franny said at once.

Marilee saw and heard, then looked over and saw Stuart was clicking another picture. She was about to step over to make him quit when Tate went before her. She did not know what Tate said, but Stuart put away his camera.

"Marilee...Marilee." Her mother walked toward her, her arms out for balance as her spike heels sank into the dirt. "Why did that boy want Willie Lee to come down here? What is this about Willie Lee healing that horse?" Her mother's eyes were anxious.

"I don't know.... I guess it was because the horse especially likes Willie Lee."

"It does? Well, I don't think Willie Lee or any of those children need to see all this gore."

"Mama, you look wrung-out. Let me help you get set down in the car."

"I need something for my nerves." Then, "I could really use a cold drink, honey. Do you suppose you could see if Winston has something in his refrigerator?"

"I'll see."

Belinda was in Winston's kitchen; she had a small Coke. She told Marilee there were a couple more bottles in the refrigerator.

"Is Willie Lee some sort of healer?" Belinda asked, raising a curious eyebrow.

"The horse likes him," Marilee said, as she pulled a small bottle of Coca-Cola from the refrigerator.

"I heard Ricky Dale say he knew Willie Lee could heal the horse."

"I'm sure that Willie Lee's love helped the horse.

And, Belinda, I really don't think it would be good for Willie Lee for the rumor to go around that he can heal.''

Belinda's speculative gaze rested on Marilee. "Oh.''

"Is the little horse gonna be all right, Marilee?''

"I hope so, Leon.''

"I was just tellin' Stella that one day last month I saw Willie Lee pick up a dead cat out of the street and now he's got it over there with y'all. I've seen him playing with it.''

"It couldn't have been dead, then, could it?''

"It looked dead. And now he come over here and healed this horse.''

"The horse likes Willie Lee. They have a special bond.''

That was her story, and she was sticking to it.

"That horse is darned lucky,'' Parker told her, in a private moment after he had sewed up the filly's leg. Sweat wetted his hair, even though the cool front had passed and temperatures had dropped. It had been a job to stitch the animal's deep wounds.

Marilee glanced over at the children, who were helping Leanne and Tate make a clean, safe stall. "Yes, it is.'' She returned her gaze to Parker. "I'm grateful that you could get here so quickly.''

"It wasn't anything I did that saved that filly. I just mopped up.'' He leveled a gaze at her. "What's this Leanne told me about Willie Lee stopping the bleeding? 'Spoke the Word,' is the term she used.''

Marilee breathed deeply. "I don't think Willie Lee spoke any word other than loving ones. I don't know,

Parker. I really don't know." The honest answer came out. She had known Parker a long time. Then she added, "The horse really likes Willie Lee. Probably that helped to give her a will to live."

He regarded her thoughtfully. "Maybe."

Franny came forward, passing him a glass of the cold tea that she had made up in Winston's kitchen and now bore around on a tray, serving everyone, as if it were an afternoon lawn party, which indeed it seemed to be, Marilee thought, looking around at knots of neighbors who had gathered.

Soon the word would be all over town, added to with all manner of embellishments, of course, as to Willie Lee's role in saving the filly.

"Marilee, your mother has fainted," Franny informed her, hurrying past with a glass of water and a wet cloth.

Marilee followed and found her mother reclining on the back seat of her car. Perry was there, bending over the door, telling her mother that he couldn't give her a sedative without a prescription. "I got aspirin." He pulled a little tin from his pocket.

Franny put the cloth on her mother's head, then passed her the aspirin, which her mother at first refused, then consented to take.

After swallowing the pills, her mother cast her a weak look and said, "I can't drive home. I just can't."

Marilee patted her mother's hand. "You won't have to, Mother."

She went into Winston's house and used the phone in the kitchen to call Carl, who had not shown up at the bachelor party, and who no one had expected anyway. He picked up on the third ring.

He had not heard of the tornado. "We've been watchin' wrestlin' on cable," he told her. She heard voices in the background and pictured her mother's husband and his friends, sitting around swilling beers and eating pretzels and cheese dip. He sounded fairly sober, however. She would trust that he was.

"Mama can't drive home," she told him, raising her voice to be heard over the television and the other voices.

"Did her car get damaged?" he asked, after a moment.

"No, Carl. Her car is fine. But mother is sixty years old and upset by this whole thing, and she is in no shape to drive. She needs taking care of, and I'm too busy down here, since my roof has been blown from my head, and I can't be running her home. You will have to come get her. Now," she added, in case he was considering waiting for his wrestling show to be over.

"O-kay," he said, as if knowing he had better not say anything else.

Marilee hung up and returned to her mother.

"Carl's comin' to get you, Mother."

"Oh, he is?" Her mother's eyes went wide.

"Yes. He hadn't heard about the tornado, and when I told him, he said he was coming right down to get you, and not to worry about your car. He will have one of his men come get it this week."

"He did?"

"Yes," Marilee lied blatantly, patting her mother's hand. She considered that Carl might tell her mother the truth, but quickly tossed off any worry over it. She was fairly certain that if she put her mind to it, she could outlie Carl Cooper any day of the week.

Marilee declined Aunt Vella's invitation for them to stay at her house. "Thank you, Aunt Vella, but I think we'll just go stay out at the Goodnight." She was intent on finding a cave and crawling in, with her loved ones around her.

Twenty-Nine

So many things we carry with us...

It was dark when Tate pulled the Cherokee beneath the yellow fluorescent lights at the old motel. Through the picture window, Mr. Goode could be seen watching television.

"Just sit here," Tate told her, squeezing her knee, and slipped out the driver door.

Marilee's eyes followed him as he entered through the glass door and crossed in front of the picture window. He had donned a faded denim shirt that stretched across his thick shoulders.

She twisted around to check the children in the back seat. Willie Lee was asleep in Corrine's lap, and Munro lay against him. Corrine, whose spine was straight against the seat back, regarded Marilee with anxious dark eyes so reminiscent of when she had first come to live with them.

Marilee sent her an encouraging smile. "Franny sent us hot chocolate packets and the electric kettle. We'll make some when we get our pajamas on, okay?"

Corrine nodded. The anxious light remained in her eyes.

"We'll sure have a story to tell your mother, won't we?"

Corrine nodded again and tried for a smile, but it didn't reach her eyes. Marilee wished the seat was not between them. She longed to hug the child back into feeling safe and secure. Of course, perhaps the hugging would be as reassuring to Marilee herself.

Tate came back, slipped behind the wheel, and tossed her a key.

"Largest cabin they got. Two double beds and a set-tee," he said, imitating Mr. Goodnight's accent.

Marilee looked at the key. One room. She looked at his profile, then turned forward, a soft smile brimming up and out. She had not known, but this was what she wanted. She wanted her loved ones close around her. And Tate had known this. And perhaps he shared the feeling.

She and Corrine gathered bags, while Tate gathered Willie Lee, carried him inside and laid him on the bed closest to the door. "Boys will bunk over here," he said.

Munro jumped up beside Willie Lee and lay down as if having an invisible tether to the boy.

Tate brought in the rest of their things, while Marilee got Corrine going in the shower and promised to have hot chocolate for her afterward. Coming out, she closed the door and stood for a moment.

Tate was typing away on his portable computer set up on the rickety table.

The sight surprised her a little, and brought a niggle of irritation. She reminded herself that Tate was a dedicated journalist.

She gazed at him for a long minute in which she beat back the annoyance. Hadn't he given everything to her and the children all day? Now was his time to see to his needs, and the needs of the paper. Many times that day, while helping others, he had also been jotting down notes on the cards he kept handy. He had already contacted Reggie and Leo, Tammy Crawford and Charlotte, about assignments for Wednesday's *Voice*. Now he was far away, deep into writing his own account for the paper. Possibly it would be picked up by the wire. This would be good for the paper, and his enthusiasm for journalism was what made him the special man that he was.

She dug into a duffel bag and brought out the electric teapot and packets of instant hot chocolate. The water heated quickly, and Marilee made two hot chocolates and an instant coffee for Tate, setting it beside him on the rickety table.

When he did not say anything, she pointed out the coffee.

"Thank you, darlin'." But he didn't stop or look up.

Holding her steaming cup with both hands, she stood beside him. He was oblivious to her. Oh, how his mind was moving, and his fingers on the keyboard were keeping up the pace.

That was a major difference between herself and Tate. He was a born journalist. He would have an entire idea and bring it to the paper. She had simply fallen into writing, and would have to think and think, because generally at least half her mind was focused always on her role as a mother and those whom she loved. The needs and desires of her children, and now Tate, took precedence. There was little left of her afterward to focus on writing anything factual, unless, of course, it pertained to her love of family.

Her gaze fell on Willie Lee, who lay sprawled on his back, arms wide, face like an angel. Her dear, precious, Willie Lee, who had saved a horse. She thought about that for some minutes, and then she looked back at Tate, who was still typing away.

She wished he would stop typing.

She moved to read over his shoulder. The title was: "Tornado Comes To Town."

Tate had the ability to personalize even a tornado.

Her eyes scanned rapidly downward, and her heart picked up tempo. He was telling the story of how neighbors came together in a time of crisis.

"Tate?"

"Hmmm?"

"Tate…you aren't going to tell about the horse being injured and Willie Lee's part in it, are you?"

"Hmmm?"

She bent around him and looked him in the face. "You aren't going to tell about Willie Lee and that filly, are you?"

"Uh…yes, I was plannin' to tell about the horse…how Willie Lee and all the neighbors came over to help." He looked confused.

"You can't do that." She sat on the corner of the bed, facing Tate firmly.

"Why not?"

"Because it is likely that Willie Lee got that horse to stop bleeding to death." She felt like closing the computer on his hands, which remained poised over the keys, as if he could barely take an instant of distraction from his task.

Tate, who felt lost at the direction Marilee was

taking but noticed her staring at his hands, felt compelled to withdraw them from their position. He turned his chair to face her fully. "Well, I think it is likely. Our Willie Lee most definitely has a way with animals."

He did not understand why this was a problem, although he did understand that something was going on with Marilee. It obviously was some woman-thing, and a voice in the back of his mind told him to go carefully. He kept a patient tone, even though he was very impatient to get back to his writing.

"That's part of the human interest story. People love to hear about animals being saved, and they especially like it when it is kids doing the saving, the way Ricky Dale came seeking help for his beloved horse, and how his friends Willie Lee and Corrine responded unselfishly in the time of need."

It was a great story. He had plans of selling it to his old Houston newspaper and hopefully some magazines.

Marilee watched Tate's face and knew exactly that he was carried away with anticipating the sale and publication of his wonderful story.

"Yes, our Willie Lee has a way with animals," she said, "and by ten o'clock tomorrow morning the information is going to be all over town that Willie Lee James is a healer. Your story will broadcast it to everyone and his cousin across the country."

She thought to calm her voice, but she got to her feet and leaned toward him. "His life is already hard enough. People treat him as if he's an imbecile, or they're afraid of him, as if he might contaminate them. I don't want...well, I don't want people getting crazy ideas and looking at him all the time, and making pilgrimages to our door with their dying dogs and canaries." She saw the frightening prospect in rapid but clear images crossing her mind.

"Darlin', don't you think you might be gettin' a little carried away with that?"

This comment struck Marilee like a slap across the face, and she stared at him for several seconds, before saying a definite, "No, I do not."

Tate knew he had misspoken.

Marilee sought to keep a firm hold on her emotions. She knew she could get overwrought, and say and do things that later she regretted. She had lived this many times, only to wish later she had contained herself. She always promised to contain herself, but one problem with this was an equal fear that she might contain herself too much and be sorry that she had. When it came to Willie Lee, she figured she would rather have to deal with regrets at actions taken rather than not taken.

She said in a hoarse whisper, "I saw a similar thing once, in Tennessee. Stuart did a story about it. A three-parter, in fact. It was reported that this little girl could heal people, and my gosh, for a month, people were streaming to her door. The poor thing could not go anywhere hardly. People just hounded her. When she wasn't able to help them, they called her and her parents charlatans, and other people, who said she had healed them from everything from ingrown toenails to skin cancer, said she was the Virgin Mary. The little girl was lost in all of it."

Tate, not wanting to put his foot in it again, tried to think of a way to show support for her position but not encourage what seemed to him making a mountain out of a molehill.

"Now, I grant you, sweetheart, that sometimes things get sensationalized. But in Willie Lee's case, I don't think we are looking at him being proclaimed a healer. In the first place, what Willie Lee did is not something new. He laid hands on a horse he cares for, and that cares for him. The horse's wound did not magically heal up before our eyes. The horse simply came back around. I've seen my own mother use laying on of hands. Sometimes a person is helped. It was said around our neighborhood that Mama could cure headaches, neuralgia, lumbago, and once she cured my hives. But she sure didn't succeed every time. Science is even recognizing the energy fields involved in this now."

He saw by her expression that he had not calmed her fears.

"Your mother is an adult who can understand," she told him. "Willie Lee might not understand, and he sure might get worn out, trying to heal every Tom and Spot. And what if he can't heal every animal? What then? He will be so hurt. You know how he loves animals. We're liable to have a zoo in our backyard."

"We don't have a backyard at the moment," he interjected, before he thought.

Marilee's reply to that was, "I am being serious here, Tate. And we do so have a backyard, we have just lost half your house."

Her voice rose again, and they both looked at the closed bathroom door.

Then Tate said, "Darlin', I know we've had a hell of a day in which our world has been blown to pieces. I know you are worried over this thing. I promise you that I will not mention Willie Lee, okay? I'll just tell about the filly, and how everyone went over to help as best they could. I'll report the heroic human capability for compassion.''

He paused a moment, and then a few more thoughts occurred to him. ''If reports on healings of this nature were done in a rational style, people would not make mountains out of them but take them as a matter of the normal course of loving each other.''

This idea sat very well with him; he thought how he would employ this line of reasoning in his article. Maybe it would require another article. He could certainly get a good editorial out of it.

His eyes slid over to his humming computer. He didn't want to waste time arguing; he wanted to get back at his writing.

''Honey, I have a real good chance of sellin' this story to a friend of mine down at my old Houston paper. I spoke to him earlier, and he's waitin' for me to send my first piece tonight.''

Marilee, who had ceased to hear, was suddenly picturing her ex-husband and his own laptop computer. ''Stuart is likely writing this story up right now.''

''Well, I imagine he's workin' on something,'' Tate agreed, and he wanted even more to be working on his own story.

''I've got to get over there and stop him.''

''You what?''

''I've got to stop him. He's got access to top magazines. He's got pictures.''

Marilee was having a panic now. She did not want anything reported about Willie Lee. Already he was a target, an innocent child who had been reported in the press last year as having gained a considerable fortune in stock, given to him as a reward for finding an important computer chip for the Tell-In Technology Corporation. After that came out in papers nationwide, Marilee became more vigilant than ever over her son, worrying about him being kidnapped.

Tate was telling her to calm down, but she told him to look after the children as she hunted around for her purse and keys.

At that point the bathroom door opened, and Corrine, with wet hair and pajamas hastily donned, came out, her eyes wide. "I heard thunder. It's lightning outside."

Marilee stopped in her tracks.

There came the unmistakeable sound of a rumble, which she and Tate had not heard because of their argument.

Tate opened the cabin door. Lightning shot across the black sky, giving evidence of an approaching storm.

Marilee set aside her purse. "It's okay, honey. We'll turn on the television and see if there's a report. Come on, climb into bed."

The television screen showed a local weatherman reporting the build up of severe storms once again. Their county was under a tornado watch, and the thunder outside became louder.

"Where will we go if there is another tornado?" Corrine asked.

"Well…Tate, did you see a storm shelter near the office?"

Tate, who had sat again at his computer and was typing, nevertheless warmed her heart by hearing her and saying, "Yes, there is," and he went so far as to rip himself from his writing and take Corrine to the window, where he pulled back the drapes and pointed to the hump of the shelter that could just be seen near the office.

Tate returned to his computer and typing, and Corrine returned to bed and sipping her hot chocolate. Marilee slipped off her shoes, curled next to Corrine and put her arm around her niece, whose thin body felt so fragile. Marilee had a sense that she would beat back the tornado with her very fists, should it try to zoom in on them again, and at the same time, she thought of Stuart, in her bungalow, typing away on his computer in the same manner to which Tate had returned.

Both of them two peas in a pod—journalists, and as such, it was the story that counted. Stuart had a special talent for sensationalism.

"Excuse me a minute, honey," she told Corrine, at a time when the thunder had abated. She snugged the covers around the child. "Tate...can I have a word with you?"

It took him several seconds to look up, and several more seconds to tear his hands and body away from his keyboard. She beckoned him outside and closed the door behind them. The concrete stoop was cool on her bare feet, and the strong humid wind whipped around them, tugging at their hair and causing her to fold her arms close.

"I want you to go talk to Stuart and tell him not to write about Willie Lee."

Tate's brows came together and then rose in unison. "Darlin', we don't know that he's doin' a story about Willie Lee."

She disliked his patent placating and ignored it.

"We had best catch him before he does. I can't leave Corrine, but you can go."

"Marilee, I don't think it is my place to tell another journalist what he can and cannot cover, and I have my own story in there to write. I've got a chance at a sale, but I've got to get it down to Skip in Houston tonight. If they don't use it there, they'll at least forward it to a string of smaller papers they own over in West Texas, and with his recommendation, it will be sold. It needs to be to those papers by tomorrow morning. News is only news for a day. Things move on."

"I think Willie Lee is a little more important than selling a news story."

That comment stood in the air a moment, while Tate ran his hand over his hair, giving her a long look. "I do, too, Marilee, but I think you are wrought up...and that is understandable after the day we have had. But Stuart is not only a journalist—he is Willie Lee's father. What he does in that capacity is up to him. I don't believe I need to be tellin' him one way or the other. And this is somethin' that needs discussing in a rational manner, not by me rushin' over there and tellin' the man what he should or should not do."

Marilee did not know what to say to his words and entire stubborn attitude. She swallowed, pain slicing into her chest. She had relied on him to help, to see how she felt and do what she needed him to do. But he would not. He was disappointing her.

"All right, then," she said and turned.

"Marilee, don't take it like that."

She did not reply to him, did not look at him, but kept going inside, where she pasted what she hoped passed for a calm expression on her face, because Corrine's gaze fastened onto her like a magnet. "There's more storms," Corrine said, indicating the television.

"There are? Well, we're snug here in this bed."

Again Marilee curled around her niece. She looked over to check Willie Lee, only just then realizing she had not gotten him out of his clothes. She enlisted Corrine's help to do so; this diverted the child from the sound of the thunder once more getting louder.

Just as they tucked Willie Lee beneath the covers, Tate got to his feet, saying, "I'll go over, Marilee. I don't know what I'll say to him, but I'll go over."

Marilee regarded him in surprise, as well as doubt. Perhaps he was just trying to soothe her, and she did not want to be soothed now, since he had already displayed his true colors in disappointing her.

Tate strode to the door, yanked it open and strode out into the night, closing the door behind him.

Marilee stared at it for long seconds, and then she raced to it, jerked it open and threw herself outside.

"Tate!" she called, raising her voice over the rising wind and thunder. "Tate!"

In bare feet, she ran almost mindlessly over the gravel, to the door of the Cherokee, taking hold of it and stopping him from closing it.

"Don't go. You're right…. It's too late tonight…the storms… Don't go." She could not, in that minute, bear for him to leave. To be away from them.

She gazed into his eyes, and he looked back at her as she struggled to find the honesty. "I'm afraid, Tate. I don't know why, I just am." It was the best she could do.

His expression softened with blessed understanding. Slipping out of the vehicle, he put his arm around her and hugged her close as they went back into the cabin, where Corrine waited in the open doorway.

When the door closed, the storm was shut outside.

Although he would have fussed over her, Marilee sent Tate back to his writing. She would not think of any of it, she told herself. *God, please handle it.*

She focused on getting herself into her pajamas, then joined Corrine in bed, where they watched the weather reports on the television, while there came the rhythmic clicking of Tate's typing. Marilee found it comforting and fell asleep.

Just before closing down his computer, Tate checked his e-mail. There were two messages. One from Stuart: *Here you go, Editor. No charge. Several other papers are paying.*

Stuart had sent pictures of Tate's damaged house, along with the damaged garage, and the tree and horse corral in the rear of Winston's property. The most striking shots, however, were of people's faces. Stuart James was very good at capturing drama.

How had he gotten the pictures developed?

Ah—Stuart had one of those newfangled digital cameras! Of course he would have, being the renowned photojournalist that he was.

The second message was from his old friend on the Houston paper: *You made a sale, buddy. Check will be in the mail tomorrow. Am forwarding these on to our affiliates out west.*

By golly, it paid to have friends! And the Internet! These were the good ol' days.

The Houston paper would run his article in tomorrow's edition, and he would run it in the *Voice* on Wednesday. It darn sure paid to own one's own newspaper, too. He felt sweet satisfaction. Pouring all his energy and finances into the newspaper had been the right thing. He had stretched his finances to the limit in order to update the *Voice* into the computer age, but he was surely now reaping the benefits. He would have done well to get Reggie one of those digital cameras, and he would, as soon as he could afford it.

For a brief moment he closed his eyes and gave thanks. Then he turned off the computer and stretched, realizing he was darn tired. He looked across the room for the first time in hours. His gaze fell first on the bed where he would sleep with Willie Lee.

Only Willie Lee wasn't there—the bed was empty.

His gaze skittered to the far bed, which was full. Sometime while Tate worked on his piece for the papers, Willie Lee had gotten up and crawled into bed with his mother, and now Marilee was tangled with the children. Even with Munro, who lay at the foot of the bed.

Tate gazed at the sight for a long minute, feeling a mixture of gratitude and guilt. He had not meant to get so busy as to shut them out.

His ex-wife's admonitions came to mind; Lucille had said over and over, "You are a newspaperman, not a husband."

This time he wanted to be a husband. He didn't want to let Marilee down, like he felt he had let Lucille down.

He had seen that he had let Marilee down in her eyes, when he had refused to go to speak to Stuart.

He thought of Stuart's pictures and winced inwardly. What had seemed a far-fetched, overwrought worry on Marilee's part began to seem quite possible. With growing unease, he wondered if he had pushed her worries aside too easily, and that maybe he had done so because he was focused on his own desires of the moment.

His desire was to provide for his family. He was supposed to work for his family, wasn't he?

In any case, there was nothing to be done about it tonight. He washed up in the vintage bathroom, where he felt very much at home, and donned pajama bottoms, which he felt necessary because of Corrine—man, there was a lot to think about for a man who had been a bachelor as long as he had. Wearily he crawled into bed.

It was lonely.

He looked over at the bed filled with bodies and had the urge to either wake one of them up or crawl in with them, if there had been room.

Just then Munro hopped off that bed and hopped up with Tate.

"Thanks, fella. I appreciate it greatly."

He would be glad when he got to sleep with Marilee, although he had a sad suspicion that, even married to her, their intimate time alone might be scant for many years.

Stuart sat with his notebook computer open on the dining-room table in Marilee's bungalow and typed onto the e-mail message screen: *Hey, Troy. I may be on to a story here. Pictures and commentary in the*

*three attachments. I'll check into it further. Get back
to me about any publications you know of that might
be doing healer stories.*

He read the black words on the white screen and
sat there staring at them, hesitating about sending the
message. At last he hit the send button.

Over the years he had encountered various people
who, it was claimed, healed. Stuart had thought it all
hogwash, either delusion or deliberate conning. From
one, though, a young girl in the Tennessee hills, he
had gotten a good spread in *Life* magazine. People
did not care if it was truth; they wanted to believe
it, and they wanted to hear about it. The pictures he
took had slanted to the belief side. It was what paid.

A certain anger came over him, and he rose. His
left leg almost gave way, and a pain seemed to go
through every bone in his body. Surprised, he
grabbed hold of the table.

He had forgotten to take his pills. He shook as he
went to the bedroom to get them from the dresser
drawer. There was water in the pitcher there; Franny
saw to that. He downed the pills, looked at the pain-
killers, and took another, then lay back on the bed,
closing his eyes, and seeing his son hold a bird that
looked dead, and then had fluffed and flown. Stuart
had thought he had not seen correctly, but perhaps
he had.

He had seen the same as everyone at the corral
that day—that horse had been dying, and then it
hadn't been.

Wouldn't it turn out ironic if years ago he had
turned his back and walked away from a really great
story just waiting to be told, as well as the one person
who could help him now?

Thirty

The best we can...

Marilee had been sitting for some time on the front stoop of the cabin, watching the sun rise, when Tate stepped out behind her.

"Here you are," he said, as if both surprised and relieved.

"Where did you think I was?"

"Well, you weren't inside," he said, sounding a little put out as he lowered himself to sit beside her. "You could have been anywhere."

"I wouldn't have gone far."

"No, you wouldn't." He grinned that boyish and charming grin she so loved and scratched his head. "I'm just a little mixed up this mornin', wakin' up with a dog in bed with me, and those bedspreads and curtains that are at war with each other. I thought maybe I was ten years old again."

She gazed at him, wondering how he could think so much first thing in the morning. "Are the children still asleep?"

"Yes, ma'am, they are, so we have a few minutes alone." He put his arm around her shoulders and faced the golden glow shining on the horizon. "Another day in paradise."

"It *is* paradise here, isn't it?" she said, running her eyes over the land that stretched in rolling hills and green pastures on the other side of the black-topped highway. It was something like a mystical drawing. "It's a good place to be."

"Hmmm…sure is."

He nuzzled her neck, sending little jolts of electricity through her body. She wanted to give in to the feeling but was frightened by the force of it. They were in no position to go anywhere with the passion, and she didn't feel up to dealing with it.

Her mind was distracted by her concerns over Willie Lee and finding a new place to live that would ease Tate's worries and helping the children deal with the trauma of the tornado. That was a lot to be concerned with.

Then Tate said, "I sold the article last night to the Houston paper. Good money."

"I'm glad for you."

"It's for us." He sounded a little hurt.

"I know, and I'm proud of you…and I'm grateful that you are looking out for us, too." She smoothed her hand on his, bringing her attention fully to him. "Why do men always get so excited about making money?"

Tate, who always had a logical answer for everything, replied, "It's the provider instinct. Togetherness, peace and love are good, but it is also nice to eat in this real world."

A sudden and very immense appreciation for him swept her. She smiled at him, and he hugged her happily. It seemed to take so little to make Tate happy. She should apologize to him for her erratic behavior the previous night, but while she was thinking of doing this, he spoke.

"You're beautiful in the morning," he told her.

"I'm sleepy in the morning," she said.

"And sexy as hell with it, too. If the children were not in the bed in there, I would drag you in there and show you how you make me feel. I guess I'll settle for a kiss right now."

The next thing she knew he kissed her in a way that made her feel hot and cold at the same time, and caused her to go limp against him.

"There. Did that knock your socks off?"

"Do it again," she whispered, and did not wait for him to move, but pressed her lips hard to his, seeking to give back the passion he had imparted to her.

When they finally broke apart, he told her that they had better slow down. "I won't be able to go in there in my condition. I don't think I'll be able to stand up."

The apology was still on her lips but wouldn't come out. She closed her eyes and felt herself safe in his arms, the scent of him around her and the warmth of the sun dawning on her face.

Then she said, "Willie Lee wants so much to be like other boys. I want to give him that, as much as I can. I want him to have a normal life. That's why I don't want people to think he's a healer." She needed to explain.

"You're doin' great at giving him a normal life, darlin'," he said, "but I think we need to face that what will be a normal life for Willie Lee isn't going to be exactly like that of other boys. He's an extraordinary boy. Maybe he is some sort of special healer, or maybe he is simply so pure with love that that horse felt it and took hold of the will to live. This is not the first healing heard of in the world, and it won't be the last. And if Willie Lee is a healer, I don't think there's anything we can do about it. But I can tell you what a really wise woman who talked to me yesterday told me.''

She twisted around to look at him.

''She said to me that what we would do is the best we can.''

Tate had not known he was going to say all that until the words came out. He was amazed to find that the advice was quite sound. He liked it.

He watched her sigh and accept, at least in some measure. He felt satisfied at having said the right thing.

But then she was frowning again.

''What about Stuart?'' she asked. ''What if he asks Willie Lee to heal him? That's fine, if it works, but what if it doesn't? What if it's as you say, just somehow Willie Lee's friendly presence helped that horse but won't be enough for a man dying of cancer? How will Willie Lee feel then?''

Tate saw immediately that his future wife could think of all possible contingencies. He felt a little foolish not to have thought of this one. In fact, this entire thing about the healing had not struck him as all that big a deal, but now, seen in the light of Stuart and the problems Marilee kept bringing up, he could understand how emotions could run deep on this.

He said slowly, ''Well, I guess we're all just going to have to have a talk about this thing. An honest talk with Stuart and with Willie Lee.''

Marilee gazed at him, then looked away.

The sun was now almost totally up. Gazing at it, he thought: another day in paradise, in which anything could happen. Tornados came, even to paradise. In an instant life changed. What person among them knew if he would be alive that night? Mostly what they had all been doing was ignoring the fact of Stuart's impending death. Death was embarrassing to people. It was like digestion problems. Messy. No one wanted to talk about constipation, diarrhea or dying, all basic and common difficulties in life; they were whispered about as if they were some secret sin.

He could get a good editorial from this. He needed his notepaper.

"Tate." Marilee entwined her hand with his. "I'm sorry about the way I acted last night...getting so upset and wanting you to stop what you needed to do in order to go speak to Stuart. I'm sorry I got so crazy." Her blue eyes were large and watery in her pale face. "I wish I could promise that I won't get crazy again, but I don't think I can." A tear overflowed and dripped on her cheek. "Parker and Mother say I'm too emotional...that I get far too upset. It's just that sometimes I get worried and fearful and carried away."

"Oh, darlin'..." He hugged her to him, feeling a fierce love in his chest. "Don't you change. Don't you dare change. Of course you're emotional, and that's what I love. I love you just the way you are. I love you crazy, I love you sane. I can't promise you I'll always understand or agree, but I can promise to always do my best to love you."

He got so choked up that his voice got hoarse. He

wanted to hold her forever and protect her forever, and she clung to him and told him in a ragged whisper, "I won't let a day go by that I don't tell you I love you, Tate Holloway."

It was, he thought, the angel of death who had taught them how to live.

Just then the door of the cabin opened, and Willie Lee stepped out, with Munro right beside him. "There is no schoo-ool, Mo-ther."

"There isn't?" Marilee would have pulled self-consciously from Tate's arms, but he held her. She blinked and did her best to appear her normal self for her son.

Willie Lee shook his head. "It was on the tel-e-vis-ion. Cor-rine said. There is no 'lect-tric-ity." He struggled with the word as he regarded her closely. "Are you cry-ing, Ma-ma?"

"Just a bit. It's from happiness, though." She smiled at Tate, and he smiled at her.

He was the most handsome and wonderful man in the world. And he loved her.

"Oh. Look." Willie Lee pointed to the motel office.

It was Mr. Goode coming out with the Valentine City flag to put in the holder on the side of the building.

He hollered over to them, "Y'all want doughnuts, we got 'em. Complemen'ry."

"I am hun-gry," Willie Lee said and started away toward the office.

"Willie Lee, you come get some shoes on," Marilee ordered, immediately thinking of a sharp rock possibly cutting his foot, or him catching cold.

But Tate jumped to his feet, grabbed up Willie Lee

and hoisted him to his shoulders, saying, "I'll carry him! We'll get chocolate, if we can," he called back to her.

"You don't have any shoes on, either," Marilee hollered, just because it seemed required on her part.

As she stood there, gazing at them and pressing the precious sight of the man and boy she loved into memory, Corrine stepped out beside her. Marilee put her arm around the child, who watched the man and boy, too. Marilee knew suddenly and deeply that whatever came their way in the days and weeks and years ahead, they would face it together and do the best they could. And it was enough.

Marilee and Corrine sat cross-legged on the bed, and Tate and Willie Lee took the two chairs at the rickety table, while Munro lay down between the table and the bed, twisting his head hopefully back and forth, anticipating chunks of doughnut that might come his way.

Eating doughnuts and milk seemed a perfect time for the discussion of an important matter. Marilee asked, "Willie Lee, what did you do to the horse to stop her bleeding?"

Willie Lee, studying the candy sprinkles on his doughnut, said, "I do not know. I just did it, and then she was bet-ter."

"You laid your head on the horse," Tate said, pouring more milk into Willie Lee's glass.

"Yes, I did," Willie Lee said in his helpful manner, then used both hands to drink from his glass.

Marilee looked at his hands, small, with dimpled fingers and not quite the cleanest fingernails.

"Have you done this before, with any other animals?'' she asked, when he finished drinking his milk.

Willie Lee looked at her. ''It is a se-cret.'' His gaze slid to Corrine.

Marilee and Tate looked at Corrine.

''Do you suppose you two could tell us this se-cret?'' Tate said. ''We won't tell anyone.''

Corrine's expression said she did not appreciate being placated like a child. She said, ''Beau. Ricky Dale's black dog,'' she added, when Marilee looked puzzled. ''That day, when the mare kicked Beau. Willie Lee told you. Beau looked dead. Willie Lee hugged on him, and Beau got back up.''

Marilee remembered the day they had come home from Winston's house, and how Willie Lee had said something about a dog getting kicked.

Corrine went on to tell about Miss Minnie's cat— ''It was ver-y old,'' Willie Lee said—and the tit-mouse, which Ricky Dale had brought down as an experiment, and Corrine reminded them about the kitten.

''My kit-ten,'' Willie Lee put in. ''He got dead-ed, but then he got bet-ter. And so did my frog.''

''Frog?'' Marilee, Tate and Corrine said in unison.

''Yes. But he went away. I have not seen him in a long time.''

Marilee, feeling a little dizzy, ran her gaze from Willie Lee to Tate.

Tate asked, ''How do you do this, Willie Lee? How do you make the animals better?''

Willie Lee looked thoughtful as he licked choco-late icing from his fingers with the tip of his pink tongue. ''I hold them, and I...I think a-bout good stuff. Some-times I see the sky, or maybe sunshine." He swung his legs back and forth, and lowered his voice, looking shy. "I think it may be an an-gel. Sometimes she sings to me." He looked downward, then peeked back up. "Can I have one more, Mo-ther—the cher-ry one?"

Just like a normal boy, she thought, leaning over to kiss his head. "You can have one more, my sweet son."

Tate handed him a cherry-filled doughnut, asking gently, "Do the animals always get better?"

Willie Lee looked closely at the jelly hole. "No. Only if I see the light big. Miss Min-nie's cat did not get bet-ter. He was old. He said he was tir-ed. And I do not think the rab-bit did, either."

Corrine said, "You mean Mrs. Yoder's rabbit at school? She's the fourth-grade teacher and has animals," she explained to Tate and Marilee. "The rabbit was losing his hair." She made a face.

"He was old, he told-ed me and Mun-ro," said Willie Lee, and then he bit deeply into the jelly doughnut, sending cherry filling onto his chin. "But the horse got bet-ter, and I am glad," he said, with his cheeks full.

"We're all glad, sugar." Marilee took a napkin and wiped jelly off the healer's chin.

"Does anyone else, other than Ricky Dale, know about Willie Lee's...way with animals?" Marilee asked Corrine.

Corrine shook her head. "Ricky Dale won't tell."

Marilee reflected on her niece's answer and attitude. Corrine had already been protecting Willie Lee, whom she loved. Already it was in Corrine to watch the ways of the world, and this was sad, and yet a blessing, too.

It was a sticky wicket to encourage a child to hide the truth. The best Marilee could offer was to say that while in normal circumstances honesty was the best policy, sometimes discretion was kinder and more prudent.

"That's one of those things I'll understand when I'm older, right?" Corrine said.

"Oh, I think you understand it full well right now." Marilee looked into the heart-shaped face of her niece and smiled.

Corrine smiled back.

She was going to be too beautiful by far, Marilee thought, experiencing a pang of worry. *Thank you, God, that you gave her uncommon common sense.*

When they passed Tate's house on the way to Marilee's bungalow, they saw a gathering of people and a van from a television station up in Lawton.

"Don't stop, Tate."

"Have to."

This was because Everett Northrup flagged them down by running into their path.

"News folks are coverin' the tornado damage, Editor. This is him," Everett called over his shoulder.

A man with a ball cap bearing Channel 2 News and a microphone came hurrying up. "Could we get a comment from you, sir? Just take a couple minutes. Folks say you were in your house, havin' a bachelor party. That's great stuff." He grinned.

Tate gave the steering wheel over to Marilee and told her he would join her later. She hit the accelerator with more pressure than she had intended and headed on to her bungalow, wondering what else folks might say to the newspeople.

It was a little difficult, getting out of the car and going into the bungalow, where she would see Stuart. She told herself her trepidation was silly. There was nothing special for her to do or say; she must simply let this all play out.

The children raced ahead, happy to be home. Marilee saw a rare broad grin on Corrine's face as she took the stairs to the porch two at a time. Even without her things here any longer, this was still home to Corrine, the only real stable home she had ever known.

Franny greeted them just inside the door with hugs, saying, "Come in, come in! No school? Aren't you the lucky ones?"

Stuart, wearing lounging pants and a sweatshirt, came ambling out from the kitchen, a cup in hand. Never a man for mornings, he obviously had not been up long. He needed a shave. She thought he looked thinner, if that was possible.

Willie Lee greeted him, gave him a hug, then wanted to know where his kitten was. The kitten was found, and the children took it out to the tree house, where they went to locate Willie Lee's bird. "I hope Bird-y did not get blown away."

Franny disappeared to take a long bath, she said, and Marilee and Stuart were left alone.

"I can offer you a cup of this tea Franny makes me drink," Stuart said, lifting the cup in his hand. "It's growing on me. There's some left in the pot."

"That's her own brew to stimulate the blood, isn't it? I need some this morning."

When she would have gotten it, he told her, rather

sharply, "I'll get it for you." With a self-deprecating grin, he added, "I'm usin' your house. The least I can do is get you a cup of tea."

She followed him into the kitchen. "You don't owe me for the use of the house, Stuart. You aren't taking anything away from us. It is the best thing, you being here. The house isn't big enough for Tate and me and the children, but it is just right for you and Franny right now. I don't want to get rid of it. I love this house," she said rather wistfully.

"Where are you going to live, since your roof was lifted?" he asked her, passing her the cup.

"We're going to find somewhere to rent until details can be worked out." She saw no need to tell him about Tate's house not being insured. "We don't know if the big house can be repaired or will have to be torn down and a new one started from scratch. And we rather like it out at the Goodnight," she added with a grin. "It's quiet, and we get free doughnuts."

He smiled softly, not looking at her, but at the floor. Childish laughter floated in through the open window, and he turned his gaze outside. He *was* thinner. His skin was getting paper-thin.

"Stuart, about what happened with the filly and Willie Lee..." She had begun, the words tumbling out, but she didn't know how to continue.

His head jerked around, and his eyebrows furrowed. "What about it?"

"What did you think of it?"

He thought several seconds before he answered. "I think it was quite remarkable to see, the boy holding the dying horse, and I got some great shots. And I think the boy kept her from dying."

Marilee nodded. "Only he isn't *the boy*. He's your son. He's our Willie Lee, who wants more than anything in the world to be considered a normal boy. He won't get that if you do a story about it and spread his name and picture in a magazine and paint a picture of a boy with healing powers."

They gazed at each other. She saw the questioning and considering in his eyes before he looked away out the window.

Seeing he didn't intend to comment, she said, "Willie Lee has a way with animals. He always has had. I've known for a long time that he talks to them, and they talk to him. He said they did, and after a while we all just accepted it. Certainly he can do things with animals that we can't. It seems that he can, on some occasions, have a healing effect on them.

"But I don't want you doing a story on him, Stuart. I don't want his name ending up splashed across magazines and tabloids because a really good story can be made out of it. People don't take kindly to others who are a little different. They poke fun, ridicule, take advantage. He'll face enough of that as it is. Do you remember that girl you did the story on in Tennessee? Do you remember how her family was thrown out of the church, and then another church took hold of them, exploiting that child all over the place?"

He looked at her, his expression carefully guarded.

She considered asking him to promise her that he wouldn't do a story. Would he tell her the truth? Could she believe him?

Then she said what she needed to say. "Stuart, he

might be able to help you. I don't know. But I don't want him hurt in the process."

Stuart's eyes narrowed.

Just then the telephone near her shoulder rang. For long seconds she gazed at Stuart and debated about answering, irritated at the interruption. Yet she thought of Tate and finally picked up on the third ring.

"Marilee?"

"Anita?" She was surprised to hear her sister's voice come across the line.

"Oh, Marilee, I'm so glad I got you. I heard the report just this mornin'. Just a blurb on the news. They said a tornado touched down in Valentine. I've been tryin' to get you, but I couldn't get through.... I don't know, maybe I got the numbers mixed up. I've been dialing from memory, without my address book. I called Mama, but no one answered there. Is everyone all right?"

At this point she finally had to pause to get a breath, and Marilee took the opportunity to tell her sister to calm down. "We are all fine, Anita.... Corrine is fine. The tornado did some damage, but no one was hurt in Valentine."

Seeing Stuart heading for the back door, Marilee had a bit of alarm. "I'll have to call you back, Anita."

"No! You can't! Marilee!"

She heard her sister's voice and caught the tears, and reluctantly put the receiver back to her ear. "I'm here. What is it?" Damn Anita, anyway.

"You can't call me back." Her sister was trying to control her soft sobs. "I'm...I'm in the hospital."

"What? What's happened?"

Her sister drew a trembling breath. "I'm in the hospital. In alcoholic rehab," she added in a faint tone.

"Oh, Anita." Marilee leaned back against the wall for support. She pictured her sister, whose ragged chuckles came over the line. Anita always tried to laugh things off. She used to say she would rather laugh than cry. Marilee had seen her after she had been beaten by a boyfriend, and she had quirked that bruised mouth into a grin. Marilee clutched the phone to her ear and listened as Anita told her that she had been given special permission to call Marilee, due to the circumstances, but she was not allowed phone calls for another month.

She had been committed, she said. An order signed by a judge, and Louis had seen to it.

"He must love you very much," Marilee said, surprised at the man, who had admitted to already being married. She wondered how that was working out.

"Yes," Anita said. "Maybe he does." Her tone was filled with ripe doubt. Anita could not believe any man loved her; Marilee understood.

She was to stay in the hospital for at least eight weeks, and she could stay longer, if she chose. "I want to do this, Marilee. I want to give it a try."

"You can do it, sister. You can." Tears streamed down Marilee's face.

"I'll miss your wedding."

Marilee decided not to mention that Anita had said she wasn't coming anyway. "That's okay. There'll be other times." Sober ones, she thought.

"I want to go ahead and give you and Tate temporary custody of Corrine. I'm having Louis draw up the papers. He knows some attorneys up in

Oklahoma City, so it will all be handled. All you will have to do is sign the papers."

Marilee was stunned. "Okay." Then she thought to say, "Do you want to talk to her, Anita? I'll call her...."

"No! Oh, no, Marilee, I can't."

"It's okay, honey."

Anita was crying softly again. "Will you tell her—about me being in rehab?"

"Yes, honey, I'll tell her. I'll tell her that her mother is very brave and wants to get well so that she can be with her and be a mother to her."

"Oh, I do, Marilee.... I really do."

When she hung up, Marilee continued leaning against the wall. *Well, God, I don't expect a miracle, but this is going in the right direction.*

She wiped her eyes, and then, remembering about Stuart going out with the children, she raced across the kitchen, through the laundry room to the back door, where she stopped, her hand up to push open the screen door, which she didn't push because of a loud whisper in her heart that said, *Stop!*

There, through the screen, she saw Willie Lee and Stuart sitting on the steps. Willie Lee hugged his father around the neck, his angel face in thick glasses pressed up against Stuart's head, his eyes closed. The sun shone down through the budding tree limbs upon them. Was it healing? Or was it the miracle of love?

She watched for a long second, hardly daring to breathe.

Willie Lee opened his eyes and saw her through the screen. "Hello, Mo-ther."

"Hello, sweetheart. Would you and Corrine like

to come in for a proper breakfast, and bring your
father?''

It was all she could think of to say.

The children, Franny and Stuart had just sat down
at the kitchen table, and Marilee was serving up fried
ham and eggs and biscuits and gravy, when Tate arrived through the back door, with a slight, blond-
haired young man in tow, whom he introduced as
Mike Owen, ''From the paper up there in Lawton.''

''Mike heard some tales this mornin' about our
Willie Lee havin' special powers and healing
Leanne's filly.''

She stared at Tate and the young man.

''I told him I didn't know about special powers,
but to come along and meet Willie Lee, and that
Willie Lee would tell how he did it.''

She wanted to wring Tate's neck. She only smiled.

Franny said, ''Perhaps Mr. Owen would like to
breakfast with us, and you could have a chance to
speak not only with Willie Lee, but visit with our
Stuart James, Willie Lee's father. He's a famous
photojournalist. All you journalists can talk shop.''

More or less trapped, the young man sat and ate
ham and eggs with gusto, and the three journalists
talked about the tornado and things that had happened.

Finally Mike Owen asked Willie Lee, ''What did
you do to save that horse?''

Willie Lee blinked behind his thick glasses. ''I
hug-ged her,'' he said, quite seriously.

Mike Owen regarded Willie Lee, then cut his gaze
to the others at the table, as if judging that his leg
was being pulled.

Tate said, ''That filly knew Willie Lee and all the people standing around were pullin' for it. It was just a lot of friendship and love that got that critter back up, right, Willie Lee?''

''Yes,'' he answered; then he looked at Marilee, ''I am go-ing to find my ant farm now, o-kay, Mama? They have mis-sed me.''

He was already down from his chair, and Corrine was following him. Marilee called after the two, ''Corrine, you get his hands washed so there aren't sticky prints everywhere.''

Tate patted the young man on the back. ''This is small-town America, where neighbors still care about each other. You can quote me,'' he added.

Thirty-One

From this day forward...

Days of early-evening sunlight shone golden on the church, and Marilee's tears caused her to see glimmering halos on everything—the concrete walk, the heads of all the people, the long, white limousine that everyone at the *Voice* had chipped in to rent to take them all the way to DFW airport.

"Good luck!"

"God Bless!"

"Have a great time!"

"Hallelujah!"

The good wishes of friends and loved ones, as well as bird seed, rained down upon Marilee and Tate as they ran hand in hand down the church steps and along the walk to the waiting limousine. Uncle Perry was just then getting in. It had been decided that Aunt Vella and Uncle Perry would serve in place of a hired nanny. Uncle Perry was being assisted by Sandy Conroy. Sandy had seemed to take on an unusual commanding air with his formal attire. Throughout the wedding and festivities, he had been on the sidelines directing traffic, caterers and band members.

Along the sidewalk, hands applauded and reached out for handshakes and hugs. Her cousin Belinda astonished Marilee by grabbing her in an enthusiastic and teary embrace. Marilee, thoroughly caught up with emotion, hugged her back.

Sheriff Oakes took hold of Tate's hand, pumping it like a pump handle, and then Tate hauled off and wrapped his arms around the big man.

"By golly, you got it done, Editor. You're a brave man."

Marilee wondered about that, and then there was Charlene MacCoy hugging her, followed by Reggie Pahdocony stepping in front of her, with a camera to her face, "Let me get a second shot here! Y'all get out of the way of the bride and groom."

Then Charlotte was taking her hand. "Come on, honey. You and Tate have to get going if you're goin' to make your flight."

"Oh, Charlotte. I love you, friend. Next time it will be your turn."

"Yes, now you all get on. They won't wait the plane," Charlotte said briskly through her tears, tugging Marilee toward the car, where Sandy stood ready with his hand extended, intending to hand her through the wide door.

"Wait! Y'all wait!" It was Franny, hurrying forward with an immense bouquet of forsythia branches. "I promised your mother to get these fixed up so you could take them with you. Here, Tate, hold on to them for her. They'll last till you get to the hotel. Oh, my, you two look beautiful!"

Franny hugged her, and then hugged Tate. Marilee watched them, watched how tenderly Tate held his mother against him, how his tanned face looked against Franny's pale one.

"Miss Marilee?" Sandy beckoned to her.

She started to put her hand in his, to enter the limousine, but someone pulled her around. It was Parker, who said, "I'm not missin' out on my kiss for the bride," and in a grand, sweeping motion, he bent her over backward and planted one on her lips, while the crowd roared and applauded.

When straight up again, she said, "Oh, Parker," and hugged him tight. *Goodbye, into your wife's hands I commit you.*

And then her gaze fell on Stuart, who was standing behind Sandy, leaning a little on the car and taking a picture of her. She paused. He took the shot.

Dropping the camera, he smiled a small smile.

She went to him, going up on tiptoe and putting her arms around his neck. He bent awkwardly, wrapping one arm around her. He felt all bones, so slight, fading away. She pressed her cheek to his for a long moment in which she whispered, "Thank you for Willie Lee.... Thank you for coming, so that we got straight with you and me." *All is forgiven, we are free for the journey.*

Pulling back, she looked long into his eyes. He looked back, as straight at her as he was capable of.

Then someone hollered, "Don't forget to throw the bouquet!"

Taking Sandy's hand, she stepped up on the running board of the limousine, braced herself on Tate's shoulder, drew back and gave a great thrust of her arm, sending the bouquet of yellow roses and forsythia and blue cornflowers far up into the bright blue sky, where it seemed to hang in the air and then to float gracefully downward, into the hands of Belinda, who yelled, "Oh, not me!" and tossed it upward like a hot potato to the small cluster of stretching hands.

But Belinda had thrown it harder than anticipated, and it went over the stretching hands to come down right at Zona Porter, who had been standing behind the pack and a little to the side, in order to see. Instinctively Zona caught it, and then she stood there, blinking behind her Coke-bottle lenses.

"Goodbye! Thank you, all!" Marilee blew kisses. She felt, suddenly, like the image of Marilyn Monroe above Tate's desk.

Then she was grabbed by the hips. It was Tate, who pulled her inside and down into his lap, as the doors were closed and the limousine began to roll out of the parking lot.

They were out in the street when Willie Lee and Corrine cried out, "Stop!

Ricky Dale was in the car, and Munro was not, because he had gotten out to do his business before the long drive.

The limousine stopped. Tate opened the doors for Ricky Dale to hop out, reluctantly, and for Munro to hop inside, eagerly.

Once more the doors closed and the limousine began to roll. Marilee and Tate turned to look out the rear window at their loved ones and friends, who flowed out into the middle of the street, an army of well-wishers sending them off, with Winston Valentine, in his capacity of town patriarch, leading the way.

Marilee's gaze lingered on Winston. In his pale summer suit and with his shock of hair that had finally gone all white, he could be seen from several blocks up the street, until the limousine turned west on Main Street and headed out of town.

Good-night kisses and hugs were exchanged, and hand in hand, Marilee and Tate retired to their bedroom. As Tate was closing the door, there came the sound of the television coming on.

"Perry, you turn that television off and come on over with the children and me to our bedroom."

"But John Wayne is fixin'…"

Tate paused, and he and Marilee cocked their ears.

"I don't care what world John Wayne is fixin' to save, shut it off. We are here to watch our great niece and nephew, and to have a wonderful time together. You just keep your eyes on me for a week. I'm sure, if you practice, you can make headway."

"Well, I guess you are entertainment," was Uncle Perry's surprising comeback.

"You bet I am…and I'm going to prove it to you," Aunt Vella said in a saucy voice.

If Uncle Perry had anything further to say to this, Tate did not hear it. The door to the bedroom on the other side of the suite closed. Tate closed the door to their own room, and he and Marilee regarded each other in what was for them a moment of surprise.

"Alone at last," Marilee said, and a soft smile bloomed on her lips.

"By golly, we are," said Tate, who had wondered if this night would ever come about. "Feels strange."

Then he saw that the woman who had become his wife was removing her robe in a most seductive manner. She tossed it carelessly to a nearby chair, in a move that sent Tate's adrenaline flowing with such strength as to compel him into the reckless act of sweeping her up into his arms and carrying her to the widest expanse of bed he had ever encountered, where they both practically tore off their clothes and made love in an incredible, mindless fashion, all hot and hard, and fast and furious.

It was a manner Tate had not known himself capable of, and it was so furious for him that Tate thought he should apologize afterward.

He did so, in a whisper, while he held Marilee close against him.

Her response was to rise up and look at him with sex-filled eyes and say, "Oh, Tate...do it again."

Tate, who at first wondered if it would be possible for him to do it again, found to his joy that it was. And he thanked God for the miracle of a man and a woman, together.

Two months later:

The Valentine Voice
View from the Editor's Desk
by Tate Holloway

The City Council has designated the coming week Valentine Days, with the theme of *Small Town on the Move*. The question always becomes on the move to where, and after receiving a lot of suggestions in this matter, some not printable, it seems to me that just where this town and each one of us is going is a matter of personal opinion and is not relevant, anyway. Just come on and celebrate our fair town.

Beginning Monday, special prizes will be awarded to customers from various merchants, so shop at home and support your town.

Also beginning Monday, on special display at City Hall will be original photographs by the late eminent photographer Stuart James, as well as historical ones on loan from our files and from a number of our longtime residents. Mr. Winston Valentine and Mrs. Minnie Oakes and some others of our senior citizens will be on hand at certain hours to provide commentary on the historical photographs. Call City Hall for the hours that you can enjoy this rare treat. Then on Saturday will be the great picnic, chili cook-off, dance and fireworks display from the high school grounds, so everyone come on out.

In what is perfect timing, we here at the *Voice* are also celebrating one full year of a new era. It hardly seems possible, but an entire year has passed since I became publisher of the *Voice* and took up residence here in Valentine. In celebration of this milestone, and in conjunction with Valentine Days, we will once again be presenting a series of special inserts each Sunday for the month, in which we give focus on life in our wonderful small town. Don't miss a one! Now revised and updated with comments and memories from our citizenry and pictures by Mr. James, these special features are sure to be collectors' items.

My wife and I would like to say thank you to all who have expressed condolences at our recent and substantial losses. I know the demolition of the great Porter-Holloway house meant the ending of an era for many of you. But I hope the new library to be built in its place will be a fitting substitute, and I'm appreciative to the people of this town for filling a long-standing need of a library for our residents. I am honored to accept the position as chairman of the library committee and promise my utmost effort in getting a facility that suits the tone of the neighborhood and the need.

We are also grateful for the condolences we have received at the passing of our son's father and our friend, Stuart James. We can feel blessed that in the brief time he was among us, Mr. James showed us ourselves and revealed our wonderful gifts of neighborliness.

It seems to me that during our journey through life, it is inevitable that we each have to come often by the corner of love and heartache. I think that corner is a little easier to stand on, here in Valentine.

Tate dropped his pen on his desk and ripped the yellow pages from the legal tablet in order to take them up to Marilee. He preferred her to read his editorials now, instead of Charlotte. Marilee was kinder in her criticism, and she seemed to appreciate his wit so much more than Charlotte.

Charlotte had pointed out that Tate did not want a critic. He wanted agreement. He conceded that this was probably true.

He shut out the light in his office, made sure the ones in the big city room were on that should be on, then stepped out the front door, locking it securely, before heading the couple of yards to the door at the edge of the building—their private entrance to the second floor of the *Voice,* where they were fashioning a temporary apartment.

Just reaching the door was Ricky Dale, lugging a small plastic animal crate, and beside him was a rather tiny girl.

"Well, good evenin', Ricky Dale."

"Good evenin', Editor." The boy set the crate down. "This here's Melody. We come to see Willie

Lee. Melody's puppy is deaf. Her daddy won't let her keep him if he's deaf.''

"Ah…well, come on up.'' He reached to take the crate, but Ricky Dale said he could carry it. Tate noticed the puppy wasn't all that big.

"It's an Australian shepherd. Sometimes if they're bred too close, they can turn out deaf,'' Ricky Dale said in a manner indicating he knew about such things. "Dr. Parker told me, when I was over there. I got a part-time job with him now.''

"That's good. You're gonna go places.''

"Yep.''

When they entered the upstairs apartment, Ricky Dale went directly off to Willie Lee's room, already knowing the way.

Tate went into the partitioned kitchen, where Marilee was preparing supper.

"We got another one…a deaf puppy.''

"Oh, well, maybe Willie Lee can help it.''

"Hmm. I wrote my editorial.''

He laid it on the table, then took Marilee into his arms and kissed her.

"Do it again,'' she said, when he lifted his lips.

He kissed her again, and kept kissing her even when a puppy raced into the room and around them barking, with children chasing after it. He'd learned not to let children interrupt his kissing his wife.

From *USA TODAY* bestselling author
Emilie Richards comes the story of a
woman who has played life by the book,
and now the rules have changed.

EMILIE RICHARDS

PROSPECT STREET

Faith Bronson, daughter of a prominent Virginia senator and wife
of a charismatic lobbyist, finds her privileged life shattered when
her marriage ends abruptly. Only just beginning to face the lie
she has lived, she finds sanctuary with her two children in a run-
down row house in exclusive Georgetown. This historic row
house harbors deep secrets of its own, secrets that force Faith to
confront the deceit that has long defined her.

Available the first week of July 2002, wherever fine hardcover books are sold!

Jan Coffey
Twice Burned

Playing with fire…

Twenty years ago Léa and Ted Hardy came home from school to find their parents dead, victims of a murder-suicide. Léa leaves the small town of Stonybrook and the painful memories behind. But Ted can't seem to escape the past. Marrying the daughter of Stonybrook's leading family, he starts a new life—until he discovers secrets that lead to the death of his wife and daughters. And to accusations of murder. Now, convicted and facing execution, Ted has given up hope.

Determined to save her brother, Léa must return to a town that harbors a fierce desire to see Ted die…taking long-buried secrets with him. Desperate, she turns to Mick Conklin, a man she is deeply attracted to but cannot fully trust. But she needs an ally, now more than ever. Because the fuse has been lit, and the bright fires of truth are about to blow Stonybrook wide open.

"With…enough twists and turns to keep you guessing from beginning to end, Jan Coffey will delight."
—*Romantic Times* on *Trust Me Once*

Available the first week of July 2002 wherever paperbacks are sold!

Curtiss Ann Matlock

66827	COLD TEA ON A HOT DAY	___ $5.99 U.S.	___ $6.99 CAN.
66599	DRIVING LESSONS	___ $5.99 U.S.	___ $6.99 CAN.
66499	LOST HIGHWAYS	___ $5.99 U.S.	___ $6.99 CAN.

(limited quantities available)

TOTAL AMOUNT	$_____
POSTAGE & HANDLING	$_____
($1.00 for 1 book, 50¢ for each additional)	
APPLICABLE TAXES*	$_____
<u>TOTAL PAYABLE</u>	$_____
(check or money order—please do not send cash)	

To order, complete this form and send it, along with a check or money order for the total above, payable to MIRA Books®, to: **In the U.S.**: 3010 Walden Avenue, P.O. Box 9077, Buffalo, NY 14269-9077; **In Canada**: P.O. Box 636, Fort Erie, Ontario, L2A 5X3.

Name:_____

Address:_____ City:_____

State/Prov.:_____ Zip/Postal Code:_____

Account Number (if applicable):_____

075 CSAS

*New York residents remit applicable sales taxes.
Canadian residents remit applicable GST and provincial taxes.

MIRA®